continued . . .

"A goofy excursion in a style reminiscent of Foglios's *Girl Genius* graphic series. . . . A highly entertaining romp."
—*Locus*

"Paying homage to the likes of *Skybreaker*, *2D Goggles*, and *Girl Genius*, *The Doomsday Vault* is *awesome*. One of my favorite steampunk-zombie novels. Abso-freaking-lutely recommended."
—The Book Smugglers

Also by Steven Harper

The Clockwork Empire

The Doomsday Vault

The Impossible Cube

THE IMPOSSIBLE CUBE

A NOVEL OF THE CLOCKWORK EMPIRE

STEVEN HARPER

A ROC BOOK

ROC
Published by New American Library, a division of
Penguin Group (USA) Inc., 375 Hudson Street,
New York, New York 10014, USA
Penguin Group (Canada), 90 Eglinton Avenue East, Suite 700, Toronto,
Ontario M4P 2Y3, Canada (a division of Pearson Penguin Canada Inc.)
Penguin Books Ltd., 80 Strand, London WC2R 0RL, England
Penguin Ireland, 25 St. Stephen's Green, Dublin 2,
Ireland (a division of Penguin Books Ltd.)
Penguin Group (Australia), 250 Camberwell Road, Camberwell, Victoria 3124,
Australia (a division of Pearson Australia Group Pty. Ltd.)
Penguin Books India Pvt. Ltd., 11 Community Centre, Panchsheel Park,
New Delhi - 110 017, India
Penguin Group (NZ), 67 Apollo Drive, Rosedale, Auckland 0632,
New Zealand (a division of Pearson New Zealand Ltd.)
Penguin Books (South Africa) (Pty.) Ltd., 24 Sturdee Avenue,
Rosebank, Johannesburg 2196, South Africa

Penguin Books Ltd., Registered Offices:
80 Strand, London WC2R 0RL, England

First published by Roc, an imprint of New American Library,
a division of Penguin Group (USA) Inc.

First Printing, May 2012
10   9   8   7   6   5   4   3   2   1

To my son, Aran, who always manages the most amazing surprises. Every day with you is a wonder.

ACKNOWLEDGMENTS

I need to thank Tim Smith, PhD, of the University of Michigan, for information about the workings of electrical turbines. Thanks also go to the Untitled Writers Group (Christian, Cindy, David, Diana, Erica, Jonathan, Mary Beth, and Sarah) for pounding through so many drafts.

THE STORY SO FAR

We include this section as a courtesy for new readers who did not have the opportunity to peruse *The Doomsday Vault*, the most excellent first volume in this series. The information may also prove useful to experienced readers who require a bit of a refresher, or who lack a mechanized cranial implant with fully realized library. Thoroughly experienced readers are encouraged to leaf their way over to Chapter One, where they will find Gavin Ennock in awkward and perilous circumstances.

The year is 1857.

Nearly one hundred years earlier, a new disease ravaged the world. The plague causes rotting of flesh, and also invades the host's nervous system, causing motor dysfunction, dementia, and photosensitivity. Victims lurching through the late stages inevitably became known as plague zombies. However, a handful of victims end up with neural synapses that, for a brief time, fall together instead of apart. Advanced mathematics, physics, biology, and chemistry become as toys to them. But as the virus slowly destroys their brains, they eventually lose their grip on reality. Their attachment to mechanical inventions and their detachment from normal human emotion earned them the name clockwork geniuses or clockworkers, and the disease itself became the clockwork plague.

Two nations—England and China—built opposing empires using the fantastic inventions supplied by captive clockworkers, and only the delicate balance of power holds the two empires in check.

In *The Doomsday Vault*, we encountered Alice Michaels, an impoverished woman of quality who had finally caught the eye of wealthy industrialist Norbert Williamson. Norbert promised to pay Alice's family's debts if she married him and provided their eventual child with a title. Alice reluctantly agreed. Mere hours later, she rescued from great danger a handsome young street musician named Gavin Ennock.

Before Gavin met Alice, he served aboard the American airship *Juniper*. An unfortunate encounter with pirates left him stranded in London with no means of employment save playing the fiddle on street corners. After Alice's dramatic rescue, Gavin found himself attracted to her, and she to him, but her circumstances and his social standing didn't allow for a romance.

A great many adventures followed. Alice's aunt Edwina turned out to be a clockworker. Plague zombies attacked London. A great mechanical beast kidnapped Alice, and Gavin rescued her with the help of a mutated walking tree designed by another clockworker. Gavin and Alice learned of a shadowy organization called the Third Ward. The Ward, led by Lieutenant Susan Phipps, has been charged by Queen Victoria herself to scour the world for clockworkers and bring them back to London, where they build inventions for the good of the Crown—and the detriment of the Orient.

Aunt Edwina's diseased mind created a pair of

cures for the clockwork plague, but such cures would upset the careful balance of power between the British and the Chinese, so the Third Ward locked Edwina's work in the Doomsday Vault, which houses only the most dangerous of inventions. Infuriated, Edwina infected Gavin with the plague in hopes of forcing Alice to retrieve the cure and, in the process, kill everyone in the Third Ward. Edwina's plan worked—almost. Alice and Gavin stole the cures, but stopped short of murder.

Aunt Edwina did not survive the release of her own airborne cure, and Alice found herself the disconcerted owner of a mechanical gauntlet that can cure the clockwork plague with a scratch. Unfortunately, neither of Edwina's cures helps clockwork geniuses; they only cure people in danger of becoming ordinary plague zombies.

Alice left her betrothed and declared her love for Gavin. She attempted to cure Gavin of the plague and failed; Gavin was becoming a clockworker.

Alice and Gavin fled London in a small airship, with Lieutenant Phipps hot on their heels. Joining them are Gabriel Stark (a clockworker who calls himself "Dr. Clef"), Feng Lung (the son of China's ambassador to England), Kemp (Alice's mechanical valet), and Click (Alice's windup clockwork cat). They are heading for China, which has its own supply of clockworkers, and may have a more powerful cure that can restore Gavin's fading sanity and save his life.

Chapter One

Gavin Ennock snapped awake. His temples pounded, his feet ached, and his arms flopped uselessly above his head. Far above him lay green grass strewn with twigs. It took him several moments to understand he was hanging upside down by his ankles. At least he wasn't naked this time.

"Hello?" he called.

Below him, nothing moved. He shifted in confusion, and the iron shackles around his ankles clinked like little ghosts. How the hell—? The last thing he remembered was walking back to the inn from a much-needed trip to the bathhouse and someone had called his name. Now he was hanging head-down amid a bunch of trees. Most were little more than saplings, but a few were full-sized. Gavin didn't know trees, but these certainly didn't seem . . . normal. Their branches twisted as if with arthritis, and the leaves looked papery. Two or three bloomed with bright blue flowers, and bees bumbled among them.

The forest itself was contained within a domed greenhouse, three or four stories tall. Gavin's head hung fully two of those stories above the ground. Glass walls broken into geometric designs magnified and heated angry summer sunlight. The whole place smelled green. Water trickled somewhere, and humidity made the air heavy. Breathing felt almost the same as drinking.

Poison ivy vines of fear took root and grew in Gavin's stomach. "Hey!" Blood throbbed in his head, and his voice shook more than a little. "Is someone going to tell me what's going on?"

From around one of the trees limped a man. His back was twisted, and his sparse brown hair clumped unevenly against his skull. This and his scarred, gnarled hands gave the initial impression that he was old, but Gavin, who wasn't yet twenty, quickly realized the man was barely older than he was himself. The man was a clockworker, and the plague had left him with physical and mental scars both.

"Shit," Gavin muttered.

"Is he awake?" The man had a French accent. "Yes, he is awake."

"I'm an agent of the Third Ward," Gavin called down to him, lying. "When I don't report in, they'll send a team to see what happened to me. You don't want that. Let me go, and—"

The twisted man threw a lever Gavin hadn't noticed before, and Gavin dropped. The ground rushed up at him. His stomach lurched, and Gavin yelled. At the last moment, the twisted man threw the lever again and Gavin jerked to a stop five feet above the ground.

His ankles burned with pain, and the headache sloshed hot lead inside his skull.

"I think he has no idea who I am." The twisted clockworker pressed a scarred hand to Gavin's upturned cheek in a strangely tender caress. The gesture created an odd convergence of opposites. Gavin's captor stood firmly on the ground. His body was as twisted and warped as his trees, his face was scarred beneath greasy, sparse hair, and he wore a filthy robe that looked like it had once belonged to a monk. Muddy hazel eyes peered at his captive. Gavin had even features, white-blond hair, and blue eyes. His black shirt and trousers contrasted sharply with his fair skin and hair, and his fingers were straight and strong.

The clockworker cocked his head, as if hearing a voice—or voices. "Then maybe he should look around and try to remember who I am. Maybe he should."

Gavin considered socking the clockworker, but discarded the idea—bad leverage, and even if he managed to knock the other man unconscious, he would still be trapped in the shackles. His earlier fear gnawed at him again, mingling with the pain.

Now that he was lower, he could see nearby a large stone worktable littered with wicked-looking gardening tools, a large control panel bristling with levers, dials, and lights, and, incongruously, a brass-and-glass pistol. A power cable trailed from the stock and ended in a large battery pack.

"Listen," Gavin said with growing desperation, "I can help you. I can—"

The man turned Gavin, forcing him to look at the trees. "I don't know if he remembers. Maybe he will if

I point out that the forest is old but the greenhouse is new. What do you all think?"

"What are you talking about?" It was useless to argue with clockworkers—the disease that stoked their brains also lubricated their grip on reality—but Gavin couldn't help himself. "You aren't making—"

One of the trees moved. It actually leaned down and in, as if to get a closer look at Gavin. The blue blossoms shifted, and a glint of brass caught the light. Long wires and strips of metal ran up the bark. Gavin's breath caught in his throat. For a moment, time flipped backward, and he was fleeing through a blur of leaves and branches that were actively trying to kill him. A tall, bearded clockworker in an opera cloak rode one of the walking trees, steering it by yanking levers and pressing pedals. His partner, Simon, shouted something as Gavin spun and fired the electric rifle attached to the battery pack on his back.

"L'Arbre Magnifique," Gavin whispered. "This is his forest. But the greenhouse wasn't here before, and you aren't him."

"I heard him mention my father, L'Arbre Magnifique," the clockworker said. "But I don't believe he asked *my* name." He paused again. "Yes, that was indeed rude of him. He should know my name is Antoine."

Gavin's mouth went dry. Fantastic. What were the odds of two clockworkers showing up in the same family, or that Gavin would run into both of them in one lifetime? The shackles continued to bite into his ankles with iron teeth.

"Look, Antoine, your father is alive and well," Gavin said, hoping he was telling the truth. "In London. We gave him a huge laboratory and he invents great . . . uh, inventions all day long. I can take you to him, if you want."

Antoine spun Gavin back around and slugged him high in the stomach. The air burst from Gavin's lungs. Pain sank into him, and he couldn't speak.

"Ah," Antoine said. "Do you think I hurt him? I do." Another pause, with a glance at the trees. "No, it was not as painful as watching him kidnap my father." He turned his back to Gavin and gestured at one of the towering trees. "That is true. My father only taught me to work with plants. I will teach myself how to work with meat. Slowly."

An object flashed past Gavin's face and landed soundlessly on the grass where Antoine couldn't see. It was a perfect saucer of glass, perhaps two feet in diameter. Startled, Gavin looked up toward the faraway ceiling in time to see a brass cat, claws extended, leap through a new hole in the roof. The cat fell straight down and crashed into some bushes a few feet away. Antoine spun.

"What was that?"

It took Gavin a moment to realize Antoine was talking to him and not the trees. "It was my stomach growling," he gasped through the pain. "Don't you feed your prisoners?"

A string of saliva hung from Antoine's lower lip. "Yes. I feed them to my forest."

The leaves on the lower bushes parted, and the

brass cat slipped under the worktable, out of Antoine's field of view. It gave Gavin a phosphorescent green stare from the shadows. A ray of hope touched Gavin.

"Your father is a genius, Antoine," he said earnestly. "A true artist. Queen Victoria herself said so."

The trees whispered among themselves, and a storm crossed Antoine's face. "You are right! He should never mention that horrible woman's name, not when her Third Ward agents took my father away from me!"

"Simon and I captured a tree with him, remember? The tree turned out to be really useful," Gavin continued, a little too loudly. The pain from the punch was fading a little, but his ankles still burned. "It helped us track down a clockworker who hurt a lot of people."

Another glance at the trees. "Ah, yes. I miss Number Eight, too. What? No, I have definitely improved your design since then. Look at yourselves. I can make you blossom and create seedlings that grow their own metal frameworks, if only you have enough minerals in your roots. The entire forest will walk at my command! I only need more money. Money to buy more metal for my hungry trees."

Through the hole in the roof flew a small whirligig, its propeller twirling madly to keep it aloft. It trailed a rope. The whirligig zipped down to a support beam close to the ground and grabbed it with six spidery limbs, leaving the slanted rope behind it. Two of the trees creaked and leaned sideways, as if they were searching for something. Antoine, sensitive to their moods, started to turn. The unnatural position of Gavin's arms started new pains in his shoulders. The aches made Gavin's concentration waver, and he had to force himself to speak up and divert Antoine's attention.

"Where are you going to get money?" he said. "You live in a forest."

Distracted, Antoine turned his attention back to Gavin. "He doesn't know that I will collect a reward for capturing him, yes, I will. But will I play with him first? Also, yes."

Gavin froze. "What reward? What are you talking about?"

"Is it a large reward? Enormous!" Antoine began to pace. The cat watched him intently, and when Antoine's twisted back was turned, it bolted out from under the table and took a flying leap onto Gavin's back. Its claws sank into Gavin's skin, and Gavin sucked in a sharp breath at the pricks and stabs of eighteen claws.

"Ow! Click!" Gavin gasped.

Antoine glanced sharply at him, but the cat was hidden from view behind Gavin's body. "Click?"

"I said I'm sick," Gavin managed. "Who could be offering a reward for me? I've been in France only a few days."

"That would be Lieutenant Susan Phipps."

Gavin's blood chilled. "No," he whispered.

"Ah. Did you see the way I frightened my new subject?" A pause, and his expression turned churlish. "But I should be allowed to play before I turn him over to Lieutenant Phipps. Just a little. Just enough."

"What about Alice?" Gavin couldn't help blurting. "Is there a reward for her, too?"

"Would I like to double the reward?" Click the cat climbed higher just as Antoine snaked out a hand and pulled Gavin closer by his hair, which gave Gavin an excuse to yelp in pain. "Where is your little baroness?"

At that moment, a woman in a brown explorer's shirt, trousers, and gloves slid through the hole in the roof and down the slanted rope. Her hair was tucked under a pith helmet, and her belt sported a glass cutlass. Her expression was tight, like a dirigible that might explode. Alice Michaels. Oh God. Gavin's chest constricted and he felt a mixture of love and alarm, devotion and dread. He was so glad to see her he wanted to go limp with relief even as he was terrified the clockworker would capture her as well.

"We split up," Gavin gasped, too aware of the cat on his back. What the hell was the damned thing doing? "Right after we left England. The Third Ward was chasing us and we decided it would be safer. You'll never find her."

"Do I believe him? No, I do not. Do I think his Alice is somewhere nearby? Yes, I—"

"*MONSEIGNEUR!*" boomed one of the trees. "*MONSEIGNEUR! ROCAILLEUX!*"

Everything happened at once. Antoine snatched up the brass pistol from the worktable. Click scrambled up Gavin's legs to his ankles and extended a claw into the shackles. Alice whipped the glass cutlass free with one hand and sliced the rope below her. Clinging to the top piece like a liana vine, she swung downward. With a *clack*, Gavin's shackles came open and he dropped to the ground, barely managing to tuck and roll so he wouldn't hit his head. Antoine fired the pistol at Alice. Yellow lightning snapped from the barrel. Thunder smashed through the greenhouse. An anguished shout tore itself from Gavin's throat. The bolt missed its target, and four windows shattered. Alice landed several yards away from the circle of trees, stumbled, regained her feet in waist-high shrubbery. Click dropped to the ground in front of Gavin. Antoine took aim at Alice again.

Now enraged, Gavin tried to come to his feet, but his legs, chained for too many hours, gave way. Instead, he snatched up Click and threw. Click landed on Antoine's head with a mechanical yowl. Antoine's arm jerked. The pistol spoke, and thunder slammed the air as the yellow bolt tore through the top of one of the trees. Another window shattered.

"*ROCAILLEUX*," the tree cursed. To a tree, anything rocky was bad.

Alice crashed through the bushes toward Antoine, who was still struggling with Click. Blood flowed from a dozen tiny cuts on the clockworker's face and head. He finally managed to fling the cat aside and bring the pistol around on her.

"Alice!" Gavin's heart wrenched with terror for her. Already he could envision the smoking hole in her chest.

Antoine's finger tightened on the trigger. Without pausing in her stride, Alice swung the glittering cutlass and severed the power cable. It spat sparks and dropped to the ground like a dying electric snake. A magnificent move, and Gavin grinned. But instead of hesitating, Antoine swung the barrel of the pistol. It clipped Alice on the side of the head, and she stumbled.

"*Pute!*" Antoine snarled. "Do I care if I get a reward for her alive? No, I do not!"

Angered again, Gavin wrenched himself to his feet and rushed at Antoine, but the clockworker was ready, and stiff-armed Gavin in the chest. Antoine looked old, but he was actually young and strong and gifted with heightened reflexes by the disease that was also burning through his brain. Gavin possessed similar strength and reflexes, but he was still hobbled by his hours in shackles, and he staggered back.

Alice recovered herself, but instead of going for Antoine, she ran for one of the brass-limned trees. Antoine snatched up a set of huge hedge-trimming shears and flipped a switch. They chattered and chopped as he ran toward her, foam and spittle trailing from his mouth. Alice scrambled up the tree. Antoine swung the shears and gouged out a chunk of brass and bark just below her boot.

"*ROCAILLEUX*," the tree said.

Knives and needles slashed Gavin's sore muscles, but he ignored them and forced himself to move. He slammed into Antoine from behind, stopping the clockworker from swinging the shears again but not knocking him over. Instead, Antoine's plague-enhanced reflexes allowed him to spin and jab at Gavin. The shears snapped at Gavin's arm, and he barely yanked it out of the way. Air puffed past his fingers as the blades closed. He grabbed Antoine's wrist and twisted, hoping to force him to drop the shears, but Antoine was stronger than he looked and Gavin's stiff muscles continued to disobey him. Antoine slowly forced the shears back around until the blades were snapping at Gavin's neck. A warm drop of saliva dribbled from Antoine's mouth onto Gavin's cheek.

"Will the boy pay?" he hissed. "He will!"

The tree Alice had climbed creaked and bent. "Gavin! Down!"

At Alice's shout, Gavin relaxed and let himself fall. It never occurred to him not to. He dropped to the grass, leaving Antoine standing above him. One of the tree's branches swung around at chest height. Gavin caught the surprise on Antoine's face just before the tree swept him aside like a toy soldier knocked off a table.

"Hurry!" Alice called. "Climb up."

Gavin struggled to his feet and jumped onto the lowered branch. Click followed, his claws digging into the bark and offering a clear advantage over Gavin, who had to cling as best he could while the branch hauled him up to the main trunk. Alice, surrounded by pedals, cranks, levers, and pulleys, was seated on a bench built into the wood. She spun one of the cranks, and the tree straightened again. Then she grabbed the front of Gavin's shirt and pulled him down for a long kiss.

The world stopped for a moment. The pain in Gavin's body receded, and Alice's warm lips pressing against his own made him feel both safe and calm, even as they stole his very breath. He kissed her back, so thankful to see her that tears came to his eyes. They parted.

"That's for being alive when I came to get you," Alice said, then slapped him lightly on the cheek. "And that's for getting captured and scaring me half to death in the first place."

"I love you, too." Gavin said. "Now, run! He'll recover in a minute, and I'm not up for fighting him. I don't suppose you brought Dr. Clef's power gun."

"Too heavy to carry down the rope, darling." Alice held out an arm and whistled. The whirligig buzzed in and settled on her shoulder. Click took up a position on the bench beside her. "We're safe for the moment anyway. These trees don't move unless you tell them to. Do you want to drive? I never handled the original Tree back home."

Below, Antoine had already regained his feet and was staggering toward the worktable.

"Antoine can control them from the ground," Gavin said tersely. "Go! Go now!"

Alice didn't hesitate or ask for further explanation, which was one of the many reasons Gavin loved her. She hauled ropes and yanked levers. The tree stomped forward on a bifurcated trunk that ended in balled roots. Antoine reached the worktable—and the control panel. Alice stomped another step forward, and another. She had nearly cleared the ring of mutated trees.

"Will I kill them?" Antoine screamed from the control panel. "Will I?"

"He's losing his mind," Gavin observed as Alice worked. "He's not even answering his own questions."

Antoine's hands moved swiftly over the panel, flipping levers and twisting dials. A low-pitched hum throbbed through the earth and vibrated even the tree.

"*FEUILLU*," said the tree.

"Is that French for *leafy*?" Gavin asked.

"Yes," Alice said. "He must like the vibrations. I find them most uncomfortable."

"It's a very low C," said Gavin.

"You and your perfect pitch. Good heavens, how I missed you, darling."

Antoine yanked a large lever, and all the other trees snapped to attention. "Destroy them!"

"Uh-oh," Gavin said. "Can you move faster?"

"The tree is trying to follow Antoine's orders instead of mine," Alice replied grimly. "But I seem to be getting the hang of it."

The tree picked up speed even as the other trees—four of them—turned as one and stomped in Alice's wake. Alice, for her part, was guiding their own tree straight toward the perimeter of the glassy greenhouse. Gavin clung to the branch with white fingers. The noise was incredible. Heavy trees thudded across the ground like an army of gods, the vibrations that controlled the others throbbed in Gavin's bones, and Antoine's shrieks chased them faster than a flock of ravens.

"It's still fighting me," Alice shouted. Her arms and legs worked the controls in a blur. "It wants to do what the others are doing."

"How are we going to get out of here?" Gavin called over the noise. "I don't see a door."

"Cover your eyes!" was all Alice said.

"*ROCAILLEUX*," screamed the tree.

They hit the greenhouse wall. Glass exploded in a thousand directions, and Gavin lurched forward. His feet left the branch, and he was flying through the air. The tree hadn't smashed completely through, and its top third was caught on the remains of the greenhouse.

Gavin tumbled forward, but the clockwork plague suddenly took over. The universe slowed. Green leaves and glittering glass surrounded him like strange snowflakes. Just below him were the tree's branches, and he was aware of the drag coefficient of the bark, which places would slow him down and by how much. He saw every bump and nub, every side branch and twig, and his brain instantly mapped out a route that would take him to safety. Behind him floated Alice, and he calculated the arc of her flight pattern as well, then readjusted his own route accordingly.

The universe burst back into motion, and his body, finally free of its earlier stiffness, turned the dive into controlled leaps and jumps down the tree's branches until he came to rest on solid ground outside the greenhouse exactly where he wanted. Then he whirled and caught Alice. Her helmet flew on without her and cracked against a boulder. Gavin nearly went over backward, but just managed to keep his feet with Alice in his arms. Thank God. He held her tight, feeling her heart pound against his chest. The universe could come to a complete stop now, and he wouldn't mind in the slightest.

"Thank you, kind sir," she gasped, pushing a lock of tousled honey-brown hair out of dark brown eyes. "That quite took my breath away."

"Clockwork reflexes," Gavin said. "I should be in a circus."

The tree was now standing with its lower branches sticking out of the glittering greenhouse, while the upper part was still trapped inside. Behind it stampeded the other trees. Click trotted out of the wreckage, his metal ears back, and the whirligig whizzed overhead, unhurt.

"Now what?" Gavin asked, setting Alice down. "You do have a plan, right?"

She took his hand. "Yes: run!"

A rutted dirt road twisted through the woods ahead of them, and they sprinted down it. The late-summer breeze should have been uncomfortably warm, but it felt refreshing after the hot, still air of the greenhouse. Behind them, glass smashed and tinkled as the trees hit the side of the greenhouse, but they were tangling up with one another, and they were further hampered by the fact that all of them were making the exact same motions under Antoine's control. Gavin, Alice, and the two little machines rounded a bend in the road, leaving the greenhouse and its howling inhabitant behind.

"Why didn't you have Click cut an exit at ground level instead of coming in through the ceiling?" Gavin puffed.

"The glass is thicker at the base to support weight," Alice pointed out. "It's thin on the roof."

"So where are Dr. Clef and the *Lady*? Shouldn't they be—?"

A crackling crash brought them up short. From out of the trees beside the road about fifteen feet ahead of them burst a pair of mechanicals. They were nearly two stories tall, with squat, round builds, heavy legs, long arms, and gleaming brass skin. A glass bubble enclosed the top of each. Inside one rode a young man with dark, curly hair that peeked out from around his hat, and inside the other sat a woman in a long skirt, puffy white blouse, and fashionably small hat. The man pointed one of his mechanical's arms at Gavin, and the hand ended in an impressively large gun barrel.

"Aw, no," Gavin groaned. "Simon, Glenda—you aren't serious."

"Surrender, Gavin. You too, Alice," said Simon d'Arco into a speaking tube. His voice, carried outside the bubble, sounded tinny and distant.

"We've got you," the woman added in a similarly tinny voice. "And you know it."

"I know nothing of the sort, Glenda," Alice shot back.

"What if we tell you to piss off, Simon?" Gavin said. "Are you going to shoot me? Squash me? We were partners in the Ward for months." *And you were half in love with me,* he added silently.

"You *destroyed* the Ward, Gavin," Simon said. "It's gone now. The Queen herself disbanded it. Our last mission is to arrest you for treason and bring you back for trial."

"Now that you've released that cure," Glenda added, "we'll have no more clockworkers to hunt down. The few we have are dead or dying."

"And millions of other people will live," Alice replied hotly. "I don't regret it for a moment."

"You thought of nothing but yourselves," Glenda snapped, showing some agitation. "Nothing! The Ward was *everything* to me, Alice. I gave you a chance with the Ward and with Gavin, and this is how you repay me?"

"We're not going back to England, Simon," Gavin said. "So are you ready to shoot me?"

"He doesn't have to shoot you," said a voice that made Gavin stiffen. "He only has to delay you. Just like Antoine did, and admirably." From the trees stepped a second woman. Her black hair, only slightly streaked with silver, was pulled into a twist. She wore a blue uniform with hat, boots, and epaulets. The coat was cut to show her left arm, which was entirely mechanical. It also had six fingers. Her name was Lieutenant Susan Phipps.

"In the name of Her Royal Majesty and the Third Ward," Phipps said, "I place you both under arrest for sedition, treason, and attempted murder."

"No," Gavin said, though some of the bravado had left him. Phipps by herself was more imposing than even two agents in mechanicals. He made himself stand upright, though he was sweating under his arms. "Sorry, Lieutenant—Susan—but we all know that Glenda and Simon aren't going to hurt us. We *saved* you from that doomsday invention Alice's aunt dropped on headquarters. I don't mean to sound disrespectful, but it wasn't very smart to bring those two. You should have brought someone who doesn't know us."

"They're loyal," Phipps said, unruffled, "and won't disappoint me. Unlike some."

Gavin couldn't help flinching at that. When Gavin was only seventeen and stranded in London, Phipps had offered him a position as an agent of the Third Ward. She had seen him through his training, encouraged him, opened doors for him. She had lifted him out of the gutter and handed him the keys to the world, and he had betrayed her.

"I'm . . . sorry, ma'am," Gavin said. "Look, I'm not happy about what I—"

"Oh, shut it, Gavin," Alice interrupted. "We learned the Empire had been keeping the cure locked away to ensure the plague continues creating clockwork geniuses. You let thousands of people die excruciating deaths, Phipps, and have no right to debate morality."

"Thousands more will die because you released the cure," Phipps said. "Because of you, China will have clockworkers for much longer than we, easily long enough to take over the world, and that conflict will cost countless British lives. So come quietly, or come noisily. It makes no difference."

"Noisily?" Gavin said. "What do you mean by—?"

Phipps reached into her pockets with both hands and came up with a pair of tuning forks. Gavin's eye automatically measured their length and thickness with clockwork precision. When struck, they would produce the notes D and A-flat. For the second time that day, his blood chilled.

"Run!" Alice screamed, but it was too late. Phipps clanged the forks together. The two notes rang down the road. Dual vibrations tore ugly ripples through the air faster than Gavin could react, and the discordant interval, a tritone, slammed into his brain. The noise made its own string of numbers inside his head, and they spun around him, refusing to coalesce into anything that made sense. A tritone has, at its base, the square root of two, and it is the only musical interval that is expressed as an irrational number, a number that does not truly exist, and yet at that moment it *did* exist in the sound Gavin was hearing. The paradox that he could hear so clearly tore at his mind and made his head dizzy with pain. He clapped his hands over his ears, but the sound was too loud to shut out.

He was vaguely aware of Alice shouting something, and he heard clunky mechanical footsteps. Hard metal hands scooped him up. The tritone began to fade, then clanged again, and Gavin cried out in fresh pain as an explosion rocked his body.

Chapter Two

Gavin landed hard. The terrible tritone faded, and the mind-numbing pain and dizziness went with it. Dust clogged his mouth and nose. Coughing and spitting, he levered himself upright. A great hole, perhaps ten feet across, had appeared in the road. Gavin lay on one side with Alice and Click and the little whirligig. Phipps and the two Ward agents were on the other. Glenda's mechanical was sitting down like a toddler who had lost its balance and landed on its backside. Phipps had kept her feet, but she had lost one of the tuning forks. That was one good thing, at least.

"That is called a warning shot," bellowed a voice from above. "I believe my energy cannon can manage another. The *boom* may not be so large or exciting, but it will suffice."

Over the road and just above the trees hovered a familiar dirigible the size of a generous cottage. A gondola shaped like an unmasted sailing ship hung from a cigar-shaped envelope that was clearly too small to provide enough lift for such a mass. A lacy blue endo-skeleton Gavin had forged and bent himself glowed like captured sky beneath the envelope's thin skin, and a long rope dangled from the stern, which sported the words *The Lady of Liberty*. Leaning over the gunwale was a portly man in a white coat and heavy goggles over a bulldog face. He was pointing a small cannon down at the road. Phipps, Glenda, and Simon didn't move. A river of relief swept over Gavin.

"Dr. Clef!" he shouted. "You're my favorite German."

"Very glad to see you are safe, my boy."

Alice looked calm and unruffled, but Gavin read a symphony of strain holding her upright. "I don't suppose," she called up, "that you could provide a ladder?"

Seconds later, one end of a rope ladder tumbled down. Alice clambered up first, and Gavin followed with Click. The whirligig flew.

"We can still follow you," Phipps shouted up at them. "We found you now, and we'll find you again!"

Ignoring her, Gavin pulled himself over the edge to join Alice. His shoes came down on solid planking, and he felt some of the tension drain away. The airship, the *Lady*, was his place, his home. Wood and hemp made their familiar creak as the envelope strained against her ropes, trying to pull the ship higher while her lacy skeleton gleamed a magnificent azure blue. The generator that ran on paraffin oil muttered and mumbled to itself on the deck, emitting steam and feeding a steady stream of power to the *Lady*'s skeleton and to her propellers. Dr. Clef, a clockworker once captured by the Third Ward, had developed the alloy that pushed against gravity when it was electrified, but Gavin had been the one to put it into the envelope of a dirigible.

At the helm stood a stocky, sharp-faced Oriental dressed in a pirate shirt that suited him perfectly. He was just over eighteen. His trousers were tucked into his boots, and like Alice, he kept a glass cutlass sheathed at his belt. He saluted Gavin with a rakish grin that made him even more handsome than before.

"No, no," Dr. Clef was calling down. He continued to aim his power cannon at the ground. "Don't move, please. My finger trigger, it itches."

"That's trigger finger," Gavin said. "And you let *Feng* pilot the *Lady*?"

"It was that or give him the cannon," Dr. Clef replied mildly. "I did consider pulling apart the clicky kitty's brain and using it to create a wireless device that would allow me to control the ship from a distance, but the young woman wouldn't hear of it."

"Bloody right." Alice picked up Click and let the whirligig land on her shoulder. "Feng, get us out of here!"

"Which way?" said Feng Lung with a trace of China in his words.

"Any way, as long as it's east," Alice said.

Feng swung the helm around. The propellers on the *Lady*'s nacelles hanging from the outer hulls whirled to life, and she picked up speed, still trailing the rope. Alice set Click down and pulled it in.

"You slid all the way down *that* to get into the greenhouse and rescue me?" Gavin said. "I must be awfully special."

"Indeed you are, Mr. Ennock." Alice coiled the rope on the deck, then turned and collapsed into Gavin's surprised arms. Her body shook against his, and wet, sloppy tears dampened his shirt. "Don't you ever do that to me again, you . . . you *cad*."

His own throat thickened and he held her, clumsily at first, then tightly. "I'm sorry. I'm so sorry." After a moment, he added, "What did I do?"

Alice gave a hiccupping laugh and straightened. "Oh, Gavin. Dear God. You scared me half to death, that's what."

"So true," Feng said from the helm. "After you went missing from the hotel, she went mad. Berserk. She would not sleep; she would not eat. When we tracked you to the greenhouse, she almost rammed it with the ship. I insisted to be pilot then."

"Oh. I'm sorry," he said again. "Should I write letters in the sky to warn you when I'm going to be captured?"

"Certainly." Alice pulled off her leather gloves, revealing a metal spider wrapping her left hand from forearm to fingers. Its legs ended in claws that tipped Alice's own nails, and tubules running up and down the spider's legs flowed scarlet with her blood. The dark iron gleamed, and the spider's eyes glowed red, indicating that she had just touched someone infected with the clockwork plague—Gavin, in this case. It was another of the daily reminders that he was dying, and it was inextricably linked to the woman he loved. The thought made him both sad and angry, and he wanted to wrench the spider off her, even though he knew it wouldn't work. The spider's joints squeaked slightly as Alice fumbled at her sleeve for a handkerchief, and then she remembered she wasn't wearing a woman's blouse. She reached into her pocket for one instead and dabbed at her eyes. "I'll *kill* the next one who captures you. I swear it."

"There's going to be a next one?"

Alice cuffed him lightly on the shoulder, then knelt in front of him to pull up his pant cuffs. "If Phipps has her way, there will be."

"Uh . . . what are you doing?"

"I need to check your ankles. Those horrible chains Antoine kept you in couldn't have been good for them. This will be easier if you sit down."

He sank into a deck chair and let her pull off his shoes, wincing as the leather came away from swollen flesh. Alice made a low sound.

"I wish you'd been wearing your boots instead of just shoes," she muttered. "They might have protected you better. Does this hurt?" She gently massaged his ankles.

"Yes," he hissed through clenched teeth. "But don't stop."

She looked up at him, and he saw tenderness in her eyes. It melted the pain and relaxed every muscle in his body. He slumped in the chair, unable to move as her strong, careful fingers went over his feet and worked at the muscles.

"Oh my God, I love you," he groaned. "Always and always."

"And I love you always," she replied. "Even when you blaspheme."

"You blasphemed just a second—"

"Now you need to explain what happened, starting from the moment Antoine took you."

"Not yet, Madam." A mechanical man emerged from belowdecks. His features were only painted on, as was his black-and-white outfit, yet he carried himself as if he were starched and fully clothed. The only hint of expression lay in the flickering firefly lights that made up his eyes. He set a laden tea tray on a deck table beside the spot where Alice knelt. "You haven't eaten since Sir was captured. And then you must have a massage yourself to ease the tension."

"Wonderful, Kemp." Dr. Clef rubbed his hands together. "Do you have any of those lacy sugar cookies? I have had quite a craving, and the patterns twist through dimensional rifts on golden wings."

"You have had your tea, Doctor," Kemp said. "I will make more if I have time, but I have more important concerns at the moment."

The cake and sandwiches on the tray sent up smells that called to Gavin's stomach, though he wasn't yet willing to move away from Alice's ministrations. "What time is it?" he asked, trying to get a glimpse of the sun around the envelope.

"Two fifteen," Kemp replied. "Tuesday."

Gavin bolted upright, and Alice released his foot. "Tuesday? How long was I—?"

"You've been missing for three days, darling." Alice took a teacup, which rattled in her metallic hand. "It's been hell."

"Three *days*?" Gavin sank back onto the chair and bit into a ham sandwich without really paying attention to it. "I thought it was only a night."

"Antoine has powerful sleep drugs," Feng said.

Gavin stared past Alice at calm, blue infinity. He should feel safe, at home in the ship he had created with his own hands. She ignored gravity, soared silent currents, explored the limits of daylight. Set him free. But all he felt was violated, stripped of his clothes and then his skin. He wondered how long he had hung unconscious in Antoine's greenhouse, a piece of meat in the hands of a twisted homunculus. His gorge rose, and then he was at the gunwale, the few bites of sandwich falling to the forest far below. The pieces seemed to fall slowly, pushing aside the billions of tiny bits that made up the air. The bits rubbed against the falling pieces and raised their temperature as they fell closer to hell.

"We could harvest the energy of the pieces," he said. "The billions of bits would make a hellfire and cook twisted hunks of homunculus."

"Sir?" Kemp handed him a cup of tea. Gavin swished and spat over the side. The tea spread in both droplets and a stream, both wave and particle. He watched it, an eternity caught in a split second. Then the tea vanished.

"Wave to particles," he muttered. "Wave them away."

Alice had had the good sense to keep her seat, though her face tightened as Gavin sat back down in his own chair. "You're talking like a clockworker," she said, her voice heavy with worry. "It's already starting, isn't it?"

"It's all mixed up inside me, Alice." He rubbed a hand over his face and tried to cheer up, but the violation and the fear dragged him down. "I'm sorry. Your aunt knocked me out, locked me in that tower of hers, and infected me with this plague. She treated me like a piece of meat. So did the pirates who captured the *Juniper* and made me fiddle for them. Now I learn Antoine held me for longer than I knew. He stole time from me, and I don't have time to steal."

She took his hand across the tea tray. "We'll get to China. If anyone can cure clockworkers, they can."

"The Dragon Men are very powerful," Feng agreed from the helm. "They can do anything."

"Hmm." Dr. Clef opened a chest and unrolled an enormous chart on a table near the helm. "Peking is approximately seven thousand miles away, if we fly over Istanbul and the Gobi Desert. We could detour south into India, around the Himalayas, but that would add another four thousand miles or so. This ship's top speed is fifty miles per hour. If we travel for twelve hours each day, the journey will take us approximately twelve days."

"That's all?" Alice said. "It doesn't seem like—"

"This is also assuming," Dr. Clef continued, "that the ship always travels at top speed—it cannot—and that we have the wind behind us—we do not—and that the engines or helium extractors never break down—they will—and that the sky never sends us any bad weather—it shall—or that any number of other delays do not delay us. I believe it will take closer to two months, perhaps three."

"Oh." Alice nibbled her sandwich as a cloud drifted past. "Well, that will still be plenty of time. He was infected last May. It's only late August."

"It is not much time," said Dr. Clef. "He is already

beginning to babble. You see things, don't you, boy? Beautiful things. Like the universe is handing you its keys, one by one."

Gavin thought about his vomit and the falling tea water. "Yes."

"And you love and hate the tritones," Dr. Clef continued. "Square root of two, lovely and deadly as infinity."

Just the memory of that horrible, enticing number and the brain-bending sound that went with it made him shudder. He nodded.

"I shouldn't be so far along," Gavin said quietly.

Dr. Clef shrugged. "There is a range. Some clockworkers last only a few months, others last for two or three years. Edwina's version of the plague was experimental, so who knows what it was like? You shouldn't have become a clockworker, but you did. You should have shown no symptoms for several weeks, but you have. Losing yourself and talking about what you see is a sign of the final phase, where I am. You have about three months left. Four months if you are lucky. You will be a raving lunatic by the time we reach Peking, and then Alice will still have to find a Chinese clockworker who can cure you, and that assumes such a clockworker even exists. So you will die, my boy. But don't worry." He clapped Gavin on the shoulder. "They say once we clockworkers go completely mad, we do not even know what is happening, and we enjoy it. We can go mad together, yes?"

"Why did you bring him with you?" Feng asked.

"He jumped on board the ship while we were running away from the Third Ward headquarters," Alice said dully. "Perhaps I should have kicked him off."

"No." Gavin straightened. "I'm not going to give in to this. We'll find a way to get to Peking, and we'll find a Chinese clockworker—"

"Dragon Man," Feng interrupted. "We call them Dragon Men."

"Dragon Man," Gavin continued, "who has a cure. If we can't find time, we'll *make* time."

An odd look came over Dr. Clef's bulldog face. "Make time."

"But we do have a more powerful problem." Feng moved the *Lady*'s helm to adjust for a current. "This ship is very easy to see. Many airships fly, but none of them glow blue."

"She's very beautiful," Gavin said, feeling defensive. The motor gave a pleased-sounding hiccup and went back to its normal quiet murmur.

"True. But beauty has its price," Feng said. "Hers is that she attracts attention. Also, if Third Ward agents are spreading word and money to look for us, we have more trouble. How do they do it so quickly?"

"Several clockworkers in England and in Europe invented wireless communication devices," Gavin said. "You can send messages at the speed of light to any other wireless device that listens to the same frequency. They're better than a telegraph because you don't need to raise poles or string wires."

"We can't outrun such a message," Feng pointed out. "As it is, we lost three days when you were captured. I imagine that was what your Lieutenant Phipps wanted—to catch us up. It is fortunate she seems to have no airship."

"Yeah. We'll have to think of some way to hide better. I just wish we had more time."

"You said that." Alice set her cup down with a clink of metal on china and came around behind his chair to put her arms around his neck. The iron gauntlet was chilly. "And you're right, darling. We'll find a way. We'll find time."

Her touch made him feel better, despite the spider. Even though he was barely nineteen and she was twenty-three, he felt no difference in their ages. Alice had been initially put off by it. The gap had been one of the reasons she had resisted admitting she loved him.

Gavin touched Alice's hand, letting himself drink in her steady presence. And she was so beautiful. Her deep brown eyes set off her honey-brown hair, and her triangle face and little nose and rounded curves all came together like the parts of an intricate fugue, compelling and hypnotic. He still found it hard to believe she was with him—and that it had taken her so long to break society's rules and leave her horrible fiancé. She leaned down. Her scent wafted over him, and he kissed her softly in the free and open sky. The kiss intensified, and a thrill went through him. He could do this. He could conquer the whole damned world, as long as Alice Michaels stood beside him.

"Very sweet," Feng said, breaking the moment. "But I have no idea where I am going."

They broke away and Alice coughed, a bit flushed. "I'd help, but I never learned how to read a navigation chart."

"Right." Gavin got up and took the charts away from Dr. Clef, who was now staring into the distance.

"My Impossible Cube had time," he muttered. "All of it. At once. But you destroyed it, my boy. My lovely, lovely Impossible Cube."

"Not this again." Alice sighed. "Click!"

Click jumped down from his vantage point on the gunwale and strolled over to rub against Dr. Clef's shins. A mechanical purr drifted across the deck. Dr. Clef glanced down.

"Ah, you send me the clicky kitty as a distraction. It will not work. I am so very forlorn." Still, he picked the cat up and stroked the metal ears. "It won't work at all, will it, clicky kitty? It will not. It will *not*."

"Germans are so good at despondent," Gavin observed. He pored over the charts. "If we keep our current course, we'll reach Luxembourg by tomorrow. I know the place—it gets a lot of airship traffic, and the *Juniper* stopped there several times."

"Do you think the other airships will give us camouflage?" Alice asked.

"Honestly? No." Gavin gestured at the softly glowing envelope. "She stands out, even among airships, and the envelope isn't big enough to lift her without turning on the generator."

"Then why did you build your ship this way?" Feng asked.

"You're such a clicky kitty," Dr. Clef cooed. "You *are*."

Gavin's stomach turned over. "Because I could. You don't think about consequences when you're in a . . . a clockwork fugue. You just build. I didn't even know I was a clockworker when I built the *Lady*. I thought I just had insomnia."

"Whatever the reason, we have a conspicuous ship," Alice said, "and the Third Ward is spreading word of a generous reward for our capture."

"Is the clicky kitty hungry? Would he like a saucer of arsenic?"

Gavin sighed and leaned over the gunwale, the fresh breeze on his face, solid wood beneath his bare feet. Forests and fields stretched to the horizon, emerald meeting azure, broken only by a railroad that ribboned through the green.

Alice joined him. "What are you thinking?"

"That you're right. The ship is too conspicuous," he said. "*We're* too conspicuous. You have that gauntlet that won't come off. Feng is Chinese. Dr. Clef is . . . Dr. Clef. And we have all these automatons. I mean, you can order Kemp to stay hidden—"

"We have to for at least a while," Alice interrupted. "Human-seeming automatons are illegal on most of the Continent."

"Only in the western part," Gavin said, "where the Catholic Church is powerful. Once you get past the four French Kingdoms and the ten Prussian Kingdoms into Poland and the Ukrainian Empire, no one cares."

"Oh." Alice looked miffed that she hadn't known this. "Kemp will be glad to hear that."

"But I was saying that Click has a way of showing up wherever he wants," Gavin continued. "We're a very distinctive group, and you know Phipps has described us carefully."

"Come, clicky kitty," Dr. Clef said. "We will go below and you will watch me while I work. Would you like that? You *would.*"

"If I took such a tone with Click," Feng said to no one in particular, "he would disembowel me. Why does he allow Dr. Clef the privilege?"

A train passed beneath them, puffing smoke and spurting steam. The whistle—a G, Gavin noted automatically—sounded high and thin up in the air. The locomotive was painted bright red, and the cars sported bright colors as well. It looked like a child's toy. Something about it tugged at him, but he couldn't say what.

"We'll have to figure something out soon," Gavin finished. "Luxembourg is the only place nearby where we can stock up on paraffin oil for the generator, and we have to stop there."

"And the food stores are nearly nonexistent," Kemp added. "Madam and everyone else were searching for Sir, and I was not allowed to shop."

"That's another worry," Alice said. "Money. We don't have much left. The Ward won't be paying our salaries anytime soon, and I rather doubt Norbert would be willing to wire me any money now that I've left him."

Gavin stared across the free sky as tension tightened his muscles again. Even here, on his own ship, problems weighed him down. He wanted—needed—to leap over the side and coast away with nothing but bright and flowing air beneath him. The clouds twisted in the air currents, droplets hovering like trillions of tiny spirits buoyed by—

Alice touched his arm. "You've been staring for a long time. Would you play for me?"

"A long time?" He blinked at her. "How long?"

"Over an hour." She handed him his bow and fiddle. "Maybe this will focus you."

Gavin looked around, bewildered. The sun had moved a considerable distance. Dr. Clef, Click, and Alice's whirligig were nowhere to be seen. Only Feng remained, still at the helm. Gavin looked down at his fiddle. It had been his constant companion ever since he could remember. His inborn perfect pitch let him pick up songs almost instantly, which meant he was able to play street corners in Boston at an early age and bring the pennies home to his mother and siblings. He had secretly fantasized that one day he would play in a music hall or even in an orchestra. But later, on his twelfth birthday, Gramps had brought him down to the Boston shipyards and introduced him to Captain Felix Naismith of the *Juniper*. From that day on, cabin boy Gavin Ennock had barely touched the ground while he played for airmen and ran their errands. Then came the attack. In seconds, both Naismith and Gavin's best friend were dead and Gavin was forced to perform for pirates. They had stranded him in London. Unable to find work on another airship, he'd gone back to playing the streets for pennies until Alice's aunt had snatched him away and locked him in her tower. For three weeks, he'd had nothing to do but play the violin until Alice had appeared and rescued him. And then he had rescued her, and then she him, and so it went.

He drew his bow over the strings and was about to begin when Alice abruptly held up a hand. For a dreadful moment, he thought he'd made a mistake and she was stopping him. It was one of his secret fears—that he'd made a mistake while playing where someone could hear. His playing, like his pitch, needed to be *perfect*. It often felt as if someone were watching over him, waiting to pounce if he played wrong, though he couldn't say why.

But Alice said only, "A moment. I want to try something first."

From her pocket, she took a small bird made of gleaming silver. Sapphires made up its eyes and glowed softly at the tips of its claws.

"My nightingale," Feng said. "Yours now, Gavin. I am glad Antoine did not get it."

"I found it in the hotel." Alice set the bird at Gavin's feet and pressed its left eye. "Now, play."

Gavin nodded and swung into a song familiar to all airmen. He played a verse, relieved when he got through it with no mistakes, then sang.

> *For to see Mad Tom of Bedlam, ten thousand miles I*
> *   traveled*
> *Mad Maudlin goes on dirty toes to save her shoes from*
> *   gravel.*
> *Still I sing bonny boys, bonny mad boys, bedlam boys*
> *   are bonny*
> *For they all go bare and they live by the air, and they*
> *   want no drink nor money.*

"Tom of Bedlam" was the unofficial song of airmen everywhere. The idea that men who lived by the air went naked and didn't want for drink or money held immense appeal, and the song's infinite verses were

made for pounding out on wooden decks. Gavin
started to sing the second verse when Alice jumped in
herself:

> *No gypsy, slut, or clockwork shall win my mad Tom*
> *from me*
> *I'll weep all night, with stars I'll fight, and the fray shall*
> *well become me.*

Gavin laughed and joined in for the chorus.

> *Still I sing bonny boys, bonny mad boys, bedlam boys*
> *are bonny*
> *For they all go bare and they live by the air, and they*
> *want no drink nor money.*

The orange sun sank to the horizon and shadows
snaked among the trees below. The sputter and hum of
the generator continued beneath Gavin's music as he
played and sang his way through "Bedlam" with Alice
clapping her hands to the beat beside him. He caught
Alice's eye, letting her know the song was for her. Her
face flushed, and he flung her a wide smile. The music
cast itself out into the darkening void, sweet as wine,
carrying Gavin's spirit with it.

"That was wonderful," Alice said softly. She picked
up the nightingale and pressed its left eye again. Then
she pressed the right eye. Instantly, the little bird
opened its beak and the sound of Gavin's fiddle trilled
forth. It was a smaller sound, with a tinny undertone,
but otherwise a perfect replica, a recording. Then
Gavin's voice joined the music, and "Tom of Bedlam"

again floated across the deck. The sound struck Gavin. He had never heard his own voice before. It sounded different than it did in his own head, but also vaguely familiar. It made him uncomfortable. He tapped the nightingale to stop the music.

"I like the real thing better," he said.

"I do, too." Alice kissed him on the cheek, and he smiled again. "Where did you learn to play? You've never said."

"Gramps—my grandfather—started me on the fiddle when I was five or six," Gavin said. The strangeness of the nightingale's reproduction stayed with him. "I mostly taught myself. It's easier when you have perfect pitch like I do, and when you never forget a song after you've heard it, like I don't."

"So the fiddle was your grandfather's?"

Gavin was all set to say *yes*, when something stopped him. For a moment, a tiny moment, he remembered something else. A man was handing him the fiddle, but it wasn't Gramps. A much younger man, tall, broad-shouldered, with white-blond hair. The memory hovered in front of him like a reflection in a soap bubble, shiny and distorted.

"You can play just like Daddy. Would you like that?"

Gavin realized Alice was waiting for an answer. "I'm . . . I'm not sure," he said. "Gramps used to have it, but . . ."

"Was Gramps your father's mother or your mother's father?"

"Hold the fiddle like this and the bow like this. They're big now, but you'll grow. Do it right."

"My father's." Gavin's voice grew distant. He felt

strange, mixed up. "He lived with us, even though Dad . . . didn't."

"Didn't? What happened to him?"

"This one is D, this one is G, this is A, and this is E."

Gavin shook his head. "I don't know. He left when I was very small. Ma refused to talk about him, and she became angry if anyone asked. After a while, I stopped wondering."

"Good! Keep that up, and you'll play 'I See the Moon' for your ma just like me."

He raised the bow again. The horsehair was new, but the wood was old, burnished from hours of skin and sweat. He waved it, and the bubble burst, taking the memory with it.

"I'm sorry, darling." Alice put an arm around his waist. "I didn't mean to awaken painful memories."

"It's all right," he said. "It was a long time ago, and I don't really remember. Though," he added wistfully, "I wonder sometimes what it would be like to have a dad. Gramps was there for me, of course, and Captain Naismith was kind of like a father, but . . . you know."

"I know," Alice said. "I find myself wondering what it would be like to have a mother. Mine died when I was so young."

"Well, between us we had a full set of parents," Gavin said with a small laugh to break the heavy mood, and Alice smiled. He buried his face in her hair and smelled her soft scent. "All I really need is you."

Feng spoke up. "The romantic moment unfortunately will not keep me awake all night. We have to anchor ourselves."

"I'll take over." Gavin took back the nightingale,

stowed the fiddle in its case, and accepted the helm from Feng. "I don't sleep much these days."

Feng disappeared belowdecks. Alice stood beside Gavin for a moment, her presence warm and solid. Gavin steered with one hand so he could put an arm around her. "We're alone for the first time in ages," she said.

"Unless you count the *Lady*," Gavin replied with a smile.

She rested her head on his shoulder. "I want more time with you, Gavin. I feel like we never have enough."

"No one ever has enough time." Gavin checked his heading on the compass set into the helm, visible thanks to the soft blue glow of the envelope, and corrected his course. "Especially not clockworkers."

Eventually, Alice kissed him good night and went below herself, leaving Gavin alone on the deck. He felt her absence, even though she was only a few yards away.

In the morning, everything changed.

Interlude

Lieutenant Susan Phipps threw her hat onto the rick-ety table. She had intended to drop into the ladder-back chair next to it, but found she couldn't, and paced the tiny room instead, her hands clasped behind her. Her brass left hand felt cool and heavy in her fleshy right one, though the sensation was so familiar to her now she barely noticed it.

Glenda Teasdale, her blouse and skirt looking worse for the wear, stood behind the other ladder-back chair while Simon d'Arco, equally disheveled, hovered near the bed. A tiny lamp shed grudging light over the table as the sun slid away. The quarters, part of what passed for a hotel in this little town, were dank and cramped compared to her spacious rooms at Third Ward head-quarters back in London, but Phipps refused to voice a single complaint, even to herself. What sort of com-mander sent her troops into conditions that she herself refused to endure?

"We were close," Glenda said in that flat voice that

was still new to Phipps. "So close. If that bloody Dr. Clef hadn't shown up—"

"It's fine," Phipps interrupted, still pacing. "They're traveling by airship. Very hard to hide an airship. We *will* catch them; we *will* bring them back to London; we *will* see them put on trial."

"It's just . . . We're very tired, ma'am," Simon said.

She suddenly realized what she was doing. They had to remain standing while their commanding officer was on her feet. "Sit, sit," she ordered. "I think better on my feet."

Simon dropped onto the bed while Glenda perched on the chair. The woman looked odd in skirts. Ever since she joined the Ward, she had put aside feminine clothing in favor of more practical male attire, like what Phipps wore. However, when female agents traveled abroad, especially in places where the Third Ward had less influence and no actual authority, they typically wore skirts to avoid attracting attention. Phipps continued to wear her uniform, partly because it conveyed authority whether she had it or not, and partly— she admitted only to herself—because it provided her with a wall that made her feel safe.

"They're heading for Luxembourg, no doubt, judging from the general direction they took and the fact that it's a major trade city," Phipps said, thinking out loud. "Alice will want to spread her cure there. And that's a fine thing for us. The Crown has strong ties with Luxembourg, and I can force a fair amount of cooperation with the local gendarmerie. They'll help us find Ennock and Michaels in no time. The mechanicals will let us catch them up fairly quickly, so we won't lose much time."

"Maybe we should check the hotels first, Lieutenant," Glenda said. "They'll have to stay somewhere, and if we find them without starting a fuss with the police first, so much the better."

"I like that," Phipps said with a small nod. "We'll start there, then use the police."

"Good plan." Simon paused, then added, "How long are we going to chase them?"

Phipps turned. The monocle that framed her left eye amplified low light and let her see better—a clockworker invention she had confiscated nearly a year before the incident that had claimed her left arm—but she didn't need it to read the tension in Simon's body.

"We'll pursue them until we catch them, Simon," she said evenly. "There's no question."

"Only I was wondering," Simon replied in a low voice, "whether it'll be worth the cost."

"Worth the cost?" Phipps repeated. "Simon, they are dangerous *criminals*. In addition to releasing a weapon from the Doomsday Vault, they let Dr. Clef out of the Ward. Have you forgotten him?"

Simon didn't answer. Dr. Clef worried Phipps. He was a classic clockworker—completely absorbed by his work and utterly oblivious to the impact any of it might have on the world around him. His Impossible Cube was one of the most powerful inventions she had ever seen, and thank God it had been destroyed. Unfortunately, he was running about loose in the world with Gavin Ennock, a new-made clockworker. The thought of the two of them creating world-class inventions together made her sweat ice water and lent new urgency to her need to capture the little group before

China got hold of them. Every hour she regretted not killing Alice Michaels beneath Third Ward headquarters. It was the biggest mistake of her career, and now the world was paying for it.

"Dr. Clef will probably be dead in a few weeks," Simon said at last. "As for the doomsday weapon Alice and Gavin released . . . Well, we can't put the cure back into the bottle, and England's clockworkers will be gone within the year. If we let them go to China, they might be able to ensure the same thing happens to the Dragon—"

"You shut it, Simon d'Arco!" Glenda was on her feet again. Two spots of color rose in her cheeks. "I'm going to capture Alice Michaels—Lady Michaels—and drag her back to London by the hair if I have to. Every damned mile over broken glass, if I can arrange it."

"Why, Glenda?" Simon asked. "What for?"

"What do I have, Simon?" Glenda snarled. "The Third Ward is dead, by the Queen's order. Once the final clockworker dies, we'll have no reason to exist anyway. Maybe a few of us will hang about to guard the Doomsday Vault, but nothing more. And where will I go? I'm a *woman*, Simon. Shall I become a seamstress? A schoolteacher? A parlor maid? A wife? For nearly ten years I've been hunting clockworkers and keeping England safe and I brought Alice Michaels into the Ward because she was small and timid and I felt solidarity for my fellow woman. Now that bloody bitch destroyed the Ward and I have nothing. I'll see her hang for treason, and I'll piss on her grave."

"Oh," was all Simon said.

"You may sit down again, Glenda," Phipps said quietly, and Glenda reluctantly obeyed. "And I don't answer to you, Simon," she added.

"Yes, ma'am." He shifted uncomfortably on the bed. "But I . . . I just . . ."

Phipps leveled a hard gaze at him. "Simon, I want the full truth from you, as a gentleman and an officer of the Third Ward."

He stiffened. "Ma'am."

"I brought you and Glenda on this assignment because you are my absolute best agents. I am not saying this as flattery or to puff you up. It's simple truth. However, I am also fully aware of your . . . romantic proclivities and of your feelings toward your former partner. I don't much care about the former, since you are an officer of the Ward, and as such, you have my complete loyalty and support. As for the latter, I assumed that your loyalty toward the Ward would be the overriding concern, but now I must ask, Agent d'Arco: Is your loyalty pure? Will your feelings for Gavin Ennock get in the way of our mission? Answer honestly. You will not be reprimanded, but I do need to know if I must send for someone else, someone who can be a fully capable man."

Simon got to his feet. His face was stony, but Phipps's monocle told her that the heat in his body had shifted into a pattern she associated with anger, exactly the emotion her final remark had been calculated to engender. He stood at attention, unconsciously making himself stiff and hard as a fully capable man should be.

"Lieutenant," he barked, "I am willing and able to carry out any orders you give me, as my oath to the Third Ward dictates."

"Excellent, Agent d'Arco," Phipps replied. "Your hard work will not go unnoticed. Dismissed."

Simon saluted. The door snapped shut behind him, and his footsteps faded down the hotel hallway as he went to his own room. Glenda coughed.

"Fully capable man," she said. "You know how to hit below the belt, Lieutenant."

"Hm," Phipps said, and stared out the window, though now it was dark and there was nothing to see.

"Just between us," Glenda said, "and knowing that I'm perfectly happy to come along because I want to see Alice pay, why *are* you doing this? You did let them go, down in the Doomsday Vault."

Phipps chose her words carefully. "Simon persuaded me not to kill Alice, but only because she had stopped Edwina Michaels's device from exploding and killing us all. Simon said I owed her, and he was right. That debt is paid, and now it's time for Alice and Gavin to pay their other debt to us. To the Empire."

"That doesn't quite answer my question," Glenda said. "Why are you *here*? You never go into the field."

"I used to," Phipps said. "It's where I started. My father was a military man, and he was away quite a lot. But he always sent home money to make sure my mother and I had food and clothes. And his brother, my uncle, visited often to ensure there was a man about."

For a moment, the reflection in the window showed a Susan Phipps much younger, without the streaks of silver in her hair, and with the smooth features of a girl not yet twenty, but who still held the ramrod posture expected by her father, her dear father, who never showed emotion but who could grind her to the ground with a tiny frown or fling her to joyful skies with a simple nod. The reflection showed her younger self hurrying home on one of the rare days when Father was in town. He met her at the door of their row house with two carpetbags in his hand.

"The world is upside down," he said simply. "I do not wish to live here any longer, so we are moving."

Susan knew better than to ask *why*, but she felt she deserved more information, so she said, "I don't understand, Father."

"I found the love letters. As far as I am concerned, your disloyal mother is dead, and so is my brother."

Susan remembered the overwhelming despair, the fear, and most of all, the anger. Not at Father, of course, but at Mother, who had committed such a betrayal of loyalty. The bedrock of Susan's life, her parents' marriage, had crumbled into sand, and it was Mother's fault. It had to be. Otherwise Father would be in the wrong, and that was unthinkable.

"Loyalty, Susan," Father had said as they climbed into a cab. "Loyalty."

For a while, Susan wondered if Father's reference to Mother's death was metaphorical or literal. She never heard from Mother again, but neither did the police come for Father. No one was even reported missing, and for the first time Susan wondered what sort of work Father did for the military. Eventually Susan dismissed the matter as unimportant. A few years later, Father introduced her to Lieutenant Lawrence Garrison, who asked if she wanted to join the Third Ward. When she replied in the affirmative, Father gave her a small nod.

Phipps's hands clutched the windowsill. Her right fingers turned white, and her left ones left dents in the wood. "I made a terrible mistake when I let them go, Glenda," she said, "so it is my duty to set it right. Gavin and Alice unloosed several dangers into the world, and we *must* bring them into custody before they do further harm."

Glenda gave her a long look, then rose. "I understand. If I may, Lieutenant?"

Phipps nodded a dismissal and continued to stare out the window. *I'll find them, Father. I'll set the world aright for you. For us.*

Chapter Three

Alice glared down at the unyielding numbers. They glared stubbornly back, hard little loops and corners that wouldn't move no matter how hard she tried. Twice she had rubbed them off the page and run through them again, but they always came out exactly the same. She resisted the urge to throw the book overboard. Instead she snapped it shut and slipped it into her trouser pocket so she could lean on the gunwale to think while cool morning air washed over her like water.

In the distance ahead, airships of all sizes and designs floated, cruised, and hovered above the sprawling city of Luxembourg like tame clouds. London controlled airship traffic, but Luxembourg apparently didn't. Alice glanced over her shoulder at Gavin, lean and strong at the helm of their ship. The rising sun caught his pale blond hair and turned it nearly white, making a stark contrast with the torn black clothes he still wore from last night. His sharp features and long jaw made her hunger for a kiss. He caught her eye and grinned that grin that always sent a delicious shiver down her back. And she felt all that when he was silent. When he sang, his voice melted her soul. She'd follow him into a volcano if he only sang to her first, and a part of her was glad he didn't seem to know that yet.

And there it was. In the end, she had betrayed her country for him. She had broken into the Doomsday Vault and released the clockwork cure, an act which would eventually destroy the British Empire as she knew it. And all for the simple reason that Alice, Lady Michaels, had fallen in love with Gavin Ennock. What would the history books say about that? The thought that schoolchildren might one day read about her both fascinated and frightened her. What gave her the right to change the course of mankind for the love of a man?

The book of figures sat heavy in her pocket. Alice leaned out into the fresh breeze, trying to feel the freedom she knew carried Gavin forward. All her life she had followed the rules of traditional society, done as her traditional father had told her. And then Gavin had innocently blasted her life to pieces. Now she was spending her days with not one, but *three* strange men, and no other woman around to chaperone. Frightening. Exhilarating. It was like standing at the edge of a cliff with one foot over.

Below the ship lay a rumpled checkerboard of fields and pastures bordered by hedgerows and stone walls that surrounded the city proper. Arteries of rail and cobblestone ran in and out of the place. Canals threaded through it, and church spires pointed at Alice like accusing fingers. Castles with rounded walls took up the hills, and square houses occupied the slopes. It looked both foreign and familiar at the same time.

Several miles from the city, the *Lady of Liberty*'s blue glow dimmed, and the ship began to sink. Startled, Alice turned to Gavin, who was moving from the generator back to the helm. "Is something wrong with her?"

"We can't dock at the shipyard," he said. "Not if Phipps has gotten word out about us and what the *Lady* looks like. But I think I know a place."

They came down in a weed-filled pasture surrounded by a scraggly hedge on three sides and a stand of trees on the fourth. Near the stand of trees were a small stone farmhouse and a large stable, both half in ruin. Kemp, Dr. Clef, and Feng emerged from below to see what was going on. Sunlight gleamed on Dr. Clef's brass goggles, and he pushed them up on his forehead.

"Cut power to twenty percent, Alice," Gavin ordered.

Alice leaned over the generator and restricted the flow of air and paraffin oil. The machine responded to her precise touch, and she thought about opening it up to poke around inside. Alice wasn't a clockworker, but she was startlingly talented with the machines clockworkers created. Usually, only a clockworker could create and maintain the fantastic steam-driven inventions that let Britain and China dominate the world. In her short time with the Third Ward, Alice had encountered a number of mind-bending inventions that frightened her out of her wits. Weightless metal and walking trees were just the beginning.

Normal people were able to reproduce a few clockwork innovations—Babbage engines that allowed machines to retain information and appear to think. Tempered glass that let airmen create weapons that wouldn't spark amid dangerous hydrogen. Designs for dirigibles. Electric light. But the vast majority of clockworker inventions were so complicated, so complex, that only clockworkers could create them, and their work seemed limited only by the materials they could afford. Normal humans couldn't assemble the materials, even with careful diagrams or instructions. Even taking most inventions apart without breaking them was nearly impossible.

Alice, however, seemed to be unique in the clock-work world. She alone could understand, assemble, and repair clockwork inventions. She had, for example, assembled Click and Kemp with instructions from Aunt Edwina, along with over a dozen spiders and whirligigs, and could strip a clockwork machine to its component cogs in minutes, though this odd ability didn't extend to the spider gauntlet currently gripping her left hand.

Alice had spent considerable time trying to pry it off, and with every tool at her disposal. It wouldn't budge. She couldn't even find a way to open it. It stoically wrapped her forearm and fingers, tipping her fingers with its claws and filling its tubules with her blood. It didn't restrict her movements, and it left the underside of her hand uncovered, so she didn't lose sensation, but she still found it . . . unsettling. It was always there, burbling to itself and dragging at her arm. The demon spider was a part of her now, and she a part of it. So far the demon did everything she required of it, except come off, but she wondered what would happen on the day her desires ran counter to its.

Under her ministrations, the generator's power dropped and the envelope's glow dimmed. The *Lady* descended toward the abandoned farm buildings and touched the ground in front of them with a delicate bump.

"Perfect landing," Feng said. "You are quite skilled."

Gavin flashed the heart-stopping grin, then cast lines over the sides. "Let's get to work. That barn— stable—is big enough to hide the ship in."

Once the passengers, including Kemp, dropped to the ground, the ship rose a few feet. Everyone took a line and towed the ship toward the two-story stable, which was really little more than an empty shell. The ship barely squeezed through the gaping space left by the missing main doors, and the group lashed her in place at Gavin's direction, then edged around her to get outside into the late-summer sunlight. Click looked down at them smugly from the stern, clearly pleased that he didn't have to do any of the work.

"How did you know about this place?" Alice asked.

Gavin shuffled a little, momentarily looking like the teenager he technically was. "Sometimes the *Juniper* carried cargo that Captain Naismith didn't want the port authority in Luxembourg to see. We used to drop it off here and pick it up later."

"Smuggling?" Alice raised an eyebrow. "Mr. Ennock, I am shocked!"

"Well, Luxembourg has high tariffs on certain items that made it more expensive to ship them in than the goods were worth, and we couldn't always be— Oh."

He caught sight of Alice's expression. "You were joking."

"The famous dry British wit," Feng observed. "So much like my father's."

"Madam," Kemp said, "I am afraid I have to report that the food stores are nearly empty. Breakfast this morning drained what little we had."

"Then we'll have to get more," Alice said. "How far away are we from the city?"

"Less than five miles," Gavin said. "A decent walk, though we might be able to beg a ride from a farm wagon or a carriage. Alice, I think you should change into skirts. A woman in trousers attracts attention."

"I was thinking the same thing." Alice sighed. "And, Kemp, you and Click will have to stay behind with the ship."

"Madam!" Kemp huffed. "It is my duty to attend to Madam's every need and comfort. I cannot do that when—"

"The Catholics have made you illegal in Luxembourg," Alice said patiently. "Besides, the Third Ward is looking for a group that's traveling with a mechanical servant and a clockwork cat."

"Madam," Kemp replied stiffly. On the ship above, Click put his ears back.

"No worrying," Dr. Clef said. "I will also stay. I am working on a new piece, and the clicky kitty will keep me company."

"What about food?" Gavin asked.

"There is sufficient for one person for a day or two," Kemp said. "I said we had little, not none."

Dr. Clef looked sly. "And it gives farms about, with

fruit and vegetables in the fields. If you are gone for a few days, it matters nothing."

"Right." Gavin rumpled his hair. "That leaves you, Feng."

"Oh?" The young man struck a pose. He was, as usual, quite good-looking, though nowhere near as handsome as Gavin, in Alice's mind. "Do *I* stand out?"

"I know!" Alice plucked the goggles from Dr. Clef's forehead and drew them down over Feng's head, then extracted a red scarf from her pocket and wrapped it around the lower half of Feng's face. "There! With the right hat, you'll look like an airman instead of a mysterious Oriental. Around here, that shouldn't attract attention."

Feng made a horrified sound. "I was hoping my exotic good looks would attract a great deal of attention, if you understand my meaning."

"Mr. Lung!" Alice admonished. "That's hardly appropriate."

"That is why my father asked you to bring me back to Peking," Feng pointed out. "Unlike my father, when I see a pretty piece of . . . a pretty face, I become a *bad* diplomat." His voice was muffled through the scarf. "But for your sake, my lady, I will try."

"Your Ladyship," Alice corrected. "A baroness isn't rightly addressed as *my lady*."

"You see? Bad diplomat." He straightened the goggles. "Let us go now. I will be hungry soon."

"Feng," Gavin said, "the jar?"

Feng's almond eyes widened. "How could I have forgotten?" He dashed for the ship.

Alice, meanwhile, quickly changed into skirts in her

tiny stateroom belowdecks and snatched up a cloth airman's cap for Feng. She also took the book of figures. Gavin had changed out of his torn black clothes into a plain workman's outfit, complete with a cloth cap of his own. He wore his fiddle case on his back, since he rarely went anywhere without it. Feng appeared with a rucksack that clinked. They bade Dr. Clef and the mechanicals good-bye and left.

"Are you still a baroness?" Gavin asked as the trio set off down the dusty, hedge-lined road toward Luxembourg. "I mean, you left the country and abandoned your fiancé and became a traitor, so—"

"Titles are for life," Alice said. "My father was the last Lord Michaels, and I was his only child. His only relative, really. When he passed away, that left me Alice, Lady Michaels, and I will be until I die, no matter how scandalously I behave, though if I have a child, things become complicated."

"How?" Feng inquired. His feet kicked up small puffs of dust that hung on the still air. Birds called from the hedges and the trees that grew among them, and cows lowed from their pastures.

"For the line to continue, any child I have must be legitimate," Alice said, flushing a little. The subject still made her uncomfortable, even though England was hundreds of miles away. "If Gavin and I don't marry in a Christian church, our children won't be . . ."

She trailed off in horror, realizing what she had just said. Gavin would never live to see children. Tears welled up, and she looked abruptly away.

Gavin squeezed her hand. "I don't care if they're titled or not," he said brightly. "We aren't going back to

England, and that's the only place the title matters. You will be my wife on our airship and the whole world will be our estate!" He spread his arms wide, then swept her into a kiss. "There! Title that!"

Alice had to laugh. "Thank you, Mr. Ennock."

"You're welcome, Miss No-Longer-Lady-Alice-Michaels," he said impishly.

"I believe I will call you Miss A," Feng said. "If you prefer."

"Actually, I would not," she said. "The Third Ward uses Christian names among themselves to show comradeship and to emphasize the fact that they operate outside the usual boundaries of society. Since we are traveling together outside the boundaries of society, and I have little use for my title anymore, I think I would prefer my Christian name. Feng."

He put his fist into his hand and bowed to her in what Alice assumed was an Oriental fashion. "Then it will be so. Alice."

"You must be looking forward to going home," Alice said as they continued to walk.

Feng blinked at her. "What a strange thing to say."

"Is it? I would think you would miss your homeland, though I would imagine it's difficult to leave your father. Your mother will certainly be glad to see you."

Feng was silent for a long moment. Then he said slowly, "I am not returning as any kind of hero, Alice. I thought you knew that."

"Sorry?"

"I am returning in disgrace. The lowest disgrace you can imagine."

"I don't understand," Gavin put in. "You and your

father don't want you to be a diplomat, so you're going home to—"

"That is exactly the point, Gavin. I am a nephew to the emperor and my father's only son. I should be following into his profession. But my father has decreed that I have failed him and the family, which includes the emperor." Feng's usual carefree demeanor had left him. The words came out slow and dull as lead pipe. "I am a failure and a disgrace. If I am very lucky, I will spend the rest of my days scrubbing chamber pots with the servants."

"Good heavens," Alice said. How outrageous this was! "Feng, I had no idea. You always seemed so cheerful. I assumed you were thrilled to get away from London and go home."

Feng swiped a surreptitious finger under one lens of his goggles. "What is the worth of moping about? I will be unhappy enough later. In any case, I am in no hurry to face my disgrace, so I am in no hurry to arrive in China."

"Why not simply disappear between here and there?" Gavin said reasonably. "You're smart and know several languages. You could vanish into any number of places and live very well."

"That," Feng spat, "would show cowardice and bring even more disgrace to my family. I will not do that to them."

"You are not a disgrace," Alice said tartly. "Just now you helped save Gavin's life. Surely that should count for something."

"Perhaps." Feng sounded more tired than convinced, and fell silent. Alice didn't know what to say, so she fell silent as well.

At that point, a farm wagon drove by, and Alice's schoolgirl French was able to persuade the drover to let them ride on the back for a penny. Less than an hour later, they passed through one of the gates of Luxembourg.

The city was cleaner than London. The air smelled of horses and wood smoke and manure, but none of the scents were as cloying as in London, and dirt didn't hang on the air with yellow coal smoke. A cheerful sun chased away the dank smell and the dampness. The people on the cobblestoned streets bustled about and shouted good-naturedly at one another. Windows stood open to catch the summer breeze instead of locked against the misty damp. A group of chattering children ran past the cart, laughing and shouting their way through a make-believe world of their own. Alice felt her own heart lighten, and wondered what it would have been like to grow up here instead of chilly, drizzly London.

The cart carried the trio to an open market, and they hopped off. A number of church bells rang to announce midday. The metal tones bounced off the hills and scampered up the side streets. Merchants shouted for attention from brightly colored stalls, and a number of surfaces sported garish advertisements for the *Kalakos Cirque International du Automates et d'Autres Merveilles*. Here and there, a mechanical horse pulled a carriage down the street, or a spider skittered by with a basket on its back.

Alice bought a loaf of bread and a bit of butter, and they shared it for lunch on a corner. Despite the heat, Alice wore bulky gloves to conceal her spider, but no one seemed to take much notice. Most ladies were wearing gloves of their own.

"What is next?" Feng adjusted his scarf and his pack.

"We need to find paraffin oil for the ship, food stores, and a way to get both back to the ship," Gavin said. "How much money do we have?"

Alice sighed. It was the moment she'd been dreading. She took the little book of figures from her skirt pocket. "Not near enough," she admitted. "I performed a few calculations based on how much oil the ship used to get this far, how much weight we need to carry, what the winds are like, and the possibility that paraffin oil prices will be stunningly low—unlikely, considering how difficult it is to make, and how rare."

"Meaning we won't have enough money to make it to Peking," Gavin finished.

"No," Alice murmured.

"Then," Gavin said brightly, "our plan is both to earn money and figure out a way to get farther on less oil. So. Feng, you buy supplies and find a way to get them back to the *Lady* without letting anyone know where the ship is hidden. And don't forget about the jar. Alice, you find a supply of paraffin oil and bargain hard."

"What are you going to do?" Alice asked.

"Earn money. Back away." He whipped out his fiddle, sprinkled a few coins into the case on the ground before him, and began to play. The merry music on the crowded corner attracted attention fairly quickly, and even as Alice watched, a few people tossed coins of their own into Gavin's case. He winked his thanks at them and continued the song. Alice let the golden song wash over her. Though the violin was playing to the crowd, the musician was playing for her. He smiled at her, and her breath caught.

Feng plucked at her elbow. "We have much to do."

She reluctantly let him lead her away. A few moments later, he dodged down a less crowded side street and opened his rucksack. "We should do this first."

"Oh!" she said. "A good idea."

From the rucksack Feng took a largish jar, the sort that might store pickles. It held a bunch of grass and twigs and bits of food. Amid all this swarmed a large number of little fireflies. They winked green in the shady side street and cast odd shadows into the corners.

"They seem to be reproducing," Alice observed. "That's good. Let me."

She took the jar from Feng and carefully opened the lid just enough to allow perhaps a dozen of them to escape and fly off before she clapped the jar shut again. For a moment, she was back in London, in Hyde Park. Aunt Edwina's shriveled corpse had just collapsed to the ground and the cloud of fireflies was pouring out. Gavin swept the jar through the cloud, capturing a number of them, while the rest descended upon London to sting and bite. Each firefly carried a tiny organism—a virion, Aunt Edwina had called it—that attacked and destroyed the bacillus that caused the clockwork plague. Eventually the hardy little fireflies would spread throughout the world and cure or inoculate the entire human population, but it would happen faster with help.

One of the fireflies landed on Alice's neck and bit her. Normal fireflies didn't bite, of course, but these were different. She only just stopped herself from slapping, allowing it to fly off instead while Feng shoved the precious jar back into his pack. "Now, let us see what we can find for food and oil," he said, sounding more like his old self. "And perhaps female company."

"Feng," Alice warned.

"Male, then."

"Feng!"

He pulled down his scarf and grinned rakishly at her from beneath the goggles. It wasn't an expression Alice associated with Orientals. "That was a joke. Maybe."

"Let's just do our—" Alice cut herself off. In an alley nearby, a shadow shifted with a small groan, and two figures shuffled into view. They were both male, and dressed in rags. Blood and pus oozed from a dozen sores on their hands and faces. In several places, skin had split, revealing red muscle. Their bodies were thin, almost emaciated, and they smelled of rotting meat. One of them reached toward Alice and Feng, but flinched from even the indirect sunlight afforded by the side street.

Feng drew back with a hiss. "Plague zombies."

But Alice was already moving. She strode forward, stripping off her left glove. One of the zombies had enough brain function left to look a little surprised. Most people shunned or fled plague zombies—anyone who touched one was at risk for coming down with the clockwork plague and joining their ranks, steadily losing brain and body function until they dropped dead.

Only one in a hundred thousand victims became clockworkers, and no one wanted that, either. Plague zombies lived as pariahs, turned out and spurned even by family. They usually survived by scavenging garbage in the streets. Most of them starved to death before the plague finished them, and their corpses rotted in alleys and sewers because police and other city workers refused to touch them.

Alice approached the first zombie. Mucus ran from its half-rotted nose, and it babbled something incoherent at her. Alice's gorge rose, and a lifetime of fear slapped her hard. Her mother and brother had died of this very plague, and it had made her father into a cripple. Still, she forced herself to raise her metal-clad hand. She couldn't save her family, but she could save the person standing in front of her, and she would.

The iron spider's eyes glowed red, and its clear tubules, which remained painlessly drilled into Alice's arm, flowed constantly with Alice's blood. She swiped at the zombie with the gauntlet and the claws made four light cuts across the zombie's shoulder. Blood from the hollow claws sprayed over the wound as the zombie recoiled. The other zombie started and slowly moved a hand to his cheek. A firefly zipped away, leaving a green phosphorescent streak in the air. Alice, who had been ready to slash at and bleed on him as well, checked herself and stepped back instead.

"Are you well?" Feng asked.

"They can't infect me," Alice said. "Or you, for that matter. I gave you the same treatment. You needn't be afraid of them."

"It is hard to remember," Feng admitted.

"It's working," Alice breathed. "Look!"

The zombies shuddered. One looked at his hands, turning them over and over, as if seeing them for the first time. The other licked his half-rotted lips and darted glances up and down the side street. Slowly, he took a step out of the darkened alley into the half-lit byway. The light didn't seem to bother him, even though extreme photosensitivity was one of the early symptoms of the clockwork plague. As Alice watched, some of his sores stopped weeping. He gave a little moan that Alice could only describe as happy and he lurched toward the entrance of the street, where the market lay. The second zombie had vanished back into the shadows. Before Alice quite realized what was happening, the first zombie entered the square. Full sunlight fell across his face, probably for the first time in months, and he lifted his eyes to the sky in exultation.

A woman screamed, and then another. Shouts and cries erupted all over the market as people scrambled all over themselves to get away. Box stalls tipped under the stampede and wood smashed. Alice only heard—the buildings at the entrance of the side street restricted her view. All she saw was the zombie standing in the sunlight like a misshapen angel, oblivious to the chaos around him.

"Oh dear," Alice muttered.

"Perhaps we move along now," Feng said.

Another sound made Alice turn. At the mouth of the alley stood the second zombie. With him was a crowd of others—males, females, children. All of them wore torn, filthy rags that dripped blood and pus. Their skin was as tattered as their clothing. Some were missing fingers or even entire limbs. All of them huddled in the alley, not daring to go into the half-light of the side street. The second zombie, the one Alice had scratched, lifted an arm toward Alice in supplication.

Alice felt abruptly overwhelmed. She couldn't move or speak. "Oh," was all she could manage.

"What do we do?" Feng asked.

A small child limped forward, dragging a useless foot. Alice couldn't even tell if it was a boy or a girl. It held up its arms to Alice like a toddler asking to be picked up. Alice wondered who its parents were, how long it had been on the streets, scrounging for food, spreading disease, hiding from painful daylight in cellars and under dustbins, in pain, wondering what was happening and why no one was helping. She jolted forward.

"I will help you," she said, addressing the child, but speaking to them all. As gently as she could, she scored the child's arm and wet the wound with her own blood. The child gasped and lurched backward, then straightened. The cure wouldn't regrow the bad foot, but at least the disease would stop devouring flesh and bone. Alice didn't pause. She flicked her claws at the next zombie, and the next, and the next, working her way through the fetid alley in a red haze. The spider grew heavier and heavier, and her arm ached from swinging. The smell of blood hung on the air, mingling with the soft groans and yelps from wounded zombie flesh. Alice's entire world narrowed to bricks and blood, and she lost all sense of time. She could save them all. Swing, slash, bleed, and move on. Swing, slash, bleed, and move on.

"That was the last one," Feng was saying. "Alice! You can stop!"

Alice came to herself. The last zombie was shuffling into the light, and the screaming had died down from the marketplace, and whether it was because the people had become tired of running away from zombies or because they had all fled, Alice didn't know. The strength drained out of her, and Feng caught her before she collapsed.

"Sorry," she murmured. "I didn't know it would be like this."

"You helped so many," Feng said. "That was a fine thing you did."

"But there are still more. I need to save them."

"They will be well. The cure will spread to them quickly enough."

"I'm thirsty." Alice's mouth was dry, and her head felt light. "So thirsty."

She was only vaguely aware of Feng half leading, half carrying her somewhere. Eventually, she found herself sitting at a table with a plate of fruit, bread, and cheese before her and a mug of cider at her elbow. A muscular arm encircled her like a warm wing and drew her close.

"Are you all right?" Gavin demanded.

She leaned in and soaked in his scent, his strength. "Yes. I just needed to eat."

"I found him at another market," Feng reported from across the table. "He was unaware that the zombie was your doing."

"I thought it was a chance event," Gavin said, "so I moved on to play somewhere else, without all the screaming and stampeding. I had no idea you were in trouble." His voice was tight with tension.

"I'm fine. Really." Alice sat up to emphasize her words and noticed for the first time the little tavern where they were sitting. It was low-end, with straw on the wood planks and a bored-looking pair of daughters serving bread and beer drawn by their mother, who held forth behind a scarred bar. Alice, Gavin, and Feng occupied a freestanding table near the fireplace, which was empty this late in summer. The faint smell of dead ashes and old alcohol hung on the air, and the working-class patrons were still talking quietly, not drunk yet. "No need to worry, darling. I was just caught a little off guard. Next time, I'll know better."

"Next time?" Gavin echoed. "What next time?"

"Next time I heal people," she said.

"You're not going to keep doing this?" he asked incredulously.

She pulled away from him. "Of course I am. I have to help, Gavin. The clockwork plague needs to be cured."

"That's what the fireflies are for."

"Every person I cure is one fewer person who dies," she said with heat. "I can't hold it back and wait on the chance that a firefly will bite."

"And you're putting yourself in danger!"

"It didn't seem to be an issue when I came to rescue *you*!"

"That was low."

Alice's voice rose. "No lower than you assuming I can't take care of myself."

"Of course you can take care of yourself." Gavin's

voice rose to match. "It's why Feng had to carry you in here."

"I often enjoy it when people stare," Feng said, "but I believe our plan was to keep to ourselves."

Most of the customers were indeed staring at them. Alice, who noticed she was on her feet, sank slowly back to her chair. Her claws had pierced the tips of her glove. "I apologize, Mr. Ennock," she said stiffly.

"Me, too, Miss Michaels."

They finished eating in silence. Alice kept her eyes on her food and fumed, despite her apology. She had a duty to spread the cure. The plague had made victims of her entire family, ruined her life, and she wasn't going to let anyone else go through the same thing. Her life was replete with sacrifices to the plague, and at last, at *last*, she could fight back. Was Gavin trying to control her the way her father and fiancé had tried to do? Infuriating! More than that, he was a mere commoner, with no right even to *speak* to her in such a tone. In some parts of England, a baroness like her could still have him . . .

. . . flogged.

Alice swallowed a bit of carrot without tasting it. Gavin had already been flogged. By the pirates who had captured his airship and shot his best friend and killed his captain. When she embraced him, she could feel the ropy scars through the thin fabric of his shirt. The thought made her ill. He had seen his share of sacrifice. He had already been hurt so badly, and now she was hurting him again. But iron pride stiffened her neck, and she couldn't quite bring herself to apologize again.

"Did you earn much money?" she asked in a quieter voice. The other patrons went back to their drinking.

"A bit," he said. "But not as much as I would have liked. I was interrupted by zombies, so—"

The temper flared red again. "Are you implying that I shouldn't have—"

"I'm not implying anything. Boy, you're hot under the corset."

"Mr. Ennock!" She found she was on her feet again. "That . . . that . . ."

"What?" he said evenly.

"That . . . will be all." She turned and marched out the door.

Angrily, she chose a direction and stalked away down the darkening street. Luxembourg had a number of yellow gaslights to light her way, but they were spaced widely, and each stood out like a giant candlestick in a pool of ink. Closed shops alternated with pubs and hotels. A lonely set of church bells rang a melody Alice didn't recognize, and the cool evening breeze smelled unfamiliar. A lonely flyer for the circus, its colors muted by the gathering dusk, blew down the street. Music and sounds of men singing in French drifted across the cobbles, and a few people were scattered up and down the walkways. Now that she was outside in the cooler evening air, Alice realized she had no idea where to go or what to do. But she wasn't going back to the pub. Not now.

A door banged open ahead of her, and a little man carrying a black bag hurried out of a building, pulling on his black coat as he went. Behind him came a woman wringing her hands. She was pleading in rapid French, but the man ignored her. Normally Alice would have averted her eyes and continued on her way, but she caught the word *peste*—plague—and halted. The man yanked a small jar of paint from his bag, scrawled a large red P on the door over the woman's protests, and jumped into a waiting hansom, which sped away. The woman watched the man go, then slowly returned to the building and shut the door.

Alice's mouth went dry, and the spider hung heavy on her left arm. Then, before she could lose her nerve, she strode up to the door and knocked. It opened almost instantly, and Alice saw the hope on the woman's face die, replaced with a guarded look.

"Oui?" The woman had straight brown hair and tired, blue-gray eyes. Her hands were red and swollen from work, and she wore a limp brown work dress.

In her halting French, Alice said, "Is someone ill?"

"Why do you ask?" the woman responded. "Who are you?"

"Someone in your house has *la peste de l'horlogerie,* yes?"

"Non, non." The woman moved to shut the door. "You are mistaken."

Alice, not quite believing her own temerity, blocked the door open with her foot. She could smell the dripping paint. "The doctor marked your door for all to see. Now everyone will avoid you and your house. I can help."

The woman paused. "Who are you? We have nothing to steal."

"I am a friend. I can help. Is it your child?"

"I . . . I am . . ." The woman licked her lips, then suddenly opened the door wider. "Enter, please."

The door led into a pair of rooms that were part of a much larger building. The front room had a stove and a few pieces of furniture. Alice assumed the back room was used for sleeping. A single candle provided the only light. On a pallet on the floor huddled a little girl, perhaps nine or ten years old. A thin blanket covered her, and her face was flushed with fever. Her hair was already falling out, and her limbs twitched as if possessed by little demons. A smell of sickness hung in the air. Alice's heart pounded behind her ribs. For a moment, she was looking at her brother in his sickbed, watching the fever make him quiver. Eventually he convulsed and died. Many victims of the clockwork plague didn't survive this early stage, and those few who did were often scarred or crippled. Most went on to become zombies. At least the early stage didn't seem to be contagious, though the victims were often shunned as a matter of course.

"My husband is working, and my other children are asleep in back," the woman said. "Please do not wake them. My name is Theresa Nilsen. This is Josette."

"I . . . would prefer to keep my name to myself," Alice said, remembering Phipps. "Did the doctor say Josette has the clockwork plague?"

"He did." The woman's voice choked. "He would not touch her, and he left. I do not know what to do. She will become a monster and die. My little Josette."

"She will not." Alice stripped off her leather glove and laid her gauntleted hand on the girl's forehead. The spider's eyes instantly glowed red, confirming the doctor's diagnosis. "This may be difficult to see, Madame Nilsen, but it is necessary."

Before Mme. Nilsen could say anything else, Alice slashed Josette's arm and sprayed a bit of her blood over the wound. The girl whimpered in her fevered dreams.

"What did you do?" Mme. Nilsen demanded. "You hurt her!"

"It is a cure for the clockwork plague," Alice said softly. "Now that Josette has it, she will spread it whenever she coughs or sneezes, but I should give it to you and your other children anyway. Let me check you. It will not hurt."

Mme. Nilsen hesitantly held out her arm, and Alice took it. The spider's eyes glowed red.

"You have the plague," Alice said, and Mme. Nilsen cried out in alarm. "But you are not showing symptoms yet. Do not worry—I have the cure." Alice slashed and sprayed. "I should check your children."

"How—?" Mme. Nilsen began, but Alice was already moving to the back room, where four other children were sleeping piled together on a large pallet of their own. Alice checked, but none of them had the plague.

"They are healthy," Alice said, and strode back to the front room to check on Josette. Already her fever had lowered. When Alice touched her, the spider's eyes glowed green, indicating a lack of clockwork contagion. Josette opened her eyes, and Alice backed away to let a tearful Mme. Nilsen take her place.

"Mama," Josette whispered. "I want water."

Mme. Nilsen hurried to bring a cup. Josette drank and fell back asleep. The fever flush was gone and her breathing was more even. Mme. Nilsen looked at her for a long moment, then burst into tears. Alice didn't know how to respond. The emotional display made her uncomfortable, but she was so very glad to have helped. Her heart felt lighter, knowing the child would grow to adulthood.

"There are no thanks," the woman cried. "I will give you everything I have!"

"Just some water, and something to eat, if you have it," Alice said, remembering what happened the last time.

Mme. Nilsen gave her water and cheese, and then said hesitantly, "Can you do this to anyone?"

"Yes." Alice swallowed the last of the water. "Until my strength runs out."

"You must come. I have a friend who also has a child."

Alice dusted crumbs from her hands. "Quickly, then, while your children sleep." She paused. "But I need to do something else first."

Chapter Four

Feng abandoned Gavin after his second pint. "The angel over there can provide me with far more pleasure than you," he said, and slid away. A moment later, Feng and his laughing female companion were strolling out the front door, arm in arm. Gavin ignored them and took a pull from his third pint. The ale here was stronger, and it hit Gavin a little harder than he was used to, but that was fine with him. Last spring, he had watched his friends die on the airship *Juniper*, a pirate had tried to rape him, and the first mate had flogged him senseless for fighting back. Now the high-and-mighty baroness was pissed at him, and he was sick with the clockwork plague. In a few weeks, he'd lose his grip on reality, spiral into a fascinated trance while studying a ladybug on a grass stem, and die in a ditch as his brain liquefied into sludge. If all that didn't deserve a few drinks, nothing did.

He took another sour gulp of red Luxembourger ale. It swirled like pale blood, though it was only red malt and vinegar that reflected red light from the lamps. The ale was more like wine than beer and would have fetched a pretty penny back home in Boston as an exotic treat, but Gavin was slugging it down like water. It made him feel light, as if he might float away. The other patrons in the bar seemed strangely happy, too. They were all happy, despite the plague around them. A small group sang a cheery tune in one corner, and laughed uproariously at every chorus. The noise floated up, taking Gavin's pain with it. It was a fine thing to be drunk and happy in Luxembourg. For the moment he felt like he had just escaped Purgatory and was now staring at a set of fine gates made of gold.

Gavin tapped the mug on the table, creating vibrations on the surface of the liquid. Everything slowed, and he tracked the tiny motions like chaotic imps that danced across the redness. Fascinating. He tapped again, muscles moving slow as granite, now able to predict where each wave of vibration would appear. Each rose and rippled precisely where he foresaw—or commanded. He tapped yet again, tilting the mug to get a different pattern, and then another and another, a sorcerer making demons dance. A machine, the *right* machine, would produce the same patterns, and those patterns could be used to—

A hand grabbed his arm. The spell broke and the world snapped into normal speed. Alice was standing next to him. Near her, hovering like a brown butterfly, stood a woman Gavin didn't know. He felt the literal iron in the grip beneath her glove and instantly knew she was exerting five pounds and six ounces of pressure on his biceps.

"I knew you'd come back," he said, and tried a grin, but it came out a sloppy grimace.

"Come along, darling," she said with a wide smile and without moving her lips. "We're leaving."

"I paid for this. I'm finishing it," he said. Around them, other drinkers pointed and winked. A few jeered. The henpecked husband and his domineering wife. Feng was nowhere in sight. He had apparently found a heaven of his own.

"Oh, good heavens." Alice snatched up the mug and drained it. A number of customers burst into applause. "There. Let's go."

He should have been annoyed, but a mild haze had descended over him and nothing could bother him now. "What the hell," he muttered, catching up his fiddle case. It weighed two pounds, nine ounces. The silver nightingale in his pocket weighed three ounces. "I'm out of money anyway."

She towed him to the door and outside. Light, laughter, and the woman in brown followed them. He felt a little less muddled in the cooler air but not entirely himself.

"Where's Feng?" Alice asked.

"There's a hotel across the street." Gavin gestured vaguely with the fiddle case. "He got a room with someone. Wanna do the same?"

Alice made a disgusted sound. "Do you do this often?"

"Argue with a pretty woman or get drunk?"

"Never mind. At least you're coherent. I need to show you something. This is Madame Nilsen. She doesn't speak English."

The woman, who was carrying a lantern, smiled shyly at the mention of her name, and Gavin gave her a lopsided grin. "Hi. I'm dying, you know. Not that *she* cares."

Mme. Nilsen shook her head. Alice spoke to her in French, and the other woman led the way with her tin lantern. Gavin said, "Do you think the clockwork plague will let me learn French? Or Chinese? It sure as hell won't do anything else useful."

"You're maudlin. I've never seen you maudlin."

"Yeah." He rumpled his hair. "Imagine."

"Just keep walking," Alice said. "It'll sober you."

"I don't want to be sober. I deserve to be drunk."

"But *I* don't deserve you to be drunk. Keep walking or I'll show you how sharp these claws can be."

Gavin almost sat on the street in a childish pique, but changed his mind and continued walking with his arms folded instead. After some time, they arrived at the top of a winding street. The climb put Gavin a little out of breath, and, as Alice predicted, cleared his head a bit. On the hills below and above, the city had darkened completely. Street- and houselights made a field of stars on wrinkled velvet, as if the night sky had fallen and shattered on the ground around them. Mme. Nilsen selected a tall, narrow house, knocked, and called out. After some time, the door opened, and a man and woman, both middle-aged, appeared. They wore nightshirts and caps. Mme. Nilsen spoke to them in rapid French, and Alice joined in. The couple looked mystified, then hopeful. At their gestured invitation, everyone entered the long, narrow house that smelled of bread and ashes.

"What's going on?" Gavin asked as they climbed a steep staircase. In Luxembourg, they were always climbing.

"There's plague here, but they don't want anyone to know," Alice murmured. "If word of it gets out, the house will be quarantined until the family throws the victims into the street."

"Why do I have to be here?"

"I want you to watch what I'm doing."

Now puzzled, Gavin followed the group into a bedroom. A boy lay on a bed, twitching in fever sleep. Loose hanks of pale blond hair lay on the pillow. Automatic fear touched Gavin when he recognized the clockwork plague, even though he was already dying of the disease in his own way. The boy's parents looked on with worried expressions as Alice pulled off her glove, revealing the spider. Its eyes glowed red when she touched the boy's bare arm. Then she swiped his skin with the claws, drawing blood and spraying a bit of her own. The parents gasped as one, but Mme. Nilsen talked to them and they calmed, though they remained watchful. Alice touched each of them in turn, but the spider eyes glowed green. The mother sat on the bed and stroked her son's forehead, her cheeks wet with tears. Gavin's throat thickened as he felt her sorrow, fear, and love.

"There," Alice said. "Now we wait."

Mme. Nilsen slipped out to go home. Gavin rocked on his feet, waiting uncertainly.

"Perhaps you should sing, Gavin," Alice said.

He stopped rocking. "What?"

"Sing. It'll pass the time." She turned her brown eyes on him. "Sing the moon song for me. Please."

Argument or no argument, he couldn't refuse her any more than the sun could refuse to rise.

> *I see the moon, the moon sees me*
> *It turns all the forest soft and silvery.*
> *The moon picked you from all the rest*
> *For I loved you best.*

As Gavin sang for Alice and the boy, a boy who struggled to heal as Gavin himself had done so many weeks ago, something inside him broke, shifted, and re-formed. The plague hurt a great many people, more than just himself, and Gavin, flying high above the earth or wrapped in music, had forgotten that. He pulled out his fiddle to accompany himself for the second verse.

> *I once had a heart as good as new*
> *But now it's gone from me to you.*
> *The moon picked you from all the rest*
> *For I loved you best.*

The leering eyes and sticky blood of Madoc Blue faded a little. The sharp memory of Tom Danforth's lifeless corpse falling from the rigging dulled around the edges. The opaque stone walls that trapped him in Edwina's tower thinned. And then another memory came back to him. He himself was lying sick in bed, hot with fever. A woman—Ma—bent over him, bathing his face with a cool cloth. A man with pale hair played the fiddle and sang just for Gavin, his voice rich and low and perfect, and Gavin felt better, enveloped in the soft love of both parents.

> *I have a ship, my ship must flee.*
> *Sailing o'er the clouds and on the silver sea*
> *The moon picked you from all the rest*
> *For I loved you best.*

The memory vanished when the song ended. The boy's twitching eased. His breathing evened out, and the fever faded. He opened his eyes and looked straight at Gavin for a long moment. A connection between them held for a second that lasted an age, and Gavin felt that the boy somehow understood what had just happened. Then the boy smiled and dropped back into sleep. Tears wet and refreshed Gavin's cheeks, and he felt both exhausted and exhilarated. The boy's mother flung her arms around him, weeping with joy, and his father swiped at his eyes with his sleeve. He said something to Alice in a choked voice, and she answered gracefully. They spoke at some length, and Alice nodded.

"What's going on?" Gavin wiped his own face and put his fiddle away as the father padded quickly out of the room.

"He knows of someone else who has the plague," Alice said. "Do you think I should refuse?"

Gavin put a hand on her shoulder. "I never wanted you to stop helping, Alice," he said. "I just don't want you to get hurt because you don't know when to stop. Look at you—you didn't even take a wrap, and you're shivering."

Even though she didn't speak English, the mother seemed to notice the same thing and with a firm gesture that she was to keep it, gave Alice a quilt to pull around herself. Alice accepted.

"You have to watch yourself," Gavin added, "or I'll tell Kemp on you."

Alice gave a little bark of laughter at that. "Then come with me."

"Anywhere. You know that."

The father returned, dressed, and led Alice and Gavin outside to another house, where two adult brothers were down with the plague. Alice, the quilt still pulled around her, cured both of them while Gavin played, and one of them begged Alice to go to his niece's house. Along the way, they encountered a pair of plague zombies rooting through a rubbish heap, and Alice swiped at them as well. At the niece's house, Gavin stopped Alice and demanded that she be given food and drink, which the newly cured niece was happy to give before asking Alice to visit yet another house. And so it continued. As the night wore on, Alice hurried from home to home under cover of darkness, her quilt drawn around her like a cloak while she cured a number of people with the clockwork plague, and each one seemed to know someone else who was sick. The chain of people took them all through Luxembourg, to homes rich and poor, lonely and crowded, wood and stone. Gavin made sure Alice was given a bite to eat and a sip to drink in every household. Alice cured priests and drunkards, bankers and thieves, doctors and patients. Some offered money, always hesitantly, as if they might offend. Alice tried to turn them down, but Gavin stepped in and accepted.

"If they can spare it, we can take it," he said, fiddle in hand.

"I won't turn down someone who can't—"

"Of course not," Gavin said. "But even saints have to eat. And get to China."

When dawn checkered the eastern sky, they left the final house. The air was crisp and clean and bright. Morning noises—horse traffic, food sellers, factory whistles, doors opening and closing, people shouting and talking—filled the street. Housewives and store-keepers swept the cobblestones in front of their homes and shops. Gavin noticed with a start that Alice was pale and shaky from the slow but steady blood loss, and she kept the quilt wrapped tightly around her body and head. Gavin himself didn't feel tired in the least—clockworkers entering the later stage of the plague often went days without sleep—and he mentally kicked himself for not remembering earlier that Alice did need rest, especially after everything she'd been doing.

He flagged down a cab and gave directions back to the pub where he'd been drinking the night before. Alice leaned against him and dozed off, and he was surprised at how light she felt.

The pub was closed, but Gavin found the cheap hotel where Feng had gotten a room and used the money Alice had earned to get them a room while Alice collapsed into a lobby chair. At the last second he remembered not to give his real name and signed them in as Mr. and Mrs. Tom Danforth, in honor of his late friend. He had no intention of actually sharing a room with Alice—Feng's room would have to do when Gavin finally felt a need for sleep and he would have to hope Feng didn't have a woman with him—but it was easier to fabricate a married relationship than explain to the clerk, who only spoke a few words of English.

They met Feng, alone, on the way up the dark and creaking stairs, which saved Gavin the trouble of tracking him down. Explanations followed, and Alice went into her room without further discussion.

"You will not follow her?" Feng said. He was wearing his scarf and goggles and on his back he wore the pack with the precious jar of fireflies in it. "My lady friend last night enjoyed herself immensely, and I can give you advice, if you need it."

Gavin sighed as they squeaked back downstairs on threadbare carpet. Although he was getting used to Feng's forthrightness and his interest in . . . romance, it was still a little unsettling, and he could understand why Feng's father had despaired of him ever becoming a diplomat. Feng's undeniably exotic good looks doubtless made matters worse—Gavin imagined he found it easy to sweet talk his way into any number of beds. Fortunately, he did seem to understand that showing even the slightest interest in Alice would result in a personal and rather brief experiment with the force of gravity from the deck of the *Lady of Liberty*, either at Gavin's hands or Alice's.

"I won't share . . . quarters with her," Gavin said. "Not until I can make an honest woman of her."

"And when will that be?"

They reached the little lobby again and a glimmer of brass caught Gavin's eye. His blood went cold and he nearly dropped his fiddle case. Susan Phipps and Simon d'Arco were talking to the clerk.

"Run," he whispered hoarsely, and bolted back up the steps.

They both smashed straight into Alice's door. It splintered open. She lay on the bed and she was still dressed, a fact for which Gavin felt grateful. He scooped Alice up while Feng grabbed the bedspread from underneath her. Alice squawked as footsteps pounded on the stairs leading up to their floor. Gavin glanced at the window, but they were three stories up. No escape that way. They would have to fight their way out. He frantically assessed the room. Bed. Bare wood floor. Window. Thin curtains. Chamber pot. Washstand. Mirror. Light. Feng. Bedspread. Sheets. Fiddle case.

"Put me down!" Alice barked.

Gavin flung her back on the bed along with his fiddle case. He ripped the curtains off the wall with one hand and snatched up the room's paraffin oil lamp in the other. Then he dug into his pockets for a match. Simon burst into the room, and Feng, who was standing beside the door, flung the bedspread over him like a net and kicked his legs out from under him. Simon went down with a muffled yelp. Phipps appeared in the doorway, more cautious. She held a pair of tuning forks in her hands.

"You!" Alice cried from the bed.

"Caught you," Phipps said, "you son of a—"

Gavin threw the lamp at her. She automatically parried it with her metal arm, and the cheap glass shattered, covering both her and the bedspread with lamp oil. Gavin popped the match alight with his thumbnail and applied it to the sheer curtain he was holding. Fear clenched his every nerve as it began to burn. Fire was the enemy of every airship, and to die in flame was the secret nightmare of every airman. He remembered Captain Naismith aiming a blazing crossbow bolt at the envelope of the *Juniper*, and how close he had come to dying in an inferno. His hands shook, making the fire dance.

"You won't," Phipps said flatly, and moved to strike the forks.

Gavin ran straight for her, trailing flame. Phipps leaped backward, her eyes wide with fear, an expression Gavin had never seen on her before. Alice recovered herself and bolted after him with Feng right behind her. A bit of blazing curtain flapped behind them, preventing the oil-soaked Phipps from pursuing right away if she wanted to avoid bursting into flame. Smoke and heat scorched Gavin's face and heated his hands. The clerk stared at the trio from behind his desk as they fled outdoors.

The sun shone on the bright, cobblestoned street. In the distance, calliope music played and people applauded. Traffic and pedestrians were currently giving the hotel a wide berth, though, because Glenda was standing on the sidewalk in one of the big mechanicals.

"Wotcha," she said, and reached for Gavin and Alice with big metal hands.

"Shit!" Gavin flung the flaming ball of cloth at Glenda's head. It bounced off the clear bubble encasing her, but the woman jerked out of reflex, which gave Gavin, Alice, and Feng a chance to dodge around the machine.

"This way!" Gavin grabbed Alice's hand and ran.

Glenda recovered quickly and spun to face them. Gavin jumped into a nearby cab, pulling Alice with him. The startled driver didn't even have time to protest before Gavin shoved him out with a "Sorry!" and snapped the reins. The horses, already nervous about the mechanical, leaped forward. Feng managed to leap aboard as well, despite the rucksack that weighed him down.

The cab jolted down the street with the mechanical in pursuit. Brass footsteps thundered behind them. Alice shouted at people to get out of the way, and Gavin grimly steered the frantic horses. Glenda swiped at the cab, missed, and gouged a chunk out of the street. People and horses screamed and scattered. Other automatons skittered out of the way. Fear gripped Gavin's heart. Even if they got away now, their situation remained dire. Phipps was a bulldog, willing and able to track them, and Gavin's conspicuous airship made the situation worse. They had to escape, not only now but in the long term.

"Where should we go?" Alice cried, echoing his thoughts. "How do we get away?"

And then he knew. It came to him in a flash of inspiration, and he had no idea whether it was inspired by the clockwork plague or his own imagination, but either way, it might work. Hope replaced some of the fear.

"I have an idea," he said. "But we left my fiddle."

"I have it," Alice said, brandishing it. "Didn't you notice?"

"God, I love you."

"Faster!" Feng shouted behind them.

Glenda swiped at the cab again, and this time she clipped it. The cab yawed sideways, and Alice clung grimly with her free hand. Gavin hauled on the reins, turning the yaw into a full-out left turn around a corner. The cab tipped on two wheels, then righted itself with a crash that slammed Gavin's teeth together. The move caught Glenda by surprise, and she had to back up to make the turn, which bought Gavin a bit of lead. He shouted at the horses, but they were already going flat out.

"Glenda!" Alice called over her shoulder. "You don't have to do this! The Third Ward is dead!"

But Glenda either didn't hear or didn't care. The mechanical came after them with implacable determination. The horses were slowing, tired, allowing Glenda to make up the lost time. Gavin listened. The streets here were nearly empty and the calliope music was growing louder. He pulled the horses to a stop and jumped out of the cab.

"Jump!" he said as Glenda brought both mechanical hands down. Feng and Alice leaped free as the mechanical smashed the cab to pieces. The panicked horses galloped away, dragging the remains with them. Glenda turned to face the trio, her expression stony.

"What are you doing?" Feng demanded, but Gavin was already moving.

"Come on!" He dashed down a side street, giving Alice and Feng no choice but to follow. There were still no people in evidence, but the narrow street was cluttered with front stoops, carts, piles of coal, and other street detritus. The trio leaped and twisted around it all, but Glenda was forced to slow a little.

"I'll catch you eventually," she shouted. "You can't keep running!"

Gavin burst out onto a main street and into a crowd lining it. The calliope music leaped into full volume. Coming up the street was a man in a red top hat and a red-and-white striped shirt with garters just above the elbows. He wore a cloak flung back over his shoulders and he carried a silver-topped cane. Behind him lurched a great brass elephant, puffing steam from its tusks. Its gait was oddly uneven. Scarlet signs on the animal's sides spelled out *Kalakos Cirque International du Automates et d'Autres Merveilles* in graceful, garish letters. Behind that came a horse wagon with an calliope on it played by an automaton, followed by the rest of the circus—clowns and acrobats and lion cages and girls on mechanical horses, all waving and smiling. The crowd that had gathered to watch stared, unsure if Gavin's actions might be part of the show.

Without a pause, Gavin shoved through the crowd and made for the ringmaster at the front of the parade. He snatched the man's hat off, revealing sandy hair.

"What the hell?" the ringmaster said, then blinked. *"Gavin?"*

"Great to see you, Dodd." Gavin flicked the cloak free. "Just go with this and I'll explain later."

"Gavin, what are you—?" Alice began, but he

shoved the top hat on her head, tossed the cloak around her shoulders, and ran around the other side of the lurching elephant without looking to see if Feng and Alice followed him. They did, however, and that was fortunate. Glenda reached the mouth of the side street, but her view of her quarry was blocked by the elephant, who bumbled along as if the people didn't exist. Up top, the mahout looked down at them warily.

"Take off your goggles and scarf and your shirt," Gavin whispered to Feng, keeping pace with the elephant. "The circus has Chinese. You'll look like an acrobat. Give me the rucksack."

"What about you?" Alice buttoned the cloak and drew it around herself, hiding her body and Gavin's fiddle case. "And how do you know these people?"

Feng handed Gavin the rucksack, pulled off his shirt, and wrapped it around his head in a crude turban. He had a build that could pass for acrobatic, at a distance. Several people in the crowd had noticed Glenda's mechanical, but they seemed to think it was part of the parade. They pointed and gasped with amazement. Glenda was momentarily stymied. She couldn't move forward without crushing people or sweeping them aside and hurting them, which Gavin didn't think she'd be willing to do.

A clown in white makeup, orange wig, and blue nose hurried up with a broom and a bucket. "What are you three doing? Do you speak English?"

"Bonzini!" Gavin said. "Remember me?"

"Gavin?" the clown gasped. "What in—?"

"*I'm looking for two men and a woman!*" Glenda

boomed from the mechanical. *"They just came this way. There's a reward!"*

"That's torn it," Alice said.

"No," Feng said. "The crowd speaks French and German."

"Thanks, Bonzini." Gavin plucked the wig and nose from the clown, jammed them onto his own head and face, and grabbed Bonzini's broom and bucket. The pack with the firefly cure in it went on Gavin's back.

"Hey!" Bonzini protested.

But Gavin was already moving farther back, now using the calliope wagon and then a lion cage for cover. Alice and Feng came with. Glenda gave up on the crowd and was now nudging people aside so she could move onto the street. The calliope continued to hoot out something in D-major.

"Split up," Gavin said.

"Why can't we just keep hiding behind the calliope?" Alice hissed.

"The wagon's high enough for her to see our feet." Gavin brandished the broom. "Hide in plain sight. Smile and wave and tell anyone who asks that Dodd said it was all right."

Gavin followed the lion cage with the broom over his shoulder, taking care that the bristles blocked Glenda's view of his face. Behind Gavin, a pair of jugglers tossed clubs and balls. Alice and Feng dropped farther back into the parade, smiling and waving as they went. The parade moved ahead with aching slowness. The horse drawing the lion cage dropped manure onto the street right in front of the spot where Glenda had finally worked her way through the parade audience to the curb. Gavin swallowed hard and kept his head down as he paused and swept the smelly stuff into the bucket. Glenda scanned the street with flat, hard eyes. Gavin felt her gaze rest on him for a moment, and he forced himself to put a jaunty spring into his step, though tension dried his mouth and tightened his knuckles on the bucket. He was just a lowly sweeper clown. Not worth examining closely. Glenda narrowed her eyes and her mechanical took a step forward. Gavin held his breath. Then Glenda turned and stomped away. The crowd cheered and pointed at her, still sure she was part of the parade. Gavin let out his breath and stole a glance over his shoulder. Alice and Feng smiled and waved near a troop of acrobats. The automaton on the calliope finished its song and swung into another one. Gavin continued on his way with the bucket full of manure.

Eventually the parade made its way to a field at the edge of town. The big striped tent—called the Tilt, Gavin remembered—rose up among a number of smaller tents and circus wagons. Off to one side waited the red locomotive and bright boxcars Gavin had seen from the airship earlier just before a clockworker fugue had taken him away. If not for the clockwork plague and the unexpected memory of his father, he might have recognized the train right away instead of recalling it later. He had also seen the flyers for the Kalakos Circus plastered about Luxembourg by the advance man, but they were in French and he hadn't paid close attention to them. He wasn't sure how he had missed the name; the French version wasn't so very different.

The parade continued right up to the complex of tents. Behind the parade came an enormous crowd, all ready to see the show. The performers quickly scattered, some toward the Tilt, some to the sideshow tents, and others to direct the oncoming crowd toward the ticket sellers, who wore stovepipe hats with oversized tickets attached to the top so people could locate them. An intricately decorated mechanical clock at the entrance of the Tilt ran backward, counting down the minutes until the performance began. A life-sized female automaton was attached to the clock, and even as Gavin watched, she jerked to life. She had only head, chest, and arms, and Gavin assumed this made her sufficiently inhuman to make her legal under Luxembourg law.

"Mesdames et messieurs!" she called in a voice that carried from one end of the circus to the other. *"Le spectacle commencera dans cinquante-cinq minutes! Mesdames et messieurs! Le spectacle commencera dans cinquante-cinq minutes!"* And then she went still.

Nearly an hour before the show, according to the clock. The extra time, Gavin recalled, gave the audience a chance to buy tickets, then get bored and decide to spend money at the sideshow.

A firm grip took Gavin's elbow. "The ringmaster wants to see you in his car," said Bonzini, "and you better not have sneezed inside my nose."

The ringmaster kept an entire train car to himself. Alice took off the red top hat. Feng pulled on his shirt and tried to smooth out the wrinkles. Bonzini ushered the three of them inside, but didn't enter himself. The car had a large bed, comfortable chairs, two wardrobes, a small stove, full bookshelves, and a perfectly functional bar. It hadn't changed since Gavin had seen it more than two years ago. Neither had Dodd, who was waiting for them.

"Good God, Gavin," he said, his face split into a wide grin. "I hope you have a good explanation for nearly wrecking my parade today. Who are these people? And where's Cousin Felix?"

He pulled Gavin into a warm embrace without waiting for an answer, and Gavin suddenly found himself at the top of an upswell of emotion. His throat thickened, and words wouldn't come. The memory of Captain Felix Naismith's last moments slammed through Gavin, and he saw the captain's expression as a pirate's glass fléchette sliced his flesh and ended his life. He heard the small sound that escaped the captain's throat and felt the thud as the captain's body slammed into the deck.

Dodd read Gavin's expression. "No."

"Yeah," Gavin said thickly. "Uh, this may take a while to explain."

"*Mesdames et messieurs! Le spectacle commencera dans cinquante minutes!*"

"I have fifty minutes," Dodd said.

Alice set Gavin's fiddle and the rucksack with the cure in the corner and everyone sat down. Gavin introduced Alice and Feng and then started in with the loss of the *Juniper* to pirates, moving to the death of Dodd's cousin, Captain Felix Naismith. Dodd's face hardened as the story progressed. Alice went to the little bar and came back with a half-full glass, which Dodd drained with a shaky hand when Gavin finished.

"I haven't seen him in almost two years," Dodd said in a hoarse voice. "I had no idea he was dead. Oh, God. What am I going to do?"

Gavin didn't know what to say. Alice and Feng, who didn't know Dodd at all, sat in uncomfortable silence.

"*Mesdames et messieurs! Le spectacle commencera dans vingt minutes!*"

"We go months without contact," Dodd said, "but that was all right. I was so glad when he got off that stupid scow he played second mate for and got on a real ship, and he was so happy when Boston Mail gave him his own command. Youngest captain in their fleet, he is. Was. Now he's gone. Shit."

Alice coughed, and Dodd raised his glass to her in apology, then stared off into space. Dodd was young himself for a circus ringmaster, barely thirty, with large brown eyes that made him look even younger, despite the side whiskers. Gavin glanced at him, then around the little car. Whenever the *Juniper* was in a European port, Captain Naismith checked to see if the Kalakos Circus was in town too, and if it was, he always took Gavin and Tom with him to visit. The cousins caught up while the cabin boys got free run of the show. After the performance, Dodd gave them treats from the grease wagon, or even a windup toy from his workshop.

"I'm sorry to bring bad news," Gavin said. "I miss him, too. And Tom. But there's more."

Gavin gave a thumbnail sketch of how Alice's aunt Edwina had used her cure for the clockwork plague to manipulate Gavin and Alice into joining the Third Ward so Edwina could destroy it, and how Lieutenant Phipps was now chasing them—

"Wait," Dodd interrupted. He pointed at Alice. "You're a baroness who can cure the clockwork plague?" He pointed at Gavin. "And you've become a clockworker?"

Gavin nodded. "Yes. Now we—"

"What do you do?" Dodd interrupted again, this time pointing at Feng. "Walk on water?"

"With a good running start," Feng replied.

"Mesdames et messieurs! Le spectacle commencera dans cinq minutes!"

A sharp knock came at the door, and a red-haired man with startling blue eyes poked his head into the car. He wore an Arran fisherman's sweater and a cloth cap. "Dodd? Show's on. Are you— Gavin! Good Lord, lad, it's been ages. Where are Tom and Felix?"

Dodd rose a little unsteadily. "They're dead, Nathan."

"Oh, Jesus." Nathan strode in and caught Dodd in an embrace that went on for rather longer than most Englishmen or Irishmen felt comfortable with. Gavin suddenly put together a number of cues that had completely escaped him when he was younger. He glanced at Feng, who cocked his head, and the ridiculousness of the situation occurred to him. A baroness with an iron spider on her arm, a plague-infested airman, and an undiplomatic Chinaman hiding from a giant mechanical with a circus ringmaster who fell in love with men. A wave of mirth suddenly overcame Gavin, and inappropriate laughter bubbled in his throat. Alice glared at him. Feng looked surprised. The laughter bubbled up again, and this time Gavin couldn't stop it. He laughed and laughed and pounded the little table with his fist and laughed some more. The odds of any of this happening were so high, they were impossible to calculate. Just the idea that his own ancestors would meet and produce offspring that would end in him while Alice's and Feng's own families were doing the same thing, completely unaware that the culmination of their work and toil and sex would end in a circus with a ringmaster who dabbed it up with men. Trillions upon trillions of events, both enormous and minuscule, had to take place in perfect sequence in order for this meeting to occur and if any one of them had failed to happen, the three of them would be somewhere else—or perhaps they wouldn't even exist. Best of all, they wouldn't even know the difference. Maybe they didn't know the difference *now*.

Gavin doubled over, cackling and howling at the joke. Voices and faces swirled in a twisted rainbow around him. A slight stinging to his face told him he'd been slapped, but it didn't faze him in the slightest. He laughed and laughed and then the world went black.

Sometime later, Gavin bolted awake. He always bolted awake. The attack by the pirate Madoc Blue and the lashing Gavin had endured afterward had destroyed peaceful sleep and gradual waking. By now, he had forgotten what it was to slip calmly out of slumber and greet the day without sweat on his forehead and his heart in his mouth. He sat up and found he was on the bed with his shoes off.

The sunlight had moved, and the car was dimmer. At the little table sat Nathan Storm, his sunset hair gleaming in the low light. The man was smoking a pipe, and the pungent tobacco smoke floated in a blue cloud near the ceiling. Everyone else was gone.

"Nice to see you among the living." Nathan puffed gently.

"Where's Alice?" Gavin asked.

"Exploring the midway. She slept and then wanted some air." He drew on the pipe again. "That was interesting. You were cackling like . . ."

Gavin found his shoes on the floor and laced them on. "Like a lunatic? Yeah. Clockworkers are mad. You know that."

"What's it like?" Nathan said.

"It's hard to describe." Gavin sighed. "The plague shows me things, strange things, *true* things. I'm not insane. Not really."

"You sounded pretty mad. You really hurt Dodd."

Gavin winced. "Shit. Oh, shit. I'm sorry, Nathan."

His pipe went out, and he tapped it into a bowl on the table. "You're apologizing to the wrong person."

"He and Felix aren't—weren't—really cousins, were they?"

That earned him a short bark of laughter. "You *were* young, weren't you? They met in Hamburg when Felix was working some leaky old airship and Dodd was still winding spiders for Viktor Kalakos. They tried to stay together, meeting up in whatever large cities they could, but it just didn't work. They did stay close friends. Dodd doesn't have any other family, so he started calling him *Cousin Felix*, and it stuck."

"And now you two . . ."

"Not 'now,' Gavin. For years. Since before Felix started bringing you to visit."

"Right." Gavin rubbed his face and remembered Simon, whose romantic tastes ran in the same direction. What were the chances? The corners of his mouth quirked, and he quickly ended that line of thought. "Even clockworkers can be stupid."

"Damn right. You want something to eat? I've got beans and bread here, unless you'd fancy a candyfloss."

At the mention of food, Gavin's stomach growled, and he went light-headed. "How long was I . . . away?"

"All the way through the first show. The second starts in a few minutes."

Nathan brought him a plate at the bed as if he were an invalid, but Gavin got up and ate at the table. He felt perfectly fine, except for the hunger.

"Where's Dodd?" he asked around a mouthful.

Nathan looked surprised. "Dodd's in the ring. The show must go on. If you're done eating, let's go find your two friends so you can tell me what you're really here for. I don't think you hid in the parade just to have an excuse to deliver bad news."

Outside, afternoon was fading into evening. The Tilt and the tents cast canted shadows over brightly painted wagons. Gavin knew from his previous visits that the wealthier performers lived in the wagons, which were rolled into the train's boxcars when circus left town. Poorer performers lived in tents. Other tents housed the sideshow exhibits and the animal cages. Smells of fried food and cooking sugar mingled with calliope music. Men, women, and children wandered about. A few stood in line outside the main entrance of the Tilt, handing over their tickets so they could file inside to find seats as the clock automaton shouted in French that the show would begin in one minute. The performers were out of sight behind the Tilt, awaiting cues and entries.

"There you are!" Alice threw her arms around his neck in a near choke hold and kissed him. "You scared the life out of me. Us."

"I'm sorry. I need to apologize to Dodd."

"You must wait," Feng said. "The performance will begin soon. Mr. Storm, could we go into the main tent? We should not be out in the open in case Phipps has tracked us here."

Nathan nodded and took them past the ticket taker into the Tilt. Inside, tall rows of bleachers were bent around a wide red ring, and chatting, laughing people filled most of the spaces. Sawdust lay scattered on the ground. Food sellers moved among them with trays of rich-smelling roasted peanuts and pink cotton candy. Off to one side, the automaton played its calliope. Just as the group arrived on one side of the ring, the tent flaps on the opposite side exploded open and Dodd strode into the Tilt. He had his red hat back, and his silver-topped cane waved in time to the music. Behind him came the mechanical elephant, its feet thudding unevenly on the packed earthen floor. The mahout looked a little seasick at the uneven footsteps. Then came a rainbow explosion of clowns and a group of horses, both live and mechanical, accompanied by slender girls in white feathered dresses, and behind them came acrobats in tight red shirts. A trainer led a lion on a leash and made it roar. For the hell of it, Gavin snatched the recording nightingale from his pocket and pressed the left eye just as the trainer made the lion roar a second time. Then he held the nightingale to his ear and pressed the right eye. It opened its beak and roared like a little lion, which made the real lion look around, startled. Alice shot him a hard look. Oops. He hadn't realized it would be so loud. Gavin stuffed the nightingale into his pocket and looked innocent. The parade, a smaller one than the one in town, stomped round the ring and stormed out to cheers and applause from the audience while Dodd went into the center and leaped onto a small platform with stars on it.

"*Bienvenue,*" he said, "*au le Kalakos Cirque International du Automates et d'Autres Merveilles!*"

The audience, pleased that Dodd spoke their language, burst into more applause just as a troupe of clowns somersaulted into the ring. Dodd got out of the way, and the show began in earnest. He caught sight of Nathan and his entourage lurking at the edge of the bleachers and trotted over.

"I'm sorry," Gavin said before he could speak. "We clockworkers do stupid things sometimes. It's not an excuse, just an explanation. I'm sorry."

Dodd nodded. "You're my last link to Felix, Gavin. I can't be angry with you."

"I need help, Dodd," Gavin told him. The audience laughed. "And only you can give it."

The ringmaster looked wary. "How?"

In the ring, a clown pedaled around on a unicycle with a bucket of whitewash, which he threatened to toss over the audience. Gavin swallowed, suddenly nervous. Dodd was part of the idea he'd gotten earlier, when Glenda was chasing them with the mechanical.

He hadn't had time to think about it further since the chase had started, and now that everything had slowed down, the day's events were catching up with him. He glanced at Alice. She and Feng were counting on him. If Dodd refused to help, they'd be in serious trouble.

"We found out that plague cures have been invented or discovered more than once," Gavin said, "but England and China have suppressed them. English cures were never able to cure clockworkers, only regular victims, but the Chinese ambassador told us the Dragon Men—Chinese clockworkers—might have a full cure."

The clown flung his bucket, but turned it aside at the last moment. The audience whooped at him, half laughing, half fearful.

"So you need to get to China," Dodd said. "I'm sorry, Gavin. We aren't going to China."

Gavin shook his head. "We don't need to go that far. I have an airship, but she's easy to spot and track. It's how Phipps and the others followed us to Luxembourg. We need to lose them and earn enough money to fuel the ship for a flight to Peking."

"What's that to do with me?"

"The circus is a perfect cover," Gavin blurted out. "You're heading east. I can hide the ship on the train, and we can hide among you, do some work to earn money. Once we get far enough along, we'll leave."

"Oh, Gavin—I don't know," Dodd said. "I like you. Hell, you're almost like a little brother to me. But the coppers already give us the hairy eye when we come to town."

Feng muttered something in Chinese that sounded like a swear word, and Gavin's heart sank. The clown

THE IMPOSSIBLE CUBE 101

drew his bucket back one more time. "Phipps has no real jurisdiction outside England," Gavin said, still trying.

"Doesn't seem to stop her. And I don't know that I have any paying work for you. Look, I want to help, but—"

"How long has that elephant been lurching like that?" Alice interrupted. The clown threw the bucket's contents, but all that came out was confetti. The audience laughed and cheered.

"What?" Dodd said. "Uh . . . two months, perhaps three. We bought it from a clockworker several years ago, but it seems to be breaking down. No one knows how to fix it."

"Is that so?" Alice said.

Interlude

"I was *that* close, Lieutenant," Glenda fretted. "I practically had them in my hands."

"So did I," Phipps reminded her. "And I am not worried. There are only so many places they can run to, and Alice is on a mission."

"What do you mean?" Simon asked. Once again, they were in a hotel room, though this one was rather better than the previous one. Clean, airy, with fresh linens on the beds and flowers on the nightstand, and a water closet on every floor. Once again, Glenda perched on a chair, Simon sprawled on the bed, and Phipps paced the floor.

"Haven't you been listening to the talk on the street? She's curing people, one by one, with that gauntlet of hers." Phipps unconsciously flexed her own brass hand. "They break local laws about entering houses of plague, Gavin Ennock sings, Alice Michaels scratches people with that 'sword' of hers, and people call them angels for breaking the law."

"They managed to hide the airship," Glenda growled. "There's been no sign of the thing."

"There's also been no sign of Dr. Clef since the affair at the greenhouse," Simon put in. "That worries me a little."

"It worries me, too," Phipps admitted. "Though it may mean he has died."

Glenda muttered, "Life is never so easy."

"You do have a point." Phipps sighed. "We must operate on the assumption that Dr. Clef is still alive and very dangerous. The trouble is, we've been underestimating them. All of them. Gavin *is* a clockworker, with all a clockworker's requisite cunning."

"And madness." Glenda poured herself a glass of water from a pitcher on the table. "I'll wager Alice is enjoying herself. At any rate, we'll never find them at hotels now. They're going to be wary of public houses. Unfortunately, they could hide any number of other places, including the homes of grateful plague victims."

Already the pieces were falling together. Strategy and planning, three and four steps ahead. If this happens, then that. If that happens, then this. Though it was difficult to think through the anger—and the fear. She wasn't afraid of what Gavin and Dr. Clef might do—not really. She was afraid of failing and earning that tiny shake of her father's head, the one that tormented her every night when she went to bed.

Phipps drummed metal fingers on the windowsill, as was fast becoming her habit. Was she doing the right thing? The just thing? Was she pursuing Gavin and Alice and Dr. Clef out of true justice, or because her father—

No. She couldn't afford doubt now. Aloud, she said,

"The smart thing would be for them to hide, true, but they won't do the smart thing. I repeat to you: Alice is on a mission, and she can't accomplish it in hiding. That's how we'll get her."

"You mean to set up an ambush," Simon said.

"Absolutely. I believe now is also the time to visit the gendarmes and cash in some Crown influence. They can search the city while we set a trap at the appropriate place."

"What's the appropriate place?" Glenda asked.

"At the highest concentration of plague victims, of course." Phipps gave a grim smile. "I want to run a check on the mechanicals first thing in the morning. And then we're going to shop for bread and wine."

Chapter Five

Alice shut the huge access panel on the elephant's left side and set the spanner on the workbench with a clank. Grease stained her face and blouse. The Tilt felt big and empty now, with its rows of vacant bleachers and high canvas roof. All the sawdust was trampled into the ground, and the bleacher rows were littered with dead peanut bags. Dodd stood nearby, watching closely, while Gavin and Feng occupied front-row bleachers.

"That was *fascinating*," Alice said. "I even made some improvements on the memory wheels and increased the visual acuity."

"Meaning what?" Dodd asked.

"It doesn't necessarily need a rider. Look." With a sidelong glance at Gavin and a certain amount of pride, she gestured at the big brass elephant, which came smoothly to its feet and plodded steadily around the ring, hissing and puffing steam. Alice gestured again, and it stopped. She felt like a sorceress who had conjured a steaming elemental from the depths of the earth.

Gavin applauded, and Alice turned a little pink. She had to admit that she had done this in no small part to impress him. After everything he had done this morning—rescuing her from Phipps, getting them away from Simon's mechanical, and ingeniously hiding them in a circus—she felt a need to impress him.

"All right," Dodd said. "We have a deal."

"So you'll take us with you?" Gavin said. Alice made the elephant sit like an enormous dog. This was fun.

"Absolutely," Dodd said. "We haven't had anyone who can service the machines in a long time. That's why we were heading to Kiev."

"Kiev?" Feng got to his feet, concerned. "Is that wise? The Ukrainian Empire is the source of the clockwork plague."

"Is it?" Alice straightened. "I've never heard that."

"It's never been proven," Gavin said slowly, "and not something everyone discusses. Kiev does seem to have the earliest cases of plague on record."

"Earliest cases?" Feng said. "That's an understatement worthy of my father. According to the histories, in 1750 the Dnepro River boiled in the center of Kiev and the plague rose up like a dragon and devoured the city."

"The river boiled?" Alice repeated. "What on earth does that mean?"

"No doubt some hyperbole found its way into the history," Feng said.

"Which only goes to show that the stories are unreliable," Dodd pointed out. "Boiling rivers indeed!"

"Then the plague rose up again ten years later," Feng continued, undaunted, "and one more time twenty years after that. Kiev seems to attract the plague. No one has more cases of it, and no one has an earlier source of it."

"Then why go there?" Gavin said.

"The plague is at an ebb right now," Dodd told him. "Besides, we have Alice, and everyone in the circus is immune by now. The Ukrainians do have world-class automatons. They do have pots of money. And they love a good circus. If we keep our noses clean, we can sell out two shows a day for a month. We've played there a dozen times before with no trouble. It's true they don't like Jews or Catholics, but we have neither in the circus."

"I was thinking we would go south, through Turkey," Feng said, obviously ill at ease.

"That would be out of our way," Gavin pointed out. "And the Ukrainians have paraffin oil, don't they?"

"They practically invented the stuff," Dodd said. "Russia pays them tribute in petroleum, and they've done some incredible things with it. I've already arranged to rent space and Linda says she saw us in Ukraine, so—"

"Linda?" Alice interrupted.

"She and her husband, Charlie, tell fortunes in the sideshow," Dodd answered. "They're very good, especially since Charlie's accident."

"You base this decision on a fortune-teller?" Feng said incredulously.

"And everything else I mentioned," Dodd said. "Look, I've already decided that we're going. If you want to come along, come. We can use Miss Michaels. The rest of you are dead weight, but—"

"Hey!" Gavin said. "I can play the fiddle!"

"And he sings," Alice pointed out, feeling defensive.

"I could walk a tightrope, too," Gavin muttered. "And learn the trapeze. Wouldn't take more than ten minutes. Stupid clockwork plague gives me stupid extra reflexes. May as well make some extra money out of it before it kills me."

"The Flying Tortellis would drop something on my head if I put you in the ring," Dodd said with a grin. "Besides, you're supposed to be hiding. I was joking about the dead weight. You really do have trouble with British humor, don't you?"

"Now, look—"

"I've never visited the Ukrainian Empire," Alice interrupted. "But if it's the center of the plague, I should certainly go there with Gavin. Why are you so unhappy, Feng?"

"They are Cossack barbarians," Feng spat. "They build and pollute and fight. They care nothing for balance or beauty."

"*You* worry about balance?" Alice asked archly.

"And the Chinese put them in power," Gavin said.

"That doesn't make them any less barbaric," Feng shot back.

"In any case, I want to go there with Gavin," Alice repeated. She stood the elephant back up and sent it to the side of the ring. "But please explain that remark about power."

Feng crossed his arms. "England had an arrangement with China," he said. "After the Napoleonic Wars ended, it became clear that parts of Europe—the west—and the Ottoman Empire—the east—could unite and become a threat to Britannia and China. Our governments didn't want that to happen. So we came to an understanding. Britannia took the west and China the east."

"I don't need a history lesson," Dodd complained. "Will the elephant work for anyone, Miss Michaels, or just you?"

Alice waved him away. "Anyone, Ringmaster. What do you mean by *took*, Feng?"

"Took charge." Feng was pacing again. "Napoleon's nephew was supposed to rule France after the old emperor was exiled, but the man died. With no strong ruler, France fell into civil war, and now it is four fragments. Why do you think that was? Prussia is ten tiny kingdoms who never agree. Why is that? Your Calvinists and Lutherans war with each other as well. Why does this happen?"

"You're going to tell me the Third Ward keeps everyone off balance."

"Indeed."

"Up!" Dodd said, gesturing. "Up! Miss Michaels, he isn't moving."

"You have to use your left hand, Ringmaster," Alice replied absently. "I assume China has a role as well?"

"China," Gavin put in, "destabilized the east. Russia

and Poland had split Ukraine in half and were draining it dry. The resources gave both countries enough power to make China—and Britain—nervous. Then the clockwork plague hit Ukraine again. For some reason, it created more clockworkers than normal in Kiev. A Cossack captain named Ivan Gonta ended up with a special talent for war machines, and his superior Maksym Zalizniak used Gonta's inventions to start a revolution."

The elephant got up and lumbered around the ring. It picked up speed, steam trailing from its tusks. Dodd waved frantically at it, but it didn't slow down.

"Oh! I vaguely remember something about that from a history book, now that you mention specific names," Alice said. "Gonta and the other clockworkers put together hundreds of war machines and slaughtered thousands of Russians and Poles until they abandoned Ukraine to the Cossacks."

"Hello there!" Dodd shouted. "Runaway elephant!"

"Did you ever stop to wonder where Gonta and Zalizniak found the money and materials to build all those machines?" Feng asked.

Alice gestured sharply, and the elephant screeched to a halt. "I have the feeling it came from China."

"Was that a malfunction?" Dodd asked. "Because I swear I did the exact same thing."

Feng nodded. "The emperor chose wisely—the Cossacks are content to defend their borders without expanding them, and they make an excellent wedge between Russia and Poland."

"I *am* your boss, Miss Michaels," Dodd said.

"Of course you are," Gavin murmured.

"At any rate," Feng concluded, "the ruling Cassocks are actually crueler to their own people than the Poles or Russians ever were. It's the nature of the warrior class."

"And we're walking right into them?"

"Steaming into them," Dodd said. "We have a train. But I told you not to worry. They *love* us. Now, show me how to work this damned elephant."

Alice gave him a wide smile. "What's the magic word, Ringmaster? As a hint, I'll tell you that it isn't *damned*."

Gavin laughed, and Alice thought it was the most musical thing she had ever heard.

Later that afternoon, Alice opened the hatchway on the *Lady of Liberty* in her hiding place at the abandoned stable and climbed belowdecks. The familiar narrow corridor faced with doors greeted her. The creaking space felt eerie and claustrophobic without Gavin here. Alice went past her stateroom all the way down to the end and slid the last door open. Inside was the tiny laboratory Gavin had built into the airship. The entire place was set up for efficiency. Tools hung on the bulkheads, tabletops folded up, tiny drawers kept everything pigeonholed. It even had a tiny forge, which was currently glowing and made the room hot and stuffy. The place was also hung with half a dozen clocks. They ticked madly, their exposed gears whirling. Stuck everywhere were pieces of paper, large and small. Every one of them had the same drawing, one of a three-dimensional wire cube that twisted Alice's eye. Part of the back passed over the front, or perhaps the front passed under the back. The drawings were done in pencil, charcoal, colored ink, and one medium that looked suspiciously like blood.

Dr. Clef was standing in the midst of all this with his back to Alice. He seemed to be scratching something in a notebook. Click leaped down from the rim of a porthole and hurried over to her, purring loudly. Alice scooped him up. His skin was cool and smooth.

"Click," she said. "Oh, I've missed you."

Dr. Clef turned and pushed his goggles up. "Alice! When did you come back, my dear? I have not seen you in weeks."

"Weeks?" Alice stroked Click's brass back. "Doctor, it's been only two days."

"Oh. Are you sure?" He glanced at the clocks. "How interesting. Did you know that gravity affects a clock?"

"Er . . . no."

"Look at these." He pointed at the ones closest to the ceiling. "They are moving at a slightly different rate than the ones down there at the floor. It gets more noticeable when I put them on top of the ship's envelope. It is because they are farther away from Earth's gravity."

"They look the same to me, Dr. Clef."

Dr. Clef shrugged. "They are not."

"Are you trying to re-create your Impossible Cube, Doctor?" she asked.

"With difficulty." He pointed at a small cable spool on the worktable. It was wound with fat, stiff-looking wire. "I have managed to reforge some of my special alloy using nails and other scraps from the barn, but I do not think I can re-create the Cube itself. And I do miss it."

"What's the problem?"

"It is—was—unique in all time and space." Dr. Clef sighed. "I am beginning to think it cannot be re-created, for that would violate the basic nature of its uniqueness. But look at what I have learned while I am trying." He held up a notebook with a number of formulae scribbled in it. "When you measure certain events, you change them. You can, for example, discover how fast a certain piece of . . . of matter is moving or you can learn its location, but you can't pin down both. It is very odd."

"Ridiculous." Alice waved her free hand. "There. You can see how fast my hand is moving and you can see exactly where it is."

"Nonetheless. It is especially true for things so tiny, they cannot be seen and who move so fast, they cannot be captured."

"Then how do you know they exist?"

"The numbers prove it," he said, brandishing the notebook again. "It all related to my poor Impossible Cube. I miss it so. The beauty. The symmetry. The way it twisted the universe about itself. Everything about it was perfect."

"Perhaps you can still rebuild it."

"As I said, I am beginning to think this is not possible. Can you tell me any more about the way it was destroyed?"

Alice remembered watching Gavin holding the Impossible Cube beneath the Third Ward as he sang a single crystal note that shattered everything around him. Everything but her. Then he dropped the Cube, which fell through every color of the spectrum and vanished in a white flash the moment it touched the floor.

"Only what I've told you already," she said. "Nothing new. Doctor, the way the Cube twists itself—"

"It does no such thing," Dr. Clef interrupted, agitated. "The Cube is a constant. It twists the *universe*, but since we are *in* the universe, we think the Cube is twisted."

"Of course, of course," Alice reassured him, though she had no idea what he was talking about. "But I meant that it might be better if you left the Cube alone. Perhaps it isn't meant to be re-created at all."

An odd light came into his eyes. "Do you think so?"

"Quite."

"Hmmm. Maybe I *should* leave it alone, then. Did you bring back any raspberry jam? I have not had any in quite some time."

"Oh!" Alice jolted back to the nonscientific world. "We did bring more food, but no jam, I'm sorry to say. Gavin and Feng are down in the barn. We think we have a way to move the ship, and we'll need your help."

Dr. Clef rubbed his hands together. "A project! I will be pleased to take part."

"Madam?" The door to Alice's stateroom opened and Kemp poked his head into the corridor. "Is that you?"

"Of course it is, Kemp."

"Thank heavens!" He bustled into the corridor. "I've been having a dreadful time keeping the little automatons under control, and I finally had to lock them up. We're completely out of food, and—"

"Yes, Kemp. You've done an admirable job and we couldn't have survived without you. Now, come down, both of you."

Kemp managed to look pleased despite his lack of facial features. "Madam."

On deck, they filed past the little generator, which had only recently been switched back on. It contentedly puffed steam and paraffin oil smoke, a shockingly daring woman smoking a cigarette. Above them, ropes creaked and the envelope's lacy endoskeleton glowed blue, indicating that it was receiving power and lifting the hull. They all climbed down to the barn floor. At the entrance of the barn was Gavin, who had abandoned his black clothes for an ordinary work shirt, brown trousers, and a cloth cap. He looked like a handsome young farmer. With him was Nathan Storm, his own cap barely concealing his sunset hair, and a team of four horses pulling a wagon, which carried a pile of material covered in canvas.

"What's this? What's this?" Dr. Clef asked, and Alice made introductions. Dr. Clef clapped his hands in glee. "The circus! A perfect place to hide ourselves, then. But how will we hide the ship?"

"With this." Gavin pulled the canvas off the wagon, revealing a pile of wheels and axles.

Dr. Clef clapped his hands again. "Of course, of course. I should have seen. Shall we work now?"

"I told you he would understand quickly," Gavin said to Nathan, who only lit his pipe. They hauled the *Lady* out of the barn and tethered her a few feet above the ground so they could set to work. The endoskeleton continued to glow its lacy blue, and Alice felt nervous and exposed, like a fat rabbit on a meadow with hawks cruising overhead, but there was nothing for it.

"Alice," Gavin said, "could you bring down your little automatons to assist? And then . . ."

She cocked her head. "And then what?"

"Uh . . . maybe you could go for a walk? Or just stay out of sight behind the barn. This shouldn't take long."

Her ire escalated. "Because you don't think I'm qualified to help? How can you possibly think—"

"No, no." He held his hands up. "I just don't think you should see this."

It was the wrong thing to say. Her voice rose and her metal fist clenched. "I'm too ladylike, is that it?"

"Not at all."

"Uh-oh," Nathan said.

"So I'm *not* a lady, then?" Alice said.

"What? No! I just . . . Alice, you've never seen a clockworker in a full work fugue before, have you?"

"And it's not appropriate to me because I'm a lady." She folded her arms. "It's foolish to give up a pair of hands because of some misguided principles. I'm helping, and the sooner we get started, the better."

Gavin closed his eyes. "All right. Let's get started, then."

They had to work quickly, before they were spotted and word filtered back to Phipps, wherever she was. Alice was no slouch at mechanical work, but even she was amazed at Gavin and Dr. Clef. They both circled the pile of parts and tools for some time, studying them, with her little automatons hovering and skittering nearby. Kemp and Click also awaited orders. A blank look came over first Gavin's eyes, then Dr. Clef's.

They dove into the parts with great glee and rushed with them toward the *Lady*, barking orders to the automatons as they went. Alice followed along, and was startled when Gavin thrust an axle into her hands.

"Grind these ends smooth," he boomed. "And be quick about it! Maybe then I can ride you into battle." Then he turned away and flung a handful of bolts at one of the little whirligigs, who caught them in midair. He didn't even seem to recognize Alice. At first she felt indignant. Then she felt sickened. She told herself it was the clockwork plague, not him, and when a clockworker entered a fugue, nothing mattered but the work, but she still felt like she'd been slapped.

"What are you waiting for, girl? The usual offer to tup you for half a sandwich?" Gavin snarled. His eyes were wild and his hair half stood up. Oil streaked his face and hands like blood. "Move!"

Face flaming, Alice did as she was told, and when she was finished, accepted another snarl from Gavin, this time to tighten bolts. The little automatons flitted and scampered about. He snatched her automatons and spiders one by one, opened them up, and changed their memory wheels around. They squeaked in protest, and Alice bit back a cry of alarm. Dr. Clef worked elsewhere, shouting orders at Kemp and Nathan. Click stayed out of the way. Alice felt as tense as the metal she tightened.

"Faster!" Gavin bellowed at her. "You're slow and clumsy. Typical of dog meat."

Alice kept her head down, feeling small and stupid and hating herself for it. Gavin had become another person, a sneering stranger, and she didn't like him.

Telling herself that it wasn't his fault didn't help much. After being barked at for the fourth time, she began to see why so many clockworkers were forced to build automaton assistants. The only saving grace was that Gavin and Dr. Clef seemed to be working three times as hard as anyone else.

"Hey!" Gavin dropped the automaton he was altering and dashed over to Dr. Clef, who was frantically reworking a set of wheels. "Those measurements are wrong, you fat idiot. You're off by a good sixteenth-inch."

Dr. Clef's jowls reddened. "You're not half the man your mother is, you grease-faced dog. The tracks are clearly—"

"Did you think I can't see the obvious?" Gavin barked. "My mind is sharper than any tool you'll ever touch, and certainly a good deal larger."

Dr. Clef picked up a sledgehammer and hefted it with an ease and power that caught Alice off guard. She had forgotten that the clockwork plague enhanced his strength and reflexes just as much as Gavin's. "We will see how large a tool I have."

"Just a moment!" Nathan plucked the hammer from Dr. Clef's hand. "Over there, Doctor. Does that axle look crooked to you?"

"And, Gavin," Alice said, hurrying forward, "I don't think that automaton is functioning properly."

Both clockworkers turned, distracted, and moved fairly quickly to their new tasks. Nathan set the sledgehammer down.

"Clockworkers don't work well together in fugue," he murmured.

"I can see that," Alice said.

"You!" Gavin snapped. "The one with an ass like a bag of laundry! Bring me that box of parts."

"Don't shout back. You just saw how it only makes them worse," Nathan said quietly. "And don't take it personally."

Alice's jaw was tight. "I'm trying."

In a surprisingly short time the *Lady* sported three sets of train wheels on her underside, and all the automatons had been modified. Still, the sun was setting, and Alice felt dirty, greasy, and half starved, and the steady stream of invective stuck like pitch to her skin. It would never come off.

"We're done," she called up to Gavin, who was busy carving ivy leaves into a box that he had mounted on the deck. The box had two buttons on it, one red and one green. His hands moved with inhuman speed. "Gavin! We're done!"

"Not close, you ignorant filth. Do something useful with your fingers besides twiddle yourself, and bring me a screwdriver."

Setting her mouth, Alice strode up the gangplank and grabbed him by the shoulders. He shook her off and snarled at her like a dog. A blob of spittle flew from his mouth and landed warm on the back of her hand. She jumped back, eyes wide at the monstrosity of it.

"How dare you lay hands on me?" he snarled. "Keep your disgusting hands to—"

Water doused him from head to foot. It plastered his hair to his scalp and ran off him in rivulets. Gavin gasped and gaped for a long moment. Alice scrambled backward and Nathan set down his bucket.

"Are you yourself, then?" he asked Gavin mildly.

There was a long pause. Gavin dropped the tools, and they thudded on the planking. "Are we done? What time is it? Why am I all wet?" His voice was normal, and held none of the sneering tone she'd been hearing all afternoon. She felt so relieved, she was afraid she would half burst into tears, but she was angry, too. Why hadn't he come out of it when *she* talked to him?

"We had to snap you out," Alice said stiffly. "Thank you, Mr. Storm. We should get moving, before someone spots the ship and gossip spreads."

Gavin uselessly mopped at his face with his sopping sleeve. "Did it work? Are we ready? Why won't anyone answer me?"

"I'm assuming it worked." Alice forced her voice to stay level. Looking at Gavin made her angry at the way he had treated her. *It's not his fault. It's not his fault. He told me to walk away,* she told herself. But it didn't help. "You and Dr. Clef were doing nothing but decoration, and we probably shouldn't wait for that."

"You're mad at me," he said. "Did I say or . . . do anything to you? God, Alice, I'm sorry. I don't—"

"Not now, Gavin," she said. "We need to move."

Gavin looked like someone had kicked his puppy. She knew she was being unreasonable, that she should apologize or offer to hear him out, but she couldn't seem to do it.

"We're ready up here," she called over the gunwale.

Nathan had disembarked. The *Lady* was still floating a few feet above the ground, and her new wheels just barely cleared the green grass. Dr. Clef, also out of his fugue, was hitching the horses to the front of the airship with Nathan's help.

"Give it a little more power, my boy!" Dr. Clef called up.

Gavin went to the paraffin oil generator and adjusted the dials. The purring grew louder and more steam emerged. The endoskeleton glowed a little brighter, and the *Lady* rose higher, but only about a foot.

"Clear!" Nathan called from the horses, and flicked the reins. The four horses started forward, towing the ship, which slid forward at a quick, even pace.

"It works," Alice said.

"So far," Gavin said cautiously. "And we can come back for the wagon later. I'm just not so sure about the rest."

Alice whistled, and whirligigs flew from a dozen different directions to hover in front of her, their brass parts glittering in the dying sunlight. Most of them were carrying at least one spider. "Thank you for your help," she said. "We're nearly set for the next step. Please stand ready."

Looking excited, they flew up into the rigging like a cloud of mechanical bats.

"Do they understand *please* and *thank you*?" Gavin asked.

"They seem to work better when I use those words, so I do," Alice said. "I can't explain it, so I don't try." Her words came out curt.

"Look, Alice, I'm sorry I--"

"Oh look—the tracks!"

The railroad tracks ran alongside the road Alice,

Gavin, and Feng had taken into Luxembourg two days ago. No one was on them at the moment. Nathan guided the horses around until the airship was hovering just above the tracks.

"Down!" Nathan called.

With another glance at Alice, Gavin slowly powered down the generator. The blue glow lessened and the *Lady* sank like a woman settling into an armchair. Alice looked over the side. Kemp, Dr. Clef, and Nathan pushed and nudged the hull as it went down, making sure the new wheels lined up with the tracks. With a *clunk*, the ship dropped into place.

"Perfect," Dr. Clef said. "Everything matches."

"We have an hour before a train comes," Gavin said. "So let's hope this works."

He put his hand over the green button on the newly mounted box on the deck, the one with half-carved ivy leaves on it, and paused. Several moments passed, and Alice finally said, "What's the matter?"

"I hate to do this to her," Gavin replied quietly. "It feels like I'm crippling my sister or my mother. But it needs to be done."

He slapped the green button. In the rigging, all the automatons instantly came to attention. The spiders rushed over the ropes and the whirligigs spun into action. Under the new instructions Gavin had spun into their memory wheels, they unfastened the *Lady*'s outer envelope. Their tiny fingers popped seams with quick precision, and the sides of the envelope peeled away like petticoats to reveal a glowing wire corset beneath. Alice realized she felt a bit embarrassed, as if the *Lady* were undressing in public, and she told herself not to be silly. The spiders dodged into the endoskeleton's framework, and got to work on the interior balloons. As the last pieces of the envelope drooped away, the four interior ballonets deflated with an unhappy sigh, leaving a pile of cloth inside the curlicue endoskeleton. The outer layer of cloth dropped to the deck, and Alice found herself buried in silk. She struggled out of it and found Gavin emerging as well. His expression was sad.

"My ship," he said.

But Alice could only manage a curt nod.

The endoskeleton, meanwhile, continued to hover, and the whirligigs rolled it up like an enormous piece of chicken wire with the deflated ballonets inside. It was still powered by the generator, however, so the roll hovered high above the deck. Without the additional lift of the envelope, the skeleton didn't have the strength to lift the *Lady*'s hull, and the ropes kept it from floating away. Gavin swept silk away from the generator and powered it slowly down. The wire roll, which was the same length as the ship and about five feet in diameter, sank slowly to the deck, drooping ropes as it came. The whirligigs and spiders rode it down, and Alice could swear they were silently cheering. She and Gavin pushed the roll a little to one side so it wouldn't land on the helm and finally eased it down to the starboard side of the deck. The hull creaked and settled as the weight shifted. Nathan snapped his reins, and the four horses jerked forward. It took them a moment to get started, but at last they moved ahead, pulling the newly wheeled airship smoothly down the tracks.

"We're not done," Gavin said to the whirligigs, which rushed down to the wagon and, working as teams, hauled up two large canvas signs. Gavin hung one over one side of the ship and Alice hung the other over the opposite side. In garish letters, they read *Kalakos Cirque International du Automates et d'Autres Merveilles.*

"It's like putting whore's makeup on a queen," Gavin muttered.

Alice was sure she wasn't meant to hear that comment, so she ignored it. She climbed down a rope ladder, dropped to the ground, and trotted a short distance from the tracks to get a good look. The airship's gunwales looked like the railings that graced the top of most circus wagons. Silk covered the name *The Lady of Liberty* painted across the stern, and the banner signs completed the trick. The airship looked like a tall wagon or high train car being hauled somewhere for repairs or a bit of publicity. Alice climbed back up. Kemp was back on deck, along with Gavin. Nathan and Dr. Clef drove the horses below. Click had disappeared, but Alice was confident he would show up again. He always did.

"Go below and hide, Kemp," Alice said. "You're illegal here. Take the little ones with you."

"Shall I bring tea first, Madam?" Kemp said.

"I'm not hungry anymore," Alice replied.

Kemp withdrew. The horses were making good time on the tracks. Already they were nearing the boundary of the city. The fields and trees were nearly dark, and the sounds of the city—voices, horses, clattering machinery, laughter, music—floated past in snips and pieces beneath shy stars. A faint breeze from the country brought smells of earth and hay. Alice drummed her mechanical hand on the gunwale with little clicking sounds.

"I tried to warn you," Gavin said quietly. "And I'm not going to fall all over myself apologizing."

"Don't expect you to."

He shrugged casually, but Alice could see the stiffness in his posture. "I didn't bring the plague on myself, and I don't like it that you're treating me as if I did."

The anger flared again. "What are you talking about? I gave up *everything* for you, Gavin Ennock. I gave up a marriage and abandoned my position in society and, God help me, I even destroyed the British Empire, all to save you."

"You wanted to watch me work and whatever you saw scared you." Gavin flung his cap away and spread his arms. "Get a good look, Alice. I'm the monster your dear aunt made me."

"Don't you bring Aunt Edwina into this!" Alice cried. "She was just as insane as . . . as . . ."

"As I am?" Gavin finished for her. "Go ahead. Blame me. Blame her. It doesn't matter. In a few months I'll be dead. Then you can rush to England and see if Norbert will take you back."

He stalked over to the other side of the deck and stared viciously out at nothing. Alice turned her back on him, stiff with fury. The city slid past with a faint rumble and scrape of train wheels. The *Lady* swayed a little. It felt distinctly odd, the familiar rhythm of a railway car on the open deck of an airship. Some of Alice's anger gave way to nerves. Somewhere out there,

Glenda and Simon and Phipps were looking for her. For all she knew, they were one street over, or just around the corner. She shivered and glanced back at Gavin. The anger came back. It didn't matter that it was the plague that—

Yes. It *did* matter. She looked back at the streets and buildings, now only lit by occasional streetlights and yellow lamps in windows. This part of the city was mostly residential, and there was little street traffic at night. Three of the doors each had ragged red P's painted on them. The deserted sidewalks and cobblestones suddenly seemed an echo of her life. The plague definitely mattered. It was *all* that mattered. It had stolen her entire family and her future, turned her into a fugitive, and forced her to make choices that would change the entire world. It wasn't fair. It wasn't *right*. And it made her so *angry*.

Movement caught her eye. A tattered, gaunt woman shuffled along the sidewalk as the airship glided past. She wore a battered straw hat and sores split her skin. The light from a streetlamp made her flinch. Plague zombie. A lifetime of reflexes made Alice flinch away, but once she recovered, she turned to tell Gavin, but then thought otherwise. What business was it of his?

Alice scuttled down the rope ladder. The airship moved slowly, and Alice easily dropped to the street. Nathan and Dr. Clef didn't see her and continued on with the horses. She didn't want to shout and call attention to herself, so she simply dashed over to the zombie woman, pulling off the glove that covered her left hand as she went. It would be easy enough to cure the poor woman and catch the ship back up. She couldn't save her family, but she could save this woman, and so many others like her. She had to do it, or what was the point of everything that had gone before?

The zombie woman barely reacted when Alice slashed her, but straightened fairly quickly. Much of the misery left her face, replaced with relief. She blinked and looked around, like a blind person seeing color again. Alice's heart lightened. Every life she changed for the better made her own existence a bit more worthy. The zombie—now a full person again—wandered away with an expression of wonder.

"Excusez-moi!" Another woman Alice hadn't noticed stepped out of a doorway. *"Êtes-vous qu'elle?"*

Alice started, and her light mood evaporated. "Am I she, who?" she asked cautiously, also in French. The woman was young and very pretty, with enormous blue eyes.

"The one who cures people," she clarified. "People with the plague."

The airship-cum-wagon was pulling out of sight, but if this woman also needed help, Alice didn't see how she could refuse.

"I am she," she said.

The woman abruptly caught Alice in a hard embrace. "Thank you. Thank you, thank you. You are an angel." She broke away, suddenly embarrassed, and said, "But where is your friend?"

"My friend?"

"The one whose music gives you power to cure them."

"Oh." Alice thought about correcting her, then thought the better of it. "He's . . . he's nearby."

"There are more who need you. Many more. Can you come? Please?"

The airship was curving away, nearly gone. Alice chewed her lip. She was still angry, but she wasn't stupid, either. "I can't come right now, but I will, I promise. Where?"

"To the Church of Our Lady," she said, "at the top of the hill in the center of the city. Ask for Monsignor Adames."

"I promise," Alice repeated, and ran back to the clattering airship. At the front with the horses, Dr. Clef was telling Nathan, "The closer one comes to its position in time, the farther one wanders from its position in space."

She had just reached the ladder when a trio of men on horses cantered around the corner, the horses' iron-shod hooves clattering on the cobblestones. The men wore smart blue uniforms, and one of them carried a torch. The woman fled into the shadows.

"You!" one of the men shouted at the airship in French. "Halt!"

Nathan and Dr. Clef stopped the team. Gavin poked his head over the gunwale, a startled and worried expression on his face. Alice hurried up the ladder, her hands chilly with apprehension.

"Where were you?" Gavin hissed at her.

"Never mind," she whispered back. "Get out that nightingale."

"What?"

"Just do it!"

"Yes, Officer?" Nathan asked pleasantly, also in French. He sucked at his pipe with outward calm, but

Alice could see tension in him. Dr. Clef had slid to the side of the team opposite the two police officers and was keeping his head down, away from the torchlight.

"What are you doing out at this hour?" the first man snapped. He was older, and wasn't carrying the torch.

"We are with the circus and had to move one of our cars," Nathan replied. "It was the only time the tracks were free."

"Where are your papers?"

"Here, sir. All signed and stamped." Nathan drew a set from his pocket and handed them over. The man with the torch held the light so his superior could examine them. The third man took his horse around the other side of the disguised airship, clearly to make sure no one slipped away and vanished. Alice held her breath, hoping they would take the explanation and leave.

The officer gave the papers only a cursory glance. "We have reports of certain dangerous criminals from England and America. A woman with brown hair and a younger man with pale blond hair."

"I was afraid of that," Gavin whispered. "The Third Ward has connections all over Europe. Phipps must have talked to the police."

"I'm from Ireland," Nathan said.

"What about him?" The older officer pointed at Dr. Clef, who was still huddled behind the horse.

"He's mute, and an idiot," Nathan said. "His mother was a sideshow freak and he was born funny, but horses love him."

"I still need to search this wagon," the officer said.

Alice's heart beat fast now. Before she could lose her

nerve, she shouted over the gunwale in her heavily accented French, "What is wrong down there? We should not stop for long, you know."

"Who's there?" the lead officer called up. He drew a sword. "Show yourself!"

Alice tied a handkerchief over her hair in an impromptu head cloth and peered over the side. "I am Lombarda, lion tamer extraordinaire. Who are you?"

"Lieutenant Ovrille of the Grand Ducal Police," he said. "Come down immediately! We are searching the wagon!"

"If you like," Alice called back. "But the lion, he will not be happy."

Ovrille paused. "What lion?"

"The cage, it has broken, you see. That is why we are using this wagon. The lion, he is up top, and I have no leash or cage right now, and it is far past his mealtime. He is quite hungry. Fortunately, he does not feel women are a threat, no?"

The other officer, the one with the torch, looked uncertain. "Sir—," he said.

"Our orders are clear," Ovrille said stubbornly. "We are to search everything even remotely suspicious."

"Yes, yes," Alice called. "Please come up, then. But make no sudden moves, especially if you ate meat for supper. I do not know how much longer I can keep him quiet." She changed her tone of voice, as if she were speaking to a child. "Can I, baby? No, I cannot. I just cannot keep ums quiet!"

Ovrille dismounted and reached for the rope ladder hanging over the side of the airship. Alice gestured sharply at Gavin, who fumbled with the nightingale and finally managed to press its right eye. It opened its beak and the lion's roar from the previous evening's parade snarled through the night, a little quiet but realistic enough. Ovrille froze.

"No, no, no," Alice cooed loudly. "It is all right, little one. The man is not here to hurt you. He is not for you to bite. You must sit quietly and let him—"

Gavin pressed the nightingale again, and it played the roar a second time. Ovrille snatched his hand away from the ladder as if the rungs were hot pokers. The officer with the torch backed his horse away, as did the man who had gone to the opposite side of the airship.

"What are you doing?" Alice said. "I believe I have him under control. Come up now before he again becomes angry."

Another roar. Ovrille went back to his horse. "Yes, well," he said. "I think we can let it go this time."

"Are you sure?" Alice said. "We would not wish for you to get into trouble. If you let him lick your hand first, he probably won't bite."

"Just go," Ovrille ordered.

"Huh. As you wish, then."

Nathan tapped the horses, which jerked forward, and the airship creaked along the tracks. Once the officers were out of sight, Alice blew out a long breath. Every muscle went limp and she collapsed to the deck.

"I never want to do that again," she half sobbed, half giggled.

"You thought it was bad for you." Gavin sank to the deck beside her. "I had no idea what you were saying and had to guess about making the nightingale roar."

"Good that you're intelligent, then."

There was a long pause. Alice wanted to say something more, except words wouldn't come. The anger curled around her heart like a dozing tiger and held everything in. Alice envied Gavin's easy way with words, how he could say whatever was on his mind.

After a while, Gavin brought his cupped hands with the nightingale in them to his face. When he brought them down again, he tossed the nightingale into the air. It spread its wings and fluttered about for a moment, then flitted over to settle on Alice's shoulder. Alice knew that the nightingale, meant to carry recorded messages, would fly back and forth between the last two people who had touched it. The moment it landed, the little bird sang in Gavin's voice.

> *I picked a rose, the rose picked me,*
> *Underneath the branches of the forest tree.*
> *The moon picked you from all the rest*
> *For I loved you best.*

Alice closed her eyes at the beauty that surrounded her but still couldn't respond.

"Most people think," Gavin said, "that if the melody of a song is written in a minor key, the accompaniment or counterpoint has to be played in a minor key, too. But that's not right. The counterpoint can be the major fifth chord, if you leave out the mediant, the one note that clashes."

She made a small, noncommittal noise. Ahead of them, the tracks stretched through the city, turning neither right nor left, taking the airship down its predetermined path.

"I've never been in love before, Alice," he continued. "And I've never been a clockworker. So I don't know what all this means. I can only play the music fate hands me. When I sing, all my songs tell me that I want to be with you. If you don't want to be with me, just say so."

Suddenly she couldn't bear it any longer. She sat up and grabbed his hand. His fingers were strong. The nightingale hopped back to his shoulder. "I hate the plague. I hate what it's doing to you. To us. I don't want to let you go. I *can't* let you go. But I'm frightened of what the plague might do."

"So am I," he said quietly. "It steals memory from me, and it steals time from us. We have to get to China and find a cure."

"What if there *is* no cure, Gavin?" she asked suddenly. "What if the Dragon Men can't do anything, or they just won't, or we can't find a cure in time?"

He squeezed her hand. "Alice, the plague might be able to steal my sanity, but it can't steal love. No matter how insane I go, there will always be a part of me that loves you."

And she still didn't know how to respond, so she didn't. That didn't seem to bother Gavin. They sat on the deck in simple silence together until the airship pulled onto the spur that led to the park Dodd had rented for the circus. When the ship came to a halt behind the dark circus train, Alice headed for the ladder.

"Get your fiddle," she said. "We aren't done yet."

"What are you talking about?"

"I'll explain below."

Nathan was already unhitching the horses with Dr.

Clef's help. Alice explained how she had met the woman. "She said there were more who need me at the Church of Our Lady."

"I know where that is," Gavin said.

"So do I," Nathan put in. "Dodd and I have gone there for confession once or twice."

Gavin blinked innocently. "What did you confess?"

"That you were an arse."

"She said to ask for Monsignor Adames," Alice said. "I need to—"

"There you are!" Dodd ran up and caught Nathan in a hard embrace. One of the horses snorted. "Jesus, you scared me out of my wits."

"I'm fine, I'm fine," Nathan gasped. "What's wrong?"

"Mingers." Dodd let him go. "Gendarmes. They turned the whole circus upside down looking for Gavin and Alice and demanding to know if we were hiding you. No one said anything, of course, but thank God you weren't here."

"Are they still looking?" Dr. Clef asked.

"I should think so. They seemed pretty intent. They called you criminals, and Dr. Clef a danger to society."

"Was a woman with them? Tall? Dark hair? Metal arm?" Gavin said.

Dodd shook his head. "You mean your Lieutenant Phipps. She wasn't there, but I heard them mention her name."

"What about Feng?" Alice said.

"He was easy to hide." Dodd waved a dismissive hand. "We have two families of Chinese. She didn't even ask about him."

"That's a relief, then." Alice tugged at Gavin's elbow. "We need to go."

"You can't go now," Dodd said. "Didn't you just hear? Phipps has patrols looking for you all over the city. You'll be safe here—they've already looked—but you can't go out."

"I promised, Ringmaster," Alice said. "Those people need my help. Every moment's delay means another plague victim might die. So unless you intend to lock me in a lion's cage, get out of my way before I knock you down."

"She will," Gavin told him.

"Fine." Dodd made the same dismissive gesture. "But you aren't going alone."

"Certainly not!" Alice said, and Dodd looked surprised that she was agreeing. "Only a fool would do that. And a number of people who aren't coming should know where I'm going so they can mount a rescue if I don't return in a reasonable amount of time. Gavin's coming, of course."

"Am I?" Gavin was grinning.

"You are. You know where the church is. Feng must come, too. That leaves Mr. Storm, who also knows where the church is, on rescue duty with Dr. Clef and the ringmaster."

"As long as you're running my circus," that man sighed, "you might as well just call me Dodd."

Chapter Six

They took several moments to gather equipment. Alice wanted to get the firefly jar from Feng, and Gavin wanted weapons. He couldn't bring himself to use actual pistols, however. A lifetime of training had instilled a healthy fear of anything that created flame, a deadly threat on an airship. Even after several weeks on the *Lady*, which used newfangled helium, Gavin still shunned gunpowder for the cutlass of shatter-proof glass favored by airmen. Unfortunately, he no longer had a fléchette pistol, which used compressed air to fire glass needles. The circus, meanwhile, had gone back to sleep, recovered from its encounter with the gendarmes Phipps had commandeered, but Gavin wondered how long before they returned—and how many they'd encounter on the way to the church, which was why he wanted weapons. He looked at Dr. Clef's power canon where it lay on the *Lady*'s deck, and sighed with regret.

"It's too heavy," Gavin said. "I wouldn't get twenty yards."

"Perhaps you could make modifications with this." Dr. Clef held up a spool of alloy wire, the same stuff as the endoskeleton rolled up and lying on the port side of the deck. "Can you do it alone? I have fear that we shall fight if I assist."

Gavin looked at the wire and at the power cannon. His brain leaped ahead, and he saw wires and pulsing power and batteries. He ran his hands over the cannon, able to *feel* how it all fit together, every bolt, every shard, every pathway, right down to the tiny pieces so small they couldn't hold a name. He saw a number of fascinating ways to reshape them, gently move matter and energy along a number of different venues. He was only vaguely aware that Dr. Clef, that annoying Dr. Clef, had withdrawn, and the vibrations of his receding footsteps on the deck came out as long, distorted strings that vibrated against the air and kicked it about. Gavin's fingers flew, snatching up tools and setting them down again, braiding wire, snipping metal, connecting pieces of the universe in new ways.

"Gavin?"

The high-pitched voice intruded, interrupted, interjected. He turned to snarl at the interruption—

—and saw that it was a woman. He knew her. He . . . had feelings for her. He struggled for a moment. She had broken his concentration, which made him angry, but she was also someone to be trusted, someone he didn't want to be angry at. The contradictory feelings warred for a split second, equally matched.

Alice. Her name was Alice. The new fact tipped the balance, and in a flash he remembered that she wasn't someone who deserved disdain. He twisted inside like a cat changing its mind in midleap and yanked back the retort.

"Alice?" he gasped, and realized he was panting. A trickle of sweat slid down his cheek. "What's going on?"

"I was going to ask you the same thing." She had changed into trousers, which Gavin found strangely attractive on a woman. They accentuated her hips and showed her legs. She was wearing a tighter-fitting blouse as well, and it clung to her neck and breasts. Her braided hair caught the moon and held it. The silvery light shifted, moving in a shower of particles, then splashing as a wave, but doing both at the same time, just as the Impossible Cube had twisted and changed before his eyes. It was beautiful and terrible all at once, and Gavin couldn't look away if he wanted to. For a moment it was hard to breathe.

"What is that?" she asked. "Did you make it?"

Gavin held up the object in question. An eight-foot braided lash trailed to the deck from a heavy brass handle, and the handle connected to a cord that ran to a backpack with a battery in it. Dr. Clef's power cannon lay dead on the deck, its brass entrails scattered across the wood.

"It looks like a whip," said Feng, who had also climbed up. He was dressed in what looked to Gavin like soft black pajamas from head to foot. "Show us, please."

Gavin shook off the last of the clockwork daze. He

shrugged into the backpack and flicked a switch on the handle. A low thrum—D-flat, he automatically noted—throbbed across his ears and pulsed against his palm. The metal lash glowed incandescent blue. The weight eased in his hand as the power pushed Dr. Clef's alloy away from gravity. Gavin swung. The whip flicked through the air, quick as a demon's tongue, and slashed at the barrel of the power cannon. The barrel didn't move. For a moment, neither did anyone else. Then the barrel fell neatly into two halves that thudded to the deck.

There was a long, long pause.

"I watched someone called the Great Mordovo cut his assistant in half this afternoon," Feng said at last. "I do not believe you should show this to him."

Alice swallowed visibly and shifted her pack. "That took you all of half an hour to make?"

"I didn't keep track of the time." Gavin flicked the switch off. The glow vanished, and the whip grew heavy in his hand again. He coiled it and hung it on the right side of his belt, opposite his glass cutlass.

"You must be careful," Dr. Clef admonished, approaching from his previously safe distance. "Every slash takes power, you know, and the battery does not last forever."

"Then let's go now," Gavin said.

"I'll carry your fiddle," Alice said.

The three of them slipped away from the circus and hurried down the city streets. Gavin led the way, since he knew where they were going, and Feng brought up the rear, with Alice in the middle. The air that stole over Gavin was growing chilly and damp, with an early breath of autumn to it. In the distance, a church bell repeated a dark F that pressed lonely against his ears. A scattering of lights glowed in houses or shops, but most windows were dark, and the moon coasted through a field of stars like a bright airship through a cloud of fireflies. Even the public houses were closed at this time of night, and the trio had no good reason to be on the street, which meant any gendarme would stop them for questioning. Gavin slid into another shadow, trying to control his nervousness. The cutlass and whip lent him a whiff of power, but one pistol shot could bring him down, or worse, bring down Alice. Gavin didn't know if Phipps intended to capture or kill at this point, but capture would mean transport back to England for hanging, so it didn't make much difference. He kept one hand on the smooth whip handle.

A pair of horses clip-clopped from around the corner ahead of them. Gavin grabbed Alice's hand and pulled her into an alleyway. Her backpack clinked slightly, and the noise made Gavin's heart jerk. Feng seemed to have disappeared. The riders rounded the corner and trotted down their street. Gavin pressed himself face-first against the rough alley wall, leaving the pack's uneven shape sticking out. He could hear Alice's butterfly breathing next to him, feel her body heat mingling with his. She clutched his fiddle case, and he felt oddly comforted that she held it. When the pirate captain had threatened to throw it off the *Juniper*, it had felt like the man's filthy fingers were running over Gavin's soul, but Alice's touch made him feel that the fiddle was safe, even with danger only a few steps away.

The horses clopped past the mouth of the alley, and moonlight gleamed off pistols holstered at the riders' belts. Gavin held his breath. He had turned his face away from the street so his fair skin wouldn't catch a stray beam of light, and he was looking right into Alice's eyes, just visible in the scattered wave of photons. They were wide and brown and beautiful, even when filled with unease.

One of the riders paused at the alley mouth and said something in French to his companion, who also paused. Fear made blood pulse in Gavin's ears. Alice's lips parted, and her breath came in short gasps, but she didn't move. The man spoke again, every word as harsh as a drop of melted lead.

And then they were gone, their horses trotting away to fade in the distance. The weight of fear vanished so quickly, Gavin thought he might float away. The tension went out of Alice's body as well. Gavin surprised himself by leaning in and kissing her. She stiffened again, then kissed back, her mouth warm on his. When they parted, he pressed his forehead against hers.

"Why were we scared?" Alice murmured. "You could have torn them in half with that whip."

"I could have," Gavin replied. "That's exactly why I was scared."

The street was still empty, no sign of Feng. A cough over Gavin's head made him grab for the whip, but Alice put her hand on his arm. Feng was perched on a windowsill two stories above them. His dark clothing made him look like the shadow of a spider. Carefully but steadily, using rough bricks and other windowsills for footholds, he descended to the sidewalk.

"I'm impressed," Alice asked.

"I have climbed in and out of a number of windows in my life," Feng said. "More than once with a husband in hot pursuit. It is interesting how well one can climb with the correct motivation."

They hurried away, dodging the gas lamps. Occasionally, they heard footsteps or horses' hooves a street or two over, and every time they hid in alleys or doorways or under stoops, though they didn't have any more close encounters with police. The streets wound steadily uphill, and Gavin's legs started to ache from the steady climbing, and the battery pack pulled at his shoulder muscles. After a while, he said, "Where are the plague zombies?"

That made Alice pause. "I don't know. We should have seen at least one or two by now."

"Perhaps the priest will know," Feng said.

They finally arrived at the Church of Our Lady. The huge stone building loomed over Gavin, buttressed high and stiff, surrounded by a low wall and a square marked off from the street by a line of stone pillars that stretched between them like an iron lattice. Stained glass windows shut themselves against the night.

"It is . . . large," Feng said. "I imagined a small stone church, not an entire cathedral."

"I think they've applied for cathedral status with the Pope," Gavin said.

"They have to apply to call it a cathedral?" Feng looked doubtfully up at the walls, which seemed half fortress, half heaven. "I would enjoy seeing the paperwork for that."

"The Papists do have their ideas," Alice said. "Where do we go in?"

The main doors, half large enough to admit a dirigible, were obviously locked and barred, and the idea of knocking on such enormous timbers felt ridiculous. They followed the wall around until they found a more normal-sized pair of doors in an alcove. Feng knocked hard, then pounded at some length. Gavin nervously dropped his hand to the whip. Time passed, and the door wrenched open to reveal an old woman in a dressing gown and nightcap. A candlestick glimmered in her hand. She demanded something in French, and Alice responded. Gavin caught the words *Monsignor Adames*. The woman looked doubtful, but finally gestured them inside and shut the door behind them. Gavin found himself in a small room, but he could sense a great echoing space beyond.

"She wants us to wait here," Alice said as the woman padded away, taking the light with her. Gavin waited in uneasy blackness with Alice and Feng beside him. None of them spoke. The emptiness beyond seemed to eat words, or even the idea of speaking. Time didn't move. Gavin sensed the weight of the pack on his shoulders, and the heft of the whip handle in his hand, and the pull of the cutlass at his belt. Alice's and Feng's breathing beside him pushed about tiny amounts of air that puffed against his face, bounced off and swirled away in chaotic forms that held patterns just beyond his understanding. He reached out and put his hand into one and felt it scatter and flee. Another swirl of breath bounced off him, creating patterned chaos on his skin, and if he just concentrated hard enough, he might be able to understand it, perhaps even control it, even—

"Gavin!" Alice's voice broke into his thoughts. "Are you coming?"

"Chaos swirls against my skin," he said, "but the pattern remains out of reach. How can I touch it?"

"We shouldn't stay up here," said a man's voice in lightly accented English. "Just bring him along."

And then Gavin was within the great empty place, standing before a half-sized statue of a woman on a pedestal holding an infant—the Virgin Mary. Behind her, windows of stained glass rose above an elaborate altar. She stood on a crescent moon and wore robes of gold and crimson. In her right hand she held a scepter. The baby Jesus cradled a ball in his hand and stretched out the other in benediction. Both mother and child wore tall crowns of gold that sparkled with jewels. Candles flickered around her feet and in the candelabra behind her, lending her an otherworldly glow.

"*Consolatrix Afflictorum*," said the man, and Gavin noticed for the first time he wore a long black robe and a white priest's collar. "Comforter of the afflicted. If you believe the legend, she dropped out of a tree trunk in 1624, right around the time the black plague struck, and she cured a number of people. In 1794, the clockwork plague appeared, and so many people overwhelmed the Jesuit chapel outside the city, we moved her in here."

"But you take her out and bring her around the city just after Easter," Gavin said softly. "Eight days afterward. The Octave."

The priest blinked. He had receding gray hair and a thin build. "You've heard of it."

"No. It's just obvious." Gavin flicked a glance at the statue's pale brown hair and dark brown eyes and rounded beauty and machine-like scepter in her hand, then glanced at Alice. "She looks like—"

"Don't," Alice said.

"But she really—"

"I said don't," Alice said again, and her voice floated to the high ceiling. She repositioned her backpack. "Monsignor Adames, I have a cure for the clockwork plague, and one of the people I helped told me to come here."

"A cure?" Adames repeated. "I don't understand."

"Her touch cures the clockwork plague," Feng said.

"Her touch," he echoed, then gave a small laugh. "I'm sorry if I seem doubtful, but . . . well, I'm doubtful. I believe in the holy miracles, including the ones that founded this very church, but—"

"I play the fiddle," Gavin interrupted, "and I sing."

Monsignor Adames fell silent. Then he said slowly, "There are rumors. I've heard of a beautiful woman with a sword and an angel with a golden voice who appear to cure the afflicted at night and who are pursued by brass demons during the day. I thought they were nothing but desperate stories from people who want comfort. But now . . ."

"How can we help?" Alice asked.

Adames hesitated only a moment. "This way." He caught up a candle from the statue's feet and led them to a door behind one of the carved, earth-colored pillars lining the cathedral. A tight spiral staircase twisted downward. Adames pulled back the skirts of his robe with his free hand and held up the candle with the other to light the way as they descended.

"You're an angel?" Feng said to Gavin on the stairs. "May I be the one to write your family about that? Please?"

At the bottom was a stone passageway, low and cramped. The top of Gavin's backpack brushed the ceiling. Soot from thousands of ancient candles streaked the walls. Damp darkness pressed in from all sides, hushing Gavin's footsteps. A number of alcoves and rooms opened at regular intervals, some with doors on them and some without. Adames led them to one alcove, and pressed against the back wall. It turned on an axis, and he ducked through the opening, motioning for them to follow.

The large room beyond was fitted out as a hospital ward. Iron bedsteads lined the walls, and about twenty patients lay in them, some asleep, some twitching or moaning softly. Gavin automatically pulled back from the smell of sickness in the place, then forced himself to enter. One corner was set up with cupboards and tables covered with medical equipment and supplies. Washtubs and buckets held both water and effluvia waiting to be disposed of. Lamps hung on the walls to provide soft light. A woman in a nun's habit bustled over, and Gavin realized with a start that she was an automaton. The habit hid her body, but her face was metallic, as were her hands.

"*Vater,*" she said quizzically, "*wer sind denn diese Leute?*"

"English, Berta, if you please," he said. "I don't think our guests speak German. Are there any changes?"

"Some." Berta's voice buzzed slightly, and the grill

that made up her mouth didn't move when she spoke. "Clarissa has become worse. I fear she won't last the night."

Adames crossed himself. "Perhaps we can help now."

"Monsignor!" Alice said. "I thought the Catholic Church strictly forbade human automatons."

"That's why we keep everyone down here," he said blandly. "Berta can minister to our patients without catching the disease herself or passing it on to others, and she doesn't require rest. I'm trusting you and God to keep the secret. We are the only hospital in Luxembourg for those afflicted by the plague."

"Is it not against priestly vows to disobey your Pope?" Feng asked.

"It wouldn't look good on our application to be declared a cathedral," Adames admitted. "And if the Pope learns of it, we will forever remain a church, and I will never become an archbishop."

"It's still a sin," Alice said. "How do you reconcile that?"

"We sin when we miss the mark of perfection," Adames replied. "None of us can hit that mark, and we can only ask forgiveness from he who managed it. My heart tells me I'm doing the right thing, however imperfect it may be."

"They all have the clockwork plague?" Gavin asked quietly.

Adames nodded. "Most of them die, but we save a few."

"And the ones who become zombies?" Alice asked.

"It's hard." Adames looked away. "I have Berta put them in the catacombs, and she leaves food out until the plague takes them. A number of them come in from the street as well. They seem to understand that we will feed them at least a little."

"This explains why we saw none on our way over," Feng put in.

"It's difficult to come up with enough food for everyone without arousing suspicion," Adames concluded.

Alice pulled off her glove and put her left hand on Adames's arm. The spider's eyes glowed green. "You don't have the plague," she said.

He looked down at the spider with a mixture of curiosity and uncertainty. "I wouldn't, no. I caught it as a child and survived." He pulled back the sleeve on his robe, revealing a scarred, withered arm. Alice's face tightened, and Gavin knew she was remembering her father, also scarred by the clockwork plague. "My mother said I owed God, so I entered the priesthood."

One of the patients cried out in pain from her bed. Berta turned, but Alice pushed past her. "Gavin, I want you with me. Please?"

Gavin shrugged out of the heavy backpack, set the whip down, and accepted his fiddle case from Alice. While he was taking the fiddle out, something occurred to him. "Alice, when did you last sleep?"

"I caught a few hours when you were in that fugue state in the train car," she said absently, bending over the first bed. "Just play for me. It's all the rest I need."

He played, and Alice led him around the room. She drew back white sheets and slashed each patient as gently as she could, spraying a bit of her own blood into the wounds while Gavin spilled liquid harmony from

how the parishioners would respond if they knew what lies beneath their feet. Prepare yourself, my son."

He pulled open a thick door. It exhaled air heavy with rot and fear. Gavin let the darkness swallow him as they moved inside, though the fireflies provided pale green light. Niches carved into the walls like short beds held dry skeletons, many with ragged cloth still clinging to them. Some clutched rosaries in yellowed fingers while the skulls stared eyelessly at the ceiling, the leavings of death. Gavin shrank away from them, not wanting to touch. He felt like an intruder, one who would be caught and thrown out by some monstrous gatekeeper at any moment. He followed Adames's candle down a side passage until he heard shuffling footsteps ahead. Bones clattered with a sound that crawled over Gavin's skin. Ahead, he saw the passage widen, and a shadowy group of zombies huddled in the dark. They shielded their eyes from the candle with ragged arms and groaned like a choir of uneasy spirits. Two of them lay sprawled on the floor, motionless. Dead. Gavin flinched at the sight. If they had arrived a day ago, an hour ago, a minute ago, could they have been saved? There was never enough time. If only there was a way to make more.

Gavin thought about what Adames had said as they entered the catacomb. He saw wealthy ladies in silk skirts and gentlemen in fine coats, their stomachs filled with a good breakfast prepared by paid servants. They spoke in hushed voices and smiled quietly to one another, their soft faces scrubbed pink, while below them moaned hungry, sick people.

"What can you do for them?" Adames asked.

The priest's voice pulled Gavin back—he had nearly fallen into another fugue. With an embarrassed cough, he stepped farther into the bone room, opened the gleaming jar, and waved a dozen of the fireflies out of it. They streaked through the darkness and landed on some of the zombies.

"What are they?" the priest asked.

"I'm not completely sure," Gavin said. "Alice's aunt made them. They spread the cure, and anyone they bite spreads the cure as well. Alice's cure works faster, but she's not strong enough to help everyone. How will they get out once they're better?"

One of the zombies reached a tentative hand toward Adames, who handed it a chunk of bread from his pocket. The creature fumbled to accept it and eat. "The same way they get in—through the graveyard. There's an entrance in one of the mausoleums. Are you sure this will . . ?"

"Yes." He looked around, feeling suddenly uneasy. "I think we should get back to—"

A crash thundered through the catacomb and vibrated the very stones. The candle danced in Adames's hand. Gavin swore.

"They found us!" he said.

Adames was already heading for the door. "Who?"

"The brass demons. We have to run!"

They met Feng and Berta at the spiral staircase. Berta had Gavin's backpack, and a worried-looking Feng was half carrying Alice. Gavin cursed himself for letting her push herself so hard. Another crash thundered overhead. Wordlessly Gavin yanked on the battery backpack, slapped the whip onto his belt, and snatched Alice out of Feng's arms. The clockwork plague roared through him, and he barely noticed her weight as he bundled her up the stairs. She clutched the firefly jar to her chest.

At the top, he burst out of the transept and into the crossing of the cathedral, the enormous open space just in front of the altar where the Consolatrix stood on her crescent moon. Two of the priceless stained glass windows, one on each of the long walls of the nave, had been shattered, and the confessional booths standing beneath them were smashed to flinders, crushed beneath stomping metal feet. Standing in the nave, the echoing pillared hall where the congregation gathered for services, were the two mechanicals, their glass bubbles gleaming like captured moons. In front of them was Lieutenant Phipps. Her brass monocle stared coldly about the pale brown chamber.

"How did you find us?" Alice gasped.

"The good father's secret hospital isn't as secret as he likes to think," Phipps said in a scornful tone. "The Ward has known of it for quite some time. It was just a matter of watching until you showed up with your cure—as you did."

"This is a house of God!" Adames roared, and before Gavin could stop him, he rushed forward to confront Phipps. One of the mechanicals—Glenda—leaned forward and almost casually knocked him aside. Adames slammed into a pillar and slid moaning to the stony floor.

"Nǐ shì shénme dōngxi!" Feng exclaimed.

A chill rage fell over Gavin, burning away all other emotion. "Why?"

"You are criminals," Phipps said through tight teeth. "You released a doomsday weapon and broke a dangerous clockworker out of custody. You are a menace to society, and I *will* bring you to justice."

"We don't want to hurt you, Gavin," Simon said. "Just . . . just come, all right? You'll get a fair trial."

"Why did you hurt the priest?" Gavin's voice was level and deadly. "He helped more people in one day than your Empire has in a hundred years."

"I'm not here to debate, Ennock. You're under arrest."

The lieutenant dipped into her pockets and came up with the tuning forks. Time slowed. Gavin saw the length of the metal forks, heard the creak of the mechanicals' joints, felt the weight of the cathedral ceiling high above. His hand moved smoothly down—impulses contracted muscle, shortened tendons, curled fingers—and came up with the whip. He stepped forward and swung. The lash sliced through the air. He saw the individual currents split and eddy away as the braid hissed them to pieces. At precisely the right moment, Gavin flicked his arm and the lash changed direction. Air swirled like water, and the tip of the lash broke an invisible barrier. Sound cracked as the tip flicked across the fork in Phipps's right hand. The fork shattered. Phipps cried out and jumped back.

"Get Alice out of here," Gavin barked over his shoulder at Feng.

"What are you waiting for?" Phipps snarled at Simon and Glenda. "Grab them! Grab *her*!"

"No." With one hand, Gavin drew his glass cutlass. With the other, he pressed the whip's power switch.

Blue energy flowed along the lash. He slashed the air, leaving a sizzling azure trail. "You won't get past me."

Glenda's mechanical lunged for him, but Gavin heard the pistons hiss, saw the machine's posture change, felt the tiny shift of air, and he was already moving. He whirled the lash and struck the mechanical's arm. Sparks flew where the braided alloy touched brass, sending a small jolt up Gavin's arm, but the cut was clean. The arm thudded to the stone floor. Before Glenda could react, Gavin swung again, catching the mechanical at the shin. The mechanical, caught in mid-step, lurched forward, leaving the lower part of one leg behind. She stumbled, fell sideways, and crashed into a pillar. It cracked, and bits of it crumbled. Glenda crashed face-first to the ground. Her glass bubble shattered, and Gavin caught the tail end of her scream. The cold anger, however, let him feel no mercy or remorse. Behind Gavin, Feng was hauling Alice toward one of the side alcoves and an exit, the firefly jar still in her hands.

Simon raised his mechanical's hand. The fingers clicked together into a gun barrel. He fired something over Gavin's head with a *whump* that thudded hard against Gavin's eardrums. The munition smashed into a pair of statues over the alcove and shattered them. Chunks of stone fell in front of the alcove entrance, throwing up a choking cloud of dust and blocking any exit. Alice cried out, and Feng pulled back.

"Don't touch her, Simon!" Gavin snarled. A skin of black ice encased his heart, and he flicked the lash, but Simon's mechanical was out of range.

Phipps pointed a metal finger at Gavin. He heard

the tiny *fft*, and barely brought up the glass cutlass in time to catch the dart. It shattered on the tempered glass.

"You've lost your edge, Susan," he said evenly. "I'm not a piece of street trash anymore. I'm a clockworker now, more dangerous than you can understand."

"And more arrogant," she said. "I've captured dozens of your kind, boy, some who wanted to destroy the world. Mere pirate toys don't measure up."

With that, she leaped at him, faster than a human should have moved. It caught Gavin by surprise, and then she was inside the circle of the lash, where the whip couldn't touch her. Her metal arm batted aside Gavin's glass cutlass and she gut-punched him with the other hand. The air burst from him, but he didn't feel pain. Not yet. He grabbed her wrist (*ninety-seven pounds of pressure*), twisted upward (*joint bending at 110 degrees*), and planted his foot behind hers. To his left (*nine feet, five inches*), the cutlass clattered on the floor. With a flick, he brought his foot up to upset Phipps—

—but she was already gone, leaping backward and away. She snapped her metallic left hand open, and a lash of her own snaked out of the palm. Gavin slapped it aside with the lash, and only then—

"Gavin! Look out!"

—did he realize it was a diversion. Simon's mechanical stepped forward and almost delicately grabbed Gavin's backpack. With easy strength he hoisted Gavin aloft. Simon's face looked pale through the glass. Gavin swung the lash as his feet dangled over empty air. The whip wrapped around Simon's forearm, but the blue glow flickered and died, drained of power.

"No," he whispered.

"You're mine, Ennock," Phipps said from below.

"Actually, he's mine, Susan," Alice called from beside the half-conscious Glenda amid the wreckage of the mechanical. With a deft motion, she spun a clockwork gear through the air at Simon. It trailed a pair of wires from Glenda's machinery. Simon twisted in his chair in time to see, but not to react. The gear clanged against his mechanical's shoulder. Electricity snapped and sparked. Ladders of it arced up and down the mechanical's body, and inside it, Simon convulsed and shuddered. Gavin, who wasn't touching metal, felt nothing. The mechanical's fist opened, and Gavin dropped to the ground as Simon and his mechanical collapsed noisily to the cathedral floor. The backpack smashed Gavin flat, knocking the breath out of him just as Phipps's punch had.

"You've lost your toys," Alice panted, "and you've lost us. There's no point in pursuing this, Susan."

"You haven't earned the right to call me by my Christian name, girl." Phipps was standing upright a few paces from the wrecked machinery, cool and unruffled, and for a moment Gavin was getting another dressing-down in her office back at Third Ward headquarters in London. She leaned a little toward Gavin and inhaled deeply, then nodded to herself, as if confirming something. From the floor she plucked a bit of stone from the cracked column and with her metal hand threw it with quiet nonchalance. It shattered a single pane of stained glass above the altar at the other end of the cathedral.

"I wonder," she said, and threw another piece. It

broke the pane next to the first one. "I wonder who your ally is. That man who's keeping to the shadows so I don't see his face. It occurs to me that the son of the Chinese ambassador vanished from London at the same time you fled. Is that he? I like his infrared pattern." She tapped her monocle. "He has a very interesting jar in one hand and a pistol in the other, but he won't fire, either because he's too cowardly or because I'm not attacking you right now. Which is it, boy?"

Feng, wherever he was, didn't answer. Phipps threw two more pieces, shattering two more priceless panes.

"Stop it!" Alice said. "It's senseless!"

"Let God stop me. If He cares." She threw more and more pieces, and each one blacked out a piece of glass. "I could hit you easily enough, you know."

"No," Gavin said. He had dropped the backpack and snatched up the cutlass again. His hands were steady as icicles. "You couldn't."

"You're probably right. Clockworker reflexes." Toss. Smash. "Those reflexes and that strength come at a price, you know. The plague burning through your body's resources." Toss. Smash. "How does it feel, Ennock, knowing that the plague is devouring your brain from the inside out? How does it feel to know you won't last the year with your lady love?" Toss, smash. "How does it feel to know that she'll cry over your grave for a while and move on to someone else? She already left one man."

Her words were light as pebbles, but they slammed Gavin with the force of cannonballs. His grip on the cutlass loosened, and he only just remembered to keep it ready. "You're just . . . trying to make me feel bad."

"Of course," Phipps replied conversationally. Toss. Smash. "I want you to feel bad about what you're doing, Gavin, because it *is* bad. You've done wrong. You *are* doing wrong."

"Don't listen to her!" Alice gasped from the safety of her mechanical barricade. The rush that had carried her through the fight was wearing off, and it was clear she was struggling to stay conscious.

Phipps flicked a rock in her direction, but Alice ducked into the mechanical, and it pinged off metal. Gavin's anger started up again. Phipps interrupted it. "You know I'm right, Gavin. It's bloody scary out here. Chaotic. Difficult. Imperfect. So many choices, so many paths, so many roads, and no resources to help with them. You always miss the mark."

"Silence!" Feng called from the shadows. "Or I shoot."

"If you were going to shoot, you would have," Phipps countered. "You're a coward, Feng. Otherwise you would have stood up to your father when he said he planned to send you home in disgrace. But you know that, don't you, Feng? It's why you're slinking home like a castrated dog with his tail tucked between his legs. The longer you stay with these people, the worse it will become, you know. They don't appreciate you. They're bringing you home to your doom."

"Quiet!" Alice was trying to shout, but the words came out in a harsh whisper that spun through the room and wrapped themselves around the Consolatrix. Feng didn't respond, but Gavin thought he heard a choked sound from the shadows.

Toss, smash. Phipps turned back to Gavin. "You can

build whatever you want at the Ward, Gavin. It's calm there. Quiet. Patterned. Perfect. Every day, every room, every meal. No chaos, no confusion, no disorder. Come back to us. You won't hang for treason, not if you're a clockworker. We like you, want you, *need* you."

Her words, her tone, her ideas were hypnotic as music. He remembered the underground rooms where the clockworkers lived and worked at Third Ward headquarters, their regular stonework walls, the patterns, the perfect schedule. When he was training as an agent, he'd found the required regularity difficult, even stifling, but now it sounded attractive, even alluring. The world would make sense there. Gavin realized he had sheathed the cutlass and taken a step toward Phipps.

"Gavin!" Alice croaked. "Don't!"

"It's beautiful down there now," Phipps cooed. "We've already made repairs after what you did, after what you hurt, after what you destroyed. We made it pretty and patterned and perfect. Patterns within patterns, spirals within spirals. No worries, no troubles, no cares. No fear, no dread, no fright. Just the machines. Orderly, mannerly, heavenly machines."

Her words wrapped him in warm velvet. It would be so fine to have a place where he didn't have to think and plan all the time, where worries evaporated, where patterns ruled. What had he been thinking, running away from all that in the first place?

He was vaguely aware of someone, another woman, shouting something at him, and the shadowy figure of a man stepping out of the darkness, but Phipps, beautiful, kind Phipps, flipped a stone at the man, and he retreated. Phipps always hit her mark. The shouting woman's words washed past him like tiny waves, easily ignored. He took another step.

"We can give you a cure, you know," Phipps said. "I told you before we had more cures than the one Edwina created in the Doomsday Vault. We can cure clockworkers, too."

This jolted Gavin. The perfection cracked, the velvet vanished, and he realized he was nearly face-to-face with Phipps. "Cure? There is no cure for clockworkers."

Too late Phipps saw her mistake. Her single eye blinked rapidly. "Of course not, of course not. What I meant was that you can look for a cure. The Ward has resources, anything you need to find one, seek one, look for—"

"You're very good," Gavin said quietly. "Distract, pacify, capture, right? That's the pattern. We do it with Dr. Clef all the time, except we use Click."

Phipps narrowed her eye. "I'll take you now, boy."

"No, you won't. Without Glenda and Simon, you're outnumbered and outmatched, and if you touch me, Feng really will shoot. You wanted me to go with you on my own. I won't, Susan. You'll put my head in a noose."

"I want *justice*, boy," she hissed. "I want what's right. You destroyed my empire and even now you hurt Simon and Glenda."

"Leave, Susan," Gavin told her. "You let me walk away from the Doomsday Vault, so I'll let you do the same here. Next time I'll probably change my mind."

"Because you'll be completely mad?"

"Go, Susan. You won't get your justice today."

For a long moment, she stared at him. Then she

tossed one final bit of column at the stained glass, turned on her heel, and stalked out.

Heart tight with worry, Gavin ran over to Alice. She had slumped over inside the mechanical wreckage, looking pale and delicate as paper with the spider gauntlet weighing her down, but she blinked up at him when he leaned into the machinery. Simon sprawled beside her, unconscious but breathing. Thank God they were all right. The thought of Alice getting hurt made him cold inside and out, and Simon . . . well, even now he still thought of Simon as a friend.

"Can you walk, Alice?" Gavin said. "We shouldn't stay."

"I think I can manage for a bit," she replied. "Those last few moments took a lot out of me."

"You were magnificent," he blurted. "Incredible!"

"Funny," she said softly, "I was going to say the same, Mr. Ennock."

"Your little friend will live," Feng called from Glenda's mechanical. "But she will have a dragon's headache when she wakes up. Should we tie them up?"

"With what?" Gavin helped Alice out of the mechanical. "How's the priest?"

But Berta had already arrived and was helping Monsignor Adames to his feet. He held his side and his face was pinched with pain.

"Two of your ribs are cracked and it is possible a third is broken," Berta said, and her mechanized voice managed to sound concerned. "You must come downstairs so I can wrap them."

Adames waved her off. "Not yet." His breath came in gasps. "Alice and Gavin have to know. I saw . . . I saw . . . the world coming to an end in flood and plague." He panted with the effort of speaking. "Dear God, the pain."

"Your ribs," Berta began.

"Not my pain," he gasped. "The world's. So many people will die if you fail, Alice. Millions upon millions."

Alice struggled to more alertness. "Me?"

"You must not fail," Adames said. "God has shown me. Oh, He has. I'm so sorry."

Something in his tone made Gavin uneasy. "Sorry?"

"Your trials aren't over, my children." He was leaning heavily on Berta now. "Flood and plague will destroy us if you don't cure the world."

"That's my intent," Alice said, holding up her gauntleted hand.

Adames shook his head. "Not you. Gavin."

"Me?" Gavin started. "But Alice has the spider, and her aunt made the fireflies."

"That's not what God showed me," Adames repeated stubbornly. "You will cure the world, and Alice . . . Alice must let go."

"Let go?" Alice asked. "Let go of what?"

He shook his head. "I'm sorry. It's not . . . it's not like looking in a picture. It's a dream that I know is real. Oh, Alice. Your love destroyed an empire. Now it will destroy the world as well."

Gavin's mouth went dry. Alice froze. "No," she whispered.

"You have to let *him* go, Alice," Adames gasped out. "You have to release him or the world will die."

*   *   *

A crowd was gathering outside the enormous church, summoned by the noise. They pointed and stared at the shattered windows, but seemed unsure whether they should go inside or not. Gavin carried Alice, who was too weak to stand, and tried to blend in. He'd been forced to leave the depowered backpack behind, but he kept the lash and his cutlass and had stuffed his fiddle into Alice's pack. Feng had the firefly jar. Alice felt disturbingly light in Gavin's arms as he worked his way toward the back of the crowd around the church, and the spider gauntlet lay inert in her lap, though its eyes glowed red when it brushed against Gavin's chest.

Flood and plague will destroy us if you don't cure the world. What the hell did that mean? Gavin had never been particularly religious, and minister and priest were really no different than musician, really. Their words spun people into other worlds just like music did. Priests has no more power than Gavin himself. Yet Monsignor Adames's words chased after him.

Your love has destroyed an empire. Now it will destroy the world.

He looked down at her in the near darkness as they moved through the bewildered people with Feng close by him. Those last words chilled him. Neither Gavin nor Alice had mentioned the Doomsday Vault or how the cure would eventually destroy the British Empire to Adames, and Phipps had said something only after Glenda had knocked Adames unconscious. He couldn't have known, but he did know. What did that mean for the rest of his words? The crowd pressed tighter around them, pointing and staring.

"We must bring her back to the circus," Feng said in his ear.

"It's all about destruction," Gavin muttered, pulling Alice tighter to him. It was getting harder to move. "Never creation. Even when we create, we destroy."

"Gavin," Feng said.

He shook his head. "I know, I know. I'm not . . . fugueing. Just thinking out—"

"No." Feng pointed. "*Look.*"

Feng, and most of the other people in the heavy crowd, were pointing at the stained glass windows at the back of the nave, the panes Phipps had flung casual stones at. The broken panes formed a pattern, one Gavin hadn't noticed backward, inside the church. Outside, the broken glass formed a clear symbol: $\sqrt{2}$.

"The signature of the Third Ward," Gavin said.

"What is the significance?" Feng asked. He was still clutching the firefly jar.

"It's a message. Phipps isn't giving up, and she has the power to touch even the church."

"Gavin!" Phipps's voice carried through the church-yard loud and clear. Alarm speared Gavin's chest and he held Alice tight. "One last gift for you and your friends."

At the last moment he spotted her on a shadowy window ledge above the crowd's head. She had a pebble in her mechanical hand, and she threw. Fearful for Alice, Gavin spun, shielding her with his body. But instead of feeling the bite of stone on flesh, he only heard one more note of shattered glass. Feng stood next to him, the pieces of destroyed jar in his hands. Blood ran from a cut on his arm. A chill ran over Gavin.

"No!" he whispered.

The cloud of fireflies hovered in place for a moment, keeping the shape of the jar. Then they scattered, swarming over the crowd, streaking green starlight in a thousand different directions. The people scattered, yipping and slapping. Hundreds of dead fireflies dropped to the ground, crushed by hands and stomped by feet.

"Damn you!" Gavin cried at the church. But Phipps was already gone.

Interlude

"When will you be well enough to travel?" Phipps asked.

Glenda lay propped up in her hotel room bed with a steak on her eye and her arm in a sling. "I don't know. Three days, perhaps four. I'm sorry, Lieutenant."

"I should be sorry, Agent Teasdale. I'm your commander, and I let you down."

Since Glenda had the bed, Simon occupied her customary place in the chair. "I'm not feeling very well myself," he said. "We wrecked a *church*, Lieutenant."

"A church that violated a number of laws regarding human-shaped automatons and the illegal sheltering of plague victims. Monsignor Adames knew the risks," Phipps replied, fighting to remain calm. This was the second time Gavin and Alice had slipped away from her, and she hated looking the fool. She was also fighting to push aside a growing unease that Simon had a point. "In any case, I'm sure the amount of money he scavenges from the wrecked mechanicals will more than compensate him."

"A church, Lieutenant," Simon repeated. "How do we justify—"

A knock interrupted him. Simon answered the door and returned with a letter addressed to Phipps. She had a good idea what it was about, and reading the heavy paper inside only confirmed her suspicion.

"It's from the office of the grand duke," she said. "The gendarmerie is no longer available to assist us in our enquiries and we have been asked, in the politest manner possible, to leave Luxembourg as soon as we are able. I suspected as much."

"Why did you break that jar?" Glenda asked.

Phipps almost grimaced and stopped herself. Breaking the jar had been a mistake, her temper getting the better of her. She had no idea what the jar had contained, only that it was somehow valuable to Gavin and Alice, and the final pebble in her hand had been too much of a temptation there in the shadow of the church. Lately, it was harder and harder to keep her emotions in check. How could she know if her decisions were based on logic or emotion when she was angry all the time? She was fighting for what was just, as Father had taught, and Father was never wrong. As long as she did that, she herself could not be wrong.

"Never let an opponent think he has the upper hand, even when he's handed you a . . . setback," she said in an explanation that sounded lame even to herself. "Better to take a small victory."

"Hm," said Glenda.

"So what now?" Simon asked, a little warily.

"Once Glenda can travel again, we will follow that circus."

Simon blinked. "The Kalakos Circus? The gendarmes searched there and found nothing."

"Of course they didn't. Alice was out and about on her little mission at the time, and circus performers won't admit anything to the police."

"Then how do you know they're with the circus?" Glenda asked.

"Didn't you catch the scent of peanuts and cooked sugar on Gavin when we were in the church? It was all over him," Phipps replied. "He's hiding there, all right. Unfortunately, we can't confront them now, not with Glenda injured and the mechanicals destroyed."

"And the gendarmerie unhappy with us," Simon put in.

"True. Fortunately, while you were out fetching the steak, Simon, I was able to make some enquiries. The circus plans to spend some time in Berlin, and from there it will travel to Kiev."

Glenda sat up straighter, and winced. "The Ukrainian Empire? Are they mad?"

"It will be an absolute hell," Phipps agreed.

Chapter Seven

The world rocked and wobbled. Alice tossed about, trying to make everything settle down, and finally she came fully awake. It came to her that she was lying on her narrow bunk in her stateroom on *The Lady of Liberty*. She wore a nightgown and cap, and the blankets lay heavy atop her. How had she come to be here? The last thing she remembered was Gavin carrying her out of the ruined church.

The room continued to sway, more like a train than the *Lady*'s usual stately glide, and Alice's sleep-addled mind finally remembered the day she had helped fit the airship with train wheels and hook her up to the circus train. They must be under way. Mindful of the low ceiling, she sat up as the door slid open and Kemp entered with a tea tray.

"So glad to see you awake, Madam," he said brightly. "I thought you might be hungry."

The sight of food and drink awoke a leonine appetite, and Alice gratefully accepted the tray. Tea, fresh bread, butter and jam, soft-boiled eggs, and . . . liver? Kemp knew very well she hated liver, and it was completely unlike him to serve her food she disliked, but when the smell reached her, something primal took over. She snatched up fork and knife and crammed in mouthfuls, heedless of ladylike manners. The spider gauntlet on her left hand clinked softly against the flatware.

"I noticed the change in your heartbeat and respiration," Kemp said, answering a question she hadn't asked, "and stepped out to prepare a meal. Sir said you had lost a fair amount of blood, and the proper remedy for that is tea and liver."

Alice swallowed a mouthful. "How long was I asleep?"

"Nearly two days, Madam. I urge you to drink as much as you can."

"Thank you, Kemp. As always, I don't know what I would do without you."

His eyes glowed. "You are quite welcome, Madam. In anticipation of your next question, Sir is in the workshop with the doctor. Shall I alert him to your present state?"

"Not if he's in a fugue." Alice tapped an egg with her spoon and unwound the shell. "Where are we? What's been going on?"

"We left Luxembourg late last night. Ringmaster Dodd became nervous at the number of 'mingers,' as he calls them, patrolling the streets to look for you. In any case, their presence seemed to have a dampening effect on the number of people who attended performances. So we are moving on to Berlin. I believe the local baron is giving a birthday party for his son and he wants a circus. Eventually, of course, we will travel on to Kiev."

Alice glanced out the porthole. Greenery rocked past in a blur, and the engine gave a long, low whistle. Sharp coal smoke and cinders mingled with the scent of liver and eggs. She remembered traveling by rail with her father and mother and brother and eating on tall-sided trays just like this one. Mother always bought a large bag of peppermint candies and shared them with Alice and Brent. Father sniffed that he didn't care for peppermint, but pinched pieces outrageously and made Alice giggle. Then Mother assigned Alice the task of counting cows in the fields they passed while Brent was to count sheep. Father joked that it was faster to count all their legs and divide by four, which made Alice giggle all over again and lose count. That had been in happier times, in the days before the clockwork plague struck her family, sending her mother and brother to the graveyard and twisting her father's body into a wheelchair. She held up the dark spider gauntlet for a moment. Her blood still coursed through the tubules. What would happen if she cut the tubes, sliced off its legs until it had nothing to grip with? It wouldn't be difficult, just time-consuming. But the spider moved with her perfectly, responding to every muscle twitch far more efficiently than a simple glove. How deeply had it bonded to her and how much would it damage her own flesh to cut it off?

She pushed the questions aside to finish her breakfast, wash up, and dress, opting for a simple blouse and skirt and not bothering with a corset. Her legs were a bit shaky. Sharing the blood cure was difficult, time-consuming, and physically draining, and although the people Alice cured would themselves spread the cure with every cough and sneeze, it took time, time, and more time to get the cure to those who needed it, and every day it took was another day someone else's mother, father, or brother died. There had to be a faster way. The fireflies would help, of course, since they could fly and spread things even faster, but they had their limitations as well. They couldn't cross an ocean or mountain range, and chance or nature might destroy all the ones in a particular area before they had the chance to do much good. Still, they were helpful, and would take some of the burden off Alice. She would have to make more use of them in the future.

That decided, Alice left Kemp to tidy up her room while she went off in search of Gavin. Out in the corridor, however, she encountered a seething mass of metal. A brass flock of whirligigs flitted and hovered in the air while spiders scampered back and forth over the corridor floor. They jumped and squeaked when Alice emerged, and crowded around her. She laughed, and put out a hand. Two whirligigs landed on her arm, and spiders crawled up her body to her shoulders and head.

"All right, all right." She laughed again. "I'm glad to see all of you, too. Good heavens."

The little automatons refused to leave her sight, so Alice wore them like odd flowers or jewelry as she went off in search of Gavin. She tapped on the laboratory door and slid it open. Gavin, clad in a leather coat and goggles, turned to glance at her. His eyes widened, and he dodged away with a yelp and snatched up a beaker, ready to throw.

Alice backed away. "Gavin! What's wrong?"

"Whirliblades chopping the chaos into wrong patterns," he babbled. "So much fluff."

Her heart lurched. He wasn't a snapping, snarling monster, but the nonsense wasn't much better. "Gavin, it's *me*," she pleaded. "Snap out of it!"

His blue eyes swam behind the lenses and he was breathing fast. Gently, she pulled the goggles off and touched his face. When had she last really touched him, just to touch him? His handsome face, so young but so old at the same time, felt warm and a little raspy under her palm. She wanted to take this man's hand and run with him somewhere safe, to a place where there was no plague, no machinery, no ticking clock. Just the two of them.

He grabbed the back of her hand and pressed it harder against his face. "Alice?"

His voice was normal, and she felt better for it. "It's me, darling."

"What are you wearing? You look like a knight who went through a threshing machine."

She laughed for the third time that day and turned. "Do you like it? Give it time, and whirligigs and spiders will become the latest rage."

"You're beautiful in everything, Lady Michaels."

The sincerity in his voice made her blush. "Well. For that, you may have a kiss."

She meant it to be a quick peck, but she found herself wrapped in his arms. The whirligigs and spiders exploded away from her in a startled cloud, and Gavin's entire body pressed against hers. He ran his hands through her hair and down her back as his mouth came down on hers. The world swirled away, and her entire universe became nothing but him. She felt his muscles move on hers, and felt his hardness press against her. Her body throbbed in response. She ran her own hands over him, touching his jaw, his smooth collarbone, the ripples on his chest and stomach. Her breath quickened as—oh God, how daring could she be—she explored lower and touched his erection. He groaned against her teeth as her hand traced its length through his clothing, and his arms tightened around her. Her skin felt feathery, and she wanted to pull Gavin into her, make him part of her and never let him go.

"Alice," he whispered hoarsely, "oh God, Alice. I don't . . . We have to stop now or . . ."

"Or what?" she whispered back.

"Or we have to keep going."

She moved her hand again, fascinated and excited by his length and hardness, by the reactions and gasps of pleasure her touch elicited in Gavin, and she ached for his hands on her, but he was barely moving now, as if he were afraid he might explode. He gave another groan.

". . . should we keep going?" he murmured. "Can we?"

She knew what he was talking about. A baby. If she got pregnant now, before they found a cure for Gavin, the baby would grow up without a father. That would destroy Gavin, not to mention what it would do to her.

Further, an illegitimate child would also be unable to inherit her title, and despite all the traditions she had flouted, this one she wasn't willing to give up.

It would be so easy to take him back to her stateroom, put him on the bunk and help him undress. She wanted to see him, feel him, touch him skin to skin, no barriers between them. And no one would know, or care if they did.

Her body hungered for him. But no. She had flouted any number of traditions, but this one . . . This one she wasn't ready to forego yet. She dropped her hands and turned aside. Gavin swallowed, then turned his back so he could adjust his clothes. When he turned around again, she couldn't help reaching out to brush his white-blond hair back into place, and she nearly leaped into his arms again.

"I'm sorry." With effort, she pulled her hand back. "I wish there was some way we could . . ."

"We'll live," he said.

But you won't, she couldn't help adding to herself. *I can save everyone else. Why can't I save you?*

The little automatons were still hovering in the doorway, some of them literally. Alice shooed them off. "What happened while I was asleep? Kemp told me only a little."

He turned back to the efficient worktable, upon which perched a new machine the size of a shoe box. A speaking trumpet was affixed to the top, and a crank stuck out of the side. One side of the box was open, and a few stray pieces lay on the table with some tools. Alice craned her neck to see what the machinery inside was for, but the angle was bad, and Gavin's body blocked the way.

"Let's see." Gavin picked up a screwdriver and set to work with it. "After Phipps broke the firefly jar, we got back to—"

"She *what*?" Alice cried.

He set down the screwdriver. "You didn't know?"

"No!" Alice's knees went weak, but there was no place to sit down. She leaned on the worktable instead. "How do you mean it broke?"

"Phipps threw a rock. All the fireflies flew away, though they bit a lot of people first. I'm sorry, Alice. I thought you were still awake when it happened."

"Dear God." She looked down at the spider gauntlet on her left hand. No possibility of cutting it off now. The escaped fireflies would infect a number of Flemish, but only a few of them would travel beyond their homes, and it would take years for the cure to reach around the world without artificial means. She had planned to release a few fireflies in every city they passed through, hastening the cure's movement, but now . . .

"I'm all of it," Alice said. "I have to spread the cure as far as I can now."

Gavin set his face and went back to work with the screwdriver. "You can only do so much, Alice."

"I have to do what I can. I have to save them, Gavin."

"It won't do the world any good if you kill yourself in the process."

Despair crashed over her, extinguishing her earlier arousal. "What should I do, then? Every day I malinger in bed, recovering from curing people, someone else dies."

"I'm working on a way to help." Gavin tightened the last piece of machinery and closed up the box. "There!"

Alice blew her nose into a handkerchief and dabbed at her eyes, a little miffed that Gavin wasn't offering more sympathy, but also curious about the machine. "What is it?"

"I call it a paradox generator. But I can't actually use it. Not directly."

"What? Why not?" Alice drew back. "Will it destroy the world or something?"

"I hope not." Gavin snagged a set of ear protectors similar to the ones Alice had seen Aunt Edwina use back in London. "But if it works, it'll . . . Look, I can't explain it. Let's take it up top and I'll show you."

The wind on the main deck was fierce. It blew Alice's hair and skirts straight behind her and roared in her ears. The disguised airship was the last and tallest car on the train, so there wasn't even any shelter from the brightly painted boxcar ahead of them. Far up the track, a plume of black smoke blew from the engine's stack backward over the rest of the train. Ash and cinders clogged the air. The little automatons, afraid of being blown away, stayed below. Gavin took Alice's hand and brought her to a three-sided, roofed shanty that had apparently been erected on the deck while she had been asleep. The opening faced the leeward side, allowing them to stand out of the wind but still be outdoors. In the shanty was Dr. Clef, who was scribbling in a notebook. Click sat beside him, but he ran over to rub against Alice's legs. Alice picked him up and cooed at him, eliciting his mechanical purr.

"So good to see you up and moving, my young treasure. I have kept your clicky kitty wound for you," said Dr. Clef over his pencil. He face and hands were gray with soot. "I find the fresh air helps me think, don't you?"

At that moment, a particularly thick cloud of cinders engulfed the shanty before being blown to shreds by the wind. Alice coughed over Click's back into her much-abused handkerchief. "Fresh air. Hm. What are we doing up here, Gavin?"

"Just listen." He set the new machine down and pulled the protectors over his ears. They were wooden cups stuffed with wool, apparently designed to keep out sound. Then he turned the machine's crank.

From the speaking trumpet emerged an unearthly sound. It sounded like a chorus of ghosts sighing from high to low and low to high all at once. Gavin continued turning, and the sound repeated endlessly. The pitch rose higher and higher and higher and fell lower and lower and lower, but it never seemed to reach the top or bottom of any scale. It turned endlessly, the tonal equivalent of a figure eight, always moving and going nowhere. It made Alice's skin crawl.

"I don't understand," she said when he stopped.

Gavin pulled the protectors off his ears. "I think I broke Dr. Clef."

Dr. Clef sat motionless. He stared into space without blinking, and only the faintest breath fluttered from his chest. A line of spittle drooled down the side of his mouth. The engine blew its whistle, high and shrill.

"Good heavens." Alice shook Dr. Clef's shoulders, and he didn't respond. Gavin handed her a bottle of smelling salts, and she opened it under his nose. He coughed awake and waved the bottle away.

"Where am I, then?" he asked. "What is happening?"

"I think only Gavin can explain that," Alice said.

Gavin gestured to the new machine. "It generates a tritone paradox," he said. "Kind of hard to explain. The machine plays a one-octave scale that goes down and another that goes up. When the machine reaches the top of the ascending scale, it drops back down to the bottom and starts over, but the volume changes so that you don't notice the switch. It does the same for the descending scale. But then things *really* get interesting."

"It's just a noise," Alice said doubtfully. Click squirmed in her arms, so she set him down.

"Not really," Gavin said. "The machine also adds another pair of ascending/descending scales, but those are a tritone above the first two. It creates the illusion of a sound that's always going up or always going down—it depends on your ear—but it never actually goes anywhere. Clockworkers, though, are sensitive to tritones and have perfect pitch—"

"—so it creates an unsolvable paradox for us," Dr. Clef put in. "And the addition of the other tones does away with the pain and makes the entire scale hypnotic. I remember only a lovely sound that— Wait! Wait!" He clapped his hands and his face flushed. *"Du Lieber! Ach, das ist ja nicht zu glauben! Wie habe ich das verpaßt?"*

"What's wrong, Doctor?" Alice asked. "What did you miss?"

"This tritone paradox is an auditory version of my Impossible Cube! Play it again! Play it now!"

"Just a moment," Alice said, holding up a hand. "We don't know everything this does yet. Is it harmful?"

"I don't know," Gavin replied. "It seems to have helped Dr. Clef. He's talking to me instead of arguing."

"Why, so I am!" Dr. Clef exclaimed. "We should be fighting, yet we are not. I am filled with goodwill toward you, my boy. What an amazing thing! Did you create it just for this purpose? So that we can work together?"

"No," Gavin said. "I created it because I think it's possible to slow time."

There followed a long, long pause. Wind whistled through the cracks in the shanty walls, and Click's steel wool tongue rasped as he cleaned his paws.

"Sorry," Alice said. "Did you say—?"

"It's possible to slow time," Gavin repeated.

"How?" Dr. Clef said in a low, steady voice.

"With your new alloy, Dr. Clef." Gavin gestured at the rolled-up wiring that still lay on the deck. "I saw your calculations, the ones that prove gravity distorts time."

Dr. Clef held up a finger. "That is not quite correct. I proved that time isn't a constant. The flow of time speeds up or slows down based on a number of forces, including the power of gravity, but we don't notice because we're *in* whatever passes for local time. If you could somehow put a clock two or three thousand miles above the surface of the planet, for example, within a few days you will find it is running faster because Earth's gravity is weaker up there. Time for an object also changes based on how fast it moves. I have reason to believe—though I have not yet proved it mathematically—that if you could somehow accelerate to the speed of light, time would stand still for you."

"This is more than I can follow," Alice admitted.

"But"—Gavin lifted a finger—"you used your electric alloy to make the Impossible Cube, and it warped the universe around itself. Have you thought of why the alloy does this?"

Dr. Clef shrugged. "I assumed it was to do with the nature of electricity. Electric current cycles back and forth between negative and positive, like a mouse running back and forth between its hole and a piece of cheese. We measure the distance between the two points and call it volts."

"But," Gavin said again, "we don't actually measure the farthest distance. I've been reading your notes. We measure from a point just below and above the two extremes. To use your metaphor, it's as if the mouse paused on the way to the cheese, and then paused again on the way back to its hole, and we actually measure how far the mouse ran from the pauses, not from the cheese or the hole. We do that for convenience because it's very hard to measure electricity at its peak and its low."

"What does this have to do with anything?" Alice asked.

Gavin turned his eyes on her, and they all but

glowed with intensity. "To get the distance between the stopping point and the peak, that is, the distance between the pause and the cheese—"

"Oh!" Alice interrupted. "You're going to tell me it's the square root of two."

"Well, you multiply by the square root of two, but yes."

"God in heaven!" Dr. Clef dropped his pencil and scrabbled for it on the rocking deck. "I knew this fact, my boy, but I never made the connection. The electricity in the alloy cycles between the average and the peak—the square root of two—and when combined with the Impossible Cube's design, it forces a constant on the universe and changes local time."

"My paradox generator might do the same thing," Gavin said. "If we used your alloy in it and powered it correctly."

Dr. Clef clapped his hands with newfound glee and cooperation. "It would take a lot of work and careful calculation."

"Wait a minute," Alice put in.

"And precise measurement, which we couldn't do here, with the lab rocking." Gavin began to pace within the shack, stepping over Click without really seeing him.

"One moment, please," Alice said.

"But we'll be in Berlin in a few hours." Dr. Clef flipped to a fresh page in his notebook. "The train will stop."

"Now, see here," Alice said.

"And we'll be able to buy more materials in a large city," Gavin said. "We may have to build a few tools first, but—"

"Wait. A. *Minute!*" Alice shouted.

Both men blinked at her, as if only then remembering she was there. Click's green eyes shuttered open and closed with little clicking noises that were clearly audible despite the rushing wind outside the shanty.

"What's wrong, my dear?" Dr. Clef asked at last. "You see how well we are working together. Is this not a fine thing?"

"You should not be discussing any of this," she said, one hand pressed to her bosom. Her heart fluttered about her rib cage like a frightened bird, and she felt a little sick. "You're treating the idea of changing something as fundamental as time itself like nothing more than some schoolboy's science experiment. This is . . . it's . . . Good heavens, I don't *know* what this is! Why would you do such a thing?"

Gavin looked at her, truly puzzled. "It's for you."

Alice hadn't thought she could be more shocked, and was even more shocked to learn she'd been wrong. His words sent an electric jolt through her gut, and she found herself pressed against the wall of the shanty. "What do you mean?"

"You need more time," Gavin said. "*We* need more time. You need to spread the cure and recover from it. And I'm . . . well, I don't have much time left. If I can find a way to change the way time flows for us, I can speed us up—or slow the world down. You'll have more time to recover. We'll have more time together. We can save the world, Alice. Just like Monsignor Adames said."

Nausea and more than a little fear sloshed around Alice's stomach. The very idea of tampering with time, let alone doing so in her name, screamed with wrongness. Alice tried to reply, but all that came out was a squeak. She tried again. "Gavin, Doctor—you can't be serious. I would never ask for such a terrible thing."

"I know. That's why I'm doing it."

He reached for her hands, but she snatched them away. "You don't understand at all. This is a horrible idea, Gavin. It's the sort of thing the Doomsday Vault was built to contain. What if you make a mistake? What if you speed time for us and the rest of the world goes ahead as normal and that tears a big piece out of the earth itself?"

"I wouldn't make such a mistake," Gavin soothed. "Truly. I don't make mistakes."

"You make mistakes all the time!" Alice felt like she was arguing with a tree. "You decided to escape the world's most powerful police force in an airship that can't fly without making a spectacle of itself. You used that whip of yours without knowing how much power was left in it, and it fizzled away right when you needed it most. Just now you tried your . . . your *thing* on Dr. Clef without considering whether or not it might damage his brain. No sane scientist would—" She clamped her lips shut and turned her face away. That was the problem, wasn't it? Gavin wasn't . . . wasn't . . .

She couldn't bring herself to complete the thought.

A hand took one of hers. Gavin looked her in the face, his expression worried and agitated at the same time. "I'm sorry," he said. "I'm so sorry. You're right. It's . . . I'm going in strange directions, Alice. I'm *changing*. My brain runs ahead of my mind, and I don't think. No, that's wrong. I *do* think. I think too much, and these ideas come to me, and it doesn't even occur to me that there might be something wrong. It scares me, Alice. I don't know what to do."

Alice squeezed his hand in both of hers, flesh on metal on flesh. The spider's eyes glowed red. "It's the plague. You have to fight it, Gavin. For as long as possible."

"Help me," he said simply. "Lead me."

"I'll try." It was hard to speak around the lump in her throat. "I'll never stop trying."

"Don't fail," Gavin said. "Adames said I can cure the world, but *you* mustn't fail. Maybe that's what he meant."

"I am confused," said Dr. Clef. "What are we doing?"

"We're realizing what we should and shouldn't do," Gavin said. "This"—he gestured at the paradox generator—"was a mistake. I'll destroy it now."

He drew back his foot to kick the generator over the side and let it smash on the rocky railroad bed. Then he hesitated.

"What's wrong?" Alice asked.

"I can't do it," he said. "I worked so hard on it, and it's so beautiful and perfect. How can I destroy it?"

"Then I'll do it." Alice leaned down to pick up the generator herself, but Gavin's arm on her shoulder stopped her.

"Don't!" he cried, then let her go with a start. "I mean, you can't . . . oh, God. I don't want . . . it's so *beautiful*, Alice."

Alice pursed her lips, frustrated but understanding. "I see, darling. Perhaps there's another way. Dr. Clef,

I'm going to take Gavin for a little walk. While we're gone, I want you to destroy this thing."

A horrified expression crossed Dr. Clef's face. "But it is as Gavin said—so beautiful! We cannot!"

"Of course we can." Gavin's voice hardened and he showed a bit of anger. "We must. Do you understand me, Doctor?"

Dr. Clef cocked his head. "I can," he said slowly. "If I must."

"You must," Gavin said. "We cooperate now, and you must."

"Then I shall." He sighed. "I promise. Ah, well. It *does* make fun to knock things apart, yes?"

Alice embraced Gavin hard, and belatedly realized her cheeks were wet. "Thank you," she said as the engine whistled again. "I love you always."

"And I love you always."

They joined hands and strode out into the wind.

Dr. Clef and Click watched them go. A look of bemusement crossed his ashy face. Then he picked up the discarded paradox generator and rocked it like a lost child. A single tear, and then another, leaked from his eye and splashed on the wooden casing. Click rubbed against his knee.

"*Mein armes Unmöglicheskubus,*" Dr. Clef moaned. "My poor Impossible Cube. He has abandoned us. Abandoned! And now I must destroy this thing of beauty."

Click continued to rub against Dr. Clef's knee, and Dr. Clef stroked his metal sides. They were gray with soot as well. "You understand, my clicky kitty. You are a delightful machine and would not alter your path, just as this train would not. Could not. But that boy, he is brilliant, far more brilliant than I, yet he follows his genitals to obey the woman. How can they save the world when they don't have enough time, my clicky kitty? How? The boy and the girl need more time. The boy needs more time. He needs more time."

Tears ran down his face and he rocked the paradox generator in his lap, lost in memory for a moment. Then a change came over his face. Sadness and despair dropped off, gave way to crafty resolve.

"We must show them they are wrong, mustn't we, my clicky kitty?" he cooed. "Yes, we must. Yes, we *must*! I can use the boy's theory and his generator to re-create my Impossible Cube, can't I, my kitty? Yes, I can. Yes, I *can*. Once I have my Cube back, I will be able to stop time forever, and that will give the boy and the girl all the time they need. At last the boy will have more time. Yes, he will. Yes, he *will*. I will stop time forever, my clicky kitty. Forever!"

Click only purred as Dr. Clef's joyful laughter poured out of the shanty.

Chapter Eight

Kiev was the opposite of Luxembourg. Funny how two places could be populated with human beings but be so completely different, Gavin mused as the train puffed and growled through town. Although the city was built on a series of seven hills with a winding river at the bottom of the valley, the place had no greenery in it whatsoever. Not one tree, flower, or blade of grass grew anywhere. Stone and steel, smoke and sludge hemmed Gavin in. Street after street of blocky buildings crouched low over cobblestoned streets. Gargoyles clung to rooftops and intricately carved monsters crawled across archways. Forests of chimneys belched out clouds of smoke or flashed plumes of yellow flame. Pipes urinated endless streams of waste into the river. A crowd of workers huddled outside a factory, hoping to be called in for a job. More people moved up and down crowded sidewalks. The men wore gray shirts, and the women wore brown dresses and head cloths, and they kept their heads down as they walked. Bright colors seemed to have been outlawed, and the lack pulled Gavin's spirits lower and lower with every passing moment. Something else bothered him about the crowds, but he couldn't put his finger on it.

Mechanicals ruled the streets. Skittering spiders and brass horses and hovering whirligigs clogged the pavement and the air above it. Automatic streetcars rattled down their tracks, drawing iron boundaries behind them. They all pumped out steam and coal smoke, turning the air thick with white mist and yellow sulfur. Gavin turned away from the window with a feeling of nausea. The something he couldn't figure out continued to bother him, and it gave him a slight headache.

"How can people live here?" he said.

"People live in all kinds of places," Dodd said philosophically from his own chair near the table. "Many of them can't go anywhere else. My usual thought is to be grateful I don't have to stay."

Gavin thought of his ship, his graceful *Lady*, now being hauled inexorably into this stony trap by an iron demon, and wondered how grateful he should be. He sighed. Once Alice had finished distributing the cure here, and once they were reasonably safe beyond the reach of Phipps, they could reassemble the *Lady* and fly for the Orient. As it was, he felt restless and out of sorts after days of inactivity. They had arrived in Berlin to find reward placards with Gavin's likeness on them plastered over nearly every empty surface and a notice about him that circulated daily in every local newspaper. Alice, who hadn't been with the Third Ward long enough to be photographed, had escaped such treatment, but her description had been bandied about, as was Feng's. This forced Gavin to stay hidden either aboard the *Lady* or in Dodd's car during the circus's entire time in Berlin. Alice and Feng risked slipping out to spread the cure around and brought back reports that underground stories of a woman with a demon's hand and a man with an angel's voice were already circulating. A number of Alice's "patients" asked Feng to sing, and he quickly demurred.

"When I sing," Feng said, "donkeys die in the street." So one night Gavin spent an hour with the little nightingale, recording the same song over and over until he was satisfied he'd done it perfectly. He gave it to Feng so he could play it for Alice on her nightly missions. But some time later, the nightingale came fluttering back to him. His careful music was gone, and the nightingale instead spoke in Feng's voice.

"The lady wants you to know that the nightingale's music is pretty, but not the same as yours," it said, "and it makes her sad to hear it."

More than once, Feng himself happily remained behind to accept from a grateful cure recipient what he called "additional gratuity," a practice that infuriated Alice and Gavin both—Alice on moral grounds and Gavin because it meant Alice was forced to travel back to the circus unescorted through Berlin streets. Feng, however, seemed unfazed by their fury, and Gavin understood more fully why Feng's father had decided not to allow him to continue as a diplomat in England.

When Alice returned from these midnight excursions, she collapsed into a deep sleep that lasted long enough to make Gavin nervous. He spent hours sitting by her bunk, just to be near her. The iron spider on her arm lay between them, glaring red and bubbling with blood. He barely got to speak with Alice, hardly even saw her awake. This mission to cure the world drove her to exhaustion, and while he couldn't fault her for it, he found himself wishing she would give up some of her intensity. Leaving London and Alice's fiancé behind was supposed to have granted them the freedom to love each other, but instead they found even less time for each other than before. How could Gavin compete with a world of plague victims? At times he wanted to shake her and shout that he was dying, that any day his life could end, and she would have all the time she wanted to spread the cure. But he didn't. The devotion and intensity made Alice herself, and changing any of it would make her into a different person, someone he wouldn't want to spend his remaining time with. He could either love her or change her, but not both.

Dr. Clef didn't seem to share Gavin's unhappiness. He stayed locked up in the ship's laboratory, scribbling with pencil on endless sheets of paper or with chalk on a slate, and manipulating long sections of his alloy into odd shapes. Gavin had been afraid that he was trying to re-create his Impossible Cube, but Dr. Clef waved this idea aside.

"It is as I told you," he said blandly. "I cannot re-create it, now or ever." But he would not say what he was working on.

As time passed, Gavin took to spending more and more time in Dodd's car. It was larger and more comfortable than any stateroom on Gavin's ship, and Dodd seemed glad to have him, his sole connection to Felix Naismith, though they never spoke of the man.

Enforced idleness didn't sit well with Gavin, and his hands worked without him. Even now, as the train puffed through Kiev, he wound wire around a wooden dowel, slid the dowel free, and snipped the length of the resulting coil with cutters, creating a pile of little rings.

At last the train screeched to a stop. It had taken a spur of track that cut past an enormous open square, perhaps three hundred yards on a side and bordered by tall buildings, beyond which rose columns of smoke and flame. Half the stone square was crowded with market carts and sooty freestanding tents. The other half, the side closest to the tracks, had been painted off, clearly set aside for the circus. Just beyond the tracks lay the slate-gray Dnepro River. Oil glistened in a rainbow sheen on its surface far below the cut stone banks. Steel boats of varying sizes chugged along in orderly procession, their stacks spewing yet more smoke into the already overburdened air.

The moment the train halted, the door to Dodd's car jerked open and in popped a portly man with long mustaches under a bowler hat. His name was Harry Burks, and he was the advance man, the person who traveled ahead of the circus to start the publicity and smooth the way with local officials. He spoke a dozen languages and loved nothing more than spending an evening in a pub making new friends. Gavin had never known him to forget a name or a face.

"Dodd!" Harry boomed. "Right on time. Good, good! You know how the Ukrainians feel about punctuality."

"What's the news, Harry?" Dodd asked.

"Nothing major, thank heavens, thank heavens. We have the southern half of the market square for as long as we need it, and we can leave the train on this side spur, though I had to promise the chief of police and the town council and their families front-row tickets along with the usual bribes. Placards are already up all over town, and I've taken out advertisements in all the usual places. I'm also trying something new—paying hansom cabs and spiders a small fee to paste placards on themselves. Walking advertisements, you know. We'll see if it helps, if it helps."

"Fine idea," said Dodd.

"And remind everyone not to go out after dark," Harry warned. "Kiev clockworkers can snatch anyone off the street after sunset, and there's nothing you can do about it, nothing you can do."

Dodd nodded. "Will do. And the other matter?"

Harry gave a sideways glance at Gavin. "Not a word, not a word. Your little friends may have been the toast of Berlin, but no one's talking about a reward for an American boy or an English girl, and clockwork cats are all the rage in Kiev. I think you can come out and breathe some smoky air at last, my boy."

A load of tension drained from Gavin, and he slumped in the padded chair. Freedom at last!

"But," Harry continued, holding up a finger, "there are other rumors. I'm hearing tales about a young woman, an angel who cures the plague with a touch, with a touch, and of her young lover who makes beautiful music for her."

"Uh-oh," Gavin said. "How is word getting around so fast?"

"Who knows, who knows?" Harry shrugged. "But there is more. The newspapers are saying there are fewer new cases of plague, and more of those who have it are recovering. Recovering! People are beginning to hope. That should give you reason to be careful, my boy, especially here."

"I'm always careful," Gavin said, though even as he said it, he knew it was mostly a lie. "But why here?"

"Don't forget that Kiev is supposedly the birthplace of the plague. She certainly has more zombies and clockworkers than anywhere else in the world, and it's a pity the Zalizniak and Gonta put all their resources into machines of war. They might have found a cure of their own, otherwise. At any rate, if the general population learns where to find you and that young lady, you'll be overrun, like Jesus and the lepers. So watch your step, my boy, watch your step."

An image of Alice caught in a mad mob of desperate plague victims flashed through Gavin's mind and his fingers went cold. "Understood, sir," he said.

Dodd rubbed his hands. "Let's get set up. I want the midway ready by nightfall so we can make parade by tomorrow afternoon."

Outside the train, a crowd was already gathering under the gloomy sky, though everyone stayed carefully outside the painted boundaries. Here, no one stepped out of line. Once again, something about the crowd nagged at Gavin. He examined the people, trying not to stare, but still he couldn't work it out. They looked perfectly normal. Perhaps a few more than the usual had clockwork pieces or prosthetics, but that wasn't it. Gavin shook his head. It would come to him later, he was sure.

Performers in work clothes spilled out of the other train cars and slid open the boxcar doors. The animals within howled, roared, and growled with agitation, glad to see sunlight, however hazy. Gavin sympathized. An official-looking man dressed in a blue uniform and accompanied by a brass spider the size of a collie strode up to Dodd and spoke in Ukrainian, to which Dodd smiled blankly. Harry stepped forward and took over, withdrawing a sheaf of stamped papers from his coat pocket while the circus buzzed to life and the drab crowd watched with interest. The cool autumn air was heavy with acrid smoke and steam, no little of which was added by the circus's own locomotive. Gavin smelled coal and ash and dust and polluted river water, but the city air wasn't as close as the air within the train car, and Gavin stretched, enjoying it.

Despite frequent visits when he was younger, Gavin had never been part of the circus setting up, and he turned to Dodd with a certain amount of excitement, especially after spending nearly a month in hiding with so little to do.

"What can I do to help?" he asked.

"You have no idea what you're doing," Dodd said frankly, "so the best thing you can do is stay out of the way."

The circus performers worked liked a well-oiled mechanical. First the mahouts led the elephants, both mechanical and biological, out of the boxcars while other roustabouts hauled out enormous rolls of canvas and bundles of wooden stakes with the ease of long practice. It wasn't possible to pound tent stakes through cobblestones, but before Gavin could wonder about that for too long, he saw a pair of roustabouts slide a stake into a hole that already existed, drilled long ago for exactly this purpose. It meant that the circus had no flexibility about what tent could go where or how big each could be, but it did allow a circus or other events to exist in the center of a city with no parks or grassy squares. The roustabout teams pounded the long stakes into the earth below the street with sledgehammers while teams of other workers laid out canvas. Once two rows of stakes were all in place and the red-striped canvas was laid out between them, the roustabouts pushed two long poles under the canvas and propped them up to create an opening underneath. Two more poles were placed farther in to lengthen the opening, which made enough space for the next step.

The mahout whistled, and the mechanical elephant puffed and snorted its way into the dark interior. Roustabouts followed with more long poles. Gavin, itching with curiosity, couldn't stand it anymore. He ran down to the tent and ducked inside. The brass elephant, now operating with perfect efficiency under Alice's careful repairs, was dragging tall, heavy tent poles upright, thereby shoving the tent's roof higher and higher. Gavin stood out of the way, feeling like a child near the enormous mechanical beast in the increasingly larger space. Once there was enough room, more elephants—live ones—were brought in, and the work went faster. The three enormous center poles took a trio of elephants to haul upright, with the trapeze artists and spiders up in the rigging to ensure they were set properly at the roof. Other spiders scampered about, fastening ropes and tying knots. The center ring was hauled in piecemeal and fitted together like a jigsaw puzzle. An automaton wheeled the talking clock woman to the entrance and wound her up, touched her metal cheek, and went off to help with other jobs. More people brought in bleacher seats to assemble, and the tent became loud with clacks, clatters, clinks, and shouts. For once, the clockwork plague kept its distance, and the analytical side of Gavin's brain remained quiet, allowing him to watch in wonder as the Tilt assembled around him like a genie rising from the desert.

"Incredible, isn't it?" said Alice.

Gavin hadn't noticed her slip up to next him. A smile automatically burst across his face, and he leaned in to kiss her. She still looked a little pale, her skin contrasting sharply with the dark metal of the spider on her hand.

"How are you feeling?" he asked.

"Not entirely myself, but one can only sleep for so long," she said with more candor than she usually allowed herself. "Thank you for watching over me."

He flushed a little. "I thought you were asleep."

"I heard you singing in my dreams and knew you were there." She squeezed his hand, and the entire circus slowed and stopped. He became aware of the softness of her skin on his, the warmth of her breath, the pulse of their hearts. He never wanted the moment to end, but the second hand on the clock outside ticked forward, and the noises smashed back into existence.

"We need to go," Alice said.

"Where?"

"Linda wants to see us."

Outside the tent, the midway and sideshow were taking shape. Animal cages and brightly painted wagons were rolling out of the boxcars, and several smaller tents were going up. No one merely talked. They shouted and hollered, bellowed and bawled, trying to attract as much attention as possible for the circus. Lions roared, seals barked, elephants trumpeted. The sounds bounced off the hard buildings that bordered three sides of the square, creating a swirling cacophony that both unnerved and exhilarated Gavin.

As they picked their way through the chaos, Gavin noticed the dam for the first time. It rose high above the oily Dnepro upriver, clearly visible in the dank air even though it sat between two hills well over a mile away. Water gushed through spillways, and Gavin's sharp ears picked up the faint roar of it all even above the noise of the circus setting up.

"Wow," he said. "How did they build that?"

"I have no idea," Alice said. "But I'm sure it's the reason Kiev has so many electric lights. Come along."

Where the sideshow was setting up, they came to a canary-yellow wagon, its wheels chocked into immobility. The door sported a sign: MADAME FABRY. The sign also showed a crystal ball, stars, and a palm, in case the viewer couldn't read English. Gavin knocked, and the door flew open to reveal a tallish woman who

Gavin happened to know was over sixty but could have passed for ten years younger. Her thick brown hair was covered with a gypsy scarf, and she wore glasses. Her overly patched skirt and blouse—part of a costume, now that they were setting up—rustled about her busy frame as she put her hands on her waist.

"Well, it's about time you got here, honey," she said brightly. Her accent was American, probably Midwestern, though Gavin had heard her speak with a Southern drawl more than once.

"Aren't you supposed to say, 'You're late,' or something like that?" Alice said.

"Why would I say that, sweetie?" she said. "Oh! The fortune-telling. Right. No, dear, I save that for the flatties. Gavin's been rude, is all. Dozens of cookies and butterscotch sweets I've given him over the years, and then he hides in the circus for weeks without coming to see me even once."

"Sorry," he said, unabashed. "I've been a little busy."

"Kemp said you wanted to see us," Alice said.

"Yes, yes, come in."

Linda ushered them into her comfortable wagon. Against the back wall stood an intricately carved bedstead with a plump featherbed and duvet covering it. Wooden cupboards hung from the walls, and a tiny stove took up one corner. A table folded down from the wall, with stools to sit on. But Gavin's eye went straight to the automaton. He stood in the corner opposite the stove in a case of glass and metal similar to a ticket booth. From the waist up he looked like a brass man wearing a brown jacket and red vest. From the waist down, he was a complicated mass of metal and gears—no legs or feet. His jointed fingers gleamed in the light of the lamp hanging from the ceiling off the rivets on his face and neck. The top half of his head was made of glass, and suspended in some sort of clear medium within which floated a human brain. Copper clips and wires were attached to it, and little electric sparks flicked and jumped about like fireflies. No matter how many times he had seen that, it took Gavin a moment to remember not to stare. Alice put a hand to her mouth.

"Hi, Charlie," Gavin said.

The automaton opened his mouth. "Gavin," he said in a metallic voice. "And this is Alice?"

"I am," she said. "You have the advantage of me, sir."

"Sorry. Charlie Fabry. I'd offer to shake hands, but . . ." He tapped the glass in front of him with a brass finger. "And you've met my wife already."

"Quite," said Alice, and Gavin knew her well enough to see she was trying to cover shock.

"Charlie used to be a wire walker," he told her. "He fell during a show and would have died, but a clock-worker happened to be in the audience, and . . . well, you can see the result."

"Gives you a whole new insight," Charlie said cheerfully. "No appetites, fewer needs, simpler wants. Liberating." He leaned forward with a creak until his nose nearly touched the glass and his voice dropped to a raspy whisper. "You can see what you never saw before."

"I don't understand," Alice said.

"We've been discussing your little trip to the church in Luxembourg, honey," Linda said.

Alice looked startled. "You know about that?"

"Everybody knows about that," Linda said. "Not much goes on without everyone hearing about it eventually. I read in the newspaper that a large piece of the church was destroyed, too, but the vicar is planning to rebuild it even bigger, which will help when he applies to have it declared a cathedral."

"Is that what you wanted to ask about?" Gavin put in.

"Lord, how I do talk. No, honey. This is." Linda lifted a handkerchief from the fold-down table, revealing three tarot cards. The first card portrayed a skeletal figure swinging a sword over a field of grain and was labeled XIII. The second showed a burning tower falling to pieces. Two men fell screaming from it, and it was labeled XVI: LA MAISON DIEU. Laid crosswise over the dying tower was the third card, on which was rendered a man in priestly red robes. He held a golden staff in one hand and made a gesture of benediction with the other. This card was labeled V: LE PAPE.

"I don't know anything about tarot cards," Alice said primly. "I avoid this sort of thing as nonsense."

"Place your hands palm-up under the window, if you would be so kind." Charlie slid aside a small opening at the bottom of his glass case, much like a ticket taker might. After a moment's hesitation, Alice obeyed. The spider on her left hand left her palm bare, but the metal clanked against the shelf beneath the window opening. Gavin watched warily. A pair of red lights beamed from Charlie's eyes and ran over Alice's hands. She jumped, but didn't pull away. The lights ran over every inch of Alice's hands, then went out.

"Very interesting," Charlie said. "You have refined tastes, but you work with your hands. You've been touched by the clockwork plague more than once, you are deeply in love, and you can't get this spider off your arm."

"And you can tell all that from my palms, can you?"

"No, that's just gossip around the circus. Your palms say the future is going to be difficult. Your fate line is ragged and rough, especially after your heart line. That means your future will be twisted and shredded by emotional decisions. You can change that, of course, but it'll be entirely up to you."

"Didn't Gavin say you were a wire walker?" Alice asked. "Why are you telling fortunes?"

"I was a wire walker first," Charlie replied genially. "But now that I'm freed of my body, I can see a great deal that other people can't. It lends itself to fortune-telling."

"So you're not reading my palms at all." Alice's tone was shrewd.

Charlie shook his head with a faint creak. "No. I pretend because no one believes pronouncements from thin air."

"That's not true," Alice said. "We believe pronouncements from teachers and parents and others in our lives."

"You didn't believe Monsignor Adames."

Gavin blinked. "How did you know we talked to Monsignor Adames? The church . . . mess was in the newspaper, and I can see how people in the circus might put that together with our absence, but we didn't even tell Dodd that we talked to Adames, or what he said."

"I saw it." Charlie ran a metal finger over the glass casing that topped his head. "Everything is connected. I told you that. Bits of pasteboard can give us a crude glimpse into the future, and the particles that run through my brain give me even clearer knowledge."

Alice said, "That's—"

"Nonsense? Ask your Dr. Clef about that," Charlie said. "According to some very interesting theories he's been busy proving as we speak, certain tiny particles affect one another over long distances. Turn one particle, and its twin, no matter how far away it is, will turn as well. Just like flipping a card. Clef also claims that time is nothing but an illusion created by our own limited senses, and that as many as eleven other dimensions exist beyond our ability to see, but they still affect what happens to us. Everything is connected in one way or another, and once you accept that idea, the possibility that three tarot cards could fall out of Linda's deck and my electrical systems could play 'Camptown Ladies' at the very moment you had a conversation with a man named Nicolas Adames doesn't seem very far-fetched."

Linda, who had been waiting near the table all this time with her hands folded, said, "Honey, let me tell you what the cards mean and then you can decide what to do about it, all right?"

"Very well." Alice sighed, clearly not convinced.

She took up a stool next to the table and Gavin stood behind her. Strangely, he didn't share her skepticism. In the long moments when he watched over Alice, he sometimes found himself drawn into deep places, places where things could exist everywhere and nowhere all at once, where tiny, graceful objects appeared and disappeared so quickly, it was difficult to say they had hardly existed at all, where almost everything was vast, empty space that threatened to swallow him up, where matter was made of an infinity of tiny, delicate strings that vibrated and sang with a wonderful perfection that made him weep with joy and envy. And just as he was reaching out to touch them and change their song, alter matter itself, Alice murmured in her sleep, and the sound snatched him backward and upward into a bumbling world of impossible hugeness that could only be manipulated by tearing it apart by fire or grinding it around gears. It was maddening. If there were a way to better understand how it all fit together, he wanted to hear about it.

Linda took up a stool opposite Alice while Charlie watched from his booth. Tiny jolts of electricity arced across his brain.

"Normally, honey, I'd dim the lights and burn some incense and have Charlie make some whoosh-whoosh noises," Linda said, "but you aren't flatties, so I'll give it to you without the show."

"We appreciate that," Alice said.

"How do you tell fortunes to people who don't speak English?" Gavin asked.

"I speak more than just English, honey, and Charlie

speaks what I don't. The pictures on the cards tell the rest. Most of my business is actually from women who are expecting."

"Why them?" Gavin said.

"They want to know if it's a boy or a girl. I dangle her wedding ring on a string over her middle and tell her what the baby will be based on which way the ring moves. Then I write it down in my book." She gestured to a leather-bound diary on a high shelf. "I have predictions going back twenty years."

Alice leaned forward, interested despite herself. "And how many come out right?"

"Lord, honey, I have no idea. Probably half. I can't tell a thing from a wedding ring. I just tell them what they want to hear. Part of the show."

"So what happens when you're wrong?" Gavin wanted to know.

"Usually we're long gone by the time the baby's born, dear. But sometimes when we come back to a city, I'll get an annoyed mother who shows up with a daughter, ready to fight because I told her she'd have a son. I tell her that I didn't get the prediction wrong. She *heard* me wrong. Then I get my book down and show her where I wrote she'd have a daughter, and I'm off the hook."

"Because you write the opposite of what you say," Alice supplied.

Linda nodded with a smile. "There you have it, honey. It won't do to have the fortune-teller come out wrong."

"So why should we believe you now?" Alice demanded.

"Do or don't." Linda shrugged. "But you aren't paying me and I like you both, so I have no reason to make anything up."

Alice didn't look convinced, but Gavin said, "Fair enough. Tell us what the cards mean, Linda."

"Sure, honey. Look closely." She gestured at the cards on the tiny table in front of her. "All three cards come from the trumps. They indicate large, important events that are difficult to control or change. The first card that fell out of the deck was the mystery trump, which everyone calls Death. Before you panic, let me tell you that it doesn't mean someone's going to die. It means one thing will end so something else can begin. You can't stop the end from coming, but you can decide which direction the new thing will take. Since it fell out first, I assume that's what's coming first."

"All right," Alice said.

"The second trump card is the House of God. It's as bad as it looks—utter destruction. Unlike the Death card, this is an end out of which nothing new can begin. It doesn't mean someone will die, but it might. It's not a good omen, honey."

Linda's words sent a chill over Gavin's skin, and her cheerful tone only made the dreadful prediction worse. Alice, however, remained unmoved.

"I see," was all she said.

"The third card landed across the House," Linda continued, seemingly oblivious to Alice's attitude. "This is why I called you in to talk to you. Charlie told me what the priest said to you, and this card is the Hierophant or Pope. He symbolizes religious leadership, power, and discipline. When one card lands across another, the crossing card is interfering with the card beneath. In this case, we have a religious leader who is interfering with total destruction. And just as these cards landed on the floor, Charlie told me what your priest said."

"That flood and plague will destroy us all if I fail," Alice murmured.

"No." Gavin put his hand on her shoulder. "He said flood and plague will destroy us all if *I* fail. He said that I can cure the world, but *you* have to let go."

"Let what go?" Alice growled. She held up her spider hand. "This? I wish I could."

"He said that you have to let *him* go," Charlie said gently.

Alice rounded on him. "How do you know that?"

"I believe I already explained that. And the fact that I *do* know lends credence to what Adames said," Charlie replied. "Gavin can cure the world, but only if you let him go. Otherwise the world will perish in flood and plague."

"How am I to let Gavin go?" Alice was getting truly worked up now. "I don't hold him. I don't chain him down. He's free to leave anytime he wishes."

But when the words left Alice's mouth, a pang went through Gavin. He shook his head. "No," he said.

Alice halted and twisted on her stool to look up at him. "What do you mean?"

"I can't leave you, Alice." His throat grew thick, and his jaw trembled. "I could never leave you. I love you always."

Her eyes softened. "I know, darling, I know." She

took his hand. "But I'm not *holding* you. I'm not forcing you or chaining you. Am I?"

"You're leading me, Alice Michaels." The snaps and sparks that danced across Charlie's brain created a hypnotic pattern of particles that blurred the edges of Gavin's vision. Words poured from his mouth in an electric river. "You go, and I follow. You pulled me out of that tower of destruction and changed me, and then you took me through the city of white and changed me again, and now you've led me down to the city of sulfur to change me one more time. You bring me places, Alice, and I can't stop you and I don't want to stop you."

"Is it a bad thing, Gavin Ennock?" she whispered.

"I don't know." The half trance fell away, and he gave a little laugh. "I've never been in love before."

Alice smacked the table with her free hand. "What's the point in making prophecies if they don't make sense? Why can't a fortune-teller—or priest—simply say, 'Don't leave the house on Wednesday; you'll be hit by a streetcar'?"

"The monsignor did say he couldn't see everything properly," Gavin reminded her. "At least now we know that I have a role in spreading the cure, too."

"There's one more card," Linda said. "I saved it for last because it landed some distance from the others."

From her pocket she pulled another card and laid it face up on the table. It showed a white-haired man seated on a throne surrounded by water. He wore blue robes, a yellow cloak, and a crown. In one hand he held a large cup and in the other he held a scepter.

"This is the King of Cups," Linda explained. "He's a fair-haired man, very artistic, patient, and unselfish, but given to flights of fancy. He cares deeply about others and shares their pain."

Gavin picked up the card to examine it. "That sounds a little like me, but—"

"It's not you, honey. Kings are older men, and fathers."

The remark sliced through Gavin like a knife made of ice. His fingers went numb and he dropped the card again. It landed on the table. For a moment he couldn't speak. Then he said, "This is my father?"

"Probably," Linda said. "Court cards are usually people, and kings are often father figures. It fell away from the others, which tells me that the person is far removed, but coming closer."

Gavin touched the card with a shaky finger. "I always thought he was dead. Where is he? What is he doing? Why did he leave me? Us?"

"I don't know." Linda looked sympathetic. "I just know he's out there somewhere, and your destinies are intertwined."

Alice gathered up the cards and handed them to Linda, her posture once again brisk. "We know nothing of the sort. I'm sorry, Linda. I know you believe what you're saying, but I simply can't."

"Listen, honey," Linda said, "the reason for casting fortunes isn't to tell you what will or will not happen. It's to let you know the choice is coming so you can look at your options and prepare yourself instead of being hit blind. Believe or don't believe—it doesn't matter. We've had the conversation, and you can't unhear it." She reached into her pocket and handed them each a small candy wrapped in paper. "Butterscotch?"

"I'm not twelve anymore, Linda," Gavin said, but the remark came out a little dazed.

"Honey, you're young enough to be my grandson. As far as I'm concerned, you're six." She shooed them toward the door. "Now, get out there and change the world before it changes you."

Chapter Nine

The zombie straightened. Its eyes cleared, and it slowly wiped the drool from its chin with a sore-encrusted hand. Alice lowered the spider gauntlet with a sigh. She'd lost count of the number of people she'd cured now, but the relief and satisfaction she felt for each case never lessened. This was seventh or eighth plague zombie she'd cured tonight, and she was feeling a little light-headed now.

Behind her, Gavin played his fiddle, something sweet and soft, and she drank the music in as the zombie shuffled off into the shadows of Kiev. Berlin had been difficult without Gavin, more than she wanted to admit. She drew strength from every note he played, and Feng was no substitute, even when he played Gavin's music with the little nightingale.

"My father taught me that song," Gavin said. "I'm sure he did."

"Hm," Feng said. "How can you miss a man you barely remember?"

"I just do." Gavin sounded testy. "You wouldn't know what it's like. You had a father all your life. You got to live with him, work with him, see him every day."

"And live with his disapproval," Feng added. "Maybe it's better not to have a father. Then you have no one to disappoint. Perhaps you should think of that."

"Now, look—"

"Boys," Alice said tiredly, "I know we're all nervous, but I'm not up for mediating an argument. I would prefer to move on now."

Gavin looked away. "Sorry."

"Now where?" Feng asked in a subdued voice.

"It doesn't really matter," Alice replied, and tried to make herself sound more cheerful. "You know, it's rather nice to walk about and not worry about being followed by Phipps."

"Phipps, no," Gavin fretted, "but Kievite clockworkers are another story. Remember what Harry said—they can take anyone they like off the streets after dark. Every time I play, it draws attention."

"That's the entire point," Alice said, trying not to show she was uneasy, too. "How will people find out the 'angels' are in town if they don't hear your music in the dark? Besides, you're armed."

"Hm." Gavin touched the glass cutlass at his belt and fingered the heavy, brass-adorned bands that encircled both his forearms.

Feng checked the pair of pistols at his own belt, a hard look on his handsome face. "We do not know for sure that Phipps has failed to follow. She will eventually notice that we twice appeared in the same city as the circus."

Alice clutched the amber-handled parasol Gavin had given her and stole a reflexive glance down the street, as if Phipps—or a clockworker—might leap out of the smoking sewers to carry them off. Then she admonished herself for being silly. It was well after midnight, and the gritty street was empty of pedestrians, if brightly lit. This latter aspect had taken Alice by surprise. By day, Kiev looked dark and moody, ready to pounce on newcomers. But at night, the city gleamed with lights. Every street and byway was hung with them, and many doors and windows shone with a steady, unwavering glow. Alice actually found it more unnerving than beautiful. Light should flicker and pulse and live, not remain steady and dead as a granite statue. She wondered whether it existed to ward zombies off the main streets, or to let prowling clockworkers see better.

"Even if Phipps does make that connection," Alice said, "it'll take her a few days to track us down, and we'll be leaving soon. How much money do we have?"

"Not as much as I would like." Gavin took off his cap for a moment and rumpled his hair. "People didn't donate much in Berlin. Dodd owes us some more for automaton repairs, and he won't pay us until the circus has done a couple more shows here. But yeah—once we get that money, we should be able to buy enough paraffin oil to make a run for Peking. Ahead of Phipps."

"*Proschennia mene,*" said a quiet voice. A young woman in a head cloth had emerged from one of the nearby houses and now edged uncertainly toward the trio, ready to run at the first sign of danger.

"That's you, Feng," Gavin said.

"I have nothing else to do," Feng muttered half under his breath. "Nowhere else to go."

Before Alice could say anything in response to this remark, Feng greeted the girl in careful Ukrainian and spoke with her at some length. Alice was glad Feng, someone she trusted, spoke a certain amount of Ukrainian—China watched the Ukrainian Empire carefully and many diplomatic families learned at least some of the language—but Feng's behavior was different of late.

"The rumors have reached Kiev," he reported, "just as Harry said. Lilya here heard Gavin playing, and she has braved the clockwork night to ask if Alice can cure the plague."

"Lead on," Alice said.

"Lady mine."

"Feng," Gavin said, "is something wrong?"

"No," he said shortly. "Please, let us merely come along."

Alice exchanged a glance with Gavin. He had noticed it, too—the closer they got to China, the more shuttered and surly Feng became. They needed to discuss this, but now was clearly not the time. In the tiny, low-ceilinged flat where Lilya lived, Alice cured the girl's parents, who were both lying abed with fever. Gavin played until their pain lessened. Feng, whose facility with the Ukrainian language was the reason they brought him along, asked Lilya if she knew of anyone else who needed help. As Alice expected, Lilya did, and she threaded them through grime-laden blocks of houses lit by dead lights, chattering volubly with Feng, who listened with animated interest.

"What's she talking about?" Gavin asked.

"Nothing in particular," Feng replied loftily, and said something in fast Ukrainian to Lilya, who giggled.

Keeping a wary eye on dark sky and narrow street, they dodged beneath gargoyles to the next flat, where Alice cured three children, her parasol under her arm. The joyful parents pressed food on Alice and money on Gavin. She still felt odd about taking cash for curing the plague, but she reminded herself that they needed to buy paraffin oil if they wanted to reach Peking, and Gavin never asked for money. He only took what was offered.

"That went well," Alice said as she brushed bread crumbs from her skirt and straightened her hat. She avoided trousers on most of these outings on the grounds that the spider gauntlet drew more than enough attention. A woman in trousers would only compound the problem. She looked about the flat's tiny kitchen, which smelled of watery cabbage and rye bread. "Where's Feng?"

They found him just outside the flat's back door, which opened onto a stone courtyard shared by several blocky houses. He was caught in a passionate embrace with Lilya. Her skirt was hiked up to an embarrassing level and her blouse was open.

"Feng!" Alice gasped from the doorway.

Feng drew away from Lilya and blinked at her in the light that spilled from the door. There were no lights out back, and the shadows had half engulfed the pair. An oily smell wafted in from the river, covering everything with an olfactory patina of chemicals and damp. "Do you mind?" Feng said.

"Not this again!" Alice blurted, shocked. "What do you think you're doing?"

"The same thing you have done for weeks," Feng said as Lilya straightened her clothes, "only you do it with Gavin."

Alice became aware that the inhabitants of the flat were standing behind her, as was Gavin, and she felt her face redden. "You're . . . This is . . ." She recovered herself somewhat. "Feng, we have to leave. Now."

"Of course." He nuzzled at the girl's cheek. "Lilya knows of another house of plague and we must go right this moment, must we not? Exactly on your schedule, and no one else's, because *you* are English."

Either he was oblivious to Alice's outrage or he was a master at ignoring it, which only added to Alice's fury. The girl was all but hanging out of her blouse and Feng's . . . arousal was all too evident. There was certainly no possibility she could reenter the house and face the looks of the two strangers, so she marched down the back stoop and around the corner of the house, her face growing hot again as she heard Feng bid the couple good night in Ukrainian. Gavin came after.

"You are quite a . . . What is it you say? A piece of work," Feng drawled. He was holding Lilya's hand, and she was all but skipping along beside him, apparently now enjoying her adventure. She was pretty, he was handsome, and they would have made an attractive couple under other circumstances.

"I don't know what you mean," Alice snapped. A few blocks away, a stack erupted in bright yellow flame, then went out with a *whump*.

"You and Gavin carry on very plainly, like two animals in—"

"Watch your words, Feng," Gavin growled.

"Why? Will you strike me?" Feng shot back. "I am tired of hypocrisy. You two have no stronger a connection than sweet Lilya and I do. You are not married or even engaged to be married, so by the rules of your own society, you are a pair of"—Gavin inhaled sharply, and Feng shifted ground—"a pair of very bad people. Yet you enjoy yourselves together for weeks. And then you have the nerve to tell me I should not do the same?"

"*Enjoy?*" Alice whirled on the narrow sidewalk to face him, almost too affronted to speak. Smoky fog curled around her body, and the amber-headed parasol banged against her shin. "What do you mean by that?"

Feng made a scoffing noise. "That is so English of you. Perfectly willing to tell everyone else what is right while you ignore your own rules. You and Gavin sent me to hide with those acrobats so you could—"

"What do you mean *enjoy*?" Gavin's face was turning red. "What are you telling people about us?"

"I need speak not at all. Which is how well I get along with those smelly monkeys you forced me to live with."

"We thought that you'd get along with them fine," Gavin said.

"Just because they are Chinese? Ha!" Feng spat, and

Lilya cast about uncomfortably, clearly uncertain about what was going on. "They are not fit company for the emperor's goats, let alone his nephew. As much to hide you with a family of Scottish coal miners."

"That isn't the point," Alice snapped. "You are accusing me of—"

"Yes, it is always *you*," Feng snapped back. "You, you, you, and that cure of yours. You dragged me all over Luxembourg and Berlin and Warsaw and now to filthy Kiev for your cure. So you can *save* everyone. The world revolves around the great Lady Michaels, who guards her chastity during the day so her not-so-secret lover can spend himself on her at—"

Alice slapped him.

Her hand left a mark that changed from white to red on Feng's ivory skin. Feng stared at her. Alice stared back, a little startled at herself. She had never struck another person in her life. But the fury continued to burn and she refused to move or flinch. Beside her, Gavin tensed, fists clenched. Lilya looked ready to run away. The narrow street stretched in both directions, its unwavering lights pinned to earth like half-dead stars.

"Keep your filthy false accusations to yourself, Feng," Gavin said evenly.

After a long moment, Feng said, "Translate on your own." He turned on his heel and stalked away.

"Should I go after him?" Gavin said.

"Certainly not." Alice turned to the still-uncertain Lilya and gestured with her iron gauntlet. "Go on, girl."

Lilya may not have understood the words, but she

got the message. Timid again, she led Alice and Gavin to another flat, laid out exactly like the previous one. Lilya explained to the mystified inhabitants why Alice had come and then fled immediately, leaving Alice and Gavin no way to speak short of smiles and sign language. Still, Alice managed to cure a man, a child, and a baby, which cried incessantly after Alice scratched and bled on it. Although the family appeared grateful, the wailing infant put a definite damper on their mood. Alice and Gavin left as quickly as they could.

"That was difficult," Alice said once they were back outside. "Now what?"

"We should probably just go back to the circus." Gavin scanned the smoky street and its looming gray buildings. He coughed at the soot in his throat. "We'll have to walk, too. Doesn't Kiev have even delivery vans that run at night?"

"That wretched Feng," Alice muttered, taking Gavin's arm as he slung his fiddle case over his back. "What's gotten into him, anyway?"

"No idea. He seemed pretty angry."

Alice's chin came up, which made her almost as tall as Gavin. "I'm certainly not going to apologize." She paused. "Do you think we should apologize?"

Like intelligent men everywhere, Gavin fell back on prevarication. "Uh . . ."

She continued talking, half to herself. "I mean, it isn't as if *we* did anything wrong. I honestly thought he'd get along better with people who spoke his own language."

"Absolutely."

"It may have been a little presumptuous to assume

he'd be happy with a troop of Oriental acrobats just because he himself is from the Orient any more than I—we—might be happy socializing with any random person we met from England—or America."

"You may have a point."

She gave a heavy sigh as they walked. Their footsteps echoed down the eerie, empty street. "You don't suppose the entire circus has been gossiping about us, have they? I mean, you don't suppose everyone thinks we . . . that we're . . ."

"If they do, it doesn't seem to bother them," Gavin pointed out. "No one seems to mind Dodd and Nathan."

"I can't quite get over that," she said. "Two gentlemen, and everyone knows."

"Which part can't you get over? The two gentlemen part or the everyone knows part?"

"Well," Alice amended, "I can't say I can't get *over* it. It's not as if one never hears of such things. It's just that one never discusses them."

"You seem fine discussing it with me," Gavin pointed out.

"Yes. It seems I can discuss any number of things with you, darling, and that's one thing that makes you so special." She sighed and laid her head on his shoulder as they walked. For a moment, it felt as if the entire city belonged to her and Gavin alone. Even the plague zombies seemed to have retreated. A number of thoughts were working their way across her mind, and with no one else about, she allowed herself freedom to express them. "I suppose I was rather self-centered. I know Feng feels disgraced and he's nervous about facing his family again, and on top of it all, we—I—drag him all around these cities to visit plague victims and zombies." She sighed again, feeling more and more guilty. "He said such awful things, though. Am I being womanish to feel bad about arguing with him?"

"I don't know what that means," Gavin said. "All the women I know would sooner smack you than sorry you."

"What women?"

"My ma, for one. She'd smack you cross-eyed if you mouthed and I don't ever remember her apologizing, but speak against one of her kids and you were in for a world of trouble."

"Do you think I'll ever get to meet her?" Alice asked.

"I don't know." Gavin's eyes grew sad. "I don't know if *I'll* ever—"

"Don't!" Alice cut off the rest of the sentence by squeezing his arm with her iron-clad hand. Her parasol knocked against her knee. "I'm being thoughtless again. We'll see her; of course we'll see her. She'll have to be at the wedding."

Gavin halted. "Is that a proposal, Lady Michaels? Come to think of it, I never did actually propose to you, did I?"

"Oh!" She colored. "Good heavens! I—I didn't mean to—"

"Yes, you did. You certainly did."

Alice floundered. The evening was turning out far more peculiar than she had imagined it might. The street seemed to skew sideways, and words spilled from her mouth in a dreadful torrent that she couldn't seem to stop. "I didn't mean to push you into anything, though I rather assumed that once we found a spare moment we would want to formalize our relationship, not that we're particularly traditional people anymore, but my title and my upbringing both mean I was hoping for something more traditional, and even though we were in a church in Luxembourg we never even had a moment to ask Monsignor Adames if—"

Gavin shushed her. "I'll make it easy for you." He got down on one knee on the cobblestones before her and swept off his cap. His new wristbands gleamed in the lamplight. Alice couldn't help clapping a hand to her mouth, not sure if she wanted to laugh or burst into tears. The horrible businessman's offer she had gotten from Norbert last year came inevitably into her mind. He had offered her an emerald ring over a delicate luncheon of poached salmon and champagne. Gavin, dear, gallant Gavin, knelt on grimy cobblestones in a foreign city that stank of oil and steam. She couldn't imagine a more perfect proposal.

"Alice, Lady Michaels," he said, "will you—"

And then he was gone.

Alice stared in uncomprehending disbelief at the stones where he'd been kneeling. Gavin had simply disappeared. It wouldn't register. What had—?

A split-second later, the clank of metal brought her head around. An enormous ostrichlike bird, easily two stories tall, was rising above her. It had come out of the alley beside and a little behind her. The bird was made entirely of brass and iron, intricately wrought and jointed. Gears spun and pistons puffed as it moved. Its head, at the end of a long segmented neck, was actually a rounded cage half the height of a man. Gavin knelt inside it, looking as startled as Alice felt.

"Good heavens!" she gasped.

The huge bird stalked forward out of the alley, revealing its body and legs now. Brass feathers shone. On the creature's broad back rode a plump woman in a pink evening gown. Blond ringlets more suitable for a young girl framed her face, and she wore opera gloves. A console before her sported levers and switches, and she worked them with idle skill. A gleaming collar made of copper encircled her throat.

"*Min!*" she called. "*Spaceeba!*"

A hunting clockworker. The city had been so quiet, they had let their guard down. Alice's heart pounded, and she was already moving, running straight toward the ridiculously sized ostrich, outraged beyond sensibility, her parasol raised. The amber head shone like liquid gold.

"Release him this instant!" she demanded.

"Stay back!" Gavin shouted.

The clockworker pulled a lever, and one bird wing fluttered downward. It caught Alice full across the chest and flung her backward. The air burst from her lungs. Red pain smashed her body and scored her arms as she tumbled over the pavement.

"Alice!" Gavin yelled from the cage. "Shit."

Alice staggered to her feet as the bird started to turn away. The pain receded under anger and adrenaline as she scrambled upright, only barely managing not to tangle herself in her skirts. Her hat was gone, but she had kept her parasol. Before she could charge the bird again, from the alleyway darted half a dozen birds, smaller ones this time, perhaps twice the size of a cat. They swarmed about the larger bird's feet, wings spread at Alice with menacing intent.

Gavin put one of his wristbands through the bars, aimed, and pressed a button. A gleaming gear shot from its magnetic release and spun toward the clock-worker. She yipped and twisted out of the way with startling agility. Even a woman of her bulk came equipped with plague-enhanced reflexes. The gear pinged harmlessly off the bird's metal back.

"What you do?" the woman called up to him in English. "Do not fight. I need the meat."

The smaller birds clacked their beaks at Alice and scratched long runnels in the stones with their claws. Their eyes glowed red. The spider on Alice's arm glowed back as if in answer. She gave the amber handle of the parasol a deft twist. It ratcheted twice, and a high-pitched whine shrilled in her ears. The parasol handle shone blue. The birds lowered their heads, ready to charge, and Alice slapped the handle. A bolt of electricity cracked from the tip of the parasol to the first bird. It froze in place. Sparks spat from its eyes and beak, and ozone tanged in the air. The bird fizzled with a smell of hot metal, but the electric arc was already jumping to the next bird, creating a wicked electric rainbow in the air. The second bird sparked and collapsed, and the power connected to the third, and the fourth. The arc of dreadful lightning poured from parasol to bird to bird to bird. Alice's hair stood out like leaves on a wild bush. The lightning arced to the fifth and sixth birds. They crackled and spat and half melted, beaks open in silent screams. Then the electricity abruptly ended. The parasol went heavy in Alice's hands, and the birds tipped to the pavement with six identical thuds. A line of smoke trickled from the end of the weapon, and Alice lowered it with shaky hands.

"Now," she said firmly, "you will let him go."

"*Hodynnyk?*" the clockworker said.

"Was that an insult?" Alice demanded.

"I think it means *clock*," Gavin said. He aimed with the wristband again and fired another cog. This one struck a lever on the clockworker's control panel and moved it. The cage holding Gavin abruptly opened from the bottom like a claw being released. Gavin, ready for this, kept hold of one bar and swung himself around to the giant bird's neck, whereupon he skimmed downward until he could safely drop to the ground. The move was magnificent to watch, and Alice couldn't help admiring it, despite the recent fight.

"You are clockworkers," the woman said, switching back to English. She clucked her tongue. "You might have said instead of destroying our little pets. There are ethics."

"Sure," Gavin said. "And you might have asked before you snatched me up."

The woman shrugged and pointed to herself. "Ivana Gonta. We see you are from other country. Would you like chocolate?" A mechanical hand emerged from the control panel with a small foil box. It extended itself down to Alice, who took the box without thinking. "You take. Is very useful."

"Thank you," she said automatically.

"Is good, is good. Because you are new, we will not kill you for hunting in our part of town, all right?"

"Oh," Alice said. "Er . . ."

"The Dnepro divides Kiev. The Gontas and Zaliz-niaks rule as one, but everyone knows we Gontas are superior, so the Gontas hunt on the much better right bank and the weaker Zalizniaks"—she spat—"have the left. You go hunt over there for when you need meat, not over here."

"Right," Gavin said. "Good advice. Thanks."

"Is good, is good," Ivana said again. "Circus is in town, you know. We have seen. Wonderful elephant. You must visit. Perhaps we will bring elephant to our house for private entertainment for important foreign guests."

"Oh, we shouldn't . . . ," Alice began.

"No, no, not you." Ivana waved a gloved hand. "You are not important. We are only telling you be-cause tomorrow night we are busy with guests and perhaps you can hunt then without that we kill you. You go now. Keep chocolate. Very good for luring chil-dren."

The large bird turned and lumbered away into the city, its cage dangling open. The six little birds lay on the street like half-melted metal candles. Alice looked at the box in her hand, then abruptly tossed it away and scrubbed her hand against her skirt.

"That was very strange," Gavin said absently.

"Do you *truly* think so?" Alice couldn't keep the dis-gust out of her voice.

"Definitely. Your parasol should have lasted much longer." He took it from her and held it up to a street-light with a critical air. The amber had turned black. "I'll have to look at the design."

"Gavin!"

"Eh? Oh! I'm sorry." He handed her the parasol, straightened his clothes, adjusted the fiddle case, which was still fastened to his back, and went down on one knee. "Alice, Lady Michaels, will you marry—"

"Oh, good heavens!" Alice was all set to be angry, but she caught a glimpse of her reflection in a window that the ever-present light had turned into a mirror. The sight of her wild hair and disheveled clothing and smoking parasol brought out a burst of laughter instead. It overcame her, and she laughed and laughed. Some baroness she was. An image of her late father's probable reaction to the entire situation popped into her mind, and for a moment, she understood why Gavin laughed so hard on that awful day in the ringmaster's travel car. The ridiculousness of the entire world was pointed in her direction, and helpless laughter was the only response. She nearly bent double under the onslaught. Gavin scrambled upright and put his arm around her.

"Are you all right?" he asked.

"Per-perfectly," she gasped. "Good heavens. Will you marry me, indeed!" And she laughed some more while the gargoyles and dead metal birds overhead looked on. "You're a true rogue, Gavin Ennock. I don't know how I ever let you go before."

Before Gavin could respond, a shot rang out from the direction Ivana Gonta's bird had taken. A second shot followed. Alice's laughter instantly ceased. Gavin's eyes met hers with the same thought.

"Feng," they both said.

Chapter Ten

"We shouldn't have let him go off on his own," Alice panted as they ran. "Foolish in the extreme. What were thinking?"

"Guilt later," Gavin said. "Run now."

The twisting, narrow streets remained eerily silent and empty—except for plague zombies. They seemed to be everywhere, rooting through garbage bins, lurking in doorways, shying away from the lights on the main streets. Male and female, adult and child, Gavin noticed enough to populate a small village, and those were only the ones he saw. He had never seen so many plague zombies in his life. Alice was noticing them too, he could tell. She flexed her gauntlet as they hurried on, itching to stop and help them, but they didn't dare. Not now. They had to keep running.

The trouble was, they didn't know exactly where they were running to. Gavin's keen ears tracked the sound of the two shots to a general area perhaps six or seven blocks away, but when they arrived at the place, they found nothing but an empty street.

"Here!" Alice plucked a pair of pistols from the pave stones as another plague zombie shuffled into shadow. The pistols were bent and broken. "Good heavens. What do—?"

"Sh!" Gavin held up a hand, hoping, and for once the clockwork plague cooperated. It rushed through him, thinning the world, making it transparent. Scents of oil and carbon and phosphorous floated on the air as conspicuous as feathers. Bits and beams of light rushed in a trillion directions, bouncing and battering against one another, trying to make a pattern amid their own chaos. Vibrations small and thunderous moved stone and brick and air and water, pressing and moving and swirling the mix. He felt the steady thrum and thud of factory dynamos in the distance, sensed thousands of heartbeats from the people tending them, felt electricity flick and dance. Through it all, he heard a steady pattern, a *click-clack*, *click-clack* combined with the hiss and swoop of steam trapped in a metal tube. The bird.

"This way," he said, taking Alice's hand. "Hurry!"

They followed Gavin's heightened hearing, tripping on curbs and stumbling on cobblestones because Gavin remained more intent on listening to directions than on watching where he was going. The neighborhood shifted from lower-class residential to a mercantile district, with signs in Cyrillic that hovered at the edge of Gavin's understanding, and he became aware that if he stopped and studied them long enough, they would begin to make sense, but he didn't stop. The *click-clack*, *click-clack* continued, growing louder. Ivana was taking her time, which allowed them to catch up. At last, puffing and sweating, they came to a street that ended in an enormous courtyard with a spurting fountain in the center. Beyond the fountain stood a high wall that surrounded an enormous mansion of white stone topped by yet more gargoyles and grotesques. An automaton in the curved armor and metal skirt of an old-fashioned Cossack warrior was opening a double-wide iron gate with a Г and a З wrought into the center to admit Ivana and her bird. The claw-cum-cage that made up the bird's head was closed again, and inside it knelt a familiar figure: Feng Lung. His face was tight with fear. The sight stabbed Gavin with guilt. It was his fault Feng was in this mess. The thought jolted him out of the clockwork fugue. The world's minutiae vanished, and he became abruptly aware of his body again. Pain and exhaustion crashed over him. His lungs and legs burned in equal parts.

Alice tried to shout something at Ivana, but she was too out of breath to make more than a squeak. Gavin was equally at a loss.

"Do . . . something . . . ," Alice panted.

Gavin aimed one of his wristbands at Ivana and triggered the polaretic magnetized pulsation device he had built only that afternoon. A gear shot from it and flicked straight at Ivana, but they were well over twenty yards away, and by the time the gear crossed the intervening distance, the automaton had swung the iron gates shut and the gear bounced off the bars. Ivana never even noticed. The automaton went to a guard box just inside the gates and stopped moving.

Alice managed a final run up to the gates with her

parasol, her loose hair streaming out behind her. For an insane moment, Gavin thought of Joan of Arc attacking an English castle. She reached the gates, grabbed one of the bars with her gauntleted hand, and jumped back with a yelp. Gavin summoned the strength to hurry over.

"An electric field?" he asked.

"I believe so." She shook out her hand. "Godd— Good heavens, Gavin. It's our fault. If we hadn't argued with Feng, he would have stayed with us and . . . Oh, I don't know what to do."

"Peasants do not approach the gate," the automaton said, coming out of its box. "Peasants go to the rear for deliveries. Remove yourselves!"

Gavin stepped back, partly in surprise and partly to avoid brushing against the electrified gate. "It speaks English?"

"I speak a number of languages, peasant!" said the automaton. "Go around to the back!"

"Who is Ivana Gonta?" Alice asked.

"One of several members of the Gonta-Zalizniak collective family. Do you have a delivery for her?"

"Yes." She held up her parasol. "Special order."

"Go around to the back and wait for a proper hour. Your package will be admitted. You will not."

"It's not going to let us in," Gavin murmured. "Can we get over, do you think?"

They both eyed the wall. It was at least eighteen feet high, studded with gargoyles, and likely contained a number of nasty surprises. All they had with them was a broken electrical parasol, a spider gauntlet that cured plague, a glass cutlass, and a set of wristbands Gavin had tested only sporadically. Although the parasol had proven marvelously effective, they had still severely underestimated the power of the local clockworkers. Meanwhile, Feng was inside the place, enduring heaven only knew what. Gavin thought of Charlie's bare brain and his hands chilled at the thought of his friend Feng in the hands of someone with the intelligence to perform such a procedure and who referred to human beings as meat. He wanted to find a way to storm the gates, flatten the automaton guard, and force Ivana to release Feng, but he couldn't think of a way to accomplish any of it. He turned helplessly to Alice. She set her mouth.

"We have to leave and come back," she said firmly. "With more tools and lots of help."

"The Gontas and Zalizniaks aren't exactly a family, strictly speaking, strictly speaking," Harry said. "They are a . . . collection, really."

"Collection," Gavin said. "What does that mean?"

Harry puffed on his cigar and cast a sidelong look at Alice. They were talking in what was euphemistically referred to as the Black Tent, though it was neither black nor a tent. It was actually a boxcar outfitted as a laboratory, with tools hanging on the walls, a portable forge heating up one corner, and half-finished machines littering the tables that lined the walls. It belonged to Dodd, who wasn't a clockworker but who did have enough of a facility with machines to repair or even build basic clockwork designs, though nothing on the level that Alice could do. It was here that he had tinkered together the windup toys for Gavin and Tom when they were children, visiting the circus with Captain Naismith. The place smelled of machine oil, bitter coal smoke, and metal shavings, and made Gavin think of a time when he was still learning his way around an airship. Dodd called it the Black Tent because the work area had once been a blacksmith's tent. When the circus became wealthy enough, Dodd had bought a boxcar for everything, but the original name had stuck.

Gavin was feeling restless again, and as happened on the train in Dodd's car when he guarded Alice's sleep, his hands went to work without him. A spool of Dr. Clef's alloy sat in his lap. He wound more of it and snipped rings free of the dowel. He had quite a collection now.

Harry continued to hesitate. Finally Alice spoke up. "If you're worrying about offending my delicate sensibilities, Mr. Burks, please stop. We don't have time for nonsense. You must speak plainly."

The rotund man moved his cigar to the other side of his mouth. "Very well, very well." He cleared his throat. "I don't know how much Ukrainian history you know—"

"Maksym Zalizniak was a Cossack who rose up at an outbreak of the clockwork plague," Alice said crisply. "He used Ivan Gonta and other powerful clockworkers to construct machines of war that forced out the Russians and the Poles—and then the Jews and the Catholics—so they could take back Ukraine and form their own empire. Get on with it."

"Yes, well," Harry said, "it didn't stop there, of course. The Zalizniak clan took the left bank, or western half, of Kiev and Ukraine, while the Gonta clan took the right, or east. At first they got along very well, but things devolved very quickly, very quickly. Cossacks fight as a way of life, you see, and once they didn't have the Russians and Poles to kick around anymore, they turned inward. The two clans bickered and sniped and fought all the time, all the time, their clockworkers ran rampant, and the people of Kiev were caught in the middle. They especially fought over the dam—and the power it generates."

"But the house we saw had the two Cyrillic letters in the gate," Gavin said. "A *g* and a *z*. They seem to be getting along fine now."

"That's the mystery," Harry said. "Clockworkers don't cooperate. Fifty or sixty years ago, the Gontas smashed the Zalizniaks flat, but instead of killing their rivals, they merged with them. How, no one knows, no one knows. Now, instead of having two collective families, they have just one, just one."

"How do you get a family of clockworkers?" Alice said. "They don't . . . they can't . . ."

Gavin held his face impassive over the growing net of rings. He knew very well what Alice was trying not to say, that clockworkers, including him, died within three years of contracting the plague. Family relationships were cut unfortunately short. A sudden longing to see his own children filled him, made all the worse for the fact that he knew it could never come to pass, and he had to turn his face away for a moment to get himself under control. China. China would have the cure, if only they could get there.

"That's the delicate part." Harry coughed and reddened. "You see, the Gonta-Zalizniaks operate on a process of . . . assimilation."

"I don't understand," Alice said.

"Nor should you, nor should you. The clans use a sort of forced adoption, you see. Any clockworker who appears in Ukraine is quickly snapped up by the Gonta-Zalizniaks and indoctrinated. I hear that by the time the process is over, they truly believe they are Gonta or Zalizniak." He coughed around his cigar. "They also engage in experiments on . . . younger folk. There's a belief that children are more likely to survive the plague and become clockworkers, so . . ."

Alice's face paled and she staggered back against one of the tables. "You mean they deliberately infect children with the clockwork plague in an attempt to create more clockwork geniuses?"

Harry looked unhappy. "It's only rumor, only rumor," he said quickly. "People are always looking for explanations about why Kiev seems to have more clockworkers than a city its size should."

"Numbers," Gavin put in, though he was speaking through greasy nausea. "If you think about it for a moment, you'll realize that *somewhere* has to have the highest percentage of clockworkers. Kiev is simply it."

"Of course, of course." Harry chewed his cigar. "It's a difficult rumor to unseat, however, when it couples with the fact that the plague got its start here."

"Is *rumored* to have gotten its start here," Alice corrected. "No one knows where the plague started. Kiev just has the first recorded cases. The eighteenth century kept very poor records, unlike modern times."

"This isn't getting us any closer to Feng," Gavin interrupted. He wound more wire around the dowel and snipped. "What is Ivana going to do with him?"

"Who knows?" Harry sighed. "He's not a clock-worker, so he won't be indoctrinated. Clockworkers have free rein here with anyone they capture, and Ivana Gonta can do as she wishes with him. Kievites have been forced to become adept at avoiding clock-workers, so there's a shortage of subjects these days. I hate to sound harsh, but she's likely experimenting on him right now."

A silence fell over the trio. In the distance, the calliope hooted a cheery song in B-flat, keeping time for one of the acts rehearsing in the Tilt. An idea stole over Gavin.

"How many clockworkers are in that house?" he asked. His fingers moved faster with wire and pliers, creating what looked like a framework of chain mail. He was adding to what already existed, which was currently the size of an evening cloak. On the floor nearby sat a framework and pack and machine parts that awaited assembly.

"No idea, no idea," Harry said. "Could be two, could be two hundred. And all of them made to specialize in instruments of war. I've said it before—it's a pity they don't turn their efforts toward a cure for the plague. They might have found one by now. At any rate, the place is a fortress guarded by bloodthirsty lunatics. I don't like to say it, but I think your friend is gone. Gone."

"No," Gavin said. "Maybe not."

"What are you thinking, darling?" Alice asked. The note of hope in her voice pulled Gavin's spirits up and gave him more confidence. He set down the growing net of links.

"I think we need to go see Dr. Clef."

* * *

Dr. Clef was working in the little laboratory aboard the *Lady* with Click watching intently from a perch on a high shelf. He looked up in surprise when Gavin slid the door open. Alice and Harry stood in the hallway behind him.

"Yes?" said Dr. Clef slowly. He was sitting on a high stool.

"I don't have time for nice," Gavin said. "I need my paradox generator back."

Dr. Clef blinked at him. "Generator? What generator, my boy?"

"I know you didn't destroy it like I asked you to," Gavin continued. "It was too beautiful for me to destroy, so how could you do it? If I hadn't been distracted at the time, I would have realized it earlier. Give it back. Now."

"I don't have it." Dr. Clef's expression remained perfectly ingenuous. "Honestly, I don't."

"Like I said," Gavin told him, "no time for nice. So." He reached up and took Click down from the high shelf. The clockwork cat looked at him with curious phosphorescent eyes until Gavin flipped him over and lightly depressed a switch on the underside of Click's throat. Click froze.

"Gavin, what on earth?" Alice demanded.

"No!" Dr. Clef said.

"Hand over the generator, Doctor," Gavin said, "or I'll press it all the way. All the power in his spring will release at once, and he'll shut down."

Dr. Clef looked horrified. "Not my clicky kitty. Please!"

"The generator, Doctor."

A torn expression crossed Dr. Clef's face. He looked at Click and at Gavin, then flicked his gaze to a low storage cupboard. Alice edged around him and from the cupboard pulled the generator, complete with its crank and speaking trumpet.

"I'll need the ear protectors, too," Gavin said, and Alice snagged them from their hook. Dr. Clef appeared crestfallen, so Gavin handed Click to him. The cat recovered quickly and shook his head. Dr. Clef smoothed the creature's wiry whiskers.

"You wouldn't have done it," Dr. Clef said, sounding like a recalcitrant child.

"It wouldn't have hurt him, Doctor," Alice said. "Though it would have taken an hour or more to wind him back up. And I might remind you that Click is *my* cat."

"That is not how he feels." Dr. Clef tickled Click under the chin. "No, he does *not*, he does *not*."

"As you like." Alice sighed. "We have to rescue Feng. Do you want to come?"

Dr. Clef looked genuinely puzzled. "Who is Feng?"

"Chinese man, little younger than me, so high," Gavin said. "Likes the ladies. And the—"

"Gavin!" Alice interrupted.

"I do not remember him." Dr. Clef cuddled Click. "Please leave me alone now."

"If that's what you want," Gavin said. "Right now we have to collect Kemp and find Dodd."

The first show of the day was just finishing up in the Tilt. A sell-out audience of all ages applauded and cheered from crowded bleachers while the Mysterious Yins, clad in red, went through their routine in the ring. Gavin thought of Feng and tried not to feel sick. Maybe Ivana was just holding him for now and hadn't started in on him yet. He tried not to think of Feng clamped to an operating table with Ivana Gonta looming over him, tools at the ready, but worry and guilt continued to gnaw at him. This was taking so *long*.

A roped-off section down in front kept a group of dignitaries and their families and attendant automaton servants separated from the rabble. Many of the men wore red military uniforms and carried wicked-looking dress swords, and the women wore rich dresses in bright blues and blood reds, with heavy brocaded skirts and fur jackets. Even the children were carefully outfitted. More than one little girl carried a clockwork doll. And then it slapped Gavin in the face. This was what had been bothering him since he had arrived in Kiev: These were the first children he had seen in public. In all the crowds he had seen in the city, every person had been an adult. No children walked with their parents, none played in streets or alleyways. Except for the wealthy ones Gavin had just noticed, none attended this very circus. The only children Gavin had seen were among the families Alice had cured and zombies on the night streets. He thought of Ivana Gonta and her chocolate. Did all of Kiev keep their children indoors?

Three Yins boosted high poles upright while three others leaped from one to the other with the agility of lemurs. The audience applauded again. Off to one side waited the clowns, ready to gently shoo the audience away once this act was done. Gavin, Alice, and Kemp slipped behind the bleachers to the place where Dodd waited between acts and found him. He wore his usual red-and-white striped shirt and red top hat.

"He's not going to like this," Alice said in Gavin's ear. "How are you going to persuade him to take a circus parade to the Gonta House?"

"The Gonta House?" Kemp said. "That would be dreadfully dangerous, Madam!"

"I don't know how," Gavin admitted. "I'm flying blind."

Dodd saw them approaching and gave them a quizzical look.

"We need to talk," Gavin said quietly. "I'm not—"

"Can it wait?" Dodd interrupted. "We're all about to be very busy."

"Busy?" Gavin said. The audience laughed at the antics of the youngest Yin. "I thought the show was almost over."

"This arrived halfway through the second act."

He showed Gavin a letter. In neat handwriting with a strange slant was written:

> Come with circus to Gonta House for private
> performance immediately. Bring magnificent elephant.
> Gonta

"Oh," Gavin said.

"It came with a bag of money," Dodd added. "Linda spouted some nonsense about the three of swords, but for that much money, I'll face the hundred of swords. We leave in ten minutes."

"Might Gavin and I ride the elephant?" asked Alice.

*   *   *

The elephant lumbered down the gritty, twisting streets at the head of another parade. Dodd, never one to give up the chance for publicity, insisted on a show. They had even installed a gaudy brass gondola atop the elephant. Normally Gavin would have enjoyed the experience—he was riding atop the elephant at the head of a parade with Alice next to him—but all he could think about was Feng.

Somewhat over a year ago, before the Third Ward, before the clockwork plague, before Alice, Gavin had been busking in London's Hyde Park. A young man from the Orient—Feng—had rushed out of the fog and begged Gavin to help him. Gavin hid Feng and persuaded the young man's pursuers that Feng had gone off in another direction. In gratitude, Feng gave Gavin the clockwork nightingale that re-created sounds. Much later, Gavin learned that Feng was the son of the Chinese ambassador to England and nephew of the emperor. When the ambassador discovered Gavin and Alice were fleeing to China, he asked them to take Feng along, since Feng clearly wasn't suited to carry on his father's career. Since none of them spoke a Chinese language, it seemed a good idea to bring him along. Besides, Gavin liked Feng. He was funny, and had a wistful air about him. It was only lately that he'd become surly, for reasons Gavin didn't understand. Maybe something was bothering him, something more than just being housed among acrobats. He should have spoken up.

But did you ask? Gavin thought. *Some friend you turned out to be.*

"I still think this seems terribly fortuitous," Alice complained. "Much too fortuitous."

"Why can't we have a piece of good luck for once?" Gavin countered, then added, "Don't answer that. I agree with you, actually, though Ivana Gonta *did* say last night that she had guests to entertain and she wanted to see the elephant. It's not that much of a coincidence. Maybe we actually *are* lucky. Those particles Charlie mentioned flipping at the same time to help us."

"Hm," was Alice's only response.

He shifted the pack on his back and checked his wristbands for the fifth or sixth time. Alice's parasol, newly repaired, gleamed as she waved it at the people crowding the sidewalk. A whistle dangled from a silver chain around her neck. Calliope music tootled behind them, drawing along stilt walkers, acrobats, horse acts, and animal cages. The parade scribbled a stream of bright colors through the gray city to the wide courtyard Gavin remembered from the previous night. By now it was noon, and Feng had been in Ivana Gonta's clutches for twelve hours.

Hang on, Feng, Gavin thought. *We're coming.*

The automaton guard flung the gates open and Alice guided the puffing elephant through. Its brass back was warm, almost hot, from the boilers contained inside it. Beyond the gate lay another wide courtyard, again all cobbles and stone. The blocky white mansion bent itself in a square C to make the courtyard. It reminded Gavin uncomfortably of a prison, and he remembered that the Gontas built the place at least partly in defense against the Zalizniaks across the river. An impressive set of steps rose up to a columned portico.

At the base of the steps looking out over the courtyard were a series of long tables all set with fine linen, gleaming silver, and faceted crystal. A crowd of people dressed even more richly than the dignitaries at the circus occupied benches and divans and chairs placed all about the tables, and they were laughing and talking. Food—roast pork and hams and birds and fruits and dumplings and potatoes and soups—crowded serving platters, and the mingled delicious smells made Gavin dizzy. His stomach reminded him that he hadn't eaten since yesterday. Automatons of many shapes bustled about. Human-shaped ones replaced food and refilled glasses of *kvas* and vodka. Spiders scampered about, cleaning up spills and delivering fresh napkins. Several clockwork cats similar to Click lounged among the dinner guests.

When the circus paraded through the gate, the dinner guests stared and pointed. A few clapped. Dodd trotted smartly to the forefront as Ivana Gonta emerged from the crowd to meet him. She wore a pink afternoon dress with a low neckline more suited to an indoor spring tea than an outdoor autumn banquet, but the chill in the air didn't seem to bother her. A red haze settled over Gavin's vision and he realized he was growling.

"If she's up here," Alice pointed out quietly, "it means she isn't doing anything to Feng at the moment. Maybe she's been busy arranging this little event and hasn't had time to touch him."

"I hope so," Gavin said through clenched teeth. "For her sake."

"We just need to wait until— Eep!" Alice whuffed

her parasol open and twirled it, effectively blocking Gavin's view of the banqueters. "Don't look."

"At what?" Gavin's muscles tensed. The calliope continued to play. Some of the clowns waved and made faces at the banqueters while they waited for a signal from Dodd to begin. "What's wrong? I can't see a thing."

"On a count of three," Alice murmured, face pale, "we'll climb out the back of the gondola, slide off the elephant's back, and sneak to the rear to get Kemp."

"Why?" Gavin demanded in a whisper. "What is it?"

"Look, but do it quick. In the center, a little to the left. What would be Ivana Gonta's right-hand place at her table."

Gavin poked his head just high enough over the parasol to get a look, then dropped back down behind it and the gondola wall. "Shit," he said. "Shit shit shit."

Sitting at the place Alice had described were three familiar figures: Simon d'Arco, Glenda Teasdale, and Lieutenant Susan Phipps.

Chapter Eleven

"**Q**uick!" Gavin took Alice's hand, and they slid down the elephant's backside even as Dodd called forward the Great Mordovo, Magician Extraordinaire. The circus had spread throughout the courtyard, leaving a wide space in front in an impromptu ring. Gavin wove his way to the rear of the waiting performers, his heart in his mouth. Bonzini, the clown whose wig and nose Gavin had borrowed back in Luxembourg, gave him a quizzical look as the banqueters gave light applause to Mordovo's first trick.

"Did she see us?" Alice asked. She clutched at the whistle hanging from its chain from around her neck.

"I doubt it. Phipps wouldn't have let us get away if she had."

At the back, near the closed gate, they found Kemp standing not far from the automaton guard in his guard house. He came forward when he saw Alice. The animal cages and other performers hid them from view. The people stood around, waiting quietly for their turn. It wasn't the entire circus, just the performers whose acts didn't require much in the way of setup—clowns, the magician, acrobats, animal acts both living and mechanical, horse girls, and the calliope. The latter played bright, happy music, which had the effect of covering noise and conversation. The acts themselves were silent, anyway. No traveling circus depended on an audience being able to hear or understand the language.

"Madam," Kemp said, "I don't think I approve of—"

"I know," Alice said, "but it's necessary." She faced the guard and gave the handle of her parasol a single turn. "You. I need to talk to you."

The automaton took a single step forward. "Peasants are not allowed to—"

Alice touched its chest with the end of her parasol. Electricity crackled. The guard sputtered and sparked while energy coruscated up and down its body. Then it went stiff and tipped over with small crash. The lion tamer and his wife turned and stared. Alice put a finger to her lips while Gavin extracted a tool kit from his rucksack. The smell of oil and feel of metal brought a strange taste to his mouth, and he felt the clockwork fugue descending on him. Very little mattered now except the machines. In no time at all, he had the automaton's head off. Alice turned back to Kemp.

"Kemp," she said.

"Madam," he said with resignation.

Alice took up the tools herself and also removed Kemp's head. The lights that made up his eyes glowed with indignation, but he didn't speak. His black-and-white body remained eerily upright. Gavin swiftly unbuttoned the front of the guard's jacket and shirt to expose and open the access panel, where he saw frozen pistons and unmoving gears. Automatically he traced the line of machinery. It was simple to understand, easy as reading a navigation chart, though a part of him was aware that only a few months ago it would have been a meaningless tangle to him. While Alice set Kemp's head on the automaton's neck, Gavin set to work resetting power. He was vaguely aware that Alice was touching his tools, and he didn't like it.

"It's not a perfect fit," she muttered, "but it'll do for now."

"That's my wrench," he said shortly.

"It's called a spanner," she replied, "and you need to keep control, please. You're not a mad clockworker. You're Gavin Ennock, and you love me."

Her words and voice penetrated the fugue and pulled him back a bit. He shook his head. "Right," he said. "Sorry. Thanks."

"I am not at all comfortable with this," Kemp complained as they worked.

"It's for a good cause." Alice connected a set of wires and tightened two bolts. In the background, a lion roared over the music and the banqueters made *Ooooo* sounds. "That should do it. Can you start the body back up?"

In answer, Gavin cranked up the spark generator and released the spring.

"Oh!" Kemp's eyes flickered. "Oh dear!"

"Are you functional?" Alice asked, helping him sit up.

"I-I-I-I b-b-believ-v-v-v-ve th-th-th-th-things a-a-a-a-a-a-a-are working at c-c-c-c-c-capacity, M-M-M-M-

M-Madam." Static overlaid his voice, and he spat out a string of Ukrainian words. "I a-a-a-a-a-am adj-j-j-j-j-j-j-justing m-m-m-m-m-my mem-m-m-m-mory wheels."

"Try this." Alice reached into his chest cavity with a screwdriver. Something crackled and she jerked her hand back with small oath. "Ow! Is that better?"

"M-much, Madam. *Spaceeba*." Kemp got to his new feet, a little uncertain at first but quickly gaining confidence. "This body is much stronger than my own, and more agile. More advanced, disloyal to my creator as that sounds."

Gavin's stomach went into knots as he shoved Kemp's body into the guard house and set the guard's lifeless head on the floor with it. As a final touch, he put the guard's helmet on Kemp's head. "I *really* don't like the fact that Phipps is here," he growled. "It makes everything too suspicious. The Third Ward has very little influence in Ukraine, but she's crafty enough to worm her way into the Gontas' good graces and persuade Ivana to invite the circus into a trap. I just wonder if capturing Feng was her idea or just a lucky coincidence."

"We can't call this off," Alice pointed out. "We have to find Feng."

"I know," Gavin said. "And it's exactly the kind of thing Phipps would count on. Let's go. Lead the way, Kemp."

The trio skirted the back edge of the circus and, following the high stone wall, came around to one of the jutting wings of the huge mansion that surrounded the courtyard where the lions were currently performing through the calliope's incessant hooting. The banqueters were alternately watching and eating and talking. Through the crowd, Gavin could make out Phipps's ramrod figure sitting next to Ivana Gonta's plump one on a shared divan. She was holding a crystal goblet in one hand and watching the lion tamer while Ivana talked to her. A polite, attentive smile creased Phipps's face, and it looked completely wrong on her. She was wearing a scarlet dress uniform with a gold sash that Gavin had never seen before. At any moment, she might turn in their direction and see them. But then they made the corner of the house and she passed out of sight.

"That's a relief," Alice sighed. "Crossing that courtyard was like walking on hot knives."

"We're only getting started," Gavin replied. They hurried alongside the house. The windows were small and thick, as if the builders were trying to maintain a fortress wall but had been forced to put glass into it. They finally came to a heavy door. Gavin tried it. Locked.

"Allow me, Sir." Kemp extended a finger into the keyhole and twisted. The door opened with a click. Beyond was a wide foyer with a stone floor faced with a number of closed doors and a large archway through which Gavin could see quite a number of human servants rushing back and forth, presumably to wait on the banquet. The moment they crossed the threshold, a pair of automatons stationed on either side of the door, duplicates of the one at the gate, instantly sprang to life. Sabers hummed in their hands and one of them said something in Ukrainian.

"Kemp," Alice said.

Kemp came forward. At the sight of the gate automaton's body, the guards lowered their sabers and the humming sound stopped. Kemp spoke to them. Gavin held his breath. This had to work. If it didn't, or if the guards shouted an alarm, an entire army of clockworkers would come down on their heads. Worse, Phipps would find them. Gavin kept his face impassive as Kemp talked, and Gavin's inability to understand the language became an agony. There was a terrible pause. Gavin's blood sang in his ears and his mouth was dry as sand. Then the automatons nodded and returned to their stations. The trio stepped quickly past the foyer. Gavin's legs went a little unsteady.

"Perfect," Alice murmured, appearing completely unruffled. "Now where?"

Gavin made himself regain calm. "Down," he said. "Clockworkers usually like nice, safe laboratories underground. Remember your aunt Edwina."

"She had two such laboratories," Alice agreed. "Which way?"

"If I may, Madam," Kemp said. He led them through the enormous house. Gavin forced himself to stand upright and act as if he had every right to be there, though he wanted to scrunch down and creep through the house like a rat. It wasn't just that he was here to steal away something—someone—that the Gontas no doubt saw as their property. It was also that he had spent his childhood in a tiny, crowded flat that in this house would probably fit into a closet. Everything here spoke of easy, intimidating wealth. Brass and gold fixtures were everywhere, along with heavy furniture of brocade and velvet. Bejeweled metal statues with a definite clockwork air occupied a number of niches. Even one of them would have kept his family going for a year back in Boston, and he felt an urge to snatch, even though he'd never stolen in his life. One of the statues in a room they passed but didn't enter looked to be of the Virgin Mary, though her face was stern, and her robes were jagged, as if made of lightning bolts. Over her heart was a cog. Two automatons knelt before the statue, hands clasped. They murmured in monotone.

"What are they saying?" Alice whispered as they went by.

"One is praying for the soul of someone, a deceased person, Dmitro," Kemp said. It was strange hearing his voice coming from a Ukrainian automaton. "The other is reciting prayers in penitence for sins committed by Ivana Gonta."

"The Gontas use automatons to *pray* for them?" Alice said, aghast.

"I wonder if it works," Gavin muttered.

"I wouldn't know, Sir," Kemp said. "This way."

They passed many servants, both human and mechanical, and neither type gave them a second glance with Kemp leading the way. One woman with a large set of keys did pause to ask something of Alice, but Kemp spoke to her, and she went on her way before Gavin even had time to get uneasy.

"What was that about?" he asked, shifting the pack on his back.

"That was the head housekeeper, Sir. She wanted to know who Sir and Madam were," Kemp said. "I told her I was giving a tour of the house to a pair of important people attached to Madam Gonta's special guests."

"You're a treasure, Kemp," Gavin told him.

"Sir."

"Where *are* we going?" Alice said. "I'm lost already."

"I'm seeing a pattern," Gavin said before Kemp could respond. "Many of the automatons seem to be coming from one direction, so I'm assuming the entry to the lower level is down that hallway."

"A memory wheel inside this body agrees with Sir," Kemp said. "Madam and Sir have their choice of a lift or a staircase."

"Staircase," Alice said promptly. "A lift is a perfect little cage."

In a marble foyer they found a double-wide lift, complete with iron gate that reminded Gavin of the one that descended to the dungeonlike cells where the Third Ward housed its captive clockworkers, no few of which Gavin himself had brought in with Simon d'Arco. Next to it was an archway opening onto a staircase that spiraled downward out of sight. Two guard automatons drew their sabers and rapped out orders in Ukrainian.

"They won't let anyone go down those stairs, Madam," Kemp said. "Only members of the Gonta family may do so."

"I see." Alice stepped forward smartly and touched the guard's saber with the tip of her parasol. A spark snapped and Gavin smelled ozone. The guard stiffened. Alice's parasol flicked like a sword at the other guard, who parried it with the saber, but the touch was all Alice needed. The spark snapped, and the second guard went still. Alice straightened her hat, pushed a tendril of honey-brown hair out of her eyes, and caught Gavin looking at her.

"What?" she said.

Gavin was grinning from ear to ear. "You are re-markable, you know that? How many other women could fence with a pair of automatons and win?"

"Oh." Alice looked flustered. "Probably not many."

"And I'm glad." He impulsively kissed her cheek. "God, I love you."

"If Madam and Sir are quite ready," Kemp said. "Someone may come at any moment."

"How much time do we have?" Alice asked, still blushing a little.

"We have been in the house for thirteen minutes," Kemp replied. "The circus was contracted for an hour's performance, leaving us forty-seven minutes."

Quickly, they posed the deactivated automatons in their original positions. Alice told Kemp to stay behind and run interference if necessary as she and Gavin headed down the stairs. The stairs, lit by a series of electric lights, twisted downward for a long, long time, and Gavin wondered how they'd manage the trip back up without using the lift, especially if they had to carry Feng.

Assuming he's still alive, he thought, and then quashed the idea. Feng had to be alive. He *would* be alive. And unharmed. Ivana hadn't held him prisoner for very long, and she must have been busy planning the banquet. Not much time to play with a new . . . acquisition.

They reached the bottom of the steps and emerged from the stairwell. Alice stopped dead and Gavin whistled under his breath.

"Good heavens," Alice murmured. "What will we do?"

The space beyond was cavernous, easily large enough to store four full-sized dirigibles, in Gavin's estimation. Worked stone arched up and away, several stories high. Rows of columns that looked too thin to hold up the ceiling—and the house above it—reached upward like graceful fingers. Staircases, ramps, doorways, and balconies studded the walls, as if a small city had exploded inside the giant room. More than forty hulking mechanicals two, three, and four times the height of a man and many times broader stood motionless on the main floor. One of them was Ivana's giant bird. The cage that made up its head hung open and empty.

Gavin felt an urge to examine the machines more closely. The clockwork plague tugged at him, and his fascinated eye measured slopes and angles, calculated area, felt volume. Forges hissed from beyond the balconies, putting out thousands of calories in heat. The sharp smell of molten metal tanged the air, and the wrenching scream of it when it hit cold water bounced and echoed. Spiders scurried across every surface, and whirligigs whooshed through the empty spaces. Most of them carried bits of machinery or wicked-looking weapons. Electric lights lit everything, as did the red glow of coals emanating from the balconies. No actual people were visible, which both puzzled and relieved Gavin. In a flash of clockwork insight, he understood that the Gonta clockworkers didn't spend much—or any—time out on the main floor, but worked in private laboratories that opened onto it. The clanking, hissing forges called to him, and the tiny laboratories on the *Lady* and in the Black Tent suddenly felt cramped and primitive. Here was a place where a man could *work*. Certainly there would be a vacant workroom somewhere in all this. In fact, he needed only to listen for empty space to find one. He could already feel the tools, see the machinery come to life under his hands. His fingers curled into fists and he started forward.

"What on earth is that?" Alice exclaimed.

Alice's voice sliced through the terrible need, and it faded. Gavin shook his head hard. "What's what?"

She pointed. "There."

Gavin followed the line of her finger. Along one wall was a row of cages with square bars, ten cages at a fast count. Inside each was a child. Some were boys, some were girls. All were under the age of twelve, some were as young as three or four. They sat or squatted within the bars, eyes listless and downcast. Each had a dog bowl of water.

"Good heavens," Alice whispered. "Oh, Gavin."

Gavin felt sick again. He didn't resist when Alice took his hand and pulled him over to the horrible enclosures. Some of the children looked up and scuttled backward in fear. Most didn't respond. A girl in a tattered gray dress reminded Gavin of his sister Violet back in Boston, and it made him want to tear the cages free of the walls.

"We have to get them out," he said. "Now."

"Look at that one," Alice said, "and that. Their faces

are flushed and their lips are cracked. It's the clock-work plague." She held up her spider gauntlet, whose eyes were glowing red. "I need to help them. I'll cure them and we'll take them out."

Gavin hesitated. He glanced around the great room uneasily, feeling torn and not a little helpless. "Alice, how are we going to get them out of here?"

"What are you talking about?"

"We can probably get these cages open with minimal work," Gavin said reluctantly, "but what then? How will we get all these children upstairs and past all the people and automatons in the house and over the wall outside? We'll get caught, the children will end up back in here, and everyone will be worse off."

Alice's expression darkened and she looked like she wanted to argue. Then she nodded once, hard. "You're right of course. But we'll find a way later."

"We will," he agreed.

"And I can still do this." She reached through the bars with her gauntleted hand and scratched one of the sick children before he could shy away. He barely whimpered, though he did shuffle to the rear of his cage, the scratches dripping blood. The others, seeing this, also drew back out of reach.

"Poor things," Alice said. "I wish I spoke Ukrainian so I could explain what's going on. At least the first one will infect the others with the cure."

One of the children began to cry, and Gavin caught something that sounded like "Mama." In that moment, Gavin nearly violated the good sense he had just quoted to Alice. He had to force himself to avoid tearing at the cages with his bare hands. His rubbed at his face and realized his cheek was wet with salt water. Damn it. He had been beaten half to death by pirates, locked in a tower by a madwoman, and infected with a disease that was killing him by inches, but *this* brought a tear to his eye?

"Let's go," Alice said, "before I pry these bars open myself."

Gavin nodded around a thick throat and, feeling wretched, forced himself to turn his back and walk away from the children. He swore to himself that the sun wouldn't set on another day before he came back for them.

"We need to concentrate," Alice said briskly. "How are we going to find Feng in all this?"

Gavin did his best to push thoughts of the children aside. Alice was right—he needed to concentrate on the mission at hand. "I already know how."

He took the silver nightingale out of his pocket. Alice reached for it, but Gavin moved it away from her. "Don't. It returns to the last person who touched it. Feng sent it back to me when the song I recorded for you in Berlin turned out not to help."

"So he was the last one to touch it," Alice finished. "Brilliant!" She paused. "Why didn't you use it when we were looking for him in the city?"

He gave her a strange look. "I didn't need to."

Alice pursed her lips, then muttered something that sounded like "Clockworker logic." "Just toss it, then. Quick!"

Gavin flung the little bird into the air. It sprang to life, fluttered in a circle, and headed for one of the staircases across the main floor. Gavin and Alice hurried to follow, dodging giant mechanicals and ducking whirligigs, feet thudding on worked stone. They dashed up the staircase with a wall on their left, just barely able to keep the little streak of silver in sight, and hurried down an arched hallway. Electric lights glared down from the ceiling.

The hallway abruptly widened into a large, dark room. Even Gavin's clockwork-enhanced eyes couldn't make out details, though he got the sense the space was round. It was certainly large enough to echo. A single beam of light from high up stabbed down to illuminate a small circle in the center of the room. In the center of the circle was a square cage six feet tall, and in the cage huddled Feng Lung. Or, Gavin assumed it was Feng. A blanket wrapped his body and head like a tattered cloak. Between the blanket and bars, Gavin could see only part of his face. It seemed to be Feng, and the nightingale zipped into the cage to land on his shoulder. The figure in the cage didn't react. Gavin wanted to run over and pull the cage open, but he also felt suspicious.

"Does this seem strange to you?" Alice whispered as they entered the room. The place was cold, almost icy. The duo stopped about twenty feet from the cage. "I mean, stranger than it should be."

"Very," Gavin whispered. He raised his voice a little. "Feng? Is that you?"

In response, the figure in the cage raised his head. The blanket fell back, revealing his face. Alice gasped. Gavin's heart jerked and nausea oozed through his stomach, though he also felt a strange and exciting fascination. Feng's hair had been shaved off, leaving nicks and cuts behind. A brass spider the size of a hand sprawled across the right side of Feng's head, its body covering his ear and its legs framing his eye, nose, and mouth. Four of the legs drilled into his skull and neck. Gavin's hand went unconsciously to his own skull, and he bit his lip. Scar tissue puckered Feng's cheek and his right eye drooped. A line of spittle ran from the corner of his mouth. He shivered with cold.

"Oh, Feng," Alice said. "What did she do?"

Feng didn't answer. He simply stared at them with his good eye. The nightingale perched motionless on his shoulder. Alice sniffled and, with a low cry, ran to the cage.

"Don't touch!" Gavin cried.

Alice halted mere inches from the icy bars. "Why?"

"It might be a trap."

Lights exploded to life all about the room. A barred gate crashed down to block the exit. Gavin flung up a hand to shield his eyes against the painful and blinding brightness. Alice cried out again.

"Really, Gavin," came the voice of Susan Phipps. "I'll have to have a word with Simon. He should have trained you better."

Gavin's heart sank. When his vision cleared, he saw the room was actually an operating theater, with Feng's cage in the bottom and high, circular walls all around. Above and out of reach, a circle of chairs ringed the room, set so anyone sitting in them could observe the events on the floor. Perhaps a dozen people in lab coats, work clothes, and formal dress occupied the chairs, including Ivana Gonta in her pink tea gown. All of them wore copper collars with buttons on them.

Among them sat Susan Phipps, flanked by Simon d'Arco and Glenda Teasdale.

"Shit," Gavin said, and not even Alice admonished him.

"Indeed." Phipps still wore the scarlet dress uniform and gold sash, though now she had added a matching hat with gold braid on the brim. "I'm actually disappointed in you both. You should have known it would be child's play to connect you with the circus and follow you here. The Countess Ivana was pleased to be involved. She has a new experimental subject, and I have you."

"You're traitors, Susan," Alice said. "All three of you. You don't even see it, do you? You're traitors to every human alive, and you live in hell."

"You're imprisoned in the circle," Glenda pointed out. Her blouse was a deep yellow. "Not us."

"Simon," Gavin said, "you were my best friend. Help me, instead of stabbing me in the back!"

Simon looked at Gavin and swallowed. His fingers clenched and unclenched. Then he looked at Phipps, set his mouth, and straightened his black jacket without saying a word. Gavin's heart dropped.

"What did you monsters do to Feng?" Alice demanded.

"Very important experiment," Ivana called down. She was sitting behind a console similar to the one Gavin had seen on her bird the night before, her hand on one of the levers. "You should be proud that he has become part of Gonta heritage."

"And Zalizniak," put in a man sitting near her.

"How did you do anything at all?" Alice continued

in the same demanding voice. She shook her parasol angrily up at them, drawing every eye to her. Gavin slowly slid his rucksack off, his eye on the lever in Ivana's hand. "You didn't even have him for a full day."

"That is Gonta-Zalizniak way," said the man who had spoken earlier. He wore a lab coat with red-brown stains that Gavin didn't want to think too closely about and a whirligig with spikes on its tiny feet sat on his shoulder near his copper collar. He pointed to himself. "Danilo Zalizniak. Our sister was not the only one to work on him. We all worked on him together."

"That's what you tell everyone," Alice huffed theatrically. "But we know clockworkers don't work together. They all want their own way and eventually tear each other to pieces. Quite literally, in some cases."

For a moment, Gavin flashed on the conflicts between himself and Dr. Clef. How long before one of them tried to kill the other? Assuming Gavin survived the next few minutes.

"Ah, that is for normal clockworkers," Danilo said. "We are not like them. We serve the family."

And Gavin saw the pattern. "That's what the collection is," he said. "You don't think of yourselves as individuals. You don't even call yourself *I*. It's always *we*. I'll bet you weren't born with the names Danilo and Ivana, either."

Danilo grinned a demon's grin. "You have good brain. We would like to see it."

"He and the baroness are mine," Phipps said. "You have the Oriental boy. As we agreed."

"So, so." Ivana removed her hand from the lever

and waved it negligently. "Perhaps we wish to change the terms of our agreement."

"What do you mean?" Glenda demanded. Simon remained silent.

"Do you think that you are the only ones who know of this cure your Alice carries?" said another woman. Her voice echoed about the chamber. "It interests us very, very much. This cure is already destabilizing Europe, and we approve. We predict that within five years, all European clockworkers will be gone because cure will destroy plague. China's machinery will continue to grow, and she will easily take all of India and Africa and possibly west coast of America before cure reaches her empire and stops creation of more dragon men. By then it will be too late. China will reign supreme."

"No," Phipps said flatly.

"Feng," Alice whispered. "Can you stand up?"

The young man stared blankly, and Gavin couldn't tell if he had understood her or not.

"Feng," Alice whispered again, "you have to stand up. Stand up!"

Feng instantly got to his feet. The blanket fell away. He was shirtless. Corded muscle moved under ivory skin recently scored with a series of terrible scars that ran across his chest and abdomen. Tiny, neat stitches held the edges together. Gavin's nausea returned. Hadn't the spider on his face been enough? What else had they done?

"Like or not like, Lieutenant," Danilo said. "It will happen. We *want* it to happen."

"Why would you want that?" Simon burst out. His voice was hoarse with stress. "It would destroy your family. Already, Alice is spreading the cure through your city. Who will become the next generation of clockworkers?"

"Is nothing, nothing," said an old man who sported a set of steel teeth. "We have our own supplies of plague. You are truly stupid man if you think that we Gontas and Zalizniaks could not manipulate plague when it started here, in our own city."

"You can cure the plague?" Alice gasped. She grabbed Gavin's hand with her bare one. "But I'd heard you couldn't."

"Of course we can," said the old man. "It is our secret. And we can infect people with it, and we have ways of increasing chances that victim will become clockworker. Is why we need children."

"Can you cure clockworkers?" Alice blurted before Gavin could ask the same question.

Ivana gave her a scornful look. "Why would we look into such things? Stupid English. Even if we wanted to destroy our clockworker family, plague changes itself when it makes clockworker and becomes quite incurable. Waste of time."

"Enough discussion," Phipps said. "I will take my prisoners and leave now."

"Nah, nah," said Ivana. "If lovely baroness fails to reach China, Chinese Emperor will rule most of world, and probably hurt Ukraine. This is bad for Gontas and Zalizniaks. Lovely baroness must reach China to spread cure more quickly and destroy Chinese Empire as well. We have agreed."

Gavin gasped. The Gontas and Zalizniaks were on their side?

"But we still think curing China is a bad idea!" Danilo Zalizniak protested. "We think that baroness must *not* reach China. Britain's weakness will let Ukraine expand west."

Ivana touched a button on her collar. Danilo cried out and clutched at his own collar with both hands, his face a rictus of pain. "We believe we came to agreement," she said mildly as Danilo rocked in his chair. "Is this not so? Speak English for benefit of our guests."

"No!" Danilo howled. "No! We— You are wrong! You Gontas are—"

Ivana touched a button on her collar again, and Danilo screamed. Alice put a hand over her mouth. Gavin stared, both sickened and transfixed. The other clockworkers watched in complete silence, though some of them—presumably Zalizniaks—looked unhappy or angry. Phipps sat in the center of them all, clearly trying to swallow her outrage. Gavin suppressed a mean smile. For once, *she* had miscalculated, overplayed her ability to persuade clockworkers.

"Baroness must reach China," Ivana said. Her tone was quiet and kind. "Do we agree, brother?"

"Yes," Danilo whimpered.

"And we should give her all aid necessary. Is this true?"

"Yes."

Another tap on Ivana's collar, and Danilo's face instantly relaxed. He slumped down in his chair. Glenda and Simon exchanged startled looks.

"What did we agree, brother?" Ivana asked, her finger still hovering over the copper at her throat.

"That . . . that the baroness should reach China," Danilo whispered. "And we should help her."

"Just so." Ivana touched a different button on her collar, and Danilo arched his back with a great gasp, but this time the expression on his face read pure pleasure instead of pain. His mouth fell open, and he groaned. Ivana released her collar, and Danilo relaxed.

"There we are," she said. "We may clean ourselves up and change into different trousers, if we desire."

"We are grateful, sister." Tears streamed down Danilo's face. "Grateful." He got up and stumbled out of the observation area.

"We are sorry you had to see that," Ivana called down to Gavin and Alice. "This is why experiment with Oriental boy is so important. If it works, we have no more arguments."

"Well," Gavin said, setting his rucksack on the floor and opening the top, "if you want Alice to reach China, I suppose that means we should be on our way. If you'll just open that gate . . ."

"We said baroness must reach China," Ivana agreed. "You, on other hand, are quite different. We need advanced clockworkers. You will join Gontas."

"Or Zalizniaks," said the old man.

Gavin had been expecting something like this, but the actual words still chilled him. Alice, meanwhile, had her traveling tools out, the ones rolled up in black velvet embroidered with *Love, Aunt Edwina* in gold thread. Ivana manipulated her console. A pair of long metal arms extended from the ceiling. They held a copper collar. Another pair of arms reached down with them, intending to grab Gavin and hold him.

"Don't fight us," the steel-toothed clockworker said. "It will go easier. Believe us."

"No!" Phipps rose. "He belongs to me!"

"Sit!" Ivana barked, and grabbed Phipps's metal hand. Two other clockworkers grabbed Simon and Glenda before the Third Ward agents could react, and handcuffed them to their chairs. Glenda shrieked in outrage. Simon kicked at his captor, who easily dodged away. The metal hands snatched at Gavin.

"Gavin!" Alice cried. She had a set of lock picks in her hands.

"Get Feng!" Gavin shouted, and the plague slowed time. He dodged the set of grasping arms and snatched the collar from the other set. Angles and trajectories drew themselves in the air for him. He moved his arm a precise two degrees to the left and half a degree down, and threw the collar. The gleaming discus spun through the air and hit the first lever on Ivana's console, the one she had been holding when the gate crashed down and the lights came up. The lever deployed, and gate cranked upward.

"What are you doing?" Ivana howled. She was still holding Phipps's arm. "How dare you?"

She reached for the lever, but Gavin raised his wristband. More angles, more trajectories. The magnetic polarizer sent a tiny gear spinning toward her, and it pinged off a button on her collar. Instantly, every clockworker in the gallery, including Ivana, screamed in pain. They clutched at their throats and howled. Phipps, her metal arm still caught in Ivana's grip, jumped and jigged in place as well, though she retained enough self-control to send Gavin a look of pure venom. The mechanical arms reaching into the cell went limp. Glenda and Simon struggled against their handcuffs, but to no avail.

"Hurry!" Gavin said to Alice. "Before the electricity stops!"

Alice already had the cold cage unlocked. She yanked it open, but Feng didn't move. "Feng!" she said. "Come on!"

At her words, Feng left the cage. Gavin snatched the set of ear protectors from his pack, put them on, and dashed out the doorway behind them. The three of them pounded down the long corridor, Gavin clutching the rucksack in front of him. They ran down the steps to the great room, and Gavin headed for the spiral staircase leading up to the main house, but Alice turned, towing Feng with her.

"What are you doing?" he asked, pulling one ear protector aside so he could hear her.

"I'm not leaving these children behind," she said.

He sighed. "I knew you were going to say that. And I agree with you. Let's go."

Alice's cure had already spread to all the children, thanks to the close quarters of the cages, and they looked healthier, more alert. She bent over the lock on the first cage, and the whistle hanging around her neck clattered against the bars. The child inside backed away from her.

"It's the same kind of lock they had on Feng's cage," she said. "I can open it almost as fast as with a key by now."

"They'll come any minute," Gavin said.

Alice didn't respond. In seconds, she had the door open, but the ragged little boy inside refused to come out. "Feng, can you tell him we're here to take him away?"

Feng didn't respond. He simply stood near the cage, the spider plastered across half his face.

"Feng!" Alice said.

And then Gavin had it. "Feng," he said, "tell the children in Ukrainian we've come to take them out of here. Tell them we've come to take them home."

Feng spoke musical Cyrillic syllables. The boy looked doubtful even as Alice unlocked the second cage. "Why does Feng listen to you?" she asked.

"You have to give him a direct order," Gavin said. "It's what the Gontas were working on—absolute obedience."

Alice looked sick. "That's horrible!"

"We'll figure it out later," Gavin said. "Open the cages before the Gontas recover."

The second and third children were more eager to leave their cages, which convinced the first child. Alice had just freed the tenth and final child when a horde of gibbering, angry Gontas appeared at the entrance of the hallway leading back to the operating theater. Ivana was at the forefront. They quickly spotted Gavin, Alice, and Feng. With a shout, they ran down the stairs. They had paused long enough to arm themselves, for they bristled with weapons—energy pistols, thunder rifles, vibration knives, quantum swords. They boiled down the steps, bounding with plague-enhanced speed, and rushed toward the three escapees and the children, who cowered in fear. Their demonic howls echoed off stone walls, and spittle sprayed from their mouths. Phipps was nowhere to be seen. Perhaps the electric shock affected her more because of her metal parts. Simon and Glenda were no doubt still in handcuffs.

Alice's lips moved, but Gavin had put the ear protectors back on and he could no longer hear her. Feng looked unfazed, but adrenaline zinged through Gavin's arteries. The Gontas and Zalizniaks weren't going to capture now. They intended to kill. Praying his plan would work, Gavin let the rucksack fall to the floor, revealing the paradox generator. He pointed the speaking trumpet toward the pack of screeching clockworkers and spun the crank hard.

This time, even through the ear protectors, he heard the faint sliding sound of the tritone paradox. It simultaneously climbed and dropped, spinning and swirling. The gaps between the intervals were all tritones, an auditory square root of two that itself stretched out into infinity, but each tritone was paired with a mirror of itself, a parallel. Instead of being painful, the sound became perfection. The sound twisted the universe into new shapes, teased the ear the way a star's gravity teased a comet. Gavin heard only a tiny part of it, and he felt a singular joy.

The effect on the clockworkers was electric. They stopped dead in their tracks, dropped their weapons, fell to their knees with the backs of their hands dragging on the floor. Every one of them stared at the generator with an open mouth. Most of them drooled like half-dead demons.

"Get the children," Gavin said, though it was difficult to speak. "We'll have to take the lift."

Alice mouthed something at Feng, who immediately herded the children toward the lift with Alice coming behind. Gavin stayed to keep the paradox generator going.

And then Danilo Gonta appeared at the top of the steps in his bloodstained white coat. He was wearing ear protectors. Gavin tensed.

"Shit," he muttered. He hadn't noticed Danilo wasn't among the crowd of Gontas he held captive with the generator, or remembered that Danilo hadn't returned after Ivana had sent him from the operating theater. Both of Gavin's hands were occupied with the generator, and Alice and Feng were already halfway to the lift with the children.

Danilo bounded down the stairs and stopped just a few steps away from Gavin. He didn't have a weapon, but that didn't mean he was unarmed. Gavin took an uncertain step backward, still cranking the generator. The faint but perfect beauty of the tritone paradox was a constant distraction.

The clockworker reached into his pocket. Gavin tensed again, and Danilo pulled out a metal stylus with a glass bulb on the end. A wire ran from the other end of the stylus and disappeared up Danilo's sleeve. He moved the stylus across the air, and it left a trail of light. Gavin stared in fascination, and he almost forgot to crank the generator.

We can hear this sound a little, Danilo wrote in glowing letters. *It creates unity! It is perfection! Name price.*

Gavin shook his head. Alice and the others were almost to the lift now.

Danilo waved the stylus and the words vanished. He started over. *We will let you and children go. We will send you on special train to China. We will stop Phipps.*

Where was Phipps, anyway? Gavin had a hard time believing she had been incapacitated for long.

"No," Gavin said, his voice muffled in his own ears. "You'll use it to control each other and other clockworkers and God only knows what else."

Danilo's face hardened in clockworker anger. *Then we destroy you and your circus and take friends for test subjects.*

Feng opened the gate to the lift and Alice herded the children aboard. She gestured at Gavin to come. He thought about an army of Cossack clockworkers and their weapons tearing through the Kalakos Circus, of Dodd and Nathan and Linda and Charlie and all the others being carted down here, infected with the clockwork plague or strapped to a table and cut open like Feng. Was that worth an invention he had intended to destroy in the first place? His hand slowed on the crank.

"You have to promise to let everyone go," Gavin said.

Done, Danilo wrote over the heads of his drooling family.

"And to arrange for that special train."

Danilo underlined the word *done*. His lips also moved as he muttered to himself, and Gavin, used to reading lips on windy airships that often swept sound away, saw him add *Ivana* and other words he assumed were Ukrainian. The clockwork plague helped him make lightning connections in Gavin's mind. Realizations snapped and clicked together, and Gavin's blood went cold. Danilo was lying. He had no intention of letting anyone go. He—they—wanted to use the generator as a weapon against the Gonta clockworkers, and Danilo Zalizniak would do or say anything to get his hands on it. The Cossacks, who had already broken a compact with Phipps, would have no compunctions about breaking one with Gavin.

He sped up the crank. "No!" he shouted. "I'll see you in hell first."

Danilo leaped at him with a snarl, smearing golden letters. But Gavin's combat training with the Third Ward took over. He jumped straight up and caught Danilo in the chest with a snap kick that barely interrupted the generator's lovely drone. Danilo fell back and slammed into Ivana, who toppled over without caring. One side of Danilo's ear protectors came off, exposing him to the tritone paradox, and a look of ecstasy descended on his face. He sprawled across Ivana's plump body, already drooling.

"Your second orgasm of the day," Gavin said, and kicked him in the crotch. "That's for Feng and the children, you son of a bitch."

The thud as his boot connected felt good. For a moment, Danilo's face vanished, and it was replaced by Madoc Blue, the pirate who had cornered Gavin on the *Juniper* and tried to take his trousers down. He was the first mate who had sliced the flesh on Gavin's back with a whip. Gavin hadn't had a normal night's sleep since. Nightmares made the dark restless, and every morning, Gavin jerked awake, his heart pounding. This terrible man drooling on the floor before him was the symbol of everything that was wrong in this world, everything that had gone wrong in Gavin's life. And he was helpless.

It occurred to Gavin with terrible certainty that he could end the entire problem here and now. It would be child's play to kill every Gonta in the room, even with the generator occupying his hands. He could knock the Gontas over, one by one, and stand on their disgusting throats until they suffocated, or break each of their loathsome necks with well-placed kicks. And all the while they would thank him for the lovely, deadly music. He and Alice and Feng and the children could walk out of the house, free and clear. How sweet that would be.

He planted himself, aimed the first kick that would snap a Cossack neck. And then a touch on his shoulder brought him around. Alice was there.

Come on! she mouthed. *Hurry!*

Gavin hesitated. Alice. Beautiful, practical Alice. She was standing beside him, in the same place, in the same danger, and yet it never even occurred to her to execute the Gontas.

She plucked at his sleeve. *Why the wait?* she mouthed. *Come!*

How would she react if he killed a group of helpless people, no matter how filthy and foul? And . . . how would *he* react later? Only a few days ago, the thought of killing a man with his energy whip had filled him with fear and disgust. Now he was calmly considering destroying a roomful of people. What was he becoming? What was this city turning him into? His skin crawled even as his hand continued to turn the generator. He wouldn't let himself become their sort of demon.

"Let's go," he said. Still playing, he turned his back on the Gontas and let Alice lead him to the lift.

Chapter Twelve

The lift gate clanged shut and Gavin stopped cranking the strange machine in his hands. Instantly the
eerie, nail-biting noise ended, and Alice breathed a
sigh of relief. Gavin popped the protectors off his ears
and hung them around his neck.

"They'll stay in that stupor for a few minutes longer," he said. "We need to hurry."

The lift was crowded with the ten children, Gavin,
Alice, and Feng. Feng, with the dreadful spider
sprawled across half his face like a brass scar. It made
Alice sick with guilt to see it and the scars that puckered his chest and torso. She felt bad enough after seeing Feng, and the thought of leaving the children
behind in those cages . . . well, that was quite impossible, no matter what the risk to her own safety might be.

Alice spun the crank on the lift control and moved
the lever, unable to read the Cyrillic characters but
hoping UP and DOWN would be in the same places as
an English lift. The lift jerked upward, making the chil-

dren gasp in fear. They shied away from Feng and clustered around Alice likes chicks around a hen. Two of them clutched her hands, despite the iron spider on her left. This was, strangely, her first prolonged contact with children, and she couldn't decide whether the odd circumstances of the occasion should make her laugh at the ridiculousness of it or howl with outrage at the injustice.

"Are you all right, Gavin?" she asked instead as the lift continued to rise.

"I'm fine." He held up the generator. "Danilo Zalizniak offered the earth for this."

"What in heaven's name for?"

"So the Zalizniaks could get the upper hand on the Gontas and—I'm guessing—expand their empire."

"Good heavens," Alice said. "I hadn't thought of that. The moment we get the children to safety, we must destroy that thing." She paused, still holding the slightly sweaty hands of the two children. Gavin was grinning at her, and the wide, handsome smile was still enough to make her breath stop, especially when it was aimed at her. "What is it?"

"Feng is in terrible trouble, we could be chopped into pieces at any moment, and the second we leave this lift, we're going to be fighting our way through god-knows-what, but you're thinking about the children." He continued to smile. "You saved me back there, you know."

She blinked. "Did I? I thought you were saving me."

"Not at all," he said seriously. "You led me into hell, Alice, and now I know you're going to lead me back out."

The lift slammed to a halt, and for a horrible moment Alice thought the Cossacks had stopped them, but through the gate she could see the main floor of the great house. "Feng," she said, "open the lift."

Feng leaped forward like a puppet on strings and slammed the iron gate aside with the sound of a death bell. Alice felt sick again at the way his scarred body obeyed, but made herself focus. Right now, they had to get out of the Gonta-Zalizniak house intact, and if success required her to bark orders at Feng, she would do it.

Kemp was waiting for them in the marble foyer. The surreal sight of his familiar head on a different body gave Alice a turn, even though she'd been prepared for it. "I see Madam and Sir were successful in their attempt," he said. "Excellent work, if I may be so bold."

"Thank you, Kemp," Alice said. She herded the children out of the lift. They were gaining confidence in her now, seemed to understand that she was there to help, and they were more willing to follow her. They were fearful, innocent, and trusting, children who had lived through things no child should dream of, let alone experience. She felt a deep need to ensure their safety and was quite sure she would die to protect them. For a moment, she wondered if this was what it was like to have children of her own, though she didn't think that she would want to start off—or even finish— with ten of them. She did a quick head count and led everyone toward the front door, her parasol at the ready. Feng and Kemp took up the rear, with Gavin among the children. He looked like a rather distracted young father on an outing, and Alice pushed the thought away to examine later.

The house seemed to be in confusion. Human servants rushed about or stood uncertainly in corners. A smell of burned food hung in the air. Alice put on the air of a lady and strode confidently, ignoring everyone around her. No one would dare challenge her; it would never occur to her that someone might. Keep moving, keep moving. Check the children, ensure none had wandered away. Push past the handwringing housekeeper who babbled at her in Ukrainian. Thread through the maze of rooms. Nearly at the exit. Keep moving, keep moving.

She found herself in the middle of an enormous two-storied room with red marble floors and pillars. A grand staircase swept up to a balcony that ran around the entire chamber. High arched windows provided light, and ten-foot-high double doors stood opposite her. A patch of floor in front of the doors gleamed like a diamond. Alice glanced around, halted in confusion. It was the wrong room. She had taken a bad turn somewhere.

"This is the entry foyer," Kemp said helpfully. "The front doors are straight ahead of Madam."

Alice hesitated and fingered the whistle on its chain around her neck. "I think we should find a side door. I don't want to walk out onto the front steps and into the middle of that party."

"Ivana Gonta sent everyone home some time after Madam and Sir took the lift down," Kemp sniffed. "According to the servants, she was quite rude about it, even by Cossack standards. It is why everyone is in such a panic. The circus left, except for the elephant, which won't obey orders from anyone. Perhaps it has broken down."

"So the entire banquet existed only to lure us here," Alice said.

"Who cares?" Gavin said. "We have a clear sky. Let's go!"

A door up on the balcony slammed open and a stream of mechanical guards, all dressed in red uniforms, stormed down the stairs. Faster than any human, they lined up in ranks in front of the main doors. The other doors in the great room crashed shut and locks clicked. The children clustered around Gavin and Alice, whimpering in fear. Alice spread her arms to embrace and reassure as many of them as she could, though her own heart was racing.

"Madam!" Kemp cried. "Madam!"

His body marched over to join the automatic army, his arms and legs stiff, his head turning left and right. Alice started to go after him, but Gavin took her shoulder.

"Wait," he cautioned. "We don't know what we're dealing with yet."

"Good advice," said all the automatons at the same time, in the same voice. Even Kemp. The absolute unity of the sound made Alice's skin crawl. "We are masters here. You will not leave."

"Madam!" Kemp added.

"Who is this?" Alice demanded as she turned the handle of her parasol.

"We are Gonta-Zalizniak," said the automatons. All of them, including Kemp, drew swords.

"You couldn't get out of the basement in time to stop us, so you took over your guards. Is one of you controlling all of them," Alice asked, not really caring but trying to stall so she could think, "or do each of you control one automaton?"

"You will not leave." The swords vibrated with a sound like a pack of snarling dogs.

"Madam! I am trying to change the memory wheels, but I cannot. Help me, Madam!"

"Where are Phipps and Glenda and Simon?" Alice asked.

The automatons and Kemp took a step forward in unison. "You will not leave."

"Stop us." Gavin shoved the ear protectors back over his ears and cranked the generator again. The eerie sound rippled through the red marble room. All the automatons and Kemp jerked their heads in unison, then laughed together. Gavin stopped playing in confusion.

"Siren song is very beautiful," the automatons said, "but not so enticing when we hear through metallic ears. Alice will exit and go to China. Gavin and pretty Oriental boy will come back downstairs with children. But first we will slice one or two open while you watch."

"What?" Alice cried. "Why?"

"To punish you and Gavin, little baroness. To show that you are not in charge here. If you behave well after that, we promise to use nitrous oxide on Gavin and children before more experiments, though little baroness will have to take our word on that."

Feng was trembling and his torso was sheathed in

sweat, though his spidery face stayed impassive and he remained where he was at the back of the group of children. Alice glanced at Kemp, then back at the children. Damn it. She twisted her parasol handle again, and the high-pitched whine shrilled. Her hands shook.

"Madam, what are you doing?" Kemp asked. "Madam, please don't!"

"I'm sorry, Kemp," she said. "I'm so sorry." And she fired a bolt of electricity. The children cried out and scrambled backward. The crackling bolt struck the center automaton square on and spread to the others, including Kemp. Alice bit her lip, but held her grip firm. All the hair on the back of her neck stood up, and the smell of ozone tanged the air.

The automatons stood still for a moment. Then they laughed again, even Kemp. One of the automatons extended a hand. Its forearm separated from its upper arm and shot across the room, still connected to the body by a stiff cable. The move caught Alice off guard, and the automaton's hand was able to snatch the parasol from her hand and haul it back. It snapped the weapon in two and flung it aside. "No, no, no. We know about electric umbrella. We saw it work."

"They're standing on glass flooring," Gavin said. "They aren't grounded."

"Good heavens," Alice whispered, staring at the gleaming patch of floor. Kemp remained silent.

"You have no weapons now," the automatons said. "You belong to us."

The little clockwork army, including Kemp, spread out into a semicircle and stormed forward, their terrible growling swords at the ready. Before Alice could react, a bolt of red energy slashed through the air and punched through the chest of one of the automatons. It keeled over backward. Its sword went still. Alice spun. On the balcony behind and above them all stood Susan Phipps in her scarlet uniform with a large rifle in her hands and a battery pack on her back. Her brass monocle stared coldly down into the stone foyer. Beside her, also armed, were Simon d'Arco in black and Glenda Teasdale in yellow.

"Sorry it took so long to get here," Phipps said. "We had to raid the Gonta armory first."

"Oh God," Gavin muttered.

"Fire!" Phipps ordered. Glenda and Simon obeyed. The air crackled with energies Alice couldn't name. Gavin dropped the paradox generator, and they pushed the children to the floor while terrible thunder boomed overhead. The smell of hot metal filled Alice's nose. It went on and on. Several of the children began to cry. Heat pressed on Alice's back.

And then it stopped. Alice raised her head and slowly got to her feet. Smoke choked the air and it took some time to make out the warped figures of the automatons scattered about the floor, arms and legs skewed at odd angles, bodies and heads half melted. The marble floor was pitted and scorched, and the glass plate in front of the door had shattered into a thousand pieces. The children coughed and continued to cry. The sound wrenched Alice's heart, but she forced herself to concentrate on the matter at hand.

"Madam," said Kemp's voice from among the wreckage. "Madam. Madam. Madam."

Alice gasped upon hearing this, heartened at this

small bit of mechanical life among the strange carnage. Beside her, Gavin got to his feet. Feng remained upright. No one had told him to duck.

"Madam. Madam. Madam."

Phipps came down the stairs, followed by Glenda and Simon. The brass barrel of the energy rifle glowed a soft red. "That was satisfying," she said. "I imagine the Cossacks themselves will come upstairs eventually, but we should have time. And *my* shackles are rather more effective than the ones those disgusting clockworkers used."

Glenda put a hand to her ear, which had a metal cup over it. "I have access to the memory engines that run the house, Lieutenant. The Gontas have abandoned the automaton controls and are coming now."

The smoke caught in Alice's throat, and she had to cough before she could speak. "Susan—Lieutenant—I can't go back with you."

"I'm not offering a choice."

In that moment, all the frustration and anger and fear she'd been keeping under control got away from her. "Why are you doing this?" she burst out. "What do you have to gain? The plague in England is dead. There are no more clockworkers. The Third Ward's purpose is no more!"

Phipps strode forward and grabbed Alice by the front of her blouse in a metal fist. Her breath smelled of stale bread and long-forgotten wine. Alice grabbed Phipps's wrist with her own metal gauntlet, but Phipps was stronger by far. "You endanger the world. You diminish me. You destroyed my reason to exist."

"Let her go, Phipps!" Gavin barked, but Simon

pointed his rifle at him, and he went still. The paradox generator sat uselessly at his feet like a half-dead flower.

"So now you've replaced your purpose with an obsession to destroy me?" Alice countered. "Is it worth the cost? You've dragged Simon and Glenda into hell, and these children are paying the price as well. Let us go to China, Susan, and we'll restore balance to the world. It won't be the balance you remember, but it'll be balance nonetheless."

"Madam. Madam. Madam."

Phipps's six-fingered hand tightened on the white cloth at Alice's throat, and Alice found it a bit hard to breathe. "Balance is restored only through justice. I will have justice."

"The Gontas will be here in two minutes, Lieutenant," said Glenda from behind her rifle.

"Susan," Gavin said evenly, "we shouldn't be talking about this here. These children need our help, our assistance, our aid. Isn't that also your duty, your responsibility, your obligation?"

"A fine try, Ennock," Phipps said. "But I'm not a clockworker."

"Listen to me, Lieutenant." The words came out half-choked, and Alice could barely draw breath through the iron grip at her throat. She fumbled for the whistle on its chain, but couldn't get to it. "You have a chance here to build instead of destroy. You can save these children and thousands like them. Just let us go."

Phipps stared at Alice, her ice-blue eyes meeting Alice's brown ones. She wavered. The grip at Alice's throat relaxed and she could breathe freely again. Relief made Alice relax. Everything was going to be fine. The children continued to huddle around Gavin, and she wanted to tell them it would be all right now, but she had no way to—

"No!" Phipps snarled. Her grip tightened again. "No! No! *No!* I will have justice! Glenda, chain them both. Simon, keep them covered. If they move wrong, shoot to kill. Alice first. That'll keep Gavin in line."

"Madam. Madam. Madam."

"We have barely sixty seconds," Glenda reported, setting her rifle aside and producing a set of heavy handcuffs.

"Feng!" Alice cried in desperation. "Attack Phipps!"

Feng instantly launched himself at Phipps. The move caught Phipps off guard and he slammed into her, knocking her down. Alice went down, too, but Phipps released her grip and she was able to roll free. Gavin's wristbands snapped a cog at Glenda, who ducked by reflex. Gavin shoved through the crying group of children and swept the rifle from Glenda's hands with a hook kick. It hit the floor and slid away. Simon spun and aimed his weapon straight at Gavin. The tip glowed red.

Feng and Phipps rolled across the floor, trading and blocking blows faster than Alice could track. "No!" Phipps chanted. "No! No! No! No!" Feng was getting tired, and Phipps landed several choice hits on him. Alice struggled to her feet, fumbling for the whistle.

Gavin faced Simon across the glowing rifle barrel. Simon's eyes were sunken, his hair disheveled, his black coat torn. "Are you going to shoot me, Simon?"

Gavin said. "Simon Peter d'Arco, the man who killed his friend and partner?"

"I have my orders," he said hoarsely.

"What orders come from your soul?" Gavin asked. "You once gave up happiness to give me Alice. I can't imagine that someone so unselfish would kill for shallow reasons."

"You never wanted me," Simon said. "So I found someone else, and Phipps ripped me away from him to follow you. It always comes back to you, Gavin. You!"

"I'm sorry," Gavin admitted. "I know you're angry. But is anger worth my life, or the lives of these children?"

"Madam. Madam. Madam."

Glenda was moving toward her lost rifle. Simon twisted a lever, and the red barrel glowed scarlet. Alice froze, the whistle at her mouth, as Simon fired. The energy beam shot past Gavin and hit Glenda's rifle. It leaped away, a molten mass. Glenda swore and jumped back.

"You traitorous bastard!" Phipps leaped to her feet, dark hair wild. Feng staggered upright, still trying to attack but not possessing the coordination. "I'll see you court-martialed, d'Arco!"

The door at the top of the balcony burst open, and clockworker Cossacks boiled into the room. Ivana was at the forefront. She waved a sword that would have looked ridiculous with her pink tea gown if the vibrating blade hadn't sheared a marble bust in half as she passed. The other Gontas bore similar weapons, including a number of projectile arms.

"Shit," said Simon and Gavin together.

Alice blew the whistle. It shrilled high and loud, like a baby chick crying for its mother. There was a small moment of silence when everyone in the giant room paused, as if startled that Alice would do something so ridiculous. Alice stood in the middle of the frozen chaos. The children huddled together, frightened and without a protector. Feng staggered about, still trying to obey orders and attack Phipps, but betrayed by his battered body. Kemp's head droned sorrowfully to itself. Gavin and Simon remained side by side, dark and light, newly become brothers. Even the Gontas and Zalizniaks paused momentarily in their charge.

And then an angry trumpeting answered the whistle. A faint rumble grew stronger, and the front doors smashed open. They wrenched off their hinges, and Alice ducked as one door flew over her head and crashed at the foot the stairs just as Ivana and two of her siblings arrived there. Ivana's dying scream was buried under six inches of solid oak. The mechanical elephant stampeded over the remains of the automaton army, trumpeted again, and came to a halt near Alice. It made a formidable wall of brass between her and Phipps.

"Get aboard!" Alice barked. "Feng, get the children on the elephant!"

But Gavin and Simon were now halfway across the room from Alice and the mechanical animal. Gavin snatched up the paradox generator and the two of them ran for the elephant, but one of the Gontas on the staircase lobbed a small device that landed in the space between Gavin and the elephant. It exploded with a strange *pop* that only rocked Alice but knocked both Gavin and Simon sprawling. Gavin slid backward across the smooth floor, away from the elephant and toward the staircase. Alice shouted his name.

Gavin managed to regain his feet. By a miracle, he hadn't lost his hold on the paradox generator. Simon, meanwhile, flew in a different direction entirely and fetched up against one of the walls. He pulled himself upright, rifle in hand. The Cossacks laughed and tried to clamber over the wreckage at the foot of the stairs. One of them gave it up and turned to aim a large, multibarreled rifle in the elephant's general direction.

"Go, Alice!" Gavin shouted. "Take the kids and go!"

"No!" Alice cried, horrified at the idea. "I can't leave you!" But the space between them was wide, and the Gontas were already aiming a number of other weapons. The air would turn deadly in seconds. The children were climbing up the elephant and into the brass gondola, using handholds welded onto its hide for just this purpose. Feng urged them along, but they were slow, and there was no way to get them all in before the Gontas started their barrage.

Gavin held up the paradox generator and grabbed the crank. Of course! The Cossacks couldn't resist it. All he had to do was freeze them in place long enough for—

Alice's eye fell upon Gavin's ear protectors lying on the floor some distance away. The bomb had flung them from their place around his neck. Her stomach clenched with terror. In that moment, she knew what he intended to do.

"Gavin, don't!" she screamed. "You can't!"

I love you always, he mouthed and gave her that heart-stopping grin. Then he turned the crank. The unearthly sound of the tritone paradox sighed through the room. Most of the Gontas and Zalizniaks, those who hadn't been crushed by the door, froze. A look of pure bliss descended on their faces. Their weapons thudded to the stairs. Gavin mirrored their expression. His handsome features passed into an ecstasy only he could understand as he mindlessly cranked the handle, transporting himself and his fellow clockworkers into rapture. Alice hated the filthy sound, and tears streamed down her face. She couldn't reach him, he couldn't reach her, and he would play until he dropped from exhaustion or a Cossack killed him.

And just as Alice feared, three Gontas had had the foresight to throw together ear protectors of their own, and they shoved past their entranced brethren. Two aimed rifles straight at Gavin.

"No, you don't!" Simon fired his own weapon. Red energy spat from the tip and shattered part of the stone banister. The Gontas ducked. Alice cried out.

"Gavin's bought us time!" Simon shouted at her, still firing. "Don't waste it! Glenda, stay where you are. Alice, get those children aboard!"

At that moment, Phipps dashed around the elephant. She had taken advantage of the confusion to retrieve her rifle, and she aimed it at Alice, but Alice made an infuriated gesture, and the elephant swung its trunk round and slapped Phipps aside like a fly. Phipps went tail-over-teakettle and landed hard. The rifle arced away, far out of reach.

"Leave, Susan!" Alice shouted above the noise of

the rifle fire and the paradox generator. "I don't have time for your pettiness. If you want justice later, run now."

Simon continued to fire. His expert marksmanship kept the three Cossack clockworkers pinned down, but Alice wondered how long the rifle's energy would last. The moment Simon stopped his attack, the Cossacks would turn their fire on Gavin, and Alice had no way to save him. Gavin played his perfect tritones, forever beyond her reach. In moments, he would be dead. Alice felt sick and helpless as the final two children climbed aboard the elephant.

"Come on, Lieutenant!" Glenda cried near the gaping front doors.

Phipps looked torn for a moment. Then she dashed outside. Glenda went after her.

Simon fired another volley at the Gontas, but the rifle's power was already weaker. "Go!" he shouted. "We're out of time!"

Alice gestured, and the elephant curled its trunk so Alice could step aboard it. "I won't leave without Gavin!"

"Madam. Madam. Madam."

"There's no choice!" Simon said. "You have to let him go."

Ice washed through Alice's veins at those words. "I . . . I . . ."

"Let him go!"

At that moment, Simon's rifle ran out of power. The room fell silent except for the ghostly sighs of the tritone paradox. The protected Cossacks, who were hiding behind the stone banister, raised their heads above the rail. Their own rifles came up. Something inside Alice snapped. The world went into a blur, and she was only half aware of what she was doing. A scream tore itself from her throat, and the elephant thundered forward with Feng and the children clinging to the gondola on its back. And then the mechanical beast was standing between Gavin and the Gontas. Rifle fire, some of it energy, some of it projectile, pinged and hissed off the elephant's brass hide. Alice leaped down, yanked the generator out of Gavin's hands, and slapped him sharply across the face. Weapons fire continued to pock and snarl on the other side of the elephant.

"Wha—?" Gavin said.

"Move!" she shouted.

He moved. In seconds, he was in the gondola. Alice hurled herself back onto the elephant's trunk and ordered the beast to turn and run. It obeyed with a lurch as the Cossacks continued to fire, though the elephant still provided protection as it picked up speed. The smell of scorched brass filled the room and a chunk of metal peeled off the mechanical's side, exposing mesh and gears like muscle and bone. Machinery squealed as if it were in actual pain. The other Cossacks remained in their trance, but that wouldn't last long. Above Alice, children cried and screamed. The elephant was limping badly, and Alice could hear the pistons labor. More than one was bent or misaligned, though it was still able to speed along faster than a man could run. Alice clung grimly to its trunk, praying it wouldn't break down. Simon ran lightly along the wall, heading for the door as well, but the Cossacks were concentrating their fire on the elephant instead of him. He arrived at the door and bent down to scoop up Kemp's head just as the elephant reached him. With a quick move, he tossed the head up to Gavin in the gondola, then grabbed a handhold as the elephant thundered past and swung himself up.

"Madam. Madam. Madam."

The elephant bolted onto the portico outside and down the front steps to the deserted courtyard. The banquet tables, still bearing the remains of the feast, stood between the elephant and the gate, which by a miracle stood open, no doubt from when the rest of the circus left. The elephant smashed the tables to flinders and charged into the street. The rifle fire died away.

A number of emotions tried to push their way into Alice's head and heart—fear, relief, pride, anger—but she forced herself to stay focused on the task at hand. Reach safe distance from the Gontas. Guide the elephant safely through the street. Bring the children back to the circus. Would the Gontas pursue? Alice had no idea. Right now, she had to get back to the circus, where there was help.

"Alice!" Gavin called from above. "Alice!"

His voice brought back the wave of sentiment. She ignored it, and him. Now that he was safe, she needed to deal with practical matters. Once they were back at the circus, they could talk. The elephant ran.

"Madam. Madam. Madam."

"Alice!" Gavin shouted again.

The journey was its own version of hell. Alice was terrified the Gontas were following, and she didn't dare slow down, but neither did she want to trample anyone, and the dirty, narrow streets were difficult to navigate. Thank God she knew where she was going. People and traffic leaped out of the elephant's way, some meekly, others with angry shouts. The elephant's feet thudded unevenly on the cobblestones. Alice turned it one way, then another, always heading for the Dnepro River and the circus. The circus became a goal unto itself, a haven she had to reach at all costs.

The elephant slowed, lurching more and more. A loud hissing started in one of the little boilers inside its chest. But Alice could see the Tilt between the buildings.

"Madam. Madam. Madam."

And then they were there. The circus was in something of a mess. People dashed in a number of directions, working and shouting and unhitching horses from wagons. Animals bellowed and screeched in their cages. And then Alice remembered that they had been rudely dismissed from the Gonta-Zalizniak house and must have only just returned.

"Alice!" Gavin called again. "God, Alice. Get up here!"

This time Alice listened. She quickly climbed up to the gondola, cursing the difficulty of doing so in a skirt. Simon helped her in. Feng stood in one corner of the gondola, his scarred face impassive, Kemp's head at his feet. Nine of the children lay or sat on the floor, some of them crying softly, most of them numb. Gavin knelt, cradling the tenth, the little girl in the ragged gray dress. It was the girl Alice had first cured. Gavin's jaw was trembling, and then Alice saw that the front of the girl's dress was stained with blood. All the strength went out of her and she dropped to the floor of the gondola beside the child.

"No," she whispered. "No, no, no. Is she—?"

"Dead," Simon said. "Rifle fire hit her when you went back."

Guilt and horror crushed Alice to the gondola floor. Tears welled in her eyes and her throat closed. She took the little body from Simon and cradled it. The little girl's body lay in her arms like a warm rag doll. Her mouth lolled open. Alice wept. This child would never see her parents or play house or bite a slice of bread or kiss a boy or breathe spring air. All her hopes and memories had vanished like fog in sunlight, as if they had never existed. A month ago, when she had eaten breakfast with her family, she'd had no idea that one day her corpse would lay in the arms of a stranger on the back of a mechanical monster. And it was Alice's doing. Alice wished desperately that she could change places with her, but God was never so kind.

Gavin touched her shoulder and Alice wanted to bury herself in his arms, but she wouldn't let herself. What solace did this girl have? Her family?

"You couldn't let go," Simon said in a flat voice. "She died because you went back for Gavin."

"Madam. Madam. Madam."

"Simon," Gavin said dangerously, "be—"

The words landed on her like stones. "No. He's right. I'm so sorry. She died because of me."

"You're not being fair to yourself, Alice," Gavin told her quietly. "The Cossacks gave her the clockwork plague, and if you hadn't stepped in—"

"I don't want to talk about this right now." Alice

wiped her eyes. "Damn it. There's too much to do. We need to take care of the other children and we need to destroy that generator."

"Alice—," Gavin began.

"Not now, Gavin." She got up, still holding the girl's body. The other children stared, both fearful and uncertain. "Feng, get the children down to the ground, please. Simon, help him."

When the surviving children were safe on the ground, Alice climbed down herself, the girl's body slung over her shoulder. She refused to let Gavin take it down for her. Blood smeared Alice's blouse. Disorder continued to simmer through the circus and a curious crowd had gathered to watch, though as before they stayed outside the marked boundaries. Just as Alice reached the ground, Dodd trotted up to them, his collar undone and his hat askew. He was so agitated, he didn't even notice Simon and Feng.

"What the hell did you do?" he demanded. "Jesus and God and Mary. Everything was fine until you got involved."

"What do you mean?" Gavin asked.

"Ivana threw us out, and without paying me the rest of what she promised," Dodd growled. "And what the bloody hell happened to the elephant? What happened to you?"

"It's complicated," Gavin said. He shot a glance over his shoulder at the streets leading back to the Gonta-Zalizniak house. "The short version of the story is that Ivana Gonta captured Feng and all these children. We had to rescue them, but we found out it was all a trick to . . . Well, never mind."

He wet his lips. Alice understood his nervousness. Even as they spoke, the Gonta-Zalizniaks were pouring paraffin oil into their deadly mechanicals and moving them up from underground.

"Look," he finished, "we have to get out of here. All of us. You, too. The whole circus."

"I don't understand." Dodd looked puzzled.

Gavin looked ready to shake him. "Weren't you *listening*? The whole thing—the invitation to perform, Ivana pretending to want you there—was just a trick to get me and Alice into that house. Except we escaped, and now they're angry. They're going to destroy the circus in revenge, and they're on the way right now."

Dodd stared, then turned and bellowed, "*Scarper!* Now, now, *now*! Scarper! Scarper!"

The word rippled through the circus. At first there was a sense of disbelief. The Kalakos Circus was enormous and well respected, not some gypsy sideshow, and most of the performers hadn't been run out of a town in a dozen years or more. The idea that it could happen now caught them off guard. Once it sank in that the order was real, the general disorder from before blew into full-blown chaos as people tried to gather family, snatch belongings, and decide whether or not to leave beloved animals—both living and mechanical—behind.

Dodd started to run off, but Gavin caught his arm. "We need to find Harry. He speaks Ukrainian, and he can help us find the children's—"

"I don't know where Harry is," Dodd snapped. "I'm glad you got these children out of the Gontas' house, really I am, but right now I'm more worried that my own people will end up *in* it."

"Why don't you put everyone on the train? It's faster," Gavin asked.

"The boilers are stone cold," Dodd snapped. "We'd never get everything heated up in time. Though I'm going to try, for the sake of the animals. Everyone else will have to run on foot or horseback and hope for the best. Maybe if we scatter in different directions, the Cossacks won't catch many of us. Oh!" He put his hands to his head. "Charlie! He can't run! Linda will have to hitch up her wagon. I have to find Nathan. Perhaps he can help her."

"Good heavens." Alice's knees felt weak and she leaned against the elephant's pitted side with the dead girl in her arms. The elephant felt uncomfortably warm, and it sighed steam. This was too much to take in. "I'm sorry, Dodd. I didn't know this would happen."

"Sorry? *Sorry?*" Dodd was nearly shouting. "You destroyed this circus. You destroyed our lives. *Thank* you, Baroness, for bringing my people into all this."

He whirled and stomped away.

Gabriel Stark, called Dr. Clef, stood on the deck of *The Lady of Liberty* and stared through a spyglass at the mechanical elephant. Time jerked and jumped. Some moments rushed ahead so quickly that his limbs moved like glaciers. Other moments slowed, froze even the daylight into clear, sweet ice. In those slow moments, he could see the entire world, perhaps the entire universe, caught in a single painting. When nothing moved, Dr. Clef saw every secret of the physical world, of time and matter and energy, as plain as an artist's brush stroke. Then the universe jerked back into motion, and an ocean of paint splashed over what he saw, obliterating it. Even his memory of it vanished. He only knew that he had known. Some flotsam did stay with him, however. Stray numbers, unified concepts, vibrating strings, the final piece of an irrational number. Concepts no sane mind could grasp. Fortunately, his mind was falling apart, and this allowed him to hold a few secrets together.

Another thing he held on to was the mission. The boy needed more time. That became plainer with every passing, precious moment. The boy's movements as he climbed down from the elephant betrayed this need. The clockwork plague altered his gait, his gestures. Only someone as brilliant as Dr. Clef could see the pattern of the plague's progression toward madness, dissolution, and death. Although Dr. Clef calculated a decent 62.438 percent chance that China's Dragon Men could cure a clockworker, he gave the boy only a 19.672 percent chance of living long enough to see it, and the largest problem came from the fact that he wouldn't have enough time.

Steam curled from the elephant's tusks, and Dr. Clef simultaneously saw the droplets both condense and evaporate. He hadn't yet gotten around to naming the minuscule particles that made up matter. He himself hadn't had the time, and he was running out. The plague was eating at his body even as it sharpened his mind. But there was a remedy to his problem and to the boy's.

A wave of affection swept over him. The dear, dear boy. The son he'd never had. Or perhaps he did have a son, or even a dozen. He didn't know for certain. Dr. Clef's memories of his own past grew more and more hazy every hour. He had vague recollections of fishing in a blue river with another boy while it rained, and another of kissing a pretty girl in a blue dress, and both colors were the same electric blue as his beautiful Impossible Cube. He remembered working in his stone laboratory in the Third Ward, but couldn't recall how he'd come to be there in the first place. He recalled the boy, whose eyes were the same electric blue as Dr. Clef's beautiful Impossible Cube, and how the boy had held the Cube and sung his way through solid stone. But then the Cube had vanished. Every day when Dr. Clef rose, he felt the pain of its loss, like a man who loses a leg might still feel pain in his missing foot. It was impossible to re-create the Cube's perfection. There was only one in all the universes and all the time they contained.

And then the dear, dear boy with the electric-blue eyes had handed him that lovely paradox generator, with its audible, irrational, and intoxicating double square root of two. Paired with his own alloy, which cycled the thrilling new power of electricity back and forth between the square root of two, the generator would give him his Cube back, and once he had both Cube and generator, he could give the boy all the time he needed. Dr. Clef needed only an enormous amount of electricity at the right frequency. And for that . . .

Dr. Clef turned the spyglass upriver. The dam strained against the current, tamed it, forced uncounted trillions of droplets around turbines and rotors. He could feel the magnets moving within their coils, changing the flow of water to a flow of electricity. Exciting! Thrilling! The key to the universe lay within the grasp of these little people, and instead of taking advantage, they scurried about gathering up foolish possessions, clumps of matter that mattered not at all. Their current existence had no point, and only Dr. Clef could change it. He *would* change it. If only . . .

He swung the spyglass back to the elephant. The girl seemed upset by the dead child in her arms, and the boy seemed upset that the girl was upset. He made the connection easily enough. The child had died because of something the girl had done, most likely save the boy, and now she was upset. Foolish. The boy offered the world quite a lot more than a stray child. But the fact that both of them were upset meant that they had probably . . .

Yes. The paradox generator was still on board the elephant, forgotten by everyone.

Except Dr. Clef.

Chapter Thirteen

Gavin stood in the center of chaos beside the hissing elephant and amid a whimpering crowd of children. Feng was deformed, Alice was upset, Simon was a turncoat, Kemp was beheaded, one of the children was dead, and he had no idea what to do next. He wanted to crawl under a blanket and let someone else handle everything. Even the clockwork plague seemed to have abandoned him. Irrationally, he wished for Captain Naismith's presence. The captain would know what to do and would tell Gavin how to go about doing it. Gavin wouldn't have to plan, think, or worry. Unfortunately, Felix Naismith was gone, leaving no one but a former cabin boy in command. That was always the way of it. Father, captain, mentor—it didn't matter. They always abandoned you. He squared his shoulders.

"All right," he said. "Alice, where are your little automatons?"

"Still on the ship." She was looking at the face of the dead girl in her arms.

"We need them to reassemble the—"

"Papa!" one of the children, a boy, shrieked. "Papa!"

A dozen yards away, a man in the crowd turned, and the boy flew toward him across the stones, arms outstretched. The man stared incredulously, surprise and disbelief writ all over his face. Then he cried "Pietka!" and opened his arms wide. Pietka leaped into his father's embrace, and the man rocked when the boy slammed into him. The man held his son tightly. Tears streamed down both their faces and mingled together as the father pressed his cheek to his son's. "Pietka," he said. "*Mi Pietka.*"

"Papa," Pietka snuffled.

Gavin discovered tears were leaking from his own eyes, and he wiped at them with his fingers.

"Well," Simon said beside him. "Well."

Pietka said something to his father, and the man trotted over to Gavin with Pietka still in his arms. Alice stepped back with the dead girl in hers, creating a tragic mirror image. The man said something to Gavin in Ukrainian, but Gavin could only shake his head.

"He wants to know if you're the one who rescued his son," said Harry, who came up at that moment. "Hello, Gavin. You've caused quite a fuss, quite a fuss."

"Tell him we all rescued Pietka," Gavin said.

Harry translated, and the man abruptly snatched Gavin into a rough one-armed embrace, tangling him with Pietka for a moment. Then he backed away, looking embarrassed.

"You're welcome," Gavin said, also feeling embarrassed.

The man spoke again, and Harry said, "He's asking about the other children. He wants to know if you need help finding their families. He doesn't know the Gontas and Zalizniaks are coming."

"Tell him yes," Gavin said. "Harry, can you—?"

"Yes, I'll go along to translate," Harry said, before Gavin could make the request. "I'm used to moving about on my own, and a few people in Kiev owe me a favor, so I can scarper off. I'll be fine, I'll be fine."

"I'll go with them, too," Simon said. "And then I think I'll disappear myself."

"We could use your help, Simon," Gavin said. "You saved us once in there."

Simon shook his head. "You don't need me. And frankly, my friend, it's too difficult being near you."

"Oh." Gavin nodded. "Where are you going?"

"The least said, the better," Simon replied, "in case Phipps gets her hooks into you. I won't be welcome in England, but the world is wide." He stuck out his hand. "Good-bye."

Gavin shook his hand, then suddenly pulled Simon into a hard embrace. "I'm glad I knew you."

When they parted, Simon wiped surreptitiously at his eyes. There was nothing else to say.

The children, meanwhile, seemed eager to follow Harry, Pietka, and his father, once explanations were made. Since Pietka had found his father, they seemed eager to believe they would find their own parents. Gavin turned to Alice.

"They should take . . . her, too," he said gently. "Her parents will want her body back."

Alice clutched the little girl to her. For a moment Gavin thought she would refuse to give her up, and he wondered if she was going mad. Then Alice nodded. Simon took the girl and wrapped her in his jacket.

"I'm sorry," he said to Alice.

Several of the children solemnly hugged Gavin and Alice, and Gavin was afraid he would cry again. Pietka's father led the group away. Pietka was already chattering in his father's arms.

"I'm sorry, too," Alice whispered. "I couldn't let go."

Gavin put his arm around her. "I wouldn't be here if you hadn't come back."

"But that little girl would be." She buried her face in his shoulder for a moment. "Oh God—I don't know how to feel right now, Gavin."

Circus people continued to rush about. Some were packing suitcases and wagons; others simply flung sacks over their shoulders and fled. Performing horses were drafted into service towing wagons. Almost everyone was heading toward a bridge over the Dnepro some distance downstream, since that road led out of town. Urgency drove their movements, and the ashy air was thick with fear. Most of the performers refused to look at Gavin or Alice. The few that did sent hard glares. Gavin felt very small, and very strange. A few minutes ago, he had been ready to die, a sacrifice to hell so that the children could live. But Alice had wrenched him around and led him out. And then it had happened, the very thing he had been trying to prevent. A stray bullet had penetrated the gondola and killed that little girl. Gavin had held her while the life slipped from her eyes. It was as if God had decided the two of them should trade places. He wanted to be angry with Alice, but he couldn't find it in himself. Instead, he felt glad to be alive, and also guilty that he felt glad, which contributed to that feeling that he was indeed a tiny, tiny man.

"We have some time yet," he said, "and we need to get to the ship. The stuff onboard is too dangerous to hand to the Gontas."

"Madam. Madam. Madam." Kemp's head was lying on the ground near Feng's feet, where Simon had left it.

Alice nodded. "Feng, please bring Kemp and follow us."

The trio hurried toward the train. Along the way, they encountered Linda high up on her brightly painted wagon. She was driving a pair of horses toward the bridge over the Dnepro. "Hello, honey!" she called down cheerfully.

"Linda!" Gavin called up to her. "Are you and Charlie all right?"

"Just fine. Charlie's in the back. I tried to warn everyone that this was coming, but no one listened. Circus folk are more cynical than most when it comes to fortune-telling." She popped a butterscotch into her mouth. "I feel like Cassandra at Troy."

"You *knew*?" Alice said.

"Of course, sweetie. You haven't learned to let go yet, so this was inevitable. Besides, I drew the three of swords not long after Dodd got the invitation from

Ivana Gonta. It means a disaster, but a necessary one. It teaches a lesson and relieves built-up tension so the journeyer can move forward. Good gracious—what happened to your friends?"

"Madam. Madam. Madam," said Kemp's head in Feng's hands.

"Too long to explain," Gavin said.

"Well, I'm sure it'll turn out all right in the end."

"Was that a prediction?" Alice asked.

"An assurance," Linda corrected. "I won't see you again, honey. You're on your own." She clucked to the horses, who hauled the wagon away.

"Was I supposed to let you die?" Alice burst out as Linda left. "Gavin, I couldn't—"

"Listen, now." Gavin pulled her to him. She burst into tears, hiding her face in his shoulder. It was the first time he had seen her cry, and it made him feel strangely old. Everyone said women were supposed to cry a lot, though now that he thought about it, he didn't see it happen very often. His mother had never cried that he remembered. He patted Alice awkwardly on the shoulder. "Didn't Monsignor Adames say I was supposed to save the world?"

"Yes," she sobbed while Feng stood quietly by with Kemp's head.

"I can't save the world if I'm dead. I was an idiot for trying to sacrifice myself like that. You *had* to come back for me. It was the right thing to do."

"How can it be the right thing to let a child die? It's my fault she died, Gavin."

"That's strange. I thought it was the fault of the Cossack who fired the rifle."

"That makes sense," she snuffled. "My head agrees with you, but my soul scourges me with fiery whips."

"It'll pass."

"I don't know if I want it to."

"Madam. Madam. Madam."

He didn't know what to say to that, so instead they headed for the train. It was partly abandoned. Several boxcars gaped open, revealing dead space within. Other cars were shut tight, and yet others hung half open. Animal cages had been shoved every which way into some of them in the vain hope that the engine boiler might heat up quickly enough to move the train before the Cossacks arrived. Dodd and Nathan themselves were working with the engineer, trying to coax enough heat out of the boiler to get the train going. The *Lady* still sat at the rear disguised as a car. Gavin, Alice, and Feng climbed up to the deck. Gavin immediately felt more at ease, more in control. This was his ship. It was home.

"I wish I knew how much time we had," Alice said as Gavin helped her off the ladder.

"It'll take them at least an hour to get all those mechanicals fired up, and then another twenty minutes or so to get here," Gavin said. "Considering how much time has already passed, I think that gives about forty minutes. Not long enough for Dodd to start the engine, unless he knows something I don't."

"Madam. Madam. Madam," Kemp said. His voice was growing fainter in Feng's hands.

"Give him to me, Feng." Alice accepted the head sadly and did something to it. The light went out of Kemp's eyes and he fell silent. "We'll get him a new body and fix him somehow. And you, Feng. What about you? In all the fuss, we haven't had a moment to figure out what happened." She touched his cheek. "I'm so sorry we didn't arrive in time."

Feng remained mute. The spider on his head twitched a little, and the scars on his torso scribbled ugly tracks across his skin.

"What did they do to you, Feng?" Gavin asked. "Please answer."

"Ivana placed this spider on my head and it drilled into my skull and spine," he said promptly. "She forced Danilo to help. It was painful. They put me in a cage until you came and brought me out."

His voice was clipped and precise, completely unlike his more usual free, lackadaisical tone. Gavin ached for him.

"What does the spider do?" he asked.

Feng remained silent until Gavin added, "Please answer."

"I do not know."

"It's obvious," Alice said. "The spider makes him tractable. He does nothing he isn't told to do, and he follows orders from anyone who speaks to him. Isn't that right, Feng? Please answer."

"I do not know," Feng said, "but that sounds true."

"That's . . . awful," Gavin said. "Can we take it off? Or shut it down?"

"It would take some study," Alice replied. "However, I am forced to admit that I'm not well versed in biology, and this device combines automatics with that science. Good heavens, why would they do such a thing?"

"The Gontas are trying to dominate the Zalizniaks permanently," Gavin said. "This is an experiment in that area. Feng can still think and act, but is perfectly obedient." And would never chase pretty girls again, he added silently. Not unless he was ordered to.

Alice thought a moment. "Feng," she said, "obey your own orders. Think for yourself and do as you wish."

Feng's entire body twitched as if he'd been jolted by electricity. His face contorted and he made a small sound. His hands flew up to the spider. The sound he made grew louder and louder, and the facial contortions showed pain.

"Never you mind, Feng!" Alice cried. "Obey me now! Go back to the way you were!"

Feng instantly calmed and went still.

"Sit down, Feng," Gavin said. "You look tired."

Feng sat on the deck and looked grateful.

"I wonder if we can have him ask for something," Alice mused.

Gavin squatted next to the exhausted Feng. He wanted to put an arm around Feng, but he couldn't quite bring himself to touch the puckered flesh or the evil spider. "I'm sorry," was all he could say. "We'll find a way to help you once everything calms down."

"Speak for yourself, if you wish," Alice said. "Say whatever you think you should say."

"Alice!" Gavin said. "No!"

"Speaking is different from acting or thinking," Alice said.

Feng had already opened his mouth. "Wha . . . Wha . . . ," he said.

"Go ahead," Alice said. "Say what you want when you please."

"Why did you come back for me?" Feng burst out. "What possessed you?"

This took Gavin completely by surprise. He floundered a response. Finally Alice said in a small voice, "We had to save you."

"So you believe." Feng's face was set like rock.

"I don't understand," Gavin said. "You'd rather we left you there?"

"Look at me!" he spat. "How do you think my family will receive me now? I already live in disgrace, and now I'm a living wreck."

"We couldn't leave you there," Alice replied stubbornly. "It was our fault you were captured, and it was our duty to save you."

"Not everyone wants to be saved, Alice!" Feng cried. "Did you ever consider that?"

Alice said, "You're talking nonsense."

"Am I? The Cossacks are coming to kill everyone in the circus because you saved me. If you had simply walked away, none of this would be happening."

"And those children would still be in cages," Gavin shot back.

"You could have taken them away without coming for me," Feng said. "The Cossacks became truly upset only when you used that . . . that music thing. Now they want it, and they are angry at you because you could not let me go."

Gavin took a step backward at that. He had never mentioned the words that Adames had spoken or the cards Linda had drawn to Feng. He looked at Alice.

"I am not discussing this," she said firmly, but Gavin recognized the stress in her voice and in the set of her mouth. "We need to find Dr. Clef and my little automatons so we can gather some things and evacuate. The Cossacks will be here any moment."

Her words hit Gavin hard. He looked about the *Lady*, the graceful, comfortable ship he had built with his own hands. They couldn't reassemble and inflate the envelope in time to fly her out of Kiev, which meant that in less than an hour she would be in the hands of the Gonta family. The thought made him sick.

"Let's look for Dr. Clef below," Alice said. "Feng, you too."

Feng checked Dr. Clef's stateroom while Alice went to her own room carrying Kemp's head. Gavin headed for the laboratory. It was a snowstorm of papers— diagrams and equations pinned to the walls and to the workbench like captured snowflakes. Gavin stared. The diagrams consistently portrayed two objects: Dr. Clef's eye-twisting Impossible Cube, and pieces of Gavin's paradox generator. Several equations, many done in purple crayon, tugged at his eye. The plague stirred, then roared to life. He dove into the equations and guzzled them down. The square root of two. Matter and energy. Parallel particles locked together. Vibrating strings. Electricity that cycled around an irrational number. And he knew what Dr. Clef wanted. A chill dropped through him, freezing him from scalp to instep.

"He's not anywhere on the ship," Alice said. She held Click in her arms, and a flock of little automatons hovered around her and perched on her shoulders.

Feng came up behind her. The lab was almost too crowded to move. "Feng didn't find him, either. Do you have any ideas?"

Before Gavin could answer, a faint rumble crept up through his boots, then died away. Another rumble that died, then another. A second chill followed the first.

"Can you feel that?" Gavin said. "Footsteps."

"Is that what it is?" Alice whispered. "Good heavens."

"What makes them?" Feng asked. He had found a shirt, which covered the scars on his chest and torso, though the spider on his face and neck still gave him a sinister appearance. He also seemed to have calmed down from his earlier rant. At least he could still speak freely.

"The Cossack mechanicals. They're coming." Gavin listened, let the vibrations shake through his body, and his brain worked out more math. "Eighteen minutes, twenty seconds."

"We need to leave," said Alice in a no-nonsense voice that was nonetheless filled with tension. "Where would Dr. Clef have gone?"

Gavin gestured at the diagrams. A strange calm came over him, and the words fell from his mouth like lead lumps. "The Cossacks are the least of our worries, Alice. Dr. Clef wants the dam."

"The dam? What for?"

"He's found a way to get back the Impossible Cube," said Gavin, "and I think he's going destroy the universe."

There was a long, long pause.

"What?" Feng said at last.

"What?" said Alice at the same time.

"He's going to destroy the universe," Gavin repeated. "With the Impossible Cube."

Feng put a hand on the spider scrawled across his face. "I do not understand."

"Nor do I," Alice said. A little automaton buzzed too close to her face and she brushed it away. "He told me himself that re-creating the Impossible Cube was . . . well, impossible."

"He isn't going to re-create it," Gavin said, trying not to get more upset. "The Cube still exists. Or it will, very soon."

"I am still not following this," Feng said.

They didn't share his fear because they didn't understand. Gavin tried to keep his voice steady to explain, but ideas formed and rushed out of him like water bursting from a dam.

"Dr. Clef has been working on a project he wouldn't tell us about, remember? And my paradox generator . . . and the cycles in electric power . . . and the alloy that warps gravity when electricity powers it . . . and his proof that time changes depending on local gravity . . . Come on!"

He pushed past them, through the flock of automatons, and ran up to the main deck. The others followed. Gavin was hoping he was wrong, praying with every fiber of his being that he had misinterpreted what he'd seen in the laboratory, but the pieces continued to thud into place like granite weights. He swore and pointed at the roll of alloy wire that had once been the endoskeleton for the ship's helium envelope and provided extra lift. The roll still lay on the deck where Alice's automatons had placed it, but one end was missing a noticeable piece.

"He needed a bit of that?" Alice said. "What's going on?"

"Not just a bit of that. He was making more in the Black Tent. I was using some of it, but he kept the rest," Gavin said. "He needs a lot of it."

"But what *for*?" Alice demanded. "I still don't— Oh! Oh! Good heavens! I understand now."

"What?" Feng ran a hand over the spider on his face. "What does he plan?"

Alice's expression grew agitated, and her spiders danced around her feet, mimicking her mood. Click sat nearby and washed a paw. "When Gavin last used the Impossible Cube in the Doomsday Vault, it disappeared and we assumed it had been destroyed. But Gavin thinks the reason it disappeared is that it went through time."

"Not quite," Gavin said. "The Cube is a constant, which means *it* didn't move. It actually twisted time around itself, and since we're in the stream of time, it appeared to us that—"

"Does it *matter*?" Alice cried, and several of her automatons squeaked in alarm. "Gavin! He's going to reach through time to snatch the Impossible Cube out of the past at the moment you destroyed it. Feng, listen—the alloy cycles electricity at frequencies of power that match the sounds made by Gavin's paradox generator. Those frequencies are the same—the square root of two. The Impossible Cube itself is built around that very number. If Dr. Clef pumps enough electricity through Gavin's generator at the right intervals, he could, I believe, create a sort of opening into the past that would allow him to bring the Impossible Cube into the present."

"Why is this bad?" Feng said. "The Impossible Cube has enormous power, does it not? We could destroy the Cossack clockworkers with a single blow." His voice became grim. "I will do it myself."

Gavin wanted to shake Feng. The other man didn't understand. Gavin remembered with clockwork clarity that awful night he had held the Impossible Cube in his own hands in the dungeons beneath Third Ward headquarters, how the Cube crackled with energy between his palms as he sang one note that the Cube twisted into pure power that pounded through stone and ripped away rock.

"Dr. Clef doesn't want to destroy the Gontas and Zalizniaks," Gavin said carefully. "He's obsessed with *time*."

"His calculations," Alice said. "When he was talking about clocks orbiting the earth and gravity changing time. It was nonsense, I thought."

"No," Gavin told her. "Look, I nearly destroyed the entire Third Ward with the Cube and the finite power of a single note from my voice. Another note made the Cube travel through time. Yet another destroyed all the visible light energy within a hundred yards of the Cube. When you feed it a single note, it affects mere energy, but what do you think would happen if Dr. Clef played the *infinite* sound of my paradox generator into it?"

"Good heavens." Alice put a pale hand to her mouth as another set of footsteps shook the ship.

Gavin nodded, unhappy that she was afraid, but glad she understood. "The paradox generator makes an infinite sound based on an irrational number: the square root of two. The Impossible Cube is a singular object, and it twists an infinite amount of time and space around itself using the square root of two as the basis for everything it does. If Dr. Clef feeds that infinite sound into the Impossible Cube, he'll have the power to stop time. Everywhere. Forever."

Now Feng went pale around the spider and his voice fell into a whisper. "Would he do such a thing?"

"Of course he would," Alice replied faintly. "He thinks he's *helping* us. We don't have enough time to do everything we need, and his own time in this world is growing shorter. This is his way of giving us more time. An infinite amount."

"I see." Feng paused, and the ship shook yet again. Gavin automatically calculated: ten minutes, five seconds before they arrived. "Except there should be no problem. He does not have your paradox generator."

Gavin blinked and relief made his muscles go limp. "That's true," he said. "I had it in the Gonta-Zalizniak house."

"Oh, thank *goodness*." Alice ran her hand over her face and sighed heavily. "We're saved. Where is the generator right now, then?"

He paused. "I . . . that is . . ."

"Gavin." Alice's face went tight again. *"Where is it?"*

Gavin bit his lip and his heart started a snare drumbeat again. He had to think for a moment. Everything had gotten so busy, and there was the little girl's death and the boy's reunion with his father and the argument with Dodd. The generator hadn't seemed important. What had happened to it? The heavy footsteps continued to shake the ship.

"I think I left it on the elephant," he said at last.

"And if Dr. Clef is not on the ship . . . ," Feng began.

They all traded horrified looks, then bolted for the ladder. In seconds, Gavin, Feng, Alice, Click, and the automatons were all racing back toward the elephant. People still rushed around the circus grounds. A number of the performers had vanished into Kiev, but those who had children or who couldn't travel easily or who were unwilling to abandon wagons were still busy. Trash and a tent or two littered the square around the Tilt. The train stood still, though a curl of smoke drifted up from the engine's smokestack. The watching crowd had vanished, scattered by the sound of mechanical footsteps. They knew what was coming. A line of circus wagons and horses moved down the street toward the stone bridge and the road out of town. Upriver, the dam housed its spinning turbines even as it held back countless tons of water beneath a cloudy sky. The sheer power in it made Gavin's fingers tingle.

A few blocks away, between the buildings, Gavin caught a glimpse of metal. The Cossack mechanicals. His stomach tightened as he saw the distance left for the circus to travel to the bridge.

"Where is the elephant?" Alice asked.

The elephant was gone.

"Bastard!" Gavin snarled. The clockwork plague thundered through him. Dr. Clef had thwarted him, deliberately disobeyed his order to destroy the paradox generator and now he had *stolen* it for himself. "He was waiting for us to leave it. He's got the elephant and my paradox generator!"

"What do we do now?" Feng asked. He seemed surprisingly calm.

Numbers clicked and spun in Gavin's head. "These people aren't going to make it. They need more time."

"We have to warn them." Alice looked increasingly desperate. "They need to abandon everything and run."

"We cannot run fast enough to warn them, either," Feng said.

Gavin glanced about. If they made for the dam, the Gontas would kill everyone in the circus, including Dodd and Nathan and Linda and Charlie. If they warned the circus, Dr. Clef would be able to stop time forever. Save a few people, or save the universe. More numbers ran through his mind, painting new realities behind them. The choice was obvious.

"Come on, Alice," Gavin said. "I'll need your help." And he ran straight toward the Cossack mechanicals.

Chapter Fourteen

Alice's heart stopped. *The plague's driven him completely mad,* she thought. *Now what do I do?*

"Come on, Feng!" she shouted, and ran after Gavin. Feng twitched once and followed with Alice's automatons. Gavin had a decent head start, however, and he wasn't wearing a skirt, so he kept his lead.

"Gavin!" she yelled. "What are you doing?"

But he ignored her. The narrow street that led into the square was packed with a single-file line of large mechanicals, the same ones Alice had seen in the dungeon below the Gonta house. She remembered counting forty, and it appeared that nearly so many thumped down this street, cracking the cobblestones with the sound of angry gods. The smallest was twice as high as she was, and most of them were at least two stories tall. All of them bristled with weaponry—swords and launchers and rifles and objects she couldn't discern. Alice remembered the clockwork revolution headed by the Gontas and the Zalizniaks that had ended the

Russian and Polish occupation of Ukraine, and she began to understand why the occupiers hadn't stood a chance. Most of the mechanicals were topped by a glass bubble, and in each sat a Gonta. The machinery spewed ashy clouds of smoke and fumes. The streets were only wide enough to allow one mechanical at a time to pass, which was why they came in a deadly single file, heading for the circus. Once they reached the square, they could spread out and follow the river. Dodd's little collection of automatons and fragile wagons wouldn't stand a chance, and when the Gontas crushed them into meat and metal matchsticks, it would be Alice's fault for bringing them here. More death on her head.

Gavin ran lightly up the street to the lead mechanical, which was close to eighteen feet tall. Danilo Gonta sat in the bubble, his expression cool and calm, his white lab coat stained with blood. Then he saw Gavin, and his face twisted into an animal snarl.

"That's right, Danilo!" Gavin shouted. "You want me, not them!"

Inside the bubble, Danilo spun something, and a rifle on the shoulder of his mechanical turned. It fired a burst of bullets, but Gavin was already moving, diving away from the gunfire and toward the mechanical. He shouldn't have been able to dodge the hail, but the plague was clearly working on him, and he flicked around almost faster than Alice could follow. Her heart climbed into her throat, and she desperately cast about for something—anything—she could do to help him.

Gavin reached Danilo's mechanical, which had stopped in its tracks to fire at him and thereby blocked the progress of the other Gontas behind it. They stomped their feet, and a few of them made *BEEP* sounds Alice had never heard before. People from the surrounding buildings fled into the streets and away. Clearly they'd seen altercations before.

Alice stayed close to a brick wall with Feng, Click, and her automatons and forced herself to remain calm, to *think* as frightened people streamed past her. Even from here, she could trace the workings of the lead mechanical, see the way it moved and how it fit together. Was there a weak spot she could exploit? If only she could figure out what Gavin was—

Gavin jumped onto one of the mechanical's broad feet and climbed like a monkey. In a flash, Alice understood what was going on. Brilliant! She hoped it was Gavin's idea, and not something dreamed up by the clockwork plague. She very much wanted to feel pride for his intelligence instead of fear for his sanity. With a quick motion, Alice snatched up Click and turned to the whirligig mechanicals hovering behind her.

"You carried Aunt Edwina when she tried to steal the giant war machine outside London last summer," she said to them. "Can you carry me?"

They squeaked and bobbed up and down in midair with obvious enthusiasm.

"Feng," she said without thinking, "wait here with my spiders. You, you, you, and you," she continued, pointing to different whirligigs, "carry me to that mechanical. Quick!"

The whirligigs took Alice firmly by the shoulders and back of her dress and lifted. Their propellers spun madly only inches away from Alice's face, but they lifted her handily from the ground.

"Wait!" Feng cried. "Alice, I cannot—"

But Alice was already rushing toward the big mechanical with Click in her arms. The sensation of flight swooped through her, filling her with exhilaration despite the danger. Why had she never tried this with her automatons before? Gavin had managed to skitter up to Danilo's bubble. The Gontas behind them were becoming angrier and angrier, but they were still hemmed in by the narrow street and unable to do anything. Gavin clambered up to the very top of Danilo's bubble. One of Danilo's hands swiped at him. Gavin leaped over it. When he landed, he made a face at the Gonta behind Danilo, a plump man in brown leather.

"Good thing I killed Ivana!" Gavin shouted at him. "They can feed China now! She had more rolls than a bakery!"

Alice held her breath. Danilo swiped at him again, like a man swatting at a fly, but Gavin nimbly leaped away. The Cossack behind Danilo was getting angry. Alice could see him turn red and purple, and it would have been funny if Gavin hadn't been dancing with death. She was almost there.

"You could stand to lose a few pounds yourself," Gavin taunted him. "Gain any more weight, and planets will orbit *you*."

The arm of the mechanical behind Danilo tracked around and its fingers revealed themselves to be rifle barrels.

"You don't have the guts," Gavin yelled. "It's all lard!"

Too late Danilo realized what was going on. *"Ni!"* he shouted into the speaking tube, but his fat brother Cossack had already fired. Gavin dropped down to the chest piece of Danilo's mechanical and hung there by his fingertips just as the fat Gonta's ammunition slammed into Danilo's bubble. The glass exploded. Danilo flew out of the mechanical and smacked the brick streets. He twitched once and lay still.

With her free hand, Alice gestured at the fat Cossack. "There! Go!"

The automatons skimmed over the mechanical with the shattered bubble. Alice caught a glimpse of Gavin hoisting himself with the incredible agility of a clockworker into the driver's seat, where he took up the controls. Then her own automatons dropped her on the bubble of the fat Cossack. Click fell from her arms and she scrabbled a moment on the smooth glass before regaining her balance. Behind, the other Gontas were still trapped in the narrow street, and unlike their brother, seemed unwilling to fire on their own family, especially now that Gavin had shown the disastrous consequences of doing so. The fat Cossack in the mechanical looked up, surprised.

"Cut, Click!" Alice ordered.

Click extended hard claws and scrawled a wide circle in the glass just as he had done on the roof of L'Arbre Magnifique's greenhouse. Alice stamped in the center, and the circle fell in, striking the Gonta on the head. He shouted at her in Ukrainian, but Alice was already giving orders to her little automatons. They zipped into the mechanical like hornets invading a beehive, snatched the fat Gonta up, and yanked him out into open air. He yelped, chins quivering. The automatons labored hard, and Alice tugged him upward as well, then kicked him over the side. He fell away, and the automatons let him go. Alice herself dropped into the opening and found herself sitting on a padded bench at the controls. Click leaped down to join her. Alice's inborn talent with automatics let her see instantly what went where. Pedals for the legs, hand controls for the arms, a number of switches and dials for other functions. She spun the mechanical around to face the other Cossacks.

All this had happened in only a few seconds. The remaining Gontas hadn't been expecting to be attacked. Their surprise combined with the confined space to render them helpless, but only for the moment. Already, rifles and launchers were clicking around to train on Alice. In a strategically placed mirror mounted on the controls, she could see Gavin behind her. The weapons were trained on him, too. A strange calm descended over her, as if she were sinking into a bath of ice water that sent all emotion into hibernation. Moving with care and deliberation, she made the mechanical scoop up the squawking fat Gonta in one metallic hand.

"You don't want the circus," Alice said into the mechanical's speaking tube. Her voice boomed against the high gray buildings on either side of the street. "You want us. Gavin and me."

"We will destroy you!" said one of the Cossacks. Alice couldn't tell which, but she supposed it didn't matter, when they spoke with one voice.

"Not today. Back up or I'll kill him."

"You risked your life to save dying children. You would not kill helpless man."

That stymied Alice. The Cossack was right. She loathed the filthy Gonta-Zalizniak family, but the thought of crushing one of them in her hands, even mechanical hands, only brought up sickening memories of the dead girl. The weapons whined with power.

"Alice!" Gavin called behind her. "Duck!"

Immediately Alice dropped the mechanical into a crouch. Something flew over her head, but instead of striking any of the mechanicals, the object hit one of the nearby buildings. The thing exploded. Smoke and the sharp smell of gunpowder enveloped Alice, and Click hissed on the bench next to her. The building leaned precariously, then toppled into the street with rocky thunder. It was higher than the street was wide, so it smashed into the building across from it, creating a diagonal barrier. Alice felt the concussion thud against her very bones, and she was suddenly glad that the people had fled the surrounding structures.

The ruined building effectively blocked the street between Alice and the rest of the Cossacks and, incidentally, prevented both sides from firing at each other. Alice dropped the fat Gonta, who yelped and hobbled away on a sprained ankle.

"If you want us, come and get us," Gavin's voice taunted.

Alice took the cue. She and Gavin both turned their mechanicals and ran with the faint howls of Cossack outrage following behind.

"If you wanted to get them even angrier, you succeeded handily," Alice called.

"At least they'll be chasing us and not going after the circus," Gavin called back. "We can't— Shit!" He brought his mechanical up short, and Alice nearly crashed into him.

"What's wrong?" she asked. "What's—?"

"Feng!"

A pang went through Alice. She spun her mechanical. Nearly half a block up the street, past where they had already run, stood Feng, exactly where she had left him. He was surrounded by her little mechanicals.

Feng, wait here with my spiders.

Idiot! She had ordered him to stay there, and now he couldn't move. Even as she watched in horror, a Cossack projectile launched itself over the stony barrier blocking the street and described an arc that would carry it straight toward Feng. He looked up at it, his eyes wide despite the spider on his head.

Desperately, Alice looked at the controls of her mechanical. Her mind made quick connections, and she remembered something she had seen a mechanical guard do in the Gonta-Zalizniak house. Praying she had it right, Alice flipped two switches and yanked a lever. The projectile began to fall, whistling as it came down toward Feng. The right arm of Alice's mechanical burst free of the main body and flew toward Feng, trailing a cable. The projectile dropped closer. Just as the mechanical's hand hit Feng, Alice yanked back, killing the momentum and closing the fingers around Feng's body. He made a *hoik* sound and Alice yanked. The spiders leaped aboard the fist right when it snatched Feng backward. The projectile hit the cobblestones and exploded, but Feng and the spiders were already well beyond its reach.

Alice held Feng up in front of her bubble. "Are you all right?"

"Do not put me through that again," he said. "You—"

"—don't need to save everyone. I know. Just . . . just shut it, Feng." She dropped him into Gavin's mechanical. "We have to find Dr. Clef."

Alice ran with Gavin past the remains of the circus, hoping that the Cossacks would indeed follow them and leave the circus alone. There was nothing for it now if they didn't—Alice and Gavin *had* to stop Dr. Clef. They had no time. Or, very soon, they would have an infinity of it.

The mechanical ran beside the gray water as fast as Alice could make it go. Half a mile upriver, the heavy dam seemed to glower down at the city. If Dr. Clef managed to stop time for the entire universe, would she even know? Would she and everyone else simply freeze like fireflies trapped in amber, aware but unable to act? Or would she simply cease to exist, along with everything else? Ice ran through her veins, and the Cossacks coming behind her suddenly didn't seem like such a big problem.

They arrived at the bottom of the dam. It made a wall four or five stories tall. Angry water boiled and roared at the base, and a number of stone buildings huddled around it. A network of heavy cables led from the dam to a snarl of iron towers on the bank. Near the entrance to one of the buildings stood the half-wrecked elephant.

"He's here!" Alice shouted to Gavin over the roaring water. "But where did he end up? I don't know a thing about dams."

"I don't, either." Gavin looked stricken. "I didn't think of that."

A faint vibration shivered up the mechanical though Alice's body. More mechanical footsteps.

Gavin felt it, too. "Fourteen minutes," he said. "At least they didn't stop to destroy the circus."

Alice cast about, looking for something, anything that might tell her where to—

"Click!" she exclaimed. The cat looked up at her quizzically from the padded bench. Alice made the mechanical kneel, popped the bubble, and climbed down. Click followed, as did the spiders and whirligigs.

"What are you doing?" Gavin called from his own mechanical. Feng sat pale next to him. Alice paused a moment to look at the elephant. Her practiced eye told her the pistons had seized and its memory wheels had frozen. The poor thing would never move again. She patted it once in sorrow. She didn't believe that living animals, let alone mechanical ones, had souls, but she hoped that somehow, somewhere, some piece of this magnificent beast survived.

"Alice?" Gavin said.

Good heavens! This was no time for philosophical rumination. She turned to the mechanical cat. "Click!" she said. "Find Dr. Clef!"

The cat cocked his head, but didn't move. Finally, he sat down.

"You're asking the *cat*?" Gavin said. "He won't—"

Alice cut him off with a gesture. "Shush! Click, go!"

Click stood up again, stretched, and with studied nonchalance, wandered toward one of the buildings. It was just occurring to Alice that a power production factory must employ a large number of people, and they should be here somewhere, when the large doors that Click seemed to have chosen burst open and a horde of men in work clothes stampeded into the street. Click and Alice only barely dodged aside. The men looked wild-eyed and fearful as they ran for it, scattering in a dozen different directions. Gavin and Feng watched from the safety of the mechanical.

"What on earth?" Alice asked when they passed.

"I do not wish to know what frightened them so badly," Feng said.

Alice ignored him. Click was already heading for the open doors. She followed him with her spiders and whirligigs.

"Come on, Feng." Gavin clambered down from his mechanical with Feng as a reluctant shadow.

They found themselves in a wide, long room that seemed to be a receiving area. Alice sniffed the air. Ozone, hot steel, and . . . something else. A chemical smell she couldn't identify, but one that made her heart beat unaccountably faster and brought a hint of fear to her chest. She glanced at Gavin and Feng. Were they feeling it too? Click seemed unbothered. He took them through another doorway and down a set of stairs. Their footsteps echoed off metal and stone. The spiders' feet clicked across the floor, and the whirligigs' propellers made a sound like hummingbird wings.

"Did you hear something?" Gavin said hoarsely. "I thought I heard something."

"We're just . . . nervous," Alice replied. Her mouth was dry and her hands were shaking. "Good heavens, I'm so nervous. I don't understand."

"I am not," Feng said.

The chemical smell was stronger down here. Alice sniffed again, and her heart lurched. "It's that smell."

"A gas," Gavin said. "Some sort of airborne chemical that causes a fear reaction. Dr. Clef must have created it to frighten the workers away. It doesn't bother Click or the little automatons because they're mechanical."

"And Feng is . . ." Alice trailed off.

Feng touched his own spider. "Yes."

"At least the worst of it has cleared out," Gavin continued quickly. "Or I think we'd be running, too. Where's Click gotten to?"

They found him waiting at the bottom of the stairs. A whining, humming noise came from the other side of a heavy door, which was marked with Cyrillic writing.

"I believe it says *Power Production*," Feng translated.

"And that's where we'll find Dr. Clef." Alice flung the door open with her iron hand.

Chapter Fifteen

The soft whine burst into full volume. The room beyond the door was long and high, fully the size of a dirigible hangar. Five turbines, nearly flush with the floor, occupied most of the space. They looked to Gavin like giant coiled seashells of segmented metal, each thirty feet across. Automatically he tried to calculate diameter and radius, but he kept running into pi, a number nearly as bad as the square root of two, and he forced himself to stop. A covered shaft in the center of each turbine was connected to an electrical generator. The shafts spun at a dizzying 180 revolutions per minute. Under Gavin's feet, he felt water rushing through the turbines and sensed immense kinetic power barely held in check by the sturdy walls of the dam. It was at the same time intoxicating and intimidating.

Near the third turbine stood an arc of lacy metal just high enough for a man to walk under. At the spot in the arc normally occupied by the keystone was Gavin's paradox generator. A table filled with a snarl of equipment sat next to the arc.

In the middle of the long floor near the pile of equipment was the plump form of Dr. Clef. He wore dark goggles over his eyes. A snarl of cables connected the central turbine's generator to the machinery, and a smell of solder in the air said Dr. Clef had been welding. He looked up and pulled his goggles off when Alice shoved the door open. His face burst into a cheerful grin.

"I thought you all might arrive soon," he called over the turbine whine. "And you brought my clicky kitty. So kind of you."

"Doctor, you have to stop," Gavin called back. "You don't want to do this."

He looked genuinely perplexed. "But I'm doing this for you, my boy. Everything is calculated and calibrated. In a moment, you'll have all the time in the universe. You can save the world at last."

Before any of them could respond to this, or even move, Dr. Clef threw a switch. The whine increased, and power snaked up the cable, through the machinery, and into the delicate arc. All the turbines slowed as the generators engaged and the arc drained their power. The arc glowed an electric blue, and the space within filled with light, first red, then orange, then yellow, green, blue, indigo, and violet. Gavin's mind flicked back to a moment in the stone corridors beneath the Third Ward, a moment when he dropped the Impossible Cube and it changed colors as it fell in exactly the reverse order he was seeing now.

"Don't!" Alice cried. She ran toward him. Gavin

grabbed Feng's arm and ran as well, though they were a good hundred feet away. Dr. Clef smiled beatifically and struck a large tuning fork on the table. A pure A rang through the room, and Gavin remembered that he had sung that same note in the same octave on the night he had caressed Alice with his voice and made the Cube vanish in the Doomsday Vault. It was the same note Dr. Clef had struck the day he had completed the Impossible Cube in his laboratory at the Third Ward and accidentally made the Cube disappear through time. Gavin had struck the fork again to bring the Cube back. A. The first note. The pure tone that rang through time and space and called the Cube to itself.

Dr. Clef pressed the handle of the fork to the arc, and the arc's light became a white so beautiful, it made Gavin's heart ache. They weren't even halfway to him when Dr. Clef reached into the opening. It snapped and growled as it swallowed his hand. Gavin stared in fascination even as horror crawled over his skin. His steps faltered. The machines were hypnotic, thrilling. He was watching the most brilliant clockworker the world had ever seen bend time itself to his will with a unique machine. He was also watching the most powerful act of destruction in the history of the universe.

"He cannot." Feng tugged at his arm now, trying to hurry him forward. "He will not."

Dr. Clef whipped his hand out of the arc. The metal glowed bright as the sun. Alice, who was several paces ahead of Gavin, stopped in her tracks and threw up her arm to protect her eyes. Her little automatons squeaked in fear, and Click hissed. The glow faded a little, and when Gavin's vision cleared, he saw Dr. Clef was holding the Impossible Cube.

"Shit," Gavin whispered.

"My Cube," Dr. Clef crooned. *"Mein liebes, schönes Kübchen."*

The Cube was just as Gavin remembered it. It was only the size of a hatbox, but its intricate metal lattice twisted the eye. The back seemed to shift to the front, or perhaps the front was fading into the back. One of the bottom struts crossed impossibly over the top. It shouldn't have existed, but it did. Behind it, the arc continued to glow with holy fire.

Gavin shook off the fascination and started forward again with Feng. Alice did the same. He was in a dream, running through tar and molasses. Dr. Clef popped a pair of protectors over his ears and flipped another switch. The paradox generator atop the arc cranked to life, and the double tritone rippled through the chamber like demons and angels at war, amplified by the arc's power so that the noise was clear even over the turbine whine. Gavin dropped to his knees at the terrible perfection of it.

Alice and Feng kept running. They had nearly reached Dr. Clef's table, with Click and Alice's automatons following in an angry brass cloud. Gavin admired her determination and tenacity, her beauty and power. Dr. Clef picked up another fork, and the small part of Gavin's brain that wasn't enthralled by the perfect, rapturous sound of his own generator noted the length of the prongs. D-sharp. Alice gathered herself to leap at him.

"*Nicht*," said Dr. Clef, though the word was barely audible over the turbines and tritones. He struck the fork and pressed it to the side of the Cube. Instantly a cone of sound blasted from the Cube and through the fork. It hit Alice and shoved her backward into Feng. The two of them toppled to the ground. The little automatons were scattered in all directions, rotors and legs bent and laboring. Click bowled over backward. A piece of Gavin's awareness flashed hot anger at Alice's injury, but the rest of him remained consumed by the tritone paradox. Then an edge of the cone caught him. It simultaneously dampened the tritone paradox and slapped him in the face. His ears rang. Abruptly, the sound was no longer so hypnotic. Gavin leaped to his feet and automatically ran toward Alice.

"I'm fine!" she gasped. "Stop him!"

"Help her, Feng," Gavin said. "Help us! Do whatever it takes to help!" And without waiting for an answer, he ran toward Dr. Clef's table. Another cable ran from the paradox generator. It ended in a clip that Dr. Clef was ready to connect to the Impossible Cube. But now Gavin was close enough. He raised his wristband, aimed fast, and fired. The cog spun through the air and knocked Dr. Clef's hand aside. He yelped but didn't drop the clip. The ringing in Gavin's ears continued to muffle the tritones, though he heard enough for it to be a distraction.

Dr. Clef blinked at Gavin, who was already aiming another cog. There was only one left, and there was only one choice of what to do with it. Grimly, he cranked the magnetic power as high as it would go. Flung at full strength, a spinning cog would slice through flesh and bone like butter. Dr. Clef glanced at the wristband, his brilliant mind making instant connections, and Gavin saw the understanding in the eyes of his mentor, a man who, despite a few arguments, had never been anything but kind and helpful to Gavin, who wanted only to help him now. Gavin's legs trembled, but his aim remained firm.

"You won't," Dr. Clef said, though Gavin was more reading his lips than hearing his voice.

"I have to," Gavin said, and started to move his finger.

"I can show you your father," Dr. Clef said.

Gavin froze.

"Yes. The Cube and the arc can see through time. I can show you your father as he was. You can see where he went—and where he is now."

"He really is alive?" The idea rocked Gavin harder than the tritone paradox. The vague memory of his father's voice sang softly in his head.

> I had a ship, my ship must flee
> Sailing o'er the clouds and on the silver sea.

He longed to hear that voice again, learn where his own voice had come from.

Learn why his father had left.

"Did he go away because of me?" Gavin whispered. "Was it because I wasn't as good at music as he was? Was I a bad son?"

"Gavin!" Alice cried. "Stop him!"

"We can look," Dr. Clef mouthed. "We can seek. We can find. It is easy, Gavin. You will discover, uncover, ascertain."

Ice slid down Gavin's spine. "No. You're lying! It's a lie!"

Gavin fired, and the entire world slowed for him. The cog spun lazily through the air, teeth catching light and splitting it into a trillion particles that scattered like drops of syrup. Dr. Clef, with inhuman reflexes, snapped the clip connecting the paradox generator to the Impossible Cube. A blue rose of a spark bloomed and just as quickly flickered into death. The cog continued its long, slow spin. The paradox generator fell silent as all its energy drained into the Cube. Dr. Clef's facial muscles stretched toward a smile. The cog whirled, heating the air an infinitesimal amount as it passed, and smashed into the paradox generator.

Utter silence fell over the entire chamber. Then a terrible, discordant sound boomed through the room. Time snapped back to its normal pace. The light within the arc flickered and spun like the eye of a hurricane. A terrible red light poured into the turbine room. Within the eye of the arc, Gavin saw gently flowing water, blue and calm, as if he were looking up from the bottom of a pool or river. His mind leaped from connection to connection, and he realized he was looking at a hole that punched through a dozen dimensions and opened into the past, into a number of time periods in the past, and he could see where the river had once flowed through this spot.

At that moment, a force very much like gravity pulled him toward the arc. He resisted and turned to flee, but it grew stronger with every passing second. It was like running through water. Two of Alice's little automatons were sucked squeaking toward the arc.

They struggled against the force that pulled at them, but their propellers had been damaged by the Impossible Cube and in the end they were dragged through the arc. The automatons sheered and shredded and vanished with a human-sounding scream. On the other side, the water bubbled and boiled like a cauldron, though it stayed on the other side. The Impossible Cube sat perfectly still on the table.

Dr. Clef managed to wrap his arms around one of the table legs and hold on. Gavin, now on hands and knees, made it back to Alice, who was still lying on the ground. She had braced her feet against an outcrop of brick on the floor and had caught hold of Feng's wrist with her iron-bound hand. The spider's eyes glowed green. How were they going to get out? Gavin felt himself being dragged backward. Alice's hair was drawn forward over her face. Fear for himself and for Alice and Feng made Gavin's heart beat against his spine. The force abruptly strengthened, and it lifted Feng bodily from the ground. Wind roared through the turbine room.

"Hang on, Feng!" Alice cried. "Don't let go!"

And then Gavin lost his grip on the floor and tumbled backward toward the arc.

Susan Phipps felt the strange pull even on the staircase, and she nearly lost her balance. So did Glenda, who only saved herself by clutching at the handrail.

"What the bloody hell?" Glenda said.

"It's that clockworker," Phipps replied. "If I read those notes we found on the train correctly, he's planning to do something with time. Michaels and Ennock must be *helping* him."

Her fury grew. It felt like she had been chasing Alice Michaels and Gavin Ennock for most of her life. She couldn't remember when she'd last had a good night's sleep or actually enjoyed a meal or simply sat and rested. Michaels and Ennock had become her entire world, and when had that happened?

A sudden urge overcame her, an overwhelming desire to simply turn and walk away. No one would know except Glenda, and she would keep her mouth shut if ordered. It would be so easy.

Then an image of her father standing on the front steps with the carpet bags at his feet sprang into her mind. Justice and fairness, always. They had gotten her where she was now. It was impossible to give them up just because it was inconvenient. She firmed her jaw and continued more carefully down the stairs, ready to do what was right.

And if her current path was wrong? Even . . . unjust? She paused for a long moment, caught between balanced concepts.

"Lieutenant?" Glenda asked behind her.

Phipps abruptly straightened her back. "I'm fine," she said sharply. "Let's keep going."

At the bottom, she found the door already open, and beyond lay an enormous room filled with giant metal snail shells, strange machinery, and the very people she'd been chasing all this time. A metal arc glowed an evil red and seemed to be sucking everything greedily into itself, gaining power with every passing moment. Even as she watched, two of Alice's little automatons were sucked into it and destroyed. The other automatons, including that stupid cat Click, managed to limp around to the back of one of the turbines and cling there as Alice braced herself against a line of bricks on the floor. The force reached outward and pulled at Phipps even more strongly.

"What's happening?" Glenda said.

"Run up and grab that rope from the top of the stairwell." Phipps drew a multiple coil dispersal pistol that she had snatched from the Cossack armory and twisted the charging unit. It whined with eager power. "We're going to end this."

Alice saw Gavin go by. Without thinking, she flung out her right hand and actually managed to catch his arm. Her shoulders burned. She was holding two men now, with her feet braced against the brick outcrop as wind tore past her face and hair. Her eyes met Gavin's. Oh God—her grip was slipping, and it felt like her arms were coming out of their sockets. Feng clutched her forearm with the power she had ordered him to use. She couldn't keep this up.

The dreadful force increased again. Alice screamed, still holding on.

"Let go!" Feng shouted. His words came out framed by the horrible spider on his face. "Alice, let me go! If you don't, we'll all die!"

The idea was unthinkable. Guilt overwhelmed her. It was her fault Feng was in this position in the first place. She could save him. She *would* save him. Both him and Gavin.

"No!" she shouted back. "I won't let you die!"

"You can't save us both," he said. "Some people don't want to be saved. Let go!"

Her arms burned like lava and her fingers quivered. Dr. Clef huddled at the table, able to use his arms and legs to resist the power of the arc. Alice swallowed. She had been forced to give up her mother, her brother, and her father. Why should she give up her friend?

"Let me go, Alice!" Feng shouted. "I can help!"

A tear formed in her eye and leaped across the room into the boiling water of the arc. She didn't have the strength to save them both, to save everyone. Either a few would die, or everyone would die. It wasn't fair, but it would be even worse to let everyone perish because she couldn't let go. She looked at Gavin again, and he nodded. With a scream of agony and anger, she let Feng go.

Feng flew backward, straight toward the arc. But as he fell, he angled his body so that he struck the table. Even over the wind, Alice heard bone snap, though Feng's face remained stoic. He bounced sideways and managed to latch on to Dr. Clef.

"Was, denn?" Dr. Clef sputtered.

Feng snap-punched him twice. Dr. Clef's eyes glazed over, and he let go of the table. Together Feng and Dr. Clef fell toward the arc and hit the eye. Alice wanted to look away, but couldn't. When the two men struck the eye, flesh and bone shredded as if forced through a sieve made of razors. A cloud of blood and meat misted before the arc, hung for a tiny moment, and was sucked into the boiling water beyond. Alice cried out again.

Do whatever it takes to help! Gavin had ordered. Feng had done exactly that and gotten just what he had wanted. Alice felt only heart-wrenching sorrow.

Gavin grabbed hold of Alice's free hand, the one with the spider on it, and the spider's eyes glowed red. It was easier to hold on to one person, though she couldn't do it indefinitely, and whatever force was pulling them toward the arc showed no signs of abating. Her desperation grew, as did the fear on Gavin's face.

"What do we do?" she shouted.

He shook his head. His feet were trying to find purchase on the brick floor, but they were continually drawn out from under him. His hand slipped, and Alice forced herself to grab harder, though she was growing more and more tired.

"You have the cure," he yelled. "Let me go and save yourself!"

A cold fist clutched her heart and her breath came hard. "Not you. Never you!"

"Alice—"

And then Susan Phipps was there. A rope was wrapped around her waist and she was playing it out with her mechanical hand like a mountain climber. Her silver-streaked hair streamed out like Alice's. The sight was so surprising, it took Alice a moment to understand what—who—she was looking at.

"You're both idiots," Phipps shouted. From a holster at her waist, she drew a fat pistol.

Alice's heart sank, though she didn't dare loosen her grip on Gavin to defend herself. Still, it was too much. "Damn you!" she shouted back. "Kill us, then! See if it makes you feel better."

"Phipps!" Gavin cried. "Don't!"

Phipps fired—straight at the top of the turbine. A

red beam lanced through the air and struck the spot where the shaft met the generator. Smoke formed and was pulled into the boiling arc. Then the generator shaft jumped away from the turbine shaft with a terrible grinding noise. Deprived of its energy source, the generator powered down. The arc's glow faded, the eye and the boiling water vanished. Gavin dropped on top of Alice as the force abruptly ceased. The Impossible Cube trembled for a moment, went still, then released a burst of red energy. Alice braced herself for another slamming, but the energy went through her with only a strange sensation, as if something briefly crawled over all her bones at once. The Cube darkened, though it continued to give off a faint phosphorescent blue light.

Alice lay panting beneath Gavin. His weight was both welcome and crushing at the same time. Her arms had the strength of wet string, and she couldn't even summon the energy to ask him to move. At last he heaved himself aside and dragged himself upright on trembling limbs to face Phipps, who was calmly untying the rope from around her waist and winding her hair back into a twist.

"If you had done that from the start, none of this would have happened," Phipps said. "For all your talent, you're still a rookie, Agent Ennock."

"Why?" Gavin gasped, echoing Alice's thoughts.

"I don't answer to you," Phipps replied coolly. "And you are welcome."

"Er . . . thank you." Alice felt like an admonished schoolgirl.

"We shouldn't stay," Phipps added. "I don't think it's safe."

Alice summoned the strength to sit up. "Oh, *come* now! After everything you put us through, you owe us an explanation and you damned well know it!"

Phipps sighed and thawed a little. "If I can make the great Alice, Baroness Michaels, curse, I suppose I can offer an explanation." She looked away for a moment. "Into the Doomsday Vault, I've put clockworker inventions that could uproot islands, let people move instantly from place to place, and make the human race immortal. But an invention that would stop time . . ." She shook her head. "I was so worried about justice itself that I lost sight of whom justice was *for*. What justice is there in letting clockworkers seize destiny from mankind? The time of the clockworker needs to end, and it needs to end now."

"What does that mean to us?" Gavin was weaving, but kept his feet.

"It means, Mr. Ennock, that I am personally going to escort you and the baroness to China to spread her cure. It is fair."

"God*damn* you, Lieutenant!" Glenda Teasdale appeared in the door to the stairwell with a pistol of her own. "After all this, you turn out like Simon? I'll see you in hell!"

"Agent Teasdale!" Phipps barked. "Lower your weapon!"

"Michaels stole everything from me!" Glenda moved farther into the room, her pistol still trained on Alice. "She stole my profession and my life! She has to pay."

"It would not be just, Agent Teasdale," Phipps said. "She's already paid, and paid, and paid. And so have we. It's time to stop. For both of us."

Glenda was breathing fast. Alice was so tired, she could barely move, but from somewhere she found a reserve of strength that let her come to her feet. "Glenda," she said, "you've done so much for me. You were an exemplar to me, and without you, I would never have struck out on my own. I did a terrible thing to you in return. I'm sorry for what I did to you. I wish I could take it back. If you want to shoot, I'll understand."

And she moved in front of Phipps. Gavin tried to stop her, but she shook him off. She stood there, unarmed but for her iron spider, her arms spread wide. Too many people had died for her. She could die for someone else now.

Glenda took aim. Alice held her breath but refused to close her eyes. Glenda lowered the pistol.

"Goddamn you," she said again, but this time to Alice.

"I'm sorry," Alice said, and was surprised at how disappointed she was that Glenda hadn't pulled the trigger.

"What am I to do with my life?" Glenda asked bitterly.

"If you can control your impulse to curse," Phipps said, "perhaps you should go into politics. I can give you a letter of introduction that will go over quite well with the Hats-On Committee in Parliament."

Gavin, meanwhile, staggered over to the table where the arc stood. Silently, he picked up the Impossible Cube. A lump formed in Alice's throat. She joined Gavin and took his hand. Click clicked across the floor as well and sat at Alice's feet. He looked at the arc as if waiting for something. Alice's remaining automatons limped over to her and crawled into her skirts or fluttered to her shoulders. They all stood in a moment of silence before the arc, now a gateway to the world of the dead. Alice fought back tears.

"Feng gave his life to save ours," Alice said. "I hope that will be enough for his father—and his family."

"The plague took Dr. Clef," Gavin said. "I knew it would happen, knew he'd leave, but I didn't think he'd try to kill us." He sighed heavily and wiped at his eyes. "In his own twisted way, he was like a father to me, and now he's gone. He and Feng both."

Alice embraced him and let her own tears wet his shoulder. They both wept for loss and unfairness while Glenda, Phipps, and the mechanical stood by in mute sympathy. At last Alice stepped away and fished in her pocket for a handkerchief.

Gavin said in a heavy voice, "His remains went into the past, you know, to a time before the dam was built. Did you see the water boil?"

"Oh!" A shock of realization went through Alice and she put her metal hand to her mouth. *The Dnepro River boiled in the center of Kiev and the plague rose up like a dragon and devoured the city.* "Do you think . . . Did Dr. Clef start the clockwork plague?"

"I don't know," Gavin admitted. "Clockworkers don't spread the plague, but Dr. Clef was pulverized and his blood was dragged into several places in the past. Maybe that did something to the disease."

"Good heavens. Good heavens," was all Alice could say. She dabbed at her eyes with a handkerchief in her metal hand.

An alarm blared, and red lights flashed all over the room. Click jumped straight up. Alice started as well, and her automatons jerked.

"Oh no," Gavin said.

"We need to leave," Phipps said. "Now."

"What—?" Glenda began.

Gavin was turning the Impossible Cube over and over in his hands so quickly it made Alice dizzy to look at it. "I think that last burst of energy from the Cube did something. Didn't you feel it? The way it dragged over your bones."

"I did feel it," Phipps said. "Singularly unpleasant, too."

"The Cube was connected to the dam, and it wrenched something inside. Deep down within the stones. At the level of . . . of the tiny things." Alice could see Gavin was floundering for words. "The bits aren't holding together anymore. Can you see the cracks?"

"No," Glenda said nervously, glancing around.

"I can." Gavin tapped his forehead. "They're small, but spreading fast. The structure isn't sound."

Fear stabbed Alice as the implications hit her. "How much time before it fails?"

"Less than an hour, I think. It'll destroy a good part of lower Kiev."

"How do we stop it?" Glenda asked.

"We can't. Not in an hour," he said. "We have to evacuate everyone we can."

They ran for the stairs—or tried to. Gavin and Alice could manage only a fast walk. Alice winced at the pain in her shoulders and her thighs, but she grimly kept going. It got better the more she moved. Gavin's jaw was also set with pain. Alice thought about having her automatons carry her, but the thought of being lifted by her arms made her shudder, and in any case, most of her automatons were as bent as she was.

Somehow, they made it up the stairs and out the main doors, where they found the wrecked elephant still standing by the two mechanicals Alice and Gavin had stolen from the Gonta-Zalizniaks. Near them, however, also stood the Gonta-Zalizniaks themselves. Nearly forty of them. All in mechanicals.

"Good lord," Phipps said.

A hundred weapons clacked, whined, and chattered as they trained on the little group.

Chapter Sixteen

"Give us sound generator," boomed one of the Cossacks. "And then we kill you."

"Shouldn't that be *or* we kill you?" Glenda shouted back.

"No."

The alarms continued to blare discordant notes in a mocking parody of the paradox generator's siren song. It was a day for loss. Gavin had destroyed his own invention, his pinnacle of perfection, and then watched his mentor and his friend die painful deaths. He had lost a chance to find out what had happened to his father, and nearly died himself. He looked at the Cossack mechanicals, and a terrible calm came over him.

"I don't have time for you," he said. "The dam is failing. You need to save your people, the ones you took responsibility to rule. If you don't, I will destroy you. This is your only warning."

The Gonta-Zalizniaks laughed as one, and the sound echoed over the warning sirens. Then their voices merged into an eerie unity. "You think we are fools. Now you die."

The weapons moved. Gavin placed one hand on top of the faintly glowing Impossible Cube. It looked heavy, but felt light and springy. Gavin opened his mouth and *sang*. A clear D-sharp reverberated in the air. The Cube glowed electric blue, and it amplified Gavin's voice to a rumble, a boom, a half-tone detonation. The cone of sound flattened the mechanicals like tin soldiers. Several of them fell into the river with spectacular splashes and sank from sight. The sound poured from Gavin, shattering windows and smashing doors on both sides of the river. The mechanicals twitched and shuddered. Glass bubbles cracked and broke. The Cossack clockworkers within clapped hands to bleeding ears and screamed in pain. Alice finally jerked Gavin's hand from the Cube, and the note died, leaving groaning, half-conscious Cossacks in its wake. The Cube darkened completely.

"Enough," Alice said. "They're down. The rest of their fate is up to them."

"You're more merciful than I," Phipps observed. "They did experiment on children, after all."

"And you sided with them," Alice said.

"That was before I knew. Can you still drive that mechanical? We're in a bit of a rush."

"How are we going to evacuate everyone?" Glenda said. "There's just the four of us."

A booming crack thudded against Gavin's ears. Gavin's stomach tightened. The dam was failing faster than he had originally calculated. Once it gave, the river would smash through the lower city. Most of

Kiev was built on hills, but the lower sector past the dam would be wiped out, including the square that housed the Kalakos Circus.

The circus.

"I have an idea," Gavin said. "Lieutenant, can you drive a mechanical?"

Phipps gave him a withering stare.

"All right, good. You take this one. Alice, if you and Glenda can use the other one to run ahead and tell Dodd we're coming, I think we can save the people. But you'll have to hurry."

"What do you intend to do?" Glenda asked.

"You'll see. Just go!"

"You drive," Alice said to Glenda. "I don't think my arms are up to the task."

In moments, Glenda and Alice had run off, picking their way through the tumbled army of Cossack mechanicals. Some of the Gonta-Zalizniaks were groaning softly in their shattered bubbles, but Gavin spared them little pity. He had given them every chance, and he had other worries.

"Let's move, Lieutenant," he said, and hoisted himself into the mechanical he had stolen from Danilo Zalizniak. Lieutenant Phipps followed, and took up a position next to him. It was distinctly odd sitting near Phipps on a padded bench instead of facing her across a desk—or the barrel of a gun. Inside the machine, Gavin pulled part of the control panel apart until he located a rubber-coated live wire. He yanked the wire loose and jammed the business end against the darkened Cube. Instantly, it glowed electric blow.

"Go!" he said. "Walking speed."

Phipps put the mechanical into a stately march up-river, toward the circus. Gavin put his hand on the Impossible Cube and sang. This time, the note was a G, blue and pure and clean. The Cube glowed, and the note flowed out like liquid silver, washing over the streets and into the factories and houses and shops. The people, who had hidden inside the moment the mechanical army had marched past, emerged and blinked beneath sooty clouds. They listened to the wondrous sound and, unable to resist, followed it. On both sides of the river, people followed it. They poured out of the city and followed. Those who could walk helped those who couldn't. And they were *happy*. They laughed and chattered among themselves and pointed at Gavin, pale blond and blue-eyed as he sang on the marching mechanical.

And then the plague zombies came. They slid out of the shadows and into the street by the river, unbothered by the dim sunlight. The people didn't seem to notice or care. In the world's strangest parade created by the world's strangest music, everyone moved without panic, without fear, down the river toward the circus.

"How long can you keep this up?" Phipps asked. She seemed unaffected by the note, perhaps because of the amount of machinery in her nature.

Gavin shrugged, took a quick breath, and kept on singing. He was already tired from the events down by the turbines, and now the Cube was taking more energy from him. He felt like a water glass with a hole in the bottom, but he kept singing. The crowd followed along. It wasn't the entire city, thank heavens—only those who could hear the note, the ones who were in danger of the impending deluge. When they encountered a bridge, the people on the far side of the river crossed over to Gavin's side. Gavin was becoming seriously tired now, and the intervals between breaths were growing shorter. He forced himself to keep up the volume, and Cube glowed like captured sky in his hands.

A booming crack in the distance behind them, louder than thunder from an angry god, told Gavin the dam was beginning to fail now. Cracks were racing through its structure. Once it went, a swath of downriver Kiev would be washed away, and his clockwork was automatically calculating the path, volume, and velocity of the water. His voice wavered, tainting the purity of the note. The Cube's glow dimmed, and a wave of fear swept through the crowd. They heard the thunder and saw the plague zombies in their midst. Screams and knots of panic broke out. Sweating, Gavin forced his voice back to the G. The Cube's blue glow steadied. The crowd calmed and continued. Phipps shot him a worried look, but she didn't dare speed up and outpace the crowd.

Gavin's body was starting to shake from the effort now. Every bit of concentration he had poured into holding that single, silver note. The vague memories of his father loomed up. He had to hold the note perfectly, with absolute precision, or Dad would—

No. It was nothing to do with his father. He needed perfection in this time and in this place because these people needed it to live, and he would do it. He would be the voice they needed. For them. Not his father.

A new strength came over him, and he sang and

sang and sang. The note held steady—and perfect. The crowd came quickly and happily and in an orderly fashion.

And he realized the mechanical was kneeling beside the circus train. Alice and Glenda were in the engine compartment wearing ear protectors, and a wave of relief swept over Gavin when he saw a healthy cloud of smoke puffing from the stack. Dodd had said he would try to get the boilers going, and Alice had warned him not to stop. The circus people who hadn't managed to flee joined the crowd, their expressions also happy and calm. Linda wasn't among them, but Nathan and Dodd were, to Gavin's relief. Click and the little automatons were perched on the engine's roof, not bothered by the heat of the boilers.

Gavin kept up the note, though he could feel his voice starting to fail. An explosion upriver boomed against his bones and startled the crowd, but set off no panic. Instead, they piled into the train, into passenger sections and boxcars. They climbed onto the roofs and clung to the sides. They boarded the *Lady* and sat on the deck. They packed themselves in with calm, ordered care because Gavin's voice led them and kept them from understanding that the river carried their deaths.

Finally everyone was on board. People clung to every surface, inside and out. Phipps disconnected the Cube from the mechanical and helped Gavin up into the engine compartment with Alice and Glenda. He hoped it would retain enough power. His tired mind tried to run the formulas to find out and failed. Alice gave him a concerned look and moved toward him, but Gavin shook his head violently. She gave a tight nod and turned back to the boilers. Gavin kept singing, barely. His legs and arms shook with exhaustion. The tiny room was crowded, so Phipps stood back, near the coal carrier. Alice, who had certainly never driven a train before in her life but whose talent with machines let her understand them quickly, pulled levers and spun wheels, giving instructions to Glenda with gestures. The engineer was part of the crowd in the back, enthralled by Gavin's voice.

A soft wind whispered over them, created by tons of unchained water pushing the air ahead of it. The train jerked forward. Wheels spun in place, caught for a moment, spun again, and caught for good. Slowly, the train moved ahead, gaining speed. The deadly flood thundered toward them, smashing stone buildings and washing away bridges.

Gavin's strength gave out. The note ended. He dropped the Cube and would have fallen if Phipps hadn't stepped forward and caught him. Glenda snatched up the Cube before it hit the ground, handed it to him, and went back to work.

"Are you all right?" Phipps asked.

Gavin felt like a sack of wet sand. He could only give a small nod. Phipps helped him slide to the metal floor, though he could see out through the space between the coal carrier and the engine, the Impossible Cube in his lap. Without his voice to keep things steady, fear swept the people on the train. Demonic howls and screams trailed behind them, and some of the people clinging to the sides and top fell off. The train rocked, but Alice didn't slow. Gavin didn't have the strength to feel sorrow for the ones they had lost. The river roared behind them, reaching for them with watery dragon hands. The train gained speed. Buildings rushed past them, then were devoured by the river. Despite the train's speed, the river was gaining on them, eating the tracks behind them.

"It's hard," Alice said, her ear protectors now around her neck. "Everyone's panicking and rocking the train. It slows us down."

Glenda looked out the window and back. "The river's getting closer, nearly to your ship."

Coal dust smudged Alice's lovely face. She looked at Gavin, and he could see the reluctance. "Darling, can you . . . ?"

He didn't have the power. He couldn't even lift his arms. But Gavin met her brown eyes. This woman had led him into hell and changed him and now she was leading him back out. She needed him. With a groan, he lifted a leaden hand and dropped it on top of the Impossible Cube, let his mouth fall open, and whispered a note.

Nothing happened. The river thundered toward them. The train rocked again as people screamed and thrashed against one another, crushing and beating one another against the walls of the cars. Gavin swallowed, took a breath. He was Gavin Ennock. He could do this.

Gavin breathed out and sang. The G came through, crystalline blue. The Impossible Cube flickered, then glowed and the sound pulsed back over the train. The people instantly calmed. The train stopped rocking and picked up speed. Alice and Glenda, who had put their ear protectors back on, worked at the engines, while Phipps hovered over Gavin. He sang and sang while the train puffed faster and faster. The water receded behind them, and then the train took a curve that brought it uphill. It lost speed, but it went away from the water. Gavin's hand was sliding away from the Cube, and Phipps reached down to press it back into place. The Cube was losing its glow, running out of the electricity it had taken from the mechanical. Half a mile flashed by, and they were at the top of the hill. Alice slowed the engine and let the train coast. It was drifting to a stop near a station.

"We did it," Alice said, but her words came from far away. "Darling, you did it!"

The Cube went black. Gavin tumbled into darkness.

He was lying on a cloud, a soft, fluffy cloud. It was so restful and fine. Delightful not having to move. He had only a tiny moment to enjoy the sensation. Abruptly, he jerked fully awake as he always did, his heart beating at the back of his throat.

The room was spacious and white. Thick rugs covered polished wood floors. A large wardrobe of pale birch took up one corner, and an icon of the Virgin Mary hung in one ceiling corner, draped with white bunting embroidered with a red design. A table and easy chairs occupied another corner. The generous bed was also white, with fine linen sheets, a feather-filled duvet, and plump pillows. Where was he, and how had he come here?

He sat up and groaned as fire tore through every muscle. Aching and sore, he forced his feet around to the edge of the bed and realized he was naked. And clean. Hissing with every movement, he found a chamber pot under the bed, used it, and replaced it. The fiery ache continued when he stood up. A soft white dressing gown hung from the door, and he gingerly tied it on, which made him feel a little more secure. To his immense relief, he found his fiddle case next to the door. Carefully, he picked it up and opened it on the bed. The fiddle inside gleamed at him, undamaged. He sighed heavily.

A quick knock made him turn. The knock repeated.

"Uh . . . hello?" he called. "Who is it?"

The door burst open and Alice rushed in with a tray of food. Click trotted in behind her. "You're awake! Thank God!"

She set the tray on the table and caught Gavin in a hug that made him howl. She instantly released him. "I'm so sorry! I should have realized—when I stopped moving, everything started to hurt worse, too, and you've been asleep for a long time."

He hobbled to an easy chair next to the table and, gritting his teeth, eased himself into it. Alice hovered over him, offering help, but he waved her away. Click jumped onto the bed and settled into a pillow, his phosphorescent eyes gleaming green.

"How long was I asleep?" Gavin asked.

"You were unconscious, not asleep." Alice took up the chair opposite his. She wore a white blouse, a pale blue skirt, and a straw hat with peacock feathers on it. All of it made her look free and bright, and Gavin was so glad to see her. "It's been three full days. I was so worried. I thought the smell of food might bring you out."

The mention of the food brought his head around to it. There was tea and some kind of dumpling in a cream sauce and peppered roast pork and dark bread and cucumbers with onions. Gavin was ravenous, and, ignoring the pain, pulled the tray toward him so he could eat. The dumplings were stuffed with soft cheese, and the tender pork was seasoned perfectly. Alice took a paper packet from her pocket and handed him two pills from it.

"Take these," she said. "They'll help with the pain."

He swallowed them and kept eating. "Where are we?"

"The mayor's house. So much has happened, I don't know where to begin."

"The last thing I remember is singing on the train."

She nodded. "Part of the dam held, so the river destroyed less than we feared—a section a quarter of a mile wide and about five miles long. We got nearly everyone within that zone to safety. We lost some people, but . . . almost everyone survived. Except the Gonta-Zalizniaks. They're all missing, presumed dead. Their house was at the bottom of the valley, you know, and it's completely underwater now. The river is returning to its original bed. Some of the city will be flooded permanently, but most of it can be reclaimed. We're being hailed as heroes."

"We are?" Gavin paused with a fork halfway to his mouth. "We destroyed the dam and killed a bunch of people."

"That's not the way the Ukrainians see it," Alice said. "The dam fed power to their hated Cossack rulers, you see. We, on the other hand, rescued their children, led the Cossacks down to the horrible dam, blew it up, and swept them away forever. The mayor—his name is Serhiy Hrushevsky—has taken over the city. He's a very nice man who used to be a professor at the Kiev Ecclesiastical Seminary but became mayor because he wanted to soften what the Cossacks were doing. His son Mykhailo is extremely intelligent as well and will probably succeed him in politics, and— Oh! I'm babbling. I'm just so relieved that you're all right, darling."

"I'm happy to see you, too," he said. "But what next?"

"Well, once the whole story came out, Mayor Hrushevsky brought us here to rest and recover as honored guests. I cured the rest of the plague zombies in the city, which only made everyone even happier, and they want to have a city-wide ball in our honor."

The medicine Alice had given him started to work, and Gavin's muscles relaxed. "I've never been a hero before. I don't know how to react."

"I don't either, to be honest. I'm letting Phipps handle most of it."

"Phipps! I'd forgotten all about her. She's still with us?"

"Oh yes." Alice folded her arms. "She insists upon coming to China with us. Glenda has already slipped off, back for London. We haven't heard from Simon, either."

"And we won't." Gavin drained his teacup, then paused. "I have to say . . . I was hoping . . ."

Alice grew more serious. "For what?"

"That we might be able to search the laboratory in the Gonta-Zalizniak house. To see if they had found . . . you know."

"I do know." She reached across the table and took his flesh hand in her metal one. "We'll find a cure. You have time yet, no matter what Dr. Clef thought. We will cure you, we will get married"—her voice began to choke—"and we will have lots of children who will get very, very tired of hearing the same stories of their parents' adventures over and over again."

"'Aw, Dad, not that boring story about Feng at the dam again,'" Gavin said, trying to lighten the mood by imitating a child, except his own voice grew thick. "'We've heard it a million times.'"

"Will they speak with an American accent, do you think? Or a proper English one?"

"Hey! There's nothing wrong with a good Boston accent," Gavin said, laughing now. Click raised his head. "Don't forget that we perfected baked beans so you beefeaters could put them on toast."

Alice was laughing too, and she dabbed at her eyes with a handkerchief. "Good heavens. I haven't even told you the best part."

"There's more?"

"The paraffin refineries are nowhere near the dam and weren't touched. Mayor Hrushevsky is insisting we take all the oil we need. The *Lady* has been restored by his own men, and she is ready to fly when we are."

Gavin spent three more days recovering. He tired easily and slept a great deal, though he insisted on spending as much time as possible on the *Lady*, which was tethered just above the mayor's modest house. It was easier to rest amid the familiar, homey creak of wood and hemp. It also seemed to Gavin that the *Lady* was pleased to see him. The ship appeared to float more freely, hold herself more steadily when Gavin was aboard, though he didn't say anything about this to Alice.

When Gavin checked the *Lady*'s workshop, he was gratified to find the metal project he'd been working on had been moved there from the train, and he spent some time fiddling with it. It was nice to work on something that wasn't a weapon. The Impossible Cube was locked away in a cupboard. Alice, Gavin, and Phipps didn't see any need to tell anyone else the particulars of how they had led everyone out of danger. The paradox generator, of course, had been destroyed along with the dam, though Gavin still felt a small twinge at its loss.

Dr. Clef's notes about the danger of time, space, and energy were also gone, burned by Phipps. Gavin didn't have the heart to tell her that he had read them and, with a clockworker's precision, memorized every numeral and symbol. He didn't intend to use the information, of course. After everything that had happened, it would be foolish in the extreme. Much more interesting to work on his little project.

Now that Gavin was out of danger, Alice set about playing the part of the baroness to the hilt, making speeches and attending parties. Phipps attended most of these events as well, moving easily among the people, pointedly making friends and contacts. Once Gavin had recovered sufficiently to travel—and appear in public—Mayor Hrushevsky declared an entire day of celebration for their send-off to China. He presented Gavin with a new outfit—white airman's leathers. Gavin found he couldn't speak.

The ball was both plain and lavish, all at once. Mayor Hrushevsky, a great shaggy man with a long dark beard, insisted that the party be held outdoors in the streets, so it was more like an all-day festival than a ball. The pall of Gonta-Zalizniak rule had lifted, and the people appeared brighter, more cheerful. Even the weather cooperated, granting them a bright, balmy day. Gavin heard Ukrainian music for the first time, and he was enchanted. Street bands and musicians played at nearly every street corner. The mayor opened up the city coffers, and free food was available from stalls every few feet. The electric lights had gone out with the dam, of course, but after sunset people put out lanterns of glass and of colored paper, tinting the city with a hundred lively hues. Alice and Gavin and Phipps wandered about the city, greeted with cheers and laughter wherever they went. They danced to the music, and Gavin held Alice tightly as they whirled through the evening streets.

"Who knew that a cabin boy from Boston would travel so far?" he said to her. "I love you always."

"And I love you always," she replied.

When it was time to go, Gavin, Alice, and Phipps returned to the square in front of the mayor's house and listened to a speech they didn't understand in the slightest. They smiled and waved to the cheering crowd, Gavin in his new whites, Phipps in her formal reds, and Alice in a Ukrainian-style blouse and skirt, heavily embroidered with tiny cogs and wheels, made just for her by a dozen grateful Kievite women. Click and the automatons, repaired and shined for the occasion, made an honor guard as the trio ascended the ladder to the hovering *Lady*. The envelope's curly endoskeleton glowed blue with power from the generator and its generous supply of paraffin oil. The cheers and applause buoyed them up to the starry sky, lifting Gavin's spirit with every step. When they arrived on the deck, Gavin took the helm and Alice increased power to the generator. The glow intensified, and the ship ascended, higher and higher, until the city became flecks of color on black velvet. A cool breeze washed over him, mixing the scent of purity with the smell of paraffin exhaust. Click took up his usual spot, peering over the side of one gunwale, and the little automatons perched on the ropes or skittered about near Alice. Phipps folded her arms and watched. It was a thrill to be back in his rightful place, back in the air where he belonged.

And yet . . .

Once they established a heading east and the nacelle propellers were pushing them along, Gavin asked Phipps to take the helm for a moment. She arched a questioning eyebrow.

"I need to show Alice something below," he said.

He led Alice down to the laboratory. She looked apprehensive. "It's not anything bad," he reassured her.

"You're not going to propose again, are you?" she said. "I don't really need—"

"It's not that, either. I'm just . . . This is important to me, and I want you to be the first to see."

Now she looked mystified. "All right."

The little laboratory had been tidied up in preparation for the trip. Most of the floor space was taken up by a large, bulky object covered in a white cloth. Kemp's head, the eyes still dark, sat on the worktable.

Gavin hoped to figure out a way to restore him, but that wasn't why he had brought Alice down. His heart was beating fast, and his palms were sweaty, though he couldn't say why.

"I've finished it," he said lamely. "It's all done."

It took her a moment to understand. Then she got it. "The project you started in the circus? That's wonderful! I'm honored you want to show me, darling. Let's see it."

Gavin took a breath and whipped the cloth away. Alice gasped. The framework he had created spread out something like a kite. A battery pack with buckles and straps took up the center. The thousands of alloy rings he wound into a cloak now hung over the framework in waterfall ripples. When extended, they would stretch more than ten feet both left and right.

"Gavin!" Alice breathed. "Are those wings?"

AFTERWORD

The fun of writing semihistorical fiction is the ability to pick and choose interesting pieces of history while ignoring or altering anything that doesn't suit the story. I will no doubt be excoriated by historians both amateur and professional who want to point out that the incandescent lightbulb wasn't widely used until at least 1885, nearly thirty years after *The Doomsday Vault* and *The Impossible Cube*, or that the first paraffin oil (kerosene) refinery was constructed in Poland in 1859, not in Ukraine by 1858. Of course, such people ignore semi-intelligent windup cats, talking mechanical valets, and artificial limbs made of brass.

For the record, the *Consolatrix Afflictorum* is a real statue of the Virgin Mary in Luxembourg, and local legend has it that she fell out of a tree trunk in 1624, right around the time the bubonic plague struck the region. The stories say her touch cured a number of the afflicted, and so many people came to visit her shrine outside the city that in the late 1790s, the statue was moved to the Church of Our Lady (Notre Dame) inside the city walls.

Also in reality, Nicolas Adames was made vicar of that church in 1863. Gavin and Alice visit Vicar Adames in 1858, so perhaps in our fictional reality, Adames's predecessor died of the clockwork plague and granted him an early promotion.

In the historical 1870, Adames was named Bishop of Luxembourg, and the Church of Our Lady became Notre Dame Cathedral. I like to think it happened in fiction, too.

Ukraine has a long and sad history. Her rich farmlands made her a target for emperors who wanted to feed their armies, and she has at various times been overrun by Russians, Poles, Mongols, and Germans. In the 1700s, in both reality and in this work of fiction, Ukraine was divided in half by Russia and Poland. (Many modern people have forgotten—or never knew—that Poland was once a world-class military power.) Russia and Poland were far from kind in their rule, and in 1768, Maksym Zalizniak and Ivan Gonta led a Cossack rebellion against their oppressors. In history, they slaughtered the Poles and took over right-bank (western) Ukraine right handily. Afraid that the rebellion would spread to left-bank (eastern) Ukraine, Empress Catherine of Russia flooded the area with troops. Ivan Gonta was captured and chopped into fourteen pieces so his remains could be displayed in fourteen different towns as a deterrent to further uprisings. Maksym Zalizniak was captured and tortured but managed to escape with fifty-one of his men. He vanished, and his final fate remains unknown. Both men became national heroes, the subject of numerous Ukrainian folktales and songs.

In my fictional world, the clockwork plague arrived just before the rebellion, thanks to Dr. Clef and the Impossible Cube, so Ivan Gonta and Maksym Zalizniak were rather more successful. Although it would have been easy to have the downtrodden Ukrainians create a utopia for themselves, I was forced to remember that the rebellion was fomented by eighteenth-century Cossacks, who weren't known for their tolerance or compassion. Fortunately, Ukraine has at last regained her independence, both in modern reality and in my semihistorical fiction, and with it, perhaps she can regain her former glory as well.

—Steven Harper

Read on for an excerpt from the next
thrilling novel of the Clockwork Empire,

THE DRAGON MEN

Coming November 2012 from Roc

"I still think this is a terrible idea," said Alice.

Gavin spread his mechanical wings, furled them, and spread them again. He shrugged at Alice's words and shot a glance across the deck at Susan Phipps, who set her jaw and tightened her grip on the helm. Her brass hand, the one with six fingers, gleamed in the afternoon sun and a stray flicker of light caught Gavin in the face. The world slowed, shaving time into transparent slices, and for one of them he felt trillions of photons ricochet off his skin and carom away in rainbow arcs. His mind automatically tried to calculate trajectory for them, and the numbers spun and swirled in an enticing whirlpool. He bit his lip and forced himself out of it. There were more important—more *exciting*—issues at hand.

"I completely agree," Phipps said. "But he's the captain of the ship, and he can do as he likes, even if it's idiotic."

"Captains are supposed to listen to common sense,"

Alice replied in tart British tones. "Especially when the common sense comes from someone with a decent amount of intelligence."

At that Gavin had to smile. A soft breeze spun itself across the Caspian Sea, winding across the deck of the *Lady of Liberty* to stir his pale blond hair. He started to count the strands that flicked across his field of vision, note the way each one was lifted by the teamwork of gas particles, then bit his lip again. Damn it, he was getting more and more distractible by minutiae. More and more individual details of the world around him beckoned—the drag of the harness on his back, the creak of the airship's wooden deck, the borders of the shadow cast by her bulbous silk envelope high overhead, the sharp smell of the exhaust exuded from the generator that puffed and purred on the decking, the gentle thrumming of the propellered nacelles that pushed the *Lady* smoothly ahead, the shifting frequency of the blue light reflected by the Caspian Sea gliding past only a few yards beneath the *Lady*'s hull. Sometimes it felt like the world was a jigsaw puzzle of exquisite jewels, and he needed to examine each piece in exacting detail.

"Gavin?" Alice's worried voice came to him from far away, and yanked him back to the ship. "Are you there?"

Damn it. He forced his grin back to full power. "Yeah. Sure. Look, I'll be fine. Everything'll work. I've been over the machinery a thousand times, and I've made no mistakes."

"Of course not." Alice's expression was tight. "Clockworkers never make mistakes with their inventions."

Gavin's grin faltered again and he shifted within the harness. She was worried about *him*, and that thrilled and shamed him both. It was difficult to stand next to her and not touch her, even to brush against her. Just looking at her made him want to sweep her into his arms, something she allowed him to do only sporadically.

"Alice, will you marry me?" he blurted out.

She blinked at him. "What?"

"Will you marry me?" Words poured out of him. "I started to ask you back in Kiev, but we got interrupted, and what with one thing and another, I never got the chance to ask again, and now there's a small chance I'll be dead, or at least seriously wounded, in the next ten minutes, so I want to know: Will you marry me?"

"Oh, good Lord," Phipps muttered from the helm.

"I . . . I . . . Oh, Gavin, this isn't the time," Alice stammered.

He took both her hands in his. Adrenaline thrummed his nerves like cello strings. Alice's left hand was covered by an iron spider that wrapped around her forearm, hand, and fingers to create a strange metal gauntlet, and the spider's eyes glowed red at his touch. Gavin had his own machinery to contend with—the pair of metal wings harnessed to his back. They flared again when he shifted his weight.

"The universe will never give us the right time." Gavin's voice was low and light. "We have to make our own."

"Dr. Clef tried to make time," Alice said, "and look where it got him."

"He wanted to keep it for himself." Gavin looked

into Alice's eyes. They were brown as good, clean earth, and just as deep. "We'll share it with the world. I can't offer you more than the open sky and every tune my fiddle will play, but will you marry me?"

"There's no minister. Not even a priest!"

"So you're saying you don't want to."

She flushed. "Oh, Gavin. I do, yes, I do. But—"

"No!" He held up a hand. "No *yes, but*. Just *yes*. And only if you mean it."

"Ah. Very well." Alice, Lady Michaels, took a deep breath. Her dress, a piece of sky pinned by the breeze, swirled about her. "Yes, Gavin. I will marry you."

With a shout of glee, Gavin leaped over the edge.

Air tore past his ears and his stomach dropped. The *Lady*'s hull blurred past him, and perhaps two dozen yards below, the calm Caspian Sea shimmered hard and sharp and a little angry. Gavin spread his arms, moved his shoulders, and the wires attached to his body harness drew on tiny pulleys. The wings snapped open. The battery pack between his shoulder blades pulsed power, and blue light coruscated across the wings with a soft chime like that of a wet finger sliding over a crystal goblet. A matching blue light current glowed through a lacy endoskeleton underneath the *Lady*'s envelope above, giving her a delicate, elegant air. The endoskeleton and the wings were fashioned from the same alloy, though the wings consisted of tiny interwoven links of metal, much like chain mail. And when electricity pulsed through the alloy—

Gavin dove toward the water a moment longer, until the glow and the chime reached the very tips of his wings. In that moment, the alloy pushed against gravity itself, and abruptly he was swooping back up, up, and up; by God, he was rising, climbing, ascending, *flying* and the wind pushed him higher with an invisible hand and the deck with Alice and Phipps upon it flashed by so fast, Gavin barely had time to register their surprised expressions and then the *Lady*'s curliblue envelope plunged toward him like a whale falling onto a minnow and the wind tore his surprised yell away as a sacrifice, giving him just enough time to twist his body and turn the unfamiliar flapping wings—God, yes, they were *wings*—so that he skimmed up the side of the envelope so close his belly brushed the cloth and with dizzying speed he was above the ship, looking down at her sleek envelope and her little rudder at the back and the fine net of ropes that cradled the ship like soft fingers and his body stretched in all directions with nothing below or above him. Every bit of his spirit rushed with exhilaration, flooded with absolute freedom. His legs in white leather and his feet in white boots hung beneath him, deliciously useless. His muscles moved, and the wings, made of azure light, flapped in response, lifting him into the cool, damp air, with bright Brother Sun calling to him, lifting body and soul. A rainbow of power gushed through him, and he was part of the heavens themselves, a whole note streaking through infinity, cleansed by wind and mist and shedding worries like grace notes. Gavin yelled and whooped, and his voice thundered across distant clouds as if it might split them in two. *This* was what he'd been born for. This was home.

He hung in the blue nothing for a tiny moment. His wings glowed and sang softly behind him. The clouds spread a cottony pasture far away, and he could almost—almost—see gods and angels striding across them. A calm stole over him. It didn't matter how many trillions of particles held him aloft or how gravity failed to function. It didn't matter that a disease was coursing through his body and killing him bit by bit. There was blessed nothing. His mind slowed and joined the stillness. The wind sighed and Gavin hummed a soft note in response as the breeze curled about his white-clad body. Harmony. Peace. How perfect it was there.

A shadow below caught his eye. The *Lady* was still hovering just above the surface of the calm Caspian Sea. This was at Phipps's insistence—if Gavin's wings had failed, he wouldn't have fallen far, and the ocean would have provided a more pleasant landing than hard ground. Perhaps five miles ahead of the ship lay a sliver of an island, and just beyond that, a rocky coast. The shadow was moving beneath the water, growing larger and larger beneath the *Lady* as whatever cast it moved up from the bottom of the sea. The thing was nothing natural. Unease bloomed quickly into concern and fear. Gavin tucked and dove, his wings pulled in tightly. He didn't dare dive too quickly—he didn't know how much the harness could take, even though his mind was automatically calculating foot pounds and stress levels. He shouted a warning to Alice and Phipps and felt the vibration of his vocal cords, sensed the compression of air, knew the sound would scatter helplessly long before it reached Alice's eardrums, and still he shouted.

Half a mile below him, a pair of enormous black tentacles rose up from the shadow and broke the surface of the water. At seven or eight feet thick, they easily looped themselves up and around the *Lady* with incredible speed, even though she was the size of a decent cottage. Fear chased Gavin's heart out of his rib cage as he dove closer. He could hear Alice shrieking and Phipps yelling in thin, tinny voices that were ballooning into full volume. Air burned his cheeks as he dove past the envelope, now wrapped in suckered black flesh, and he caught the rank smell of ocean depths and old fish.

Instinct rushed him ahead. He had to reach Alice. No other thought but to reach her, to get her to safety. Even the *Lady*'s distress didn't matter.

Below and just behind the ship, a black island rose from the waves. Eight other tentacles trailed in oily shadows beneath the ship, and a wicked horned beak large enough to crack an oak tree snapped open and shut. A single eye the size of a stagecoach stared up at Gavin, and he caught his own reflection in the dark iris. Inside Gavin a monster equal to the one below roared its anger. For a mad moment, he wondered if he could dive into the eye, punch both fists straight through cornea into vitreous goo and force the creature away. Grimly, he ended that line of thought, as it was foolish. Instead he made himself fling his wings open and end the dive with a sharp jerk that sent a red web of pain down his back and into his groin, where the flight harness was strapped to his lower body. He skimmed through a gap in the tentacles and the rope web that supported the *Lady*'s hull, twisting his body in ways that were already becoming reflexive, until he could drop to the deck. His wings folded back into a metallic cloak that dragged at his back and shoulders once the blue glow faded and the chime stopped.

Susan Phipps had drawn a cutlass of tempered glass—only fools used sparking metal on an airship—and was hacking at one of the loops of tentacle that encircled the ship in a rubbery tunnel. Her mouth was set in a hard line and her graying black hair was coming loose from under her hat and spilling over her blue lieutenant's uniform. The blade gleamed liquid in the sun and it distorted the black tentacle as Phipps slashed again and again, but the edge made only shallow cuts in the rubbery surface, and if the creature noticed, it gave no indication.

Alice, meanwhile, kicked open a hatchway on deck, and a finger of relief threaded through Gavin's anger when he saw she wasn't injured.

"Are you all right?" he demanded.

"I'm fine," she barked, then shouted into the hatchway, "Out! Out out out!"

From belowdecks burst a cloud of little brass automatons. Some skittered on spider legs, others flew on whirligig propellers. They sported arms and legs and other limbs of varying sizes and shapes, but most had points, and a little pride fluttered in Gavin's chest at the way they obeyed Alice. She pointed at the tentacle above Phipps's head with her gauntleted hand. "Attack!"

ABOUT THE AUTHOR

Steven Harper Piziks was born in Saginaw, Michigan, but he moved around a lot and has lived in Wisconsin, in Germany, and briefly in Ukraine. Currently he lives with his three sons in southeast Michigan.

His novels include *In the Company of Mind* and *Corporate Mentality*, both science fiction published by Baen Books. He has produced the Silent Empire series for Roc and *Writing the Paranormal Novel* for Writer's Digest. He's also written novels based on *Star Trek*, *Battlestar Galactica*, and *The Ghost Whisperer*.

Mr. Piziks currently teaches high school English in southeast Michigan. His students think he's hysterical, which isn't the same as thinking he's hilarious. When not writing, he plays the folk harp, dabbles in oral storytelling, and spends more time online than is probably good for him. Visit his Web page at www.the clockworkempire.com, and his Twitter feed at www .twitter.com/stevenpiziks.